STAR WARS

X-WING
MERCY KILL

BY AARON ALLSTON

STAR WARS

X-WING
MERCY KILL

AARON ALLSTON

BALLANTINE BOOKS • NEW YORK

Star Wars: X-Wing: Mercy Kill is a work of fiction. Names, places, and incidents either are products of the author's imagination or are used fictitiously.

2013 Del Rey Mass Market Edition

Copyright © 2012 by Lucasfilm Ltd. & ® or ™ where indicated.

All Rights Reserved. Used Under Authorization.

Excerpt from *Star Wars: Crucible* by Troy Denning copyright © 2013 by Lucasfilm Ltd. & ® or ™ where indicated. All Rights Reserved. Used Under Authorization.

Published in the United States by Del Rey, an imprint of The Random House Publishing Group, a division of Random House, Inc., New York.

DEL REY is a registered trademark and the Del Rey colophon is a trademark of Random House, Inc.

Originally published in hardcover in the United States by Del Rey, an imprint of The Random House Publishing Group, a division of Random House, Inc., in 2012.

ISBN 978-0-345-51115-7
eBook ISBN 978-0-345-53480-4

Printed in the United States of America

www.starwars.com
www.delreybooks.com

9 8 7 6 5 4 3 2 1

Del Rey mass market edition: July 2013

Longtime readers of the X-Wing series have persisted for years in asking me, Del Rey, Lucasfilm, and possibly passing strangers, "When will there be another X-Wing novel?"

The answer is "now," and I suspect that a lot of the credit for *Mercy Kill* goes to your dogged and tireless insistence that this project should happen.

Thanks, guys.

ACKNOWLEDGMENTS

Thanks go to:

My editor, Shelly Shapiro; Jennifer Heddle and Leland
Chee of Lucas Licensing;
My agent, Russell Galen;
My eagle-eyes, Kelly Frieders, Roxanne Quinlan, Luray
Richmond, Janine K. Spendlove, and Sean Summers;
and Michael A. Stackpole, for setting the X-Wing
novel series in motion all those years ago.

THE STAR WARS NOVELS TIMELINE

BEFORE THE REPUBLIC
37,000-25,000 YEARS BEFORE
STAR WARS: A New Hope

c. 25,793 *YEARS BEFORE STAR WARS: A New Hope*

Dawn of the Jedi: Into the Void

OLD REPUBLIC
5000-67 YEARS BEFORE
STAR WARS: A New Hope

Lost Tribe of the Sith[†]
  Precipice
  Skyborn
  Paragon
  Savior
  Purgatory
  Sentinel

3954 *YEARS BEFORE STAR WARS: A New Hope*

The Old Republic: Revan

3650 *YEARS BEFORE STAR WARS: A New Hope*

The Old Republic: Deceived

Lost Tribe of the Sith[†]
  Pantheon
  Secrets

Red Harvest

The Old Republic: Fatal Alliance

The Old Republic: Annihilation

2975 *YEARS BEFORE STAR WARS: A New Hope*

Lost Tribe of the Sith[†]
  Pandemonium

1032 *YEARS BEFORE STAR WARS: A New Hope*

Knight Errant

Darth Bane: Path of Destruction

Darth Bane: Rule of Two

Darth Bane: Dynasty of Evil

RISE OF THE EMPIRE
67-0 YEARS BEFORE
STAR WARS: A New Hope

67 *YEARS BEFORE STAR WARS: A New Hope*

Darth Plagueis

33 *YEARS BEFORE STAR WARS: A New Hope*

Darth Maul: Saboteur*
Cloak of Deception
Darth Maul: Shadow Hunter

32 *YEARS BEFORE STAR WARS: A New Hope*

STAR WARS: EPISODE I
THE PHANTOM MENACE

Rogue Planet
Outbound Flight
The Approaching Storm

22 *YEARS BEFORE STAR WARS: A New Hope*

STAR WARS: EPISODE II
ATTACK OF THE CLONES

22-19 *YEARS BEFORE STAR WARS: A New Hope*

The Clone Wars
The Clone Wars: Wild Space
The Clone Wars: No Prisoners

Clone Wars Gambit
  Stealth
  Siege

Republic Commando
  Hard Contact
  Triple Zero
  True Colors
  Order 66

Shatterpoint
The Cestus Deception
The Hive*
MedStar I: Battle Surgeons
MedStar II: Jedi Healer
Jedi Trial
Yoda: Dark Rendezvous
Labyrinth of Evil

19 *YEARS BEFORE STAR WARS: A New Hope*

STAR WARS: EPISODE III
REVENGE OF THE SITH

Dark Lord: The Rise of Darth Vader

Imperial Commando
  501st

Coruscant Nights
  Jedi Twilight
  Street of Shadows
  Patterns of Force

The Last Jedi

*An eBook novella
**Forthcoming
[†] Lost Tribe of the Sith: The
  Collected Stories

THE STAR WARS NOVELS TIMELINE

DRAMATIS PERSONAE

Bhindi Drayson; retired intelligence officer (human female)

Garik "Face" Loran; retired intelligence officer (human male)

Jesmin Tainer; Antarian Ranger (human female)

Myri Antilles; gambler (human female)

Stavin Thaal; general (human male)

Trey Courser; mechanical engineer (human male)

Turman Durra; actor (Clawdite male)

Viull "Scut" Gorsat; biofabricator (Yuuzhan Vong male)

Voort "Piggy" saBinring; mathematics professor (Gamorrean male)

Wedge Antilles; retired pilot (human male)

A long time ago in a galaxy far, far away. . . .

STAR
WARS®
X-WING
MERCY KILL

CHAPTER ONE

Imperial Admiral Kosh Teradoc paused, irritated and self-conscious, just outside the entryway into the club. His garment, a tradesbeing's jumpsuit, was authentic, bought at a used-clothes stall in a poverty-stricken neighborhood. And the wig that covered his military-cut blond hair with a mop of lank, disarrayed brown hair was perfect. But his *posture*—he couldn't seem to shake off his upright military bearing, no matter how hard he tried. Loosening his shoulders, slumping, slouching . . . nothing worked for more than a few seconds.

"You're doing fine, Admiral." That was one of his bodyguards, whispering. "Try . . . try *smiling*."

Teradoc forced his mouth into a smile and held it that way. He took the final step up to the doors. They slid aside, emitting a wash of warmer air and the sounds of voices, music, and clinking glasses.

He and his guards moved into the club's waiting area. Its dark walls were decorated with holos advertising various brands of drinks; the moving images promised romance, social success, and wealth to patrons wise enough to choose the correct beverage. And they promised these things to nonhumans as well as humans.

One of Teradoc's guards, taller and fitter than he was and dressed like him, kept close. The other three held back as though they constituted a different party of patrons.

The seater approached. A brown Chadra-Fan woman who stood only as tall as Teradoc's waist, she wore a gold hostess gown, floor-length but exposing quite a lot of glossy fur.

Teradoc held up three fingers. He enunciated slowly so she would understand. "Another will be coming. Another man, joining us. You understand?"

Her mouth turned up in the faintest of smiles. "I do." Her voice was light, sweet, and perhaps just a touch mocking. "Are you the party joining Captain Hachat?"

"Um . . . yes."

"He's already here. This way, please." She turned and led them through broad, open double doors into the main room.

Teradoc followed. He felt heat in his cheeks. The little Chadra-Fan—had she actually *condescended* to him? He wondered if he should arrange an appropriate punishment.

The main room was cavernous, most of its innumerable tables occupied even at this late hour. The music and the din of conversation grew louder. And the smells—less than a quarter of the patrons were human. Teradoc saw horned Devaronians, furry Bothans, diminutive Sullustans, enormous, green-skinned Gamorreans, and more, and he fancied he could smell every one of them. And their alcohol.

"You're upright again, sir. You might try slouching."

Teradoc growled at his guard but complied.

There was one last blast of music from the upraised stage, and then the band, most of the players nonhuman, rose to the crowd's applause. They retreated behind the stage curtain.

Moments later the noise of the audience, hundreds of voices, changed—lowered, became expectant in tone. A new act filed out onstage. Six Gamorrean males, dressed in nothing but loincloths, their skin oiled and gleaming, moved out and arrayed themselves in a chevron-shaped formation. Recorded dance music, heavy on drums and woodwinds, blasted out from the stage's sound system.

The Gamorreans began moving to the music. They flexed, shimmied, strutted in unison. A shrill cry of appreciation rose from Gamorrean women in the audience, and from others as well.

Teradoc shuddered and vowed to sit with his back to the dancers.

The Chadra-Fan led him to a table only a few meters from the stage. A human man sat there already. Of medium height and muscular, he was young, with waist-length red hair in a braid. Costume jewelry, polished copper inset with black stones, was woven into the braid. He wore a long-sleeved tunic decorated with blobs of color of every hue, mismatched and discordant; it clashed with his military-style black pants and boots. He stood as Teradoc and his guard arrived.

"Captain Hachat?"

"The one and only." Hachat sat again and indicated the guard. "Who's your friend? He looks like a hundred kilos of preserved meat."

The Chadra-Fan seater, satisfied that she had discharged her duty, offered a little bow. "Your server will be here in a few moments." She turned and headed back to her station.

Teradoc glared after her and seated himself, facing away from the stage. He waited until his guard was in a chair before continuing. "Your messenger hinted at names. I want to hear them now . . . and to see proof."

Hachat nodded. "Of course. But first—would it help you to stop smiling? It looks like it's hurting your face."

"Um . . . yes." Teradoc relaxed, realized that his cheek muscles were indeed aching. He glanced around, noted the postures of many of the patrons around him, and slid down a little in his chair to match their slouches.

"Much better." Hachat sipped his drink, a poisonous-looking yellow concoction that glowed from within. There were two glasses, mostly empty but with a similar-looking residue at the bottom, beside it. "All right. I run a private space naval operation specializing in covert operations, especially retrievals."

Teradoc suppressed a sigh. *Why can't they ever just say, "I'm a pirate, a smuggler, a low-life piece of scum with something to sell"? Honesty would be so refreshing.*

"We recently found a prize vessel . . . one whose value could enable us to retire in luxury."

Teradoc shrugged. "Go on."

"The Palace of Piethet Brighteyes."

"I *thought* that was what your messenger was hinting at. But it's preposterous. In the centuries since it disappeared, the Palace has never been sighted, never reported. It will never be found."

Hachat grinned at him. "But it has been. Abandoned, intact, unplundered, in an area of your sector well away from settlements or trade routes."

"If you'd found it, you'd be selling off its jewels, its furnishings, all those paintings. Through a fence. Yet you come to me. You're lying."

"Here's the truth, Admiral. The vessel's antipersonnel defenses are still active. I lost a dozen men just getting into a secondary vehicle bay, where I retrieved one artifact and some lesser gems. Oh, yes, I could fire missiles at the palace until it cracked . . . but I would prefer to lose half its contents to a worthwhile partner than to explosions and hard vacuum. At least I'd get a partner and some goodwill out of it."

Teradoc rubbed at his temple. The *boom-boom-boom* from the sound system onstage behind him was giving him a headache. He returned his attention to Hachat. "Don't use my rank. Don't speak my name here."

"Whatever you want." Hachat took another sip of his drink. "You have access to Imperial Intelligence resources, the best slicers and intrusion experts in the galaxy. They could get past those defenses . . . and make us both rich."

"You mentioned an artifact."

"I have it with me. A show of faith, just as you proposed."

"Show me."

"Tell your bruiser not to panic; I'm only reaching for a comlink."

Teradoc glanced at his guard, gave a slight nod.

Hachat pulled free a small device clipped to his shirt collar and pressed a button on the side. "All right. It's coming."

They didn't have to wait long. A meter-tall Sullustan male in the blue-and-cream livery of the club's servers approached, awkwardly carrying a gray flimsiplast box nearly as tall as himself and half as wide and deep. He set it on the table beside Hachat's empty glasses. Hachat tipped him with a credcoin, and the Sullustan withdrew.

Teradoc glanced at his guard. The man stood, pulled open the box's top flaps, and reached in. He lifted out a glittering, gleaming, translucent statuette, nearly the full height of the box, and set it down in the center of the table. Hachat took the empty box and set it on the floor behind his chair.

The statuette was in the form of a human male standing atop a short pedestal. He was young, with aristocratic features, wearing a knee-length robe of classical

design. And it was all made of gemstones cunningly fitted together like jigsaw puzzle pieces, the joins so artful
that Teradoc could barely detect them.

All the color in the piece came from the stones used to
make it. Cloudy diamondlike gems provided the white
skin of the face, neck, arms, and legs. Rubylike stones
gave the eyes a red gleam. The robe was sapphire blue,
and the man's golden-yellow hair, unless Teradoc
guessed incorrectly, was lab-grown, gold-infused crystals. The pedestal was the only portion not translucent;
it was made up of glossy black stones.

The piece was exquisite. Teradoc felt his heart begin
to race.

There were *oohs* and *aahs* from surrounding tables.
Teradoc noted belatedly that he and Hachat were now
the object of much attention from patrons around them.

Hachat grinned at the onlookers and raised his voice
to be heard over the music. "I have a cargo bay full of
these. They go on sale tomorrow in Statz Market.
Twelve Imperial credits for a little one, thirty for a big
one like this. Stop by tomorrow." Then he turned his
attention back to Teradoc.

The admiral gave him a little smile, a real one. "Thus
you convince them that this piece is valueless, so no one
will attack us outside in an attempt to steal it."

"Thus I do. Now, are *you* convinced?"

"Almost." Teradoc reached up for his own comlink,
activated it, and spoke into it. "Send Cheems."

Hachat frowned at him. "Who's Cheems?"

"Someone who can make this arrangement come true.
Without him, there is no deal."

A moment later two men approached. One was another of Teradoc's artificially scruffy guards. The other
was human, his skin fair, his hair and beard dark with
some signs of graying. He was lean, well dressed in a
suit. Despite the formality of his garments, the man

seemed far more comfortable in this environment than Teradoc or the guards.

His duty done, the escort turned and removed himself to a distant table. At Teradoc's gesture, the man in the suit seated himself between the admiral and Hachat.

A server arrived. She was a dark-skinned human woman, dressed, like the Sullustan man had been, in a loose-fitting pantsuit of blue and cream. Her fitness and her broad smile were very much to Teradoc's taste.

She played that smile across each of them in turn. "Drinks, gentlemen?"

Hachat shook his head. The man in the suit and the guard did likewise. But Teradoc gave the server a smile in return. "A salty gaffer, please."

"You want a real bug in that or a candy bug?"

"Candy, please."

Once the server was gone, Hachat gave the new arrival a look. "Who is this?"

The man spoke, his voice dry and thin. "I am Mulus Cheems. I am a scientist specializing in crystalline materials . . . and a historian in the field of jewelry."

Teradoc cleared his throat. "Less talk, more action."

Cheems sighed. Then, from a coat pocket, he retrieved a small device. It was a gray square, six centimeters on a side, one centimeter thick. He pressed a small button on one side.

A square lens popped out from within the device. A bright light shone from the base of the lens. Words began scrolling in red across a small black screen inset just above the button.

Cheems leaned over to peer at the statuette, holding the lens before his right eye. He spoke as if to an apprentice. "The jewels used to fabricate this piece are valuable but not unusual. These could have been acquired on a variety of worlds at any time in the last several centuries. But the technique . . . definitely Vilivian. His work-shop, maybe his own hand."

Teradoc frowned. "Who?"

"Vilivian. A Hapan gemwright whose intricately fitted gems enjoyed a brief but influential vogue a few centuries back. His financial records indicated several sales to Piethet Brighteyes." Cheems moved the lens up from the statuette's chest to his face. "Interesting. Adegan crystals for the red eyes. And the coating that maintains the piece's structural integrity . . . not a polymer. Micro-fused diamond dust. No longer employed because of costs compared with polymers. Beautiful, absolutely beautiful." He sat back and, with a press of the button, snapped the lens back into its casing.

Teradoc felt a flash of impatience. "Well?"

"Well? Oh—is it authentic? Yes. Absolutely. I believe it's the piece titled *Light and Dark*. Worth a Moff's ran-som."

Teradoc sat back and stared at the statuette. The Pal-ace of Piethet Brighteyes—with that fortune in hand, he could resign his commission, buy an entire planetary system, and settle into a life of luxury, far away from the struggles between the Empire and the New Republic. A warmth began to suffuse his body, a realization that his future had just become very, very pleasant.

The dark-skinned server returned and set Teradoc's drink before him. He smiled at her and paid with a cred-coin worth twenty times the cost of the drink. He could afford to be generous. "Keep it."

"Thank you, sir." She swept the coin away to some unknown pocket and withdrew—but not too far. It was clear to Teradoc that she was hovering in case he needed special attention.

Teradoc glanced back at Hachat. "I'm convinced."

"Excellent." Hachat extended a hand. "Partners."

"Well . . . we need to negotiate our percentages. I was thinking that I'd take a hundred percent."

Hachat withdrew his hand. Far from looking surprised or offended, he smiled. "Do you Imperial officer types study the same *How to Backstab* manual? You are definitely doing it by the book."

"Captain, you're going to experience quite a lot of enhanced interrogation in the near future. You'll endure a lot of pain before cracking and telling me where the Palace is. If you choose to antagonize me, I might just double that pain."

Hachat shook his head wonderingly. "What I don't get is this whole Grand Admiral Thrawn thing. Every hopped-up junior naval officer tries to be like him. Elegant, inscrutable . . . and an art lover. Being an art lover doesn't make you a genius, you know."

"That's an extra week of torture right there."

"Plus, unlike Thrawn, you're about as impressive as a Gungan with his underwear full of stinging insects."

"Three weeks. And at this moment, my guard has a blaster leveled at your gut under the table."

"Oh, my." Hachat glanced at the guard. He raised his hands to either side of his face, indicating surrender. "*Pleeeeease* don't shoot me, foul-smelling man. Please, oh please, oh pleasepleaseplease."

Teradoc stared at him, perplexed.

Onstage the porcine Gamorrean dancers moved through a new rotation, which brought the slenderest of them up to the forward position. He was slender only by Gamorrean standards, weighing in at a touch under 150 kilos, but he moved well and there were good muscles to be glimpsed under his body fat.

With the rest of the troupe, he executed a half turn, which left them facing the rear of the stage, and followed up with a series of fanny-shakes, each accompanied by a lateral hop. Then they began a slow turn back toward the crowd, the movement accentuated by a series of belly-rolls that had the Gamorrean women in the crowd yelling.

Just as, with a final belly-roll, he once again faced forward, the slenderest dancer could see Hachat's table . . . and Hachat with his hands up.

He felt a touch of light-headedness as adrenaline hit his system. Things were a go.

Near Hachat's table, the dark-skinned server moved unobtrusively toward Teradoc.

The Gamorrean dancer, whose name was Piggy, stopped his dance, threw back his head, and shrilled a few words in the Gamorrean tongue: "It's a raid! Run!"

From elsewhere in the room, the cry was repeated in Basic and other languages. Piggy noted approvingly that the fidelity of those shouts was so good that few people, if any, would realize they were recordings.

Alarm rippled in an instant through the crowd, through the dancers.

Suddenly all the Gamorreans in the place were heaving themselves to their feet, sometimes knocking their table over in panicky haste, and the non-Gamorrean patrons followed suit. Confused, Teradoc took his attention from Hachat for a moment and turned to look across the sea of tables.

There were *booms* from the room's two side exits. Both doors blew in, blasted off their rails by what had to have been shaped charges. Tall men in Imperial Navy Special Forces armor charged in through those doors.

A flash of motion to Teradoc's right drew his attention. He saw the dark-skinned server approach and lash out in a perfectly executed side kick. Her sandaled foot snaked in just beneath the tabletop. Even over the tumult in the room, Teradoc heard the *crack* that had to be his guard's hand or wrist breaking. The guard's blaster pistol flew from his hand, thumped into Teradoc's side, and fell to the floor.

The server stayed balanced on her planted foot, cocked her kicking leg again, and lashed out once more, this time connecting with the guard's jaw as he turned to look at her. The guard wobbled and slid from his chair.

Then the server dived in the opposite direction, rolling as she hit the floor, vanishing out of Teradoc's sight under the next table.

Teradoc grabbed for the blaster on the floor. He got it in his hand.

Hachat hadn't lost his smile. He turned to face the glasses on the table and shouted directly at them: "Boom boy!"

One of the drink glasses, mostly empty, erupted in thick yellow smoke. Teradoc, as he straightened and brought the blaster up, found himself engulfed in a haze that smelled of alcohol and more bitter chemicals. It stung his eyes. Now he could not see as far as the other side of the table.

He stood and warily circled the table . . . and, by touch, found only empty chairs. Hachat was gone. Cheems was gone.

The statuette was still there. Teradoc grabbed it, then stumbled away from the table, out from within the choking smoke.

While the dancers and patrons ran, Piggy stood motionless onstage and narrated. He subvocalized into his throat implant, which rendered his squealy, grunty Gamorrean pronunciation into comprehensible Basic. The implant also transmitted his words over a specific comm frequency. "Guards at Tables Twelve and Forty maintaining discipline and scanning for targets. But they've got none. Shalla, stay low, Table Forty's looking in your direction."

Small voices buzzed in the tiny comm receiver in his ear. "Heard that, Piggy." "Got Twelve, Twelve is down." "Forty's in my sights."

Now the guard who had brought Cheems to Teradoc approached that table once more. This time he had a blaster pistol in one hand. With his free hand, he shoved patrons out of his way. He reached the verge of the yellow smoke, then began circling it, looking for targets.

He found some. His head snapped over to the right. Piggy glanced in that direction and saw Hachat and Cheems almost at the ruined doorway in the wall. The guard raised his pistol, waiting for a clear shot.

Well, it was time to go anyway. Piggy ran the three steps to the stage's edge and hurled himself forward. He cleared the nearest table and came down on Teradoc's guard, smashing him to the floor, breaking the man's bones. The guard's blaster skidded across the floor and was lost, masked by yellow smoke and patrons' fast-moving legs.

Piggy stood. He'd felt the impact, too, but had been prepared for it; and he was well padded by muscle and fat. Nothing in him had broken. He looked at the guard and was satisfied that the unconscious man posed no more danger.

Now he heard Hachat's voice across the comm. "We have the package. Extract. Call in when you get to the exit."

Most of the bar patrons, those who weren't running in blind panic, were surging toward and through the bar's main entrance, which inexplicably had no Imperial Navy troopers near it. Piggy turned toward the exit Hachat and Cheems had used. That doorway did have a forbidding-looking Imperial trooper standing beside it. Heedless of the danger posed by the soldier, Piggy shoved his way through toppled furniture and scrambling patrons. He made it to the door.

The armored trooper merely nodded at him. "Nice moves, Dancer Boy."

Piggy growled at him, then passed through the door, which still smoked from the charge that had breached it.

Once in the dimly lit service corridor beyond, Piggy headed toward the building's rear service exit. "Piggy exiting." He reached the door at the end of the corridor. It slid open for him, and he stepped outside into cooler night air.

"Freeze or I'll shoot!" The bellow came from just beside his right ear. It was deep, male, ferocious.

Piggy winced, held up his hands. Unarmed and nearly naked, his eyes not yet adjusted to the nighttime darkness, he didn't stand a chance.

Then his assailant chuckled. "Got you again."

Piggy turned, glaring.

Situated by the door, armed not with a blaster but with a bandolier of grenades, stood a humanoid, tall as but not nearly as hairy as a Wookiee. The individual was lean for his two-meter-plus height, brown-furred, his face long, his big square teeth bared in a triumphant smile. He wore a black traveler's robe; it gapped to show the brown jumpsuit and bandolier beneath.

Piggy reached up to grab and tug at the speaker's whiskers. "Not funny, Runt."

"Plenty funny."

"I'll get you for that."

"You keep saying that. It never happens."

Piggy sighed and released his friend. His eyes were now more adjusted. In the gloom, decorated with distant lights like a continuation of the starfield above, he could make out the start of the marina's dock, the glow rods outlining old-fashioned watercraft in their berths, not far away.

Much nearer was the team's extraction vehicle, an old airspeeder—a flatbed model with oversized repulsors and motivators. It was active, floating a meter above the ground on motivator thrust. Signs on the sides of its cab proclaimed it to be a tug, the sort sent out to rescue the watercraft of the rich and hapless when their own motivators conked out. There were sturdy winches affixed in the bed.

In the cab, a Devaronian man sat at the pilot's controls. He turned his horned head and flashed Piggy a sharp-toothed smile through the rear viewport. Cheems and Hachat were already situated in the cab beside him.

Piggy moved up to the speeder and clambered into the cargo bed. The vehicle rocked a little under his weight. He looked around for the bundle that should have been waiting for him, but it was nowhere to be seen. He sighed and sat facing the rear, his back to the cab. Then he stared at the club's back door, at Runt situated beside it. "Come on, come on."

The door slid open long enough to admit the dark-skinned server. Unmolested by Runt, she ran to the airspeeder, vaulted into the bed, and settled down beside Piggy. "Shalla exited." She glanced at Piggy. "Weren't you supposed to have a robe here?"

He knew his reply sounded long suffering. "Yes. And who took it? Who decided to leave me almost naked here as I wait? I'm betting I'll never know."

Shalla nodded, clearly used to the ways of her comrades. "You made yourself a lot of fans tonight. Those Gamorrean ladies were screaming their brains out. And not just the Gamorreans. You could have had so much action this evening . . ."

Piggy rolled his eyes. As far as he was concerned, those Gamorrean women had no brains to scream out.

Augmented by biological experiments when he was a child, Piggy was the only genius of his kind. And unlike some, he could not bear the thought of pairing up with someone whose intelligence was far, far below his.

So he was alone.

Hachat turned to glare back through the cab's rear viewport. "Kell . . ."

Piggy heard the man's response in his ear. "Busy, Boss."

"Kell, do I have to come in there after you?"

"Busy." Then the door slid open for Kell, the armored trooper who had let Piggy pass. He fell through the doorway, slamming to the ground on his back, one of Teradoc's guards on top of him.

Runt reached down, grabbed the guard by the shoulder and neck, and pulled, peeling the man off as though he were the unresisting rind of a fruit. Runt shook the guard, and kept shaking him as Kell rose and trotted to the speeder.

By the time Kell was settling in beside Shalla, the guard was completely limp. Runt dropped him and regarded him quizzically for a second. Then he pulled two grenades free from his bandolier. He twisted a dial on each and stepped over to stand in front of the door. When it slid open for him, he lobbed them through the doorway. He waited there as they detonated, making little noise but filling the corridor entirely with thick black smoke. Then he joined the others, settling in at the rear of the speeder bed, facing Piggy. "Runt exited. Team One complete."

Cheems expected them to blast their way as far as possible from the Imperial Navy base and the city that surrounded it. But they flew only a few hundred meters along the marina boundary. Then they abandoned their speeder in a dark, grassy field just outside the marina gates and hurried on foot along old-fashioned wooden docks. Soon afterward, they boarded a long, elegant yacht in gleaming Imperial-style white.

Within a few minutes, they had backed the yacht out of its berth, maneuvered it into the broad waters of the bay, and set a course for the open sea beyond.

Eight in all, they assembled on the stern deck, which was decorated with comfortable, weather-resistant furnishings, a bar, and a grill. Cheems sat on a puffy chair and watched, bewildered, as his rescuers continued their high-energy preparations.

The Devaronian, whom the others called Elassar, broke top-grade bantha steaks out of a cold locker and began arraying them on the grill. Piggy the Gamorrean located and donned a white robe, then began mixing drinks. Kell shed his armor, dumping it and his Imperial weapons over the side. Hachat disappeared belowdecks for two minutes and reemerged, his hair now short and brown, his clothes innocuous. Runt shed his traveler's robe and set up a small but expensive-looking portable computer array on an end table. A yellow-skinned human man who had not been on the speeder joined Kell and stripped off his own Imperial armor, throwing it overboard. Shalla merely stretched out on a lounge chair and smiled as she watched the men work.

Cheems finally worked up the courage to speak. "Um . . . excuse me . . . not that I'm complaining . . . but could I get some sort of summary on what just happened?"

Hachat grinned and settled onto a couch beside Cheems's chair. "My name isn't Hachat. It's Garik Loran. Captain Loran, New Republic Intelligence. Runt, do you have the tracker signal yet?"

"Working on it."

"Put it up on the main monitor, superimpose the local map."

No less confused, Cheems interrupted. "Garik Loran? *Face* Loran, the boy actor?"

Face did not quite suppress a wince. "That was a long time ago. But yes."

"I love *The Lifeday Murders*. I have a copy on my datapad."

"Yeah . . . Anyway, what do you think this was all about?"

"Getting me out of the admiral's hands, I suppose." Cheems frowned, reconstructing the sequence of events in his mind. "Two days ago, as I was being led from my laboratory to my prison quarters, I felt a nasty sting in my back. I assume you shot me with some sort of communications device. Little buzzy voices vibrating in my shoulder blade."

Face nodded. He gestured toward the man with yellow skin. "That's Bettin. He's our sniper and exotic-weapons expert. He tagged you from a distance of nearly a kilometer, which was as close as we could get to you."

Bettin waved, cheerful. "Kriffing hard shot, too. Crosswind, low-mass package. Piggy was my spotter. I had to rely pretty heavily on his skills at calculation."

"Yes, yes." Face sounded impatient. "So, anyway, that was step one. Getting in contact with you."

Cheems considered. "And step two was telling me that I was going to be called on to authenticate an artifact, and that I absolutely had to do that, regardless of what I was looking at. You told me that doing this was the only way I'd ever get off that naval base alive."

Face nodded.

"What *was* I looking at? The material had a crystalline structure, definitely, but it wasn't diamond or any other precious stone. In fact, it looked a bit like crystallized anthracite."

Kell, standing at the bar, grinned at Cheems. No longer concealed by his helmet, his features were fair, very handsome. His brown hair was worn in a buzz cut, retreating from a widow's peak. "Very good. It's a modified form of anthracite in a crystallized form."

"So I was within centimeters of ten kilos of high explosive?" Cheems thought he could feel the blood draining from his head.

"Nearer fifteen. Plus a transceiver, power unit, and some control chips in the base." Kell shrugged, accepted a drink from Piggy.

Cheems shook his head. "And I was passing it off as a work of art!"

Kell stared at him, clearly miffed. "It *was* a work of art."

Face caught Cheems's attention again. "Teradoc's habits and methods are well known to Intelligence. We had to have bait that required a gem expert to authenticate; we had to have a sneaky profit motive so Teradoc would bring you off base to do the authentication; and we had to have the bait be very valuable so when trouble erupted he'd grab it and run."

"Back to his base." Cheems felt a chill grip him. "Back to his most secure area, where his treasures are stored. His personal vault."

Face gave him a *now you get it* smile. "Which is where, exactly?"

"Directly beneath his secure research-and-development laboratories."

"Where, if Intelligence is right, his people are experimenting with plague viruses, self-replicating nonbiological toxins, and the project for which Teradoc kidnapped *you*, Dr. Cheems."

"A sonic device. The idea was that sound waves

pitched and cycling correctly could resonate with light-saber crystals, shattering them."

For once, Face looked concerned. "Could it actually work?"

Cheems shook his head. "Not in a practical way. Against exposed crystals, yes. But lightsaber hilts insulate the crystals too effectively. I couldn't tell the admiral that, though. To tell him *This can't work* would basically be to say, *Kill me now, please, I'm of no more use to you.*" Belatedly Cheems realized that he'd said too much. If this miracle rescue was itself a scam, if he was currently surrounded by *Imperial* Intelligence operatives, he'd just signed his own execution order. He gulped.

Runt turned to Face. "I have it." He repositioned the main monitor at his table so others could see.

The monitor showed an overhead map view of the planet's capital city, its Imperial Navy base, the huge bay that bordered both to the east. A blinking yellow light was stationary deep within the base. Then, as they watched, the light faded to nothingness.

Cheems glanced at Face. "Did your device just fail?"

Face shook his head. "No. It was taken into a secure area where comm signals can't penetrate. Its internal circuitry, some of which is a planetary positioning system, knows where it is—the research-and-development labs. Atmospheric pressure meters are telling it how deep in the ground it is. At the depth of Teradoc's personal vault, well . . ."

There was a distant rumble from the west, not even a *boom*. Everyone looked in that direction. There was nothing to see other than the city lights for a moment; then spotlights sprang to life all across the naval base, sweeping across the nighttime sky.

Faraway alarms began to howl.

Face settled back into the couch, comfortable. "Right

now, the lower portions of the labs have been vaporized. Pathogen vaults and viral reactors have been breached. Sensors are detecting dangerous pathogens escaping into the air. Vents are slamming shut and sealing, automated decontamination measures are activating. Before the decontamination safety measures are done, everything in that site will be burned to ash and chemically sterilized. Sadly, I suspect Teradoc isn't experiencing any of that, as he was doubtless admiring his new prize when it went off. But we owe him a debt of gratitude. He saved us months' worth of work by smuggling our bomb past his own base security all by himself."

Cheems looked at Piggy. "I could use something very tall and very potent to drink."

Piggy flashed his tusks in a Gamorrean smile. "Coming up."

Face turned to Piggy. "I'll have a salty gaffer. In Teradoc's honor. Candy bug, please." He returned his attention to Cheems. "We'd like you to do one more thing before we get you offworld and into New Republic space. I'd appreciate it if you'd go below and appraise any gemstone items you find. We'll be turning this yacht and everything on it over to a resistance cell; I'd like to be able to point them at the more valuable items."

Cheems frowned. "This isn't your yacht?"

"Oh, no. It's Teradoc's. We stole it."

CHAPTER TWO

It was only two kilometers from his office to his home, but on nights like this, when he was weary, Professor Voort saBinring chose not to make the walk. This affluent university town was blessed with rolling walkways, locally known as rumblers, and tonight Voort chose just to stand and let the campus buildings, houses, and apartment blocks roll serenely past. Many of these homes were dark at this hour, but he could see through the windows of others, into lit interiors where families dined, talked, watched holodramas.

He wasn't physically tired, not really. And it wasn't that he was old. He was middle-aged, yes, but he exercised and saw the medics at regular intervals. Yes, by human standards, he was overweight, but he was actually a touch lean for a Gamorrean.

No, the weariness came from within him. Internal and eternal. There was nothing at either end of his two-kilometer daily commute to beckon him, to invigorate him. His students seemed to be blocks of permacrete, immobile and emotionless, enduring his courses as though to do so were a condition of parole. His home was a place where he could sleep, nothing more.

The rolling walkway was elevated, situated above and beside the stationary walkway he usually took. Glow rods on the rumbler's underside illuminated pedestrians on the stationary walk. As he reached the halfway point on his trip home, Voort saw a pedestrian standing at ground level on the other side of the street, beneath the rumbler headed back toward campus. The figure, a shadow in a wide-brimmed hat and a traveler's over-coat, looked up as Voort passed and stepped forward to cross the street. The shadow moved to the near walk, stepped on an open-air lift plate, and rose to the level of Voort's rumbler. He stepped off onto the moving walkway and turned in Voort's direction. Hands in his coat pockets, he began walking toward Voort.

Voort felt a mixture of curiosity and alarm. It had been five standard years since he'd experienced that mixture of emotions: the day a high-strung immigrant from nearby Lorrd had come flying across his office desk at him in a genuine effort to murder him. Alarm had faded once Voort had knocked the wind from the boy and returned him to his chair, and curiosity had faded once Voort learned the boy felt that perfect scores were his birthright.

Perhaps this stalker would assault him for the dogged-ness with which Voort taught Lulagg's Third Theorem. Or perhaps a coalition of students had pooled their al-lowances and food servers' wages to buy a hit on their professor. If so, the assault would be an interesting side item in tomorrow's news briefs.

Voort tallied his resources: one gray suit, dull both in cut and color; one datapad; identicard, credcards, cred-coins; fists and tusks. He waited.

The shadowy man drew to a stop a couple of meters from him and spoke, his voice rich and deep. "Hello,

Piggy." He tilted his head up so that his hat brim no longer cast his face into shadow.

His dark, trim beard and mustache, his features, timeless and handsome—Voort had learned long ago what types of appearance humans found pleasing in one another—were instantly familiar. Voort brightened "Face! I feel let down. I was looking forward to being assaulted."

Face shook it off. "Well, if you like, I can try to wrestle you off this walkway. That's a good three-meter drop."

"Perhaps later." Voort let a number of possibilities run like columns of numbers through his head. "No."

Face's eyebrows shot up. "No, what?"

"In the last fifteen years, we've only encountered each other by appointment. Such as your wedding. This is an ambush. So you're up to something. No, I will not work for you. And, by the way, you know it's not Piggy anymore. Call me Voort."

"Voort, then. I want you to come work for me."

Voort slumped. "What did I just tell you?"

"I've been working myself up just to *say* those words for thousands of light-years. You can't deny me the right to say them. So, how about it?"

"I just said no."

"Refusals offered before the offer is made don't count."

Voort sighed. "We're only a few hundred meters from my quarters. Let's talk there." He stepped off the walk onto the next lift plate.

Face stepped off with him. "There's less buzz to your voice these days. Is that a new implant?"

"Upgraded, yes. The dean of the School of Mathematics insisted. Less buzz means less menacing, or something."

At ground level they stepped off. Face looked around, taking in the gently aging neighborhood, the cheerful-looking monitor droid, round and immobile as a bronze snow figure, on the street corner. "You enjoying the work?"

Voort took a moment to answer. "Sometimes."

"Ah."

"What about you? You enjoying retirement?"

Face smiled. The expression was more sinister than happy. "When Jacen Solo's war ended, pretty much every officer who'd failed to denounce him starting when he was a teenager was booted. I really don't call that retirement."

"Well, what's the word for being purged but not killed or arrested, then?"

"Retirement."

"Ah. What about your family?"

"Dia's doing great. She's now chief trainer and a full partner in the transport company she bought into. She was on HoloNet News a lot a while back, offering perspectives on the slave uprisings popping off all over the galaxy. I did adopt Adra; she's my daughter now, too. She's sixteen and dating, and if I had any hair left, it would all be white. But she's a good kid."

Voort grunted an acknowledgment of Face's words. He hadn't really been interested in all those details. But the social contract that existed between old friends, however distant they might now be, insisted that one ask such things.

They walked in silence until Voort gestured to indicate the building where he lived, a square, four-story greenstone. Entering, he took the stairs rather than the turbolift to the second story, then led Face into his quarters. Face shed his overcoat and hat, revealing his head to be as shiny-bald as Voort remembered. His clothes were his favorite sort, black and expensive but of an unobtrusive cut.

Voort gave Face the brief tour of sleeping quarters,

office, kitchen, and social room. Face made dutifully appreciative noises at the home's utilitarian, undecorated simplicity, then spent a few minutes doing a sweep for listening devices and micro-holocams. When he was done, the two of them returned to the social room.

Face sat on the couch and arrayed himself as if posing to advertise the clothes he wore. "I'm getting the band back together."

Voort lowered himself into his easy chair more quickly and awkwardly than he had intended to. "The Wraiths?" He gave Face an incredulous look. "When Bhindi Drayson told me they'd been decommissioned, she made it sound like it had been a personal mission of Chief of State Daala to scrub them out of existence."

Face nodded. "It was. Not only was it part of the same purge that got me, Daala took a special delight in getting rid of rogue operatives who play by their own rules. Not that we actually ever had rules."

"So how, in just three years, have you and the Wraiths been redeemed so that you can put the unit back together?"

Face turned a conspiratorial smile on his old friend. "We haven't. I'm putting the Wraiths back together again . . . and the government doesn't know a thing about it."

Voort narrowed his eyes suspiciously. "I'm having a hard time decrypting that. You're putting the Wraiths back together without government permission or oversight? Are you going pirate?"

Face grinned. "Not . . . exactly. What do you know about Borath Maddeus?"

"The head of Galactic Alliance Security, including Intelligence, for the last three years. He replaced Belindi Kalenda when she was swept off by the same purge."

"I barely know him. A very competent organizer, that's his reputation. And a team player, perfect for the new regime. Got along very well with Daala during her tenure, gets along great with Chief of State Dorvan now." Face put his hands together and looked at Voort over the steeple formed by his fingers. "He arranged to see me—away from his offices, away from his handlers and subordinates—a while back."

"To ask you to put the Wraiths back together."

"Yes. But not as an official Intelligence unit. You're aware of the Lecersen Conspiracy?"

Voort snorted. "Who isn't?" In the most recent set of crises facing the Galactic Alliance government, a combination of slave uprisings and government coups, it had been revealed that one of the major influences unbalancing the government was a conspiracy among Moff Drikl Lecersen of the Imperial Remnant, Senator Fost Bramsin, Senator Haydnat Treen, Admiral Sallinor Parova, General Merratt Jaxton, and others, who were maneuvering to assume control of the Alliance and then merge it into the Imperial Remnant, subordinating all the Alliance's objectives to the Empire's.

"General Maddeus has heard some disquieting rumors that General Stavin Thaal, head of the Alliance Army, might have been part of that same conspiracy." Face shrugged. "Nothing more than rumors, though."

"Still, Thaal's one of the most powerful individuals in the Alliance." Feeling unsettled, Voort stood. He moved to the undecorated wall and pressed a code sequence on the keypad there. The large window beside it slid open, revealing a view of the nighttime street outside. The rumble of the distant rolling walkways was audible again. Cool air washed over him, which was the effect he wanted.

He turned back to Face. "Maddeus doesn't trust his own people to determine whether there's any truth to the rumors?"

"No, he doesn't. He didn't select most of them, remember. Some he inherited from his predecessor, and the majority of the rest were appointed by the same committees and political factions that appointed *him*."

"Huh. Well, good luck."

"Come on, Piggy—Voort. Don't be that way."

"Face, I'm a *professor of mathematics*. All that Wraith Squadron craziness ended for me fifteen years ago."

Face nodded, his expression sympathetic. "The Yuuzhan Vong War ended a lot of things for a lot of people. But people have bounced back from what they've lost. They've started over."

"As I have."

"No, you haven't." Face gestured, a sweeping, circular move that took in Voort's quarters plus the community outside the window. "You've gone to ground; you've hidden. You've licked your wounds, and I know how deep they were. But Voort, you either need to rejoin the ranks of the living . . . or acknowledge to yourself that you're actually dead."

Voort broke out in the grunting, wheezing noises that were Gamorrean laughter. "Master motivator. When did you write that little speech? On the shuttle trip in to Ayceezee?"

"No shuttle. Maddeus provided me with a hyperdrive-equipped space yacht, *Quarren Eye,* just about the only resource he could give me. But yes, I wrote that line on the trip here. What do you think of it?"

"It would play well on a holodrama. But in real life, no."

Face sighed. "Speech or not, it's the truth, Voort."

"I'm a math instructor now. I take mathematical concepts, I shape them into spikes, and I spend months hammering them into the heads of students who'd much rather be involved in amorous pursuits or playing games, and all because they need it, even if their heads are as hard as durasteel."

"And *that* little speech might have impressed *me* . . . except that when I asked you if you were enjoying your work, your answer sounded like, *It's slightly better than being tortured by pirates.*"

Voort was quiet for a moment, then answered. "Toward the end, being a Wraith was considerably worse than being tortured by pirates."

"That was then. Look, Voort, I'm going to stop wasting both our time and jump straight to my final argument."

"Also pre-scripted?"

"In part. I'd like to be able to convince you with the fact that you're wasting your time here, but you already know that. You're a mathematical genius, capable of doing hyperspace navigation calculations in your head, a strategist capable of factoring in more variables than anyone I've met, a capable starfighter pilot, and an organizer second to none, and here you are convincing undergraduates that dabbling with calculus won't cause them to lose the will to live. But again, you know that. What you don't apparently understand is that they actually *don't* need you. A teacher droid can do everything you're doing for your students, except maybe burp."

"A droid can't instill into them a love of mathematics."

"Neither can you, not anymore. *Those students don't need you* . . . and I do." Face shrugged. "I'm not even asking as an old friend. We could be strangers, and I'd still need you.

"And Voort, now you're thinking that it could be Chashima all over again, that no matter how much you're needed, you can fail. But you *didn't* fail on Chashima. What you did was lose everything that was important to you." His gesture again took in Voort's quarters. "This is the result. It's time to come where you're needed. So, what's it going to be?"

CHAPTER THREE

They moved along the corridor that connected the spaceport's arrivals-and-inspections facilities to the spaceport exits. In front walked a redheaded business-man wearing a tired, droopy suit. Beside and a step be-hind walked a jumpsuited Gamorrean porter pushing his hover-rack of luggage.

Voort sighed. "Years of laying down the law on human and other students has caused me to forget that the Gamorrean in disguise is always going to be a me-nial laborer." He didn't bother to activate his voice im-plant; Face knew enough Gamorrean to understand.

Face nodded, scratching at an itchy spot on his fore-head where his red wig met his scalp. "We could dress you up as a master chef or a fleet admiral . . . but then people would remember you."

"They *should*. Have you ever tasted my bantha cutlet with spicefruit reduction? And speaking of my skills—are we being compensated for any of this?"

Face grinned. "You know it's not about the money. The new Wraiths all signed on to prove themselves. Or because they had a grudge."

"It's not about the money for me, either. It's about

not being exploited. About a free economy. About being able to negotiate your own worth—"

"We'll find some compensation when the assignment's all done. If the general's crooked, we'll steal his favorite vessel and sell it. If he isn't . . . we'll find a crooked general, steal *his* favorite vessel, and sell *that*."

Voort nodded. "Just so long as we're clear on that."

They came to the spaceport's main exit lobby, a cavernous space with a lofty ceiling. The chamber was decorated with monitors and midair holograms showing ever-changing views of distant vacation worlds and spectacular starfields. Opposite were the banks of doors leading out into daylight. The brilliance beyond the doors threatened to dazzle Voort's eyes.

But Face gestured and the two of them stopped where they were, along the wall just where the corridor tunnel emptied into the lobby. Men and women of every imaginable species moved past on their way to or from commercial spaceflights.

A young human woman in clothes styled to resemble a starfighter pilot's jumpsuit and jacket but made of crinkly gold cloth, her hair a more striking and unnatural red than Face's, bumped into Face, made a vague noise of apology, and hurried past, continuing onward toward the exit.

Voort scowled at Face. "I saw that."

"Of course you did."

"What did she slip you?"

Face reached into a suit coat pocket and drew out a datapad. It was small, its once-gleaming surface scratched and dull. "This. It's wired to overheat and ignite in about three minutes."

"Well, then, don't hold it in your mouth."

Face grinned again. He loosened a seal on one of the bags on the rolling rack and slipped the datapad inside, then resealed the bag. "By the way, that girl was Myri Antilles."

Voort felt his knees wobble. He held up his hand, palm down, at about waist level. "Wedge's daughter? Little Myri?"

"They grow up fast, don't they? Don't *ever* get in a sabacc game with her: she'll end up owning everything you possess."

Voort looked after the young woman. She was still in sight, her gold outfit and mane of poisonous red hair making her easy to pick out of the crowd. "She's a Wraith?"

"Wraith Three. You're Wraith Seven, by the way. You need to go catch up with her."

"You're staying here?"

Face nodded. "In two and a half minutes, this bag will ignite. Safety workers will put out the fire. Soon after, they'll examine the burned bags, finding evidence that will tie in to a munitions heist that's happening in a few minutes, and they'll review the holocam images of who was with these bags, so they'll see you and me. Remember not to scrub off your makeup and appliances until after you're through with the heist."

"Wait. Heist—*now*?"

"Go catch Three, she'll fill you in."

"Right." Voort extracted his travel bag from the pile of containers on the hover-rack and dashed off in Myri's direction.

Face turned and headed back along the spaceport tunnel, leaving the rack hovering where it was.

Voort caught up to Myri at the pickup lane where arriving travelers could arrange airspeeder trips to homes and hostels. She was in the act of waving down an oncoming speeder, an enormous blue thing so scratched and dented that no other traveler seemed to want to engage it. She smiled up at Voort. "Hello, Seven. No need to trigger your speaker. I understand Gamorrean."

Voort stared at her. The face under that preposterous wig was faintly familiar, despite the effects of too-thick green makeup surrounding her eyes and making them look like hieroglyphs rendered by a child—Voort could see traces of Wedge and Iella, her parents, in her fine-boned features. But he shook his head. "I did *not* give you permission to become an adult."

"Silly. If I'd grown up, would I be doing this?"

"You make a good point."

The battered blue speeder descended to curb level and slowed to a halt before them. Voort opened the door for Myri like any dutiful porter, then tossed his bag into the baggage compartment at the rear. He clambered into the rear seat and slid the door shut. The speeder slid smoothly away from the spaceport crowd and rose into a traffic lane.

The pilot was a human man. From behind, Voort could see that he had fair skin, short brown hair that clearly lightened toward yellow in sunlight, and a tanned neck. And he had shoulders so broad and muscular that Voort had only ever seen their like in holoventure actors, muscle models, and hardworking narcissists. Voort glanced at Myri, an interrogation—*One of us or a civilian?*

She grinned at him. "Voort saBinring, Seven, this is Trey Courser, Wraith Four."

Trey glanced over his shoulder and offered a brief wave. His features suggested he was younger than Voort would have guessed—barely out of his teens. "Heard a lot of stories about you, Seven." His voice was light, pleasant.

Voort snorted and activated his throat implant. "Either you've already swept this vehicle for listening devices or we're already in trouble."

Trey returned his attention to the traffic lane. "Both, probably. But I rebuilt this junker from bow to stern and I sweep it regularly. We're good."

Myri rested her chin on her seat back. "Four's our machine and droid fabricator. Light-duty computer slicer. Come to think of it, most of us are light-duty computer slicers. And he'd be our trainer, if any of the rest of us ever exercised."

The words *unit strongman* crossed Voort's mind, but he didn't speak them. "Where are we going and what are we doing?"

"We're not going, we're there." Trey slid the airspeeder sideways until it was out of the traffic lane. Moving in beside a low permacrete wall, he cycled the speeder's repulsors and thrusters, causing the vehicle to buck, nose down, and descend awkwardly. He set the speeder down and killed the motivators. Landspeeders and airspeeders swung wide of it as they passed.

". . . and what are we doing?"

Myri pulled a chrono out of a pocket and checked it. "Four's about to hide under a blanket. You and I are going to exit this vehicle, not allowing ourselves to be smashed flat by other pilots, and stand at its back. You're wearing something on your palms and fingers to prevent prints, yes?"

"As per instructions."

"Good. C'mon." She exited the speeder on the side away from traffic, leaving her door open, and dashed to the rear of the vehicle.

Sighing, Voort followed. "Face sort of left out until the last moment the fact that I'd be arriving in the middle of an operation in progress."

Myri gave him a blank look. "Face? Face who?"

"The man you slipped the overheating datapad to. Face Loran."

Her eyes got wide. "That was *Face Loran*? He's in on this?"

"Don't you know?"

"No. Now I need you to menace me. Loom over me. Give me some good Gamorrean insults." As if he'd already begun, she leaned away from him, bending backward over the tail of the speeder, and assumed a frightened expression, her hands near her face as if anticipating a blow.

Voort was startled into silence for a moment, then struggled to comply. He switched off his translator implant and began bellowing in Gamorrean. "*You have the color sense of a monkey-lizard and I suspect you pour sugar on your meat loaf.*"

Myri giggled. "Insults are not your field of expertise, are they?" Then she schooled her expression back into a frightened look. She raised her head a bit to peek over his shoulder, then slumped backward again. "Ten more seconds. Wave your fists."

Voort felt a prickling sensation in the small of his back. He was sure trouble had to be arriving from behind, but he couldn't break character to look. He merely raised two meaty fists and waved them as if deciding where to punch Myri first. "*Your scores in calculus are an atrocity, and you think square roots refer to artificial hair!*" Actually, there was no Gamorrean word for "calculus," but he made do with an expression meaning "big nasty math."

Through gritted teeth, Myri told him, "Don't make me laugh . . ."

Voort heard a set of repulsors approach from behind. Instead of gaining altitude or sideslipping to the left to pass, these roared with the application of retrothrust; then the vehicle, a big one by the sound of it, set down heavily on the permacrete lane behind Voort. Boots clattered on the permacrete and a loud, resonant voice sounded: "Is this man troubling you?"

Finally Voort did turn.

A few meters behind Trey's speeder, a military hauler-speeder had set down, its doors lifting to admit three men and one woman, all human and all wearing the uniform of the Army of the Galactic Alliance. The speaker, who'd been piloting, was already approaching; he was a big human male, and his right hand rested meaningfully on the holster on his right hip.

Voort suppressed a rueful sigh. He'd been on Coruscant for less than half an hour and already he was about to be beaten to a pulp.

"Save me!" Myri's voice was an uncharacteristically high squeak. She maneuvered past Voort and ran to stand behind the tall trooper.

The trooper and two of his comrades advanced on Voort. The fourth put his arms around Myri, a gesture that was half false comfort, half self-gratification.

The soldiers advanced on Voort. Voort glanced at Myri, his eyes asking the question: *Do I give them a beating, or take one?*

Then the troopers stopped where they were, their eyes growing wide as they looked past Voort.

Myri put her elbow into the solar plexus of her would-be comforter. As he sagged away, gasping, she gestured at Voort—a lowering-hand *get down* motion.

Voort got down. He hit the permacrete lane so fast and so hard that it knocked the wind from him. He wondered if the appliance he was wearing to change the look of his snout might have been jarred loose by the impact.

The lead trooper took a rifle-intensity stun bolt, fired from Trey's speeder, in the chest. He went down as hard as Voort had—harder, since he made no effort to diminish the impact.

Myri's comforter tried ineffectually to grab a holstered blaster pistol. Myri smoothly drew a hold-out blaster from her jacket pocket and shot him, a stun bolt that took him right where her elbow had landed a moment before. He staggered back into the side of the military hauler and collapsed.

The female trooper charged toward Trey's speeder, while her companion dived back to seek shelter in the hauler. A second rifle stun bolt took the woman in the gut, dropping her. Myri vaulted into the open front door on her side of the hauler, firing as she leapt, and the last trooper fell back out of the vehicle, his eyes closed.

Trey, a blaster rifle in his hands, raced past Voort and slid into the front passenger seat of the hauler. He shot a glance back at Voort. "Get your bag!" The speeders roaring by in the lanes beside and above the stopped vehicles swung even farther to the side.

Voort growled. He heaved himself upright, retrieved his bag from the blue speeder, and trotted back to the military hauler. Only the door beside the pilot's seat was still open. Voort climbed in, tossing his bag to Trey, and reactivated his implant. "My—Three, your briefing skills are inadequate."

Myri, in the rear seat, modulated her voice, making it sound like that of a holodocumentary narrator. "Seven, you'll become pilot at this stage of the operation."

"*Thank* you." Voort slammed his door shut, sealed it, and activated the hauler's repulsors. The hauler lifted into the air.

Trey tossed his blaster rifle and Voort's bag into the backseat with Myri. Then he inverted himself, ending up head-down in the passenger-side foot well, and began reaching into and tearing things out of the instrumentation wiring behind Voort's controls.

Voort kicked in the thrusters, slowly bringing the un-gainly hauler up to speed. "Where to?"

"Your next step will be to ascend two traffic lanes, to the western exit traffic lane. In a few moments, if our distractions don't all work, you'll be pursued and threat-ened by all the military police vehicles within thirty kilo-meters."

Voort felt his shoulders begin to relax. "Better."

Trey jammed his hand into the wiring and chips that governed the proper operation of a high-tech, mil-spec speeder. His body spasmed as his hand contacted some-thing it probably shouldn't have. "Ow."

Voort glanced at him. "Should you be doing that?" There was no sign of pursuit yet on the sensors, and most pilots in the lane into which he'd merged were ap-parently unaware of the violence of a moment earlier; they did not shy away from the military hauler.

"Unless you want to broadcast our position to the army, yes."

"As you were." Voort experienced an unsettling feel-ing of familiarity. This *was* a lot like the old days. Face Loran had operated on the principle that no one should be told anything he didn't need to know. The result had been improved security and a lot of temporarily con-fused Wraiths. "What distractions?"

"Well, the overheating datapad and luggage fire was one. The whole spaceport will be shut down and in con-fusion for an hour or so. As for the other distraction . . ." Myri began counting off on her fingers. "Three, two, one, zero . . ."

In the rearview holocam monitor, Voort saw Trey's battered blue speeder disappear in a vast cloud of gray-black smoke. There was no sound of an explosion—the cloud had to be from a smoke bomb, not an explosive charge designed to destroy.

"There are going to be some minor wrecks as a result

of that." Myri sounded matter-of-fact. "One fire, space-port shutdown, hauler theft, four troopers knocked unconscious . . . they could sue us for so much. Let's not get caught."

Voort joined the westbound flow of airspeeder traffic leaving the spaceport surroundings. He snorted, amused. "*Let's not get caught.* Replacing *What do we blow up first?* as the Wraith motto for a gentler era."

"No, I like the *blowing up* one better." Trey tugged, and all of Voort's gauges flickered. Then Trey's hands came up, cupping a small, gleaming blue cube with wires trailing from it. "Military transponder. Catch." He tossed it up and back.

Myri caught it. She hit a button on her door. When the viewport there slid down, filling the hauler's cab with fast-moving air that beat at Voort's eardrums, Myri tossed the box out, then sealed the viewport shut. "Oops." She looked around, gauging their current location; the speeder was entering a deep skytower zone, mostly commercial, its skies thickly populated with airspeeder traffic lanes, self-motivated flying advertisement banners, floating traffic-monitor droids, and rigid pedestrian walkways that crossed the gaps between buildings at intervals. "Seven, go one block south, turn west again, ascend to the middle westbound traffic lane."

Obligingly, Voort banked into a leftward turn, joined a southbound lane for one long block, banked rightward, and climbed to the designated lane. He performed all these maneuvers with brisk, starfighter precision.

Meaning that Myri had to hold on to the seat back with both hands to avoid being tossed around. Trey, in the act of climbing up into a normal seated position, didn't grab a stable surface in time. He bounced into the cab's ceiling and ended up in the backseat.

Myri cleared her throat and leaned forward. "What, exactly, was that?"

Voort shrugged. "A Wraith from long ago, Sharr, would have called it a passive-aggressive response."

"Ah. I get it. I'll play nice. Up ahead two blocks, between this lane and the next one above, there will be a banner stretched between buildings. A yellow banner advertising nothing. Fly directly into it."

"Center?"

"Center."

"I feel we're communicating better already."

There it was, a broad stretch of what looked like yellow flexiplast fluttering in the wind at about the one-hundred-story level. Voort waited until the last moment, then rose out of his lane, sideslipped into the middle of the gap between business towers, and hit the banner straight-on.

The flexiplast stretched and then, as the tension became too great, snapped free of the cords holding it to the buildings. It collapsed around the military hauler, fitting as snugly as if vacuum-sealed.

Voort felt his heart lurch, then checked his gauges. "We're not dropping . . . It's vulnerable to thruster and repulsor wash?"

Myri nodded. "Melted away from the thrusters and repulsors, not impeding them. So we're now a yellow civilian hauler."

"That's new. And clever." Voort gestured at the viewports all around, which were coated in a yellow surface that was translucent but not transparent. "But I can't see."

"Fly on sensors." Myri scrambled over the seat back and dropped into the front passenger seat. She withdrew a datacard from a jacket breast pocket and slid it into the hauler's onboard computer.

Voort put the sensors on the vehicle's main display. It showed other airspeeders all around as wire-frame images. As soon as the computer read Myri's card, the sensors also showed a dotted yellow line in the air, a line not corresponding to any airborne objects.

Voort returned to his westbound lane, where the dotted line hovered. "That's our path?"

"It takes us right to the unsafe house."

". . . Maybe a safe house instead?"

"That's for later."

CHAPTER FOUR

Ten minutes later and thirty stories down in the twilight cast by permacrete canyons between long stands of office and industrial complexes, a wire-frame grid representing a warehouse door slid up and open ahead of the hauler. Voort slowed and turned into the opening. Beyond was a medium-large warehouse chamber, virtually empty but for two wire-frame blobs, their exact shape and function unclear. One was bipedal and moving—an organic being or a droid.

Voort set the hauler down in the center of the open space. Hearing the main door grinding down into place, he opened his door, tearing the yellow material clinging to it, and could finally see the warehouse interior.

The moving blob was indeed a person—a human male with pale skin. He was big, his head bald, his ears a trifle large and protruding, and he wore a baggy gray jumpsuit and an incongruous smile. Another blob turned out to be a hover cart, bigger than but otherwise similar in function to the one Voort had been pushing in the spaceport. The bald man pushed the hover cart up to the rear of the hauler, then began ripping yellow material off the hauler's rear.

Metal sections had been pulled off the left warehouse wall to reveal an old-fashioned incinerator unit. Voort could feel the heat radiating from the thing the moment he pushed his way out of the hauler.

"Don't forget your bag." Trey climbed from the rear seat and ran back to join the bald man.

Myri exited and stretched. Then she cupped her hands around her mouth and raised her voice. "Phase Three! Open up!"

A durasteel panel on the wall not far from the incinerator swung open. Its seams and hinges had not been visible to Voort. Three people emerged, two females and a male, all humanoids. Voort recognized their baggy gray jumpsuits as breakaway garments. Made of flashcloth, the clothes would burn away in an instant if exposed to fire; they were a danger to their wearers in any environment that included sparks or flames but an invaluable tool to an Intelligence unit that needed to perform quick changes.

The man was an exotic—humanoid but not human. His rough-textured skin was a light green. His eyes, with narrow, slitted pupils, were blue. He was hairless, with a skin crease running from the center of his forehead to the top portion of his narrow nose. His mouth was small, a narrow horizontal line in his face. Voort's hairless eyebrows rose toward his horns; he hadn't seen many Clawdites in his day. But the man's role with the Wraiths was instantly obvious. Clawdites could exert great control over their skin, its color, texture, and features, and thus could appear to be any of many humanoid races. A chameleon like that would be a valuable spy. Watching the Clawdite run over to join Trey and the bald human, Voort barely registered the approach of the two women.

Then one of them spoke, her voice familiar. "I think I'm being insulted."

Voort turned to look. Two fair-skinned human women, a generation apart in age, stood there. The older one was lean, her face angular. She had dark hair cut short and dark eyes that he knew looked judgmental even when she was thinking of nothing more profound than what to order for dinner. Her features, by human standards, would be classed as striking, perhaps even unlovely, features suited to a senior military officer or a captain of industry. But she wore a smile for Voort.

The younger woman was taller, with an athlete's build and long blond hair pulled back in a ponytail. Over her jumpsuit she wore a plain black worker's belt with numerous snap hooks and attachment points on it; incongruously, a lightsaber dangled from one of them, its hilt plain and unadorned. Voort suspected that the woman's features did constitute beauty to other humans, but, curiously, she wore no makeup and her hairstyle seemed to be chosen for ease of maintenance rather than its ability to draw the eye. Her features were oddly familiar to him.

He returned his attention to the older woman. "Bhindi! And your friend is . . ." Voort glanced at the younger woman again. "Is it Jesmin? Jesmin Tainer?"

Bhindi stood taller to kiss Voort on the cheek. "I'm One, or Leader, until we're at the safe house. And it is so good to see you, Seven."

The younger woman offered him an uncertain smile. "Good to see you again. I'm surprised you remember me."

"You look more like your mother than yourself now." Once more Voort held his hand up at waist level, indicating the woman's height when he'd last seen her.

"Reunions will have to wait." Bhindi's voice was friendly but brisk. "Five, I need you at your station. Seven, join Three at the furnace. Good job on the heist." She moved past Voort to join Trey and the others at the back of the hauler.

Jesmin's smile became apologetic. She turned to dash back the way she'd come.

Voort moved to stand near the furnace—not too near: it really was putting out an uncomfortable level of heat. The furnace was a sturdy-looking durasteel column stretching from floor to ceiling, its black, grimy exterior marred by various analog readouts and a large hatch at waist level. The hatch was open, revealing a wall of yellow-red flame beyond. Voort knew that the column extension up to the ceiling was part of the conveyor setup; on floors above this one, residents of the skytower would drop waste into destruction hampers, which would then funnel the waste into this shaft and drop it straight into the incinerator.

Back at the hauler, the Wraiths had the cargo bed unsealed and open. They were in the process of removing its contents, a large number of blue-black duraplast cases one and a half meters long, and half a meter wide and deep. From their evident weight and their origin, Voort suspected they held blaster rifles.

Myri, carrying a cloth bag, joined him. She jerked the red wig from her head and tossed it into the furnace's open hatch. Her real hair, apparently short and black, was held down tightly by a mesh cap. "You'll want to burn your clothes, anything that might have picked up chemical or material traces from the speeder." She reached into her bag, retrieved a red wig that looked identical to the first, and dropped it on the floor in front of the furnace. "I've got a new jumpsuit, just as awful as the one you're wearing, in here for you."

"I find myself thrilled." Voort glanced at the red wig. "Full of forensic evidence for the army investigators to find, I assume?"

She smiled at him. "Oh, you know that one."

"A scam as old as the stars. But if you're meticulous enough, it works wonders." Voort bent over to unseal

his boots. He pulled them off, then straightened to unseal the jumpsuit he was wearing.

Back at the hauler, an assembly line of sorts was in full
operation. The bald human was unloading the blaster
rifle cases, piling them on the floor. Bhindi picked up
each one in turn to set it at one end of the hover cart,
which was now switched off, resting on the floor. Trey,
with a set of tools, meticulously unlocked the seals holding each case closed. The Clawdite removed one blaster
battery pack from the case and replaced it with an
identical-looking pack from a pile on the floor. Then
Trey resealed the case and Bhindi stacked it on the far
end of the hover cart. The Clawdite took the discarded
military battery pack and placed it in a large flexiplast
bag at his feet.

"Guess." Myri sounded amused.

Voort glanced at her. She'd removed the crinkly gold
costume and shoved it into the furnace; she wore only
gray shorts and a sleeveless gray undershirt. An identical
costume to her original one lay on the floor atop the
wig. She held out a mass of cloth to him, another jumpsuit.

He took it, then looked away, returning his attention
to the assembly line. In his experience, actors, dancers,
and spies were not self-conscious while dressing or un-
dressing in the presence of others, but he still preferred
to give her the pretense of privacy. He stared at the batteries. "You have transceivers in those new battery packs
so you can track their movements."

"Far too simple. Those new battery packs are actually
droids with some movement and manipulation functions . . . plus they're functional battery packs, though
they don't contain as many shots as their displays
claim."

"Ah, the 'King of the Droids' ploy."

"You're familiar with it?"

"It was invented by a teammate of mine and her astromech a long, long time ago. Before you gave your father his first gray hair. Each of your battery droids can reprogram and subvert simple droids, like housekeeping droids. Correct?"

"Aww." Even over the sound of rustling clothes, Myri's voice sounded disappointed. "I thought we'd invented that."

Voort struggled into his new jumpsuit, then slipped on and sealed his boots. "So, for this ploy to work, you have to let those rifles be recaptured, correct? Or will you be selling them to a criminal cartel?"

"Recaptured."

"Where?"

"Here. In a few minutes."

Startled, he looked at her again. She was fully dressed. Her hair, a new wig, was a metallic silver bob. Her makeup was scrubbed away and replaced by a visor that looked opaque from the outside, and she was in a jumpsuit that matched those of the others. The replacements for her incinerated previous costume lay on the floor at her feet.

She took his used jumpsuit and tossed it into the furnace. "All done? Go around the corner where Jezzie went. The grenades there are yours, the blaster's mine."

"Jezzie?"

"I mean Five. I've known her since we were kids. Old nicknames are hard to forget."

Together they exited the furnace nook and moved into the cooler, quieter gap in the wall from which Bhindi, Jesmin, and the Clawdite had emerged. Voort took a look around. It looked as though the Wraiths had broken their way into a sealed-off corridor, possibly a maintenance access or just space that had been sealed off during a renovation, and installed doors indistinguishable from wall panels at both ends. He could peer down the unpainted corridor they had made, which appeared to open, a few meters away, into another warehouse space. He could hear repulsors and thrusters being revved in what had to be a motivator test.

Closer at hand, there were two grenades and a blaster rifle on the floor against the wall. He picked up the grenades. They were of types familiar to him—one smoker and one dazzler, preset to detonate on impact once the activator buttons were pressed. He hefted them, familiarizing himself with their weight. "How are your parents?" He felt awkward asking it, but he wanted to introduce the subject of Wedge and Iella so he could ease the conversation around to what he really wanted to ask.

Myri picked up the blaster rifle, ejected the battery pack to check its contacts, and reinserted it. She flipped the switch on the side to its stun setting. "Daddy's great. Did you read his memoirs?"

"*Ace in the Hole: A Cockpit's-Eye View of Turbulent Times*. Oh, yes. Sad that he had to leave out far more than he could write about."

"More volumes for later, when things are declassified. Anyway, he's having a great time doing speaking tours, doing consulting work for Incom, things like that. *Mom*, though—she hates retirement. I think she's going to start a revolution somewhere to cope with the boredom."

"Myri, I thought you were making your living gambling. Nice and safe on the *Errant Venture*. Making a fortune, from what I heard."

She nodded, her attention on her rifle.

"So? Why this?"

She smiled. "You must be so proud."

"What? Of whom?"

"That's what they tell me. Mostly about Daddy.

'Wedge Antilles's daughter? You must be so proud.' And I am. Some people know about Mom's career. 'You must be so proud.' And I am. Some people know about my sister's record in the last war. 'You must be so proud.' Yes, yes, I am. But maybe it's time for someone to be proud of what I do. Maybe even me."

"Most of the people I'm proud to have known died making me proud, Myri."

She shot him a reproving glance. "Your heart's really not in this, is it?"

"No. And the thought of what your parents would do if—"

A speaker popped into life. Bhindi's voice came over the system: "Take your number two positions, please. We'll be attacked within three minutes."

Myri positioned herself so that her back was to the corridor wall. She could not be seen by anyone entering the warehouse through the main doors. "You want a briefing?"

"It would be nice."

"A unit of army specialists are going to blow their way in here. You and I open up on them to give the others time to get here and past us to where the extraction vehicle is. Jez—Five's piloting. When the other Wraiths are past, we bring up the rear and everybody gets away."

Voort nodded. "I like that part."

In the main room, Trey, Bhindi, and the Clawdite arrayed themselves between the stolen hauler and the exit corridor. The bald human remained at the rear of the hauler and powered up the hover cart. It rose twenty centimeters, humming, and blaster rifle cases atop it vibrated. The bald man flexed as if stretching in anticipation of an athletic contest. The Clawdite, nearest the exit corridor, held the bag of discarded battery packs.

Bhindi was nearest the hauler. She paid close attention to an open datapad in her hands, and Voort could see the image on its small screen. It switched between holocam views of the warehouse exterior. There, blue-uniformed Galactic Alliance Army troopers, special forces by the unit markings on their uniforms and the way they moved, were getting into position on the surrounding walkways, ushering pedestrians back and sending scouts forward.

Voort gulped. Confronting special forces was an easy way to get seriously killed. He took up position beside Myri.

Myri glanced around the corner, took in the scene, and drew back. "Scut drew the low card, then. Well, he's a fast runner."

"The bald human, he's Scut?"

"Human?" Myri sounded confused. "Oh. The bald man with the ears like solar arrays. That's him. Wraith Six."

The main door into the warehouse, the same portal Voort had flown through just minutes before, blew in, propelled by the concussive *boom* of a shaped charge. In the same instant the warehouse lights went out; suddenly the only light sources were the hole in the door and the fiery glow from the incinerator.

Uniformed men and women poured in through the hole, already picking out targets with their blaster rifles.

If they were attacking in darkness, they'd be using light-amplification visors, Voort thought. He stepped into the corridor opening, blocking Myri, pressed home the button on the dazzle-grenade, and hurled it.

It wasn't his best throw. The dazzler had been in his left hand, and he was right-handed. But it flew fifteen meters and landed five meters in front of the hole in the door. It detonated on impact, filling the entire chamber with a brief, brilliant glow.

Not that Voort saw it. He had his eyes closed, and he waited until the glow died before opening them. There were cries of outrage and surprise from the invading troopers. He pressed the button on his other grenade, threw, and stepped back. Myri moved up in front of him, took aim, and began squeezing off shots. Voort watched over her head.

The dazzler had done a good job. Some of the invaders were firing, but it seemed to be defensive sprays of blaster bolts, unaimed. Myri's shots were far more accurate—methodically, she picked off one, two, three, four troopers.

And she traversed rightward, aiming away from her comrades, giving them a safer approach. The Clawdite made it to the corridor, ran past Voort.

Trey was next, his run lumbering as he brushed past Voort on his way to safety.

Despite the way Myri had reduced their numbers, the troopers began to return fire with more discipline. Bhindi, narrowly missed by a pair of shots, hit the ground and scrambled on all fours with startling speed, her datapad still in hand. She got past Voort and rose, resuming a full run.

Scut was now in motion, pushing the hover cart at a dead run as if intending to escape with its cargo—despite the fact that the exit corridor was too narrow to admit it. A few crates of blasters, jostled by his motion, slid off the cart and clattered to the floor, leaving a trail behind him.

And then a blaster bolt at full lethal strength hit Scut in the center of the back.

The bald man went down on his face, sliding forward a couple of meters. The hover cart, uncontrolled, slid into the wall a few meters from the exit panel. The impact scattered most of the crates on it; they slid into the metal wall, then off the cart and onto the floor.

Myri said something that, to Voort, sounded both Rodian and very unpleasant. She concentrated her fire on the source of the blaster bolt that had hit Scut, a trooper wreathed in smoke from Voort's grenade.

Voort crouched, preparing for the last thing on Coruscant he had any desire to do: a run back into the chamber to grab Scut. But then the bald man was on his feet and running again. Voort ducked aside. Scut, still grinning, his jumpsuit on fire and burning away to ash all across his body, ran past Voort as if out on a daily jog. Voort stared after him, baffled.

Myri grabbed Voort's arm, spun him toward the far warehouse, and pushed. She raised her voice to be heard over the tumult from the chamber they'd just left. "Extracting!"

The near doorway swung shut with a clang. Voort belatedly began running, the floor plates booming under his boots, and emerged into a smaller but similar warehouse chamber. That chamber's main door was grinding open. The only thing in the chamber was an airspeeder, a bulky orange delivery vehicle, the lettering on its side reading FOOD THE COLOR YOU ENJOY MOST.

Jesmin, at the pilot's controls, was visible through the forward port viewport, and the vehicle was already floating on its repulsors. Scut half ran, half dived through the side door into the main compartment.

Myri overtook Voort and was next in. Voort followed, slapping the door controls. The compartment door slid shut. He was taken off his feet by the vehicle's sudden acceleration. He landed in a forward-facing seat beside Myri. Directly ahead of him, strapping himself into a rear-facing seat, sat Scut. Bhindi was beside him, in the center seat opposite. The Clawdite had the rear-facing seat on the starboard side, Trey the forward-facing seat opposite him.

Bhindi breathed a sigh of relief. "Well, that was closer than I like."

Voort stared at her, eyes wide. "It's not over yet. It'll

take them about thirty seconds to spot a vehicle this distinctive and you have a critically wounded Wraith. Who's our medic?"

Bhindi shook her head. "Still trying to recruit one. We've been pressed for time."

Scut stared at Voort, his eyes serene, that ridiculous smile still on his lips. "A mild burn, of no consequence. There is no need to worry." His voice was curiously rough and did not at all match his demeanor.

"*No need*—Bhindi, he's in shock and he's going to die if we don't get medical care for him *right now*. You can smell the wound!"

Bhindi waved his objection away. "As for our color scheme, in a couple of turns, Five will hit a console button. Our exterior will turn black and the lettering will fall off. We're *fine*."

Voort opened his mouth for another protest, but Scut raised a hand to forestall him. "Here. I will show you how it is. I'm wearing a body pad of living tissue similar in composition to my mask." He reached up as if to scratch his neck, but then he gripped rather than scratched, and pulled.

He pulled his face off.

It came away in a single piece, not just the face but every bit of his scalp and neck. The tissue made a repellent sucking noise as it came free.

Beneath it were not denuded bone and muscle, but another face, this one thinner, a light gray in color. It had lean, angular features and black eyes that stared with an alien intensity. A sloping forehead and a heavy supraorbital ridge did nothing to soften his fierce aspect. This man had hair, thin and black, worn short.

Voort felt himself grow faint, and the hair-bristles all over his body seemed to stand up. "You're Yuuzhan Vong."

CHAPTER FIVE

"I am called Viull Gorsat." The Yuuzhan Vong dropped the false face onto the floorboards between him and Voort. Next, he reached under the cuffs of his sleeves and peeled the skin of his hands away—clinging gloves of the same material as his false face. His true hands, underneath, were as gray as his true face. "My body pad was intended to give me dimensions suited to my face, not to act as armor. But it was a durable organism and gave its life to save mine."

Voort stared at Bhindi. "You're working with a Yuu-zhan Vong."

Bhindi nodded, placid, as if she'd just been informed that the atmosphere was breathable. "And a Clawdite and a Gamorrean and several humans, and, worst of all, a Corellian."

Myri shot her a dirty look from underneath her mop of silvery hair. "Cheap shot."

Bhindi returned her attention to Voort. "Voort, Scut is one of the Extolled—the caste they used to call the Shamed Ones. He suffered more at the hands of their military and ruling classes than you have."

"The Extolled are just as crazy as all the rest of them." Voort stared at Bhindi, stunned that, with all her experience, she didn't grasp this simple fact.

Scut's brow seemed to deepen as he frowned. "As a child, at the height of the war, I was on a work crew. The warriors left us behind as a diversion. Most of us died in a New Republic counterattack. I was captured. Given to a human couple. So I have Yuuzhan Vong parents who rejected me as my body rejected Yuuzhan Vong implants, and human parents who raised me. I am of two people. As you are."

Voort gave him a look he hoped the Yuuzhan Vong understood, a look that said, *Come one centimeter closer and I'll kill you.* "You're nothing like me."

"Voort." Bhindi's voice was suddenly chilly. "Are you questioning my judgment?"

Yes, I am. Yes, yes, yes. Voort wanted nothing so much as to leave right now, even if that meant jumping from the side door and hoping he'd find a speeder underneath while falling.

But he kept that thought to himself. He knew Bhindi. She would not respond well to having her decisions challenged.

Of course, Voort could leave, immediately return home and get back to teaching. But that would leave Bhindi, someone he cared about, and Myri and Jesmin, children of people he cared about, associating with this Yuuzhan Vong.

So he composed himself and shook his head. "No."

"Good. Scut's a biofabricator. He made the mask and gloves you saw—"

"Ooglith masquers." It took an effort on Voort's part not to spit out those words. During the Yuuzhan Vong War, alien Vong wearing ooglith masquers to pass as member species of the New Republic had infiltrated, sabotaged, assassinated.

Scut's voice remained neutral. "*Neoglith* masquers. The concept is similar. But I use tissues of species native to this galaxy. Nor are they complete organisms unto themselves, as ooglith masquers were. They have no brains, they do not suffer. When the nutrients suffusing their tissues are absorbed, they die—they do not propagate as species."

Voort suppressed a shudder. "Perhaps we should talk about our objectives. I'm . . . behind."

"Soon." Bhindi glanced through the small forward viewport into the cockpit. "When we're at our safe house."

It was the sort of safe house Voort was used to from his years with the Wraiths, a small tapcaf whose operators, already struggling on the edge of insolvency, had been financially ruined by a fire. The fire had damaged the tapcaf interior, blistering one duraplast wall with signs of char, embedding a sharp smoke odor in all the cheap furnishings, but it had not affected the structural integrity of the midlevel skytower floor where the business had been housed. Bhindi, posing as a repair crew operator, had offered a low, low bid on repairs. Now the Wraiths were free to move in and out of the tapcaf's vicinity, using its loading dock, arriving and departing with all variety of vehicles, and the owners of surrounding businesses paid them no mind so long as they wore workers' garments.

Nor were they entirely abusing the business owners with this deception. While Voort moved from booth to booth, wiping down sparkly purple flexiplast tabletops with a cloth dipped in a fluid that smelled like flowers— chemicals that would remove the stink of smoke now embedded in the flexiplast—other Wraiths also moved around the main room, working as they talked. Trey removed and replaced wall sensors, chronos, attachment points for powered advertisements. Scut, now somewhat leaner with the padding portions of his disguise discarded, was visible on the other side of the midsection-high barrier separating main room from kitchen, mopping. Turman Durra—that was how the Clawdite had been introduced, and Voort had heard his name in the past, the name of a well-regarded stage actor—methodically removed smoke-discolored sound-absorbing tiles from the ceiling and tossed them into a waste receptacle. Jesmin and Myri sat at a booth, a datapad before them, scanning HoloNet News and other news streams for reports on the spaceport shutdown and the army hauler hijack.

Bhindi, sitting opposite Voort at another booth, kept her voice pitched very low. "Piggy, is this going to be a problem?"

"The only problem will be if you keep calling me Piggy. You know better. You were there."

"Don't deflect my question."

He met her gaze square-on. "No. If you're certain he's not an insane genocidal freak who belongs in another galaxy altogether, I'll take your word for it."

"That's not very reassuring."

"Then I'll spell it out for you. *This will not be a problem.* You just surprised me, that's all. Imagine that we held a celebration for you, we wheeled in a giant pastry, and Emperor Palpatine popped out of it. That kind of surprise. But it's not a problem."

Bhindi took a deep breath, then apparently chose to let the matter pass for the time being. She turned her attention to the others and cleared her throat. The Wraiths gathered around, Myri sliding into the booth beside Voort and Turman beside Bhindi. The rest pulled up chairs in a semicircle beside the booth.

Bhindi indicated her own datapad on the tabletop before her. "The recordings burst-fired to us by the holo-cams we left behind outside the engagement zone show the army hauling off the blasters and bringing in a forensics team. Everything there seems to be going as planned, assuming we didn't mess up on any of the evidence we planted. So let's turn our attention back to the next stage: determining General Thaal's guilt or innocence. Voort, what does the old school have to say about this?"

Voort switched his implant to a normal conversational volume. "Assuming he's guilty, we don't know his precise motivation. So in the old days, what we'd do is set up a series of baits for him, each designed to appeal to one of his most likely motivations, and see which, if any, he bites on. In other words, we run a series of confidence games until we see which one he wants to play." He saw some nods from the others.

Bhindi nodded, too. "Good. So what are his likely motives for joining the Lecersen Conspiracy, what is he likely to be doing now, and what sorts of bait will draw him out?"

Jesmin was first. "Wealth. He might want to be made an Imperial Moff or just given a payoff from the Empire. Either way, he would become a very, very rich man."

Bhindi gave her a little smile of sympathy. "You really have been scarred by dealing with the black market, haven't you?"

Jesmin ignored the comment. "So we set up a bogus big-credit score, something that would require him to betray the Alliance."

"Good. Next?"

Turman sat up a little straighter. "Reestablishment of the Empire as it was at the height of its powers." His voice, like Face Loran's, was indeed that of an actor—controlled and vibrant. "If he's an Imperial patriot, he may have no profit motive to speak of. He's in a position to betray army secrets, maybe even the security of the entire Alliance, to the Empire . . . but he's not going to do that until the Empire has settled down under a stable leadership. We might have to convince him that this stable leadership is actually already in place or waiting for him to assume that throne."

Bhindi gave him an approving look. "So all we'd have to do is simulate the wealth and grandeur of a resurgent Empire on our available budget of pocket change and lint."

"That's about the size of it, yes."

"Next?"

Scut spoke next, the harsh tones of his voice at odds with what seemed to be well-considered words. "Many Alliance veterans carry grudges against the instigators of wars they fought. Deep down, Thaal may want to destroy the Yuuzhan Vong . . . or the Jedi who once supported Jacen Solo. Politics will not let him do that now. But given an opportunity to strike such a blow, to end a perceived menace once and for all . . ."

Bhindi winced. "But that calls for running at least two confidence schemes, one for each major likely target."

Scut shrugged. "Or determining what it is he truly hates before launching the confidence game."

Myri shook her head. "If it's one of those two, it's the Yuuzhan Vong. No offense."

Scut blinked. "I take no offense. But why the Yuuzhan Vong above the Jedi?"

"It's in his history. Thaal was an army colonel stationed here on Coruscant when the Yuuzhan Vong invasion came. Instead of evacuating, he volunteered to lead a unit of elites to set up on Vandor-Three."

Scut frowned. "Where?"

"It's actually here in the Coruscant system. The next planet sunward. Lightly populated by Coruscant standards. It has old links to the armed forces—back in the Clone Wars, there were clone trooper training grounds near Vangard, the capital. But now it's mostly agricultural, with a petroleum industry. It supplies Coruscant with a lot of its food and raw material for plastic products. Most people here consider Vandor-Three to be beyond the borders of civilization and culture. Like an uneducated cousin who doesn't bathe." She shrugged. "Anyway, he and his unit hid in a base built years earlier by the Tech Raiders, a crime organization.

"Thaal's group reported on the Yuuzhan Vong occupation of the system, data vital to the New Republic. They launched raids. They called themselves the Pop-Dogs, after a burrowing rodent from Carida—pop-dogs pop up out of their burrows, run over, grab their prey or food that's been left unguarded for just a second, and scurry back to their burrows. The Pop-Dog unit was very brave and very useful, and when that war was over, Thaal was promoted to the rank of general. And he built up elite army units nicknamed the Pop-Dogs. My guess is that he still hates the Yuuzhan Vong for all the suffering he saw."

Jesmin looked unhappy. "That's logical, but it doesn't clear up the situation for us at all. The same logic would make him hate the Jedi *more*."

Myri looked at her, clearly confused. "How?"

"A little detail buried in his career history. You mentioned that the pop-dogs, the rodents rather than the military unit, were from Carida. So was Thaal. He was an Imperial officer, a small-unit tactics instructor at the Imperial Academy there."

Myri grimaced. "That does make a difference."

Jesmin nodded. "He was *on* Carida when Kyp Durron destroyed the system. He was on one of the last shuttles to evacuate successfully before the Sun Crusher hit. He defected to the New Republic during all that chaos, and his record suggests he's been a loyal officer ever since. But when you've been through that kind of horror . . . Who knows what it does to your mind?"

Voort frowned, thoughtful. That *did* complicate the

picture. Kyp Durron, at the time only a Jedi trainee but a very powerful Force-user, had performed a horrifying act of vengeance. He had used an experimental super-weapon to destroy the star of Carida, a world where an Imperial military academy was situated, and the star's destruction had obliterated Carida itself. Evacuation efforts saved a portion of Carida's population. Though many people believed then and still believed today that Durron should have been tried and punished for the action, the destruction had been a boon for the New Republic, still at war at the time with the Empire; that, and support for Durron from Luke Skywalker, who testified to Durron's redemption, secured Durron's freedom.

Bhindi sighed. "All right. Any other likely motivations?"

There was a general shaking of heads.

"So Thaal's motivation is still unclear." Bhindi pulled a datachip from her breast pocket and handed it to Myri. "I want you, Voort, and Trey to take charge of the droid subversion effort on Vandor-Three. The rest of us will begin putting together operations to expose Thaal's motivation. Break and scatter, people."

On the trip back to the spaceport, Voort, up in the delivery speeder's cockpit, glowered over at Myri in the center seat. "I don't want to complain."

She grinned at him. "You know what people do, one hundred percent of the time, immediately after saying they don't want to complain? They complain."

"I got to Coruscant this morning. I'm leaving in the afternoon. Who comes to Coruscant for a few hours? Does that make any sense?"

"I suppose not."

"I just wanted to point that out."

"You might as well stop frowning. For good."

Voort stared at her, confused. "Why?"

"Almost nobody but another Gamorrean can tell when you're frowning. I can because I learned the expressions, the body language, and especially the species tells of lots and lots of races when I was gambling for my living. But—Trey, can you tell when he's frowning?"

Trey, at the pilot's controls, shook his head.

"See?" She fell silent for a second and just watched the skytowers sweep by on either side. "You could smile once in a while. You never smile."

"Give me something to smile about."

"I'll have to work on that."

CHAPTER SIX

The shuttle flight from Coruscant to Vandor-3 had been brief, but that was the last thing Voort found favorable about this phase of their mission.

The civilian spaceport lay halfway between Fey'lya Army Base to the north and Ackbar City to the southwest, about twenty kilometers in either case. It actually was a massive spaceport for a world with a population so small, and most of its traffic came in the form of container ships hauling grain, other produce, and meats offworld. The terminal building for visitor and other noncargo traffic was actually quite small, a two-story gray truncated pyramid with two associated landing pads.

The three Wraiths were delayed nearly an hour in that terminal while a small landspeeder rental booth struggled to find them a vehicle. Voort spent that time staring balefully at the hologram projected overhead, a tourism program extolling the virtues of the planet, especially the army base and the nearby city.

The hologram program, on infinite loop, confirmed again and again that there hadn't been an army base on Vandor-3 prior to the Galactic Alliance regaining control of the Coruscant system at the end of the Yuuzhan Vong War. But when General Thaal decided to make Vandor-3 the system's new base of army operations, the base—named for Borsk Fey'lya, Chief of State of the New Republic at the time of Coruscant's fall—had sprung up and flourished rapidly.

Finally the attendant brought the Wraiths outside and presented them with their speeder, a huge, clanking, deep-bedded hauler, its cab spacious enough for the three of them. Finally they could escape. With Myri at the controls and Trey in the middle, they flew out of the spaceport, following the route map displayed on Trey's datapad.

They all kept silent, Voort in irritation and the others sensing his mood, until they reached the first large sign leading from the spaceport, pointing in one direction toward Fey'lya Army Base and the other toward Ackbar City. Myri followed the second arrow. Voort offered the sign a rubbery noise of contempt.

"What is it with you?" Myri glowered across Trey at Voort. "You've been on the verge of a killing spree since we got here."

"Fey'lya Army Base. Newest, best-funded army base out there." Voort shook his head. "Named for Borsk Fey'lya, a conniving, self-centered son of a wampa if ever there was one. The fact that he should be *honored* like that . . ."

Myri shrugged. "So?" She returned her attention to the treetop-level signs that marked the airspeeder lane to their destination. The signs paralleled a paved ground-vehicle roadway beneath. All around them were grain fields being worked by humans, Gamorreans, droids, and self-guided farm machinery. Close to harvesttime, the fields reflected a brilliant yellow-white in the sunlight. "I was pretty young when it happened, but didn't he die, you know, heroically? Blowing himself up with a bunch of Yuuzhan Vong warriors?"

"Some people live *and* die heroically and are never honored for it. Fey'lya managed one act of contrition, of redemption, at the end of a life of scheming. Myri, he made decisions that affected people in the field. Soldiers, spacers, spies. He would make choices based on self-interest and get people *killed*."

"Oh." She kept her voice mild. "Well, people remember what they choose to remember. I guess they choose to remember him blowing up the enemy as the capital fell."

"I'm just saying . . ." Voort tamped down his irritation. He didn't need to be venting it against someone who hadn't earned his anger. It wasn't as though Myri were one of his students, after all. "I met Admiral Ackbar several times. I worked with his niece Jesmin. She was one of the first Wraiths, and died in combat."

"I know; Jesmin Tainer is named for him."

"I'm just saying that if they're going to name a huge, overfunded, state-of-the-art army base for Fey'lya, the city named for Admiral Ackbar had better be glorious."

They spotted the city from a couple of kilometers off. A broad brown patch in the midst of glowing white-and-yellow fields, it was heralded by a sign reading ACKBAR CITY. MAXIMUM AIRSPEEDER ALTITUDE SIX METERS.

"You have *got* to be kidding." Grudgingly, Myri brought the speeder's altitude down to the legal limit.

Then they reached the outskirts, a strip of dusty ground bordering a haphazard accumulation of buildings, mostly sheet durasteel bolted onto metal frames, set into permacrete foundations, and painted in a variety of dull colors. Some of those coatings of paint, beaten upon by a few years of summertime sun, were beginning to crack and peel. Some streets were paved, others covered in a rough coating of gravel, others hard-packed soil.

Myri scanned their surroundings as she piloted. When she spoke, her voice was glum. "There's nothing else flying even at this altitude. Going to landspeeder mode." She dropped altitude to a mere meter off the ground. When they passed dirt-topped cross-streets and alleys, their repulsors kicked up great clouds of brown dust. Civilians on the pedestrian walkways shouted and made rude gestures at them. "You win, Voort. I'm prepared to hate this place."

"Maybe it gets better farther in." Trey's tone was mild, more conciliatory. "Hey, that's better." He pointed through the forward viewscreen.

Myri and Voort looked in that direction. All Voort could see was a business, perhaps more gaudily painted than the others, a two-story dome whose marquee sign announced it as EAT'S.

Voort glowered. "Unless the owner is named Eat, the apostrophe is superfluous. I'm inclined to beat up the owner for bad grammar. Why, Trey, is that *better*?"

"It was a prefab! Built in the factory to be exactly that way. Not assembled here. Costs more. Better, right?"

Myri sighed. "At least there are signs for some gambling halls. I can earn some spare credits here."

The population was mostly human, but a variety of nonhumans were scattered throughout. Most seemed to be civilians, dressed in casual or work clothes, but Voort saw occasional groups of soldiers as well.

Trey had apparently done his research on the distinctions among local soldiery. He pointed to one pair of troopers standing on a street corner, their uniforms brown, their rank insignia indicating they were privates. "Off-duty troops. The city's economy runs on catering to off-duty soldiers."

Voort crossed his arms. "So we can expect most of the businesses hereabouts to be—what's the word in Basic?—sleazy."

"Maybe not." Myri sounded hopeful.

Voort snorted. "I'll bet you ten credits Ackbar City doesn't even have an orchestra."

"You're on."

"An orchestra of living musicians. Not a droid orchestra."

Myri made an unhappy face. "Bet's off."

Trey pointed out another group of soldiers, a quartet. They were in brown uniforms as well, but carried blaster rifles and wore torso armor and helmets in black. "Guard patrols. The city gets its city guard services from the army base." The four troopers were in fact keeping a close eye on passing landspeeder and pedestrian traffic.

"Interesting." Voort filed that fact away. Any deviation from normal social or governmental structure was a potential weakness or wrinkle to exploit.

Trey pointed ahead and to the right. "Pop-Dog."

Voort peered in that direction, curious about General Thaal's favorite brand of elite troopers.

The woman Trey had indicated was of average height and fit. Her uniform was similar to those of the on-duty guards, but with some embellishments. Sewn along the collar of her brown tunic was a pattern of white triangles—Voort took a moment to recognize them as stylized teeth. There were single tooth insignia on either side of her helmet. Ruddy of complexion and stern-faced, she stood listening to the words, apparently pleas, of a tan-skinned Bith shop owner. They stood outside the door of a bakery; across the door was a strip of broad red tape reading CONDEMNED. The Bith, the dome of his hairless head and his black eyes gleaming in the morning sun, gestured persuasively as the Pop-Dog shook her head. Then that scene, too, was past.

Voort kept his eye on the Pop-Dog as long as he could. "If General Thaal is the enemy, that, too, is our enemy. And if he's not corrupt, the Pop-Dogs are still elite soldiers whose backyard we are rooting around in uninvited. So keep alert."

"Yes, Dad." Trey consulted his datapad. "Myri, next left."

Two minutes later they pulled into their destination, the parking area of a small collection of corrugated durasteel buildings, all uniformly gray and weathered. The faded sign on the largest roof advertised the place as TOOZLER'S SPEEDER REPAIR AND MAINTENANCE. Weeds had broken through the lot's pavement in several places, indicating that the establishment had been abandoned for some time.

The main building of the little business was a long two-story structure, enclosing the bays for vehicle repairs, now stripped of lifts and hoists and tools. To its left was an office building with a waiting area and a refresher downstairs and a small apartment upstairs. To its right, a storage building, now empty but for the smell of chemicals and plastic parts. The three buildings were joined by short duraplast-walled passages no more than a meter in length. The unlined walls of the main building rippled and rattled when the wind blew.

Voort, Myri, and Trey spent a few minutes sweeping the place for transmitters; finding none, they spent a few more minutes planting some of their own, tiny listening devices and holocams that would show them movement on the traffic lanes outside and alert them to stealthy visitors. They taped lengths of opaque black flimsiplast over all the windows. Trey went up on the roof to add a banner proclaiming COMING SOON—BINI'S SPEEDERIUM to the sign there.

They parked the speeder in the main building. Their bags went into the office building, where Trey set up, on what had been the business counter, the communications and computer gear they had brought. He glanced over the monitor and shook his head. "No burst traffic yet from the blaster battery droids."

Voort peered over Trey's shoulder but could make no sense of the numbers and flashing updates on the screen. "What does that mean? Have they been discovered? Maybe the army will keep them for months as evidence on Coruscant."

Trey shook his head. "Noooo . . . They were bound for Fey'lya Base, so they'll get there soon enough. But if the base has all the blasters it needs for the time being, it might be days or weeks before they get uncrated and issued."

Voort grunted. "Well, let's hurry things along."

Myri and Trey stared blankly at him.

He stared back, slowly shaking his head. "You don't have the faintest idea of what I'm talking about, do you?"

"No." Myri sounded confused. "We're supposed to wait until some of the droids are activated, then begin collating the data they send . . ."

"Which, as Trey said, could be days or weeks." Voort tried not to let impatience creep into his voice. "But what if, say, several base troopers have an encounter here, planetside, that puts their blaster rifles out of commission?"

"They'd be assigned new ones." Trey brightened. "And the new ones they're assigned might be ours, or ours might just move up the queue, have to be checked out, allowing the droids to become active . . ."

Voort gave him an approving nod. "You don't wait

for things to happen in this business, son. You *make* things happen."

Myri grinned, obviously relishing the lesson in old-school Wraith techniques that was to come. "Tell us."

"This scam relies on the fact that Ackbar City does not have its own police or guard force." Voort pondered for a moment. "We'll need . . . one smallish hydraulic metal press, not traceable to us, transportable in our speeder. Six or eight addresses of abandoned homes in low-rent districts. Six to eight comlinks with unregistered ownership, disposable, to make calls to the military police on. A second pseudo-safe house a lot like this one, again not traceable to us. Spray paints in assorted colors. Disguises for you and Trey. And, if we can, sound recordings of Kowakian monkey-lizards in a state of rage."

Trey grinned. "I think I'm going to like this job."

Hours later, two army troopers, one male, one female, both human, paused at the front door of the small dwelling. It wasn't much of a home, a prefab that looked as though it had begun its existence as a section of dura-steel pipe some three meters in diameter and fifteen in length. Saw the pipe in half lengthwise, set it cut-edges down on a permacrete foundation, cap it at both ends with walls with doors in them, and paint the whole thing an unappealing dirt color, and there it was, a dwelling fit for people with no money, no taste, or both. The dwelling matched the low-income neighborhood that surrounded it.

The female trooper, whose name tag read SGT. DOBI, pressed the signal button beside the door. "I hate domestic disturbance calls. The people get into knock-down drag-outs with one another, then we show up to restore order and they come after us with vibroblades."

The male, whose badge read CPL. VITKINS, shook his head. "This one had animal noises. How many of them include animal noises?"

"Well, all right, maybe they'll end up throwing sand panthers at us instead."

"You're a pessimist."

The light above the doorway came on and the door slid aside. Just inside stood a human man—tall, strongly built, dressed in a worker's gray clothes. It was impossible to make out much of his features, for half his face was swathed in white bandage and the other marked with livid bruises. His right arm was supported in a forearm-to-elbow sling that looked as though it had been improvised from torn bedsheets.

He peered out at them from under a mop of black hair, his eyes miserable. "Cah I hep you?"

Sergeant Dobi suppressed a wince of sympathy. "A pedestrian commed the local guard station with complaints of a disturbance. We need to speak to you. Inside."

"Ob courfe." The resident stepped aside to let them enter.

Inside, they looked around. The room was almost bare—two folding durasteel chairs and a rickety table of local wood, a monitor atop it, constituted all the furniture.

The resident began explaining before the front door had quite slid shut. "Mah houfemate and I had ad argoomenf."

Sergeant Dobi nodded. "It looks like you got the worst part of it."

"Ah ahwayf do."

"Always do—this is a regular occurrence?"

"Efery time he getf Cowellian applef."

The troopers looked at each other. Corporal Vitkins

pulled out his datapad. "What sort of species gets violent after eating Corellian apples?"

"One ob a kind. Genetically augmented Kowakiad monkey-lifard."

Sergeant Dobi checked her blaster rifle, made sure it was set on stun and at full power. "Tell me you're joking. Genetically augmented?"

"Oh, he'f huge. A metew an a haff tall."

Corporal Vitkins gave the resident an appalled look, then ran a couple of quick searches on his datapad. "Look, I'm not seeing a rental or purchase contract on this dwelling, nor any record that there's a modified Kowakian monkey-lizard *anywhere* on Vandor-Three."

"We juff moved in yefterday. And he'f not on the record. I . . . fmuggled him onplanet."

Vitkins hurriedly tucked away his datapad and checked his rifle. "A dangerous animal—"

"He'f not dangewouf! The applef have wown off. You want to fpeak wif him? He's in the neft woom, napping."

Dobi nodded. "Yes. Call him out here."

"Palpy? C'mere, Palpy."

Noises sounded from the door into the next room, a heavy thump followed by a shambling, scraping sound that caused Dobi's hair to rise.

That door slid aside, revealing darkness beyond.

And the resident, behind the troopers, spoke again, his voice no longer pained or slurred. "Don't move. I have blaster pistols aimed at your backs, and you're also being covered from the other room. Troopers, you are now prisoners of the Quad-Linked Militant Pacifists."

Dobi heaved a heartfelt sigh. "I *hate* domestic disturbance calls."

* * *

It wasn't until a fourth set of troopers responded to a fourth domestic disturbance call and took a suspiciously long time in reporting completion of the assignment that the night-shift officer on duty at the local military police guardhouse noticed the discrepancy. He dispatched a follow-up unit to the first address. They found Dobi and Vitkins, expertly tied and furious, in the abandoned dwelling. The bound troopers' blasters, both rifle and pistol, were gone. Units dispatched to each of the other disappearance sites found the same thing—bound and disarmed troopers with stories of an unseen genetically augmented monkey-lizard. The officer of the day issued an advisory mandating that all domestic disturbance calls be approached with maximum caution and that units of no fewer than four troopers do the responding.

There were no more false disturbance calls that night. By dawn, army investigators had found the local headquarters of the hitherto-unknown Quad-Linked Militant Pacifists—a small metal shack with an aging hydraulic press in it. Crumpled rubbish that had once been the blasters of eight troopers littered the floor. Fresh graffiti decorated the shack's inner walls—slogans denouncing all acts of violence. All except those of the Quad-Linked Militant Pacifists.

The army issued orders for the arrest of two suspects, a heavily bandaged human man and a heavily robed woman of indeterminate species, but the trail of the pacifist terrorists seemed to have completely dried up.

Voort sat watching the monitor of Trey's computer, which received a visual feed from the holocam on the roof. The holocam was trained a few blocks away on the metal shack, where the hydraulic press had been set up. Even now there were army airspeeders parked in front, and forensics personnel moving in and out of the building. "Anyway . . . That's how Wraiths spend their first day in a new town."

Myri, stretched out on a cot at the back of the office but not sleeping, yawned. "Tiring. But fun."

Voort nodded. "With an extra day or two, we could have come up with a giant monkey-lizard costume for me. But you have to work within your operational limitations."

"I'm going to tell Bhindi she ought to blame the original blaster heist on Coruscant on the Quad-Links." Myri yawned again. "After I get some sleep. You know, to make the Quad-Links sound more widespread. More formidable."

Trey, slumped in a chair, popped awake for a brief moment. "Good idea." Then he focused on the monitor and frowned. "Hey. We've received a burst message from one of the droids." He reached up to brush at the monitor screen, sweeping away the image of the distant shack, replacing it with a screen of data fields. The contents of some of the fields blinked.

Trey blinked, too. "Battery Droid Twelve has just signaled itself active."

Voort permitted himself a satisfied look he knew Trey couldn't interpret. "Might have nothing to do with what we did last night. But—"

Trey scanned the screen of data. "But it's always better to be active than reactive. Lesson learned."

CHAPTER SEVEN

Over the next two days, the trio of Wraiths spent considerable time in front of that monitor, watching footage and interpreting data sent by the battery-pack parasite droid—and then by Droid 12 and Droid 38.

Droid 12 waited nearly a day in its blaster rifle before the conditions surrounding it were such that it could begin activity. When nothing larger than an insect had moved in its vicinity for a couple of hours, it ejected itself and fell to the permacrete floor of a trooper ready room, recognizable on the recording by its weapons racks, equipment lockers, and benches.

On the floor, Droid 12 extruded miniature treads and crawled at a torturously slow pace to conceal itself beneath the bottom shelf of a wall-mounted weapons rack. There it waited for hours, motionless and undetected, its holocam watching ankles and feet during a trooper shift change.

After an hour of stillness and darkness in the room, a tan-colored, dome-shaped floor-cleaning droid rolled into the chamber, and Droid 12 got to work. It crawled out from beneath the weapons rack and transmitted a brief command to the cleaning droid, identifying itself as a floor stain and instructing the droid to scour it up. The cleaning droid obligingly rolled over and atop Droid 12.

"At this point, magnets activate, clamping Droid Twelve to the underside of the cleaning droid." Trey indicated the screen, which showed only Droid 12's fish-eye point of view experiencing a slight change of altitude as it rose a majestic two or three centimeters off the floor to adhere to the cleaning droid's underside. "Now Droid Twelve will extend leads to plug into the cleaning droid's primary communications jack. It'll begin reprogramming it soon."

Voort nodded and stretched. "I'm assuming Droid Twelve will detach and subvert more base droids, then find a good place to hide. All the droids it has subverted will transmit their recordings to Droid Twelve at irregular intervals. Droid Twelve will send all that data to us in burst-transmission packets. You'll integrate and collate the data. Correct?"

Trey gave him a dirty look. "You take all the fun out of it by knowing everything."

By nightfall, they had portions of the buildings Droids 12 and 38 were in mapped and had their locations superimposed on a satellite map of Fey'lya Army Base. Droid 38 seemed to be locked in a high-security chamber in a storage building where weapons and munitions were kept before being deployed, but Droid 12 was loose in the base's southern operations center. As the hours passed, Trey began building a three-dimensional walk-through of that ops center and then surrounding buildings as more and more domestic droids fell under its sway.

Trey left off maneuvering a virtual point of view around the portions of the base they had mapped. He tapped to activate a persistent blinking light in the upper right-hand corner of his screen. A series of password and security queries popped up. Once he'd typed in a succession of correct answers, the computer opened a screen of text for him.

He glanced at the others. "Orders from Leader."

Voort and Myri looked up from their sabacc game—Voort with relief, for Myri was annihilating him.

Trey ran through the message's contents. "Congratulations from Bhindi on the activation of the parasite droids. She says the Wraiths on Coruscant sabotaged a turbolaser assembly line in the name of the Quad-Linkers to lend even more authenticity to the name."

Myri smiled. "Nice of them."

"This cell, though. Here on Vandor-Three, we're to go into maintenance mode and just acquire data until otherwise notified. Voort and I are supposed to rendezvous with the others at Gagrew Station, Si'klaata Cluster. Myri, you remain in charge here."

"Alone?" Voort frowned.

Myri gave him a suspicious look. "What, you don't think I'm old enough?"

"That's not it." Blast it, that *was* it, part of the problem. "I just have a . . . dislike of leaving a team member alone, without support. It's bad tactics." But more than that, the thought of leaving Myri behind, of something happening to her, of having to look Wedge in the eyes afterward . . . Voort tried to force himself to think of her as an adult colleague, someone who'd signed on knowing all the risks of the trade.

He failed. "Trey, send a reply. Ask if we can leave someone behind in addition. To back up Myri."

Trey shook his head. "No, I don't think so. If Bhindi thinks she needs both of us, she needs both of us."

"Stang."

"Besides . . ." Myri suddenly sounded cheerful. "Did you hear what Trey said? You're going to Si'klaata Cluster. That's Hutt space. I can stay here, wallow in the mud, and eat worms all day, and I'll still be in a cleaner, nicer place than you two will."

"Point taken."

ABOARD THE RINKIN IV, CORELLIAN RUN HYPERSPACE ROUTE

"You know you don't sing well." The pilot, an Ortolan, old enough that his trunk was graying, sounded resigned. He sat in the double-wide pilot's seat, which was reinforced against his great weight, and leaned away from the navigator as though those extra centimeters might save him from a few sour notes.

The navigator, a young human ensign in the blue of the Alliance Navy, smiled and replied in song, his voice cracking and off-key. *"I know I don't, but the more I sing—"*

"The more I suffer."

"—the better I get."

"That remains to be proven."

The navigator smiled and stretched. Things were looser in the support-and-supply division of the navy. Its personnel were almost irregulars, expected to observe all naval regulations when planetside in uniform or on regular navy ships, but more like civilians the rest of the time. The bridge of this cargo vessel was spacious, the captain was tolerant, the crew was loose, and the pilot was a good sport despite his grumbling.

And the view out the forward viewports was gorgeous. The ship was now in hyperspace, somehow sideways from realspace, and abstract lights that might be glimpses of stars in realspace twisted and flowed past in a dazzling stream.

The navigator sang again: *"Comin' out of the Deep*

Core, headin' for home. Gettin' leave in Corellia, gonna put on my dance shoes. Gonna find me a lady—"

"Gonna sing to her, at which point she will shoot you. You're making my tusks crack."

"*Gonna*—hey!" A light on the main control board blinked, then went out.

The streams of colors outside suddenly stopped their movement, contracting into single points of light.

There was no sensation of deceleration, not like in an atmospheric craft, but the navigator felt as though he should have been thrown out of his seat by the sudden departure from hyperspace. He turned to the pilot. "What the *hell*—"

"Our escorts are not on the sensor screen. What's our position?"

The navigator checked his star map, did a quick calculation. "Two hours out of Corellia. Empty space."

The comm board clicked and a woman's voice sounded over it. "Bridge, Captain. What's going on?"

"Captain," the pilot reported, his voice beginning to climb in pitch. "We had a sudden unexpected departure from hyperspace. We're showing no damage. Our escorts did not drop with us. Correction, there's one—wait a second, that's not ours. We're being approached by a capital ship, unknown type. It's not signaling."

"Sound alert, all hands to battle stations. Send an emergency signal to the nearest naval base. I'll be right up." The comm board clicked again.

The navigator felt himself break out in a sweat. He looked at the pilot. "Should I—"

"Is the hyperdrive functional?"

"Negative."

"Then handle the comm. Don't need a navigator to point away from the enemy and hit all thrusters."

As the navigator flipped through the unfamiliar maze of communications screens, he felt himself being pressed back in his seat, just a little, as the ship's inertial compensators did not quite keep up with the pilot's acceleration. Finally he found the screen to activate the ship's hypercomm on an emergency naval frequency. "This is Galactic Alliance Ship *Rinkin Four*, inbound to Corellia. We have an emergency. Please reply. Over."

The door into the bridge slid open. The captain, a middle-aged woman with posture as straight as a spear, strode in. "Situation?"

Something clattered on the deck behind her. Out of the corner of his eye, the navigator saw it—a silvery ovoid some seventy-five centimeters long, with a small dial and a tiny screen on one side.

Something in the navigator's memory whispered, *Grenade*.

He acted without thinking, acted with the decisiveness and honor that others had once seen in him, that would have eventually forced him to become a fine officer. He threw himself atop the grenade. "Get—"

Curiously, the detonation did not lift him off the deck plates, did not hurl his burning body to one side. It didn't even really make a *boom*, just a *pop* noise. Then there was a *hiss* and the navigator saw opaque white smoke flow out from underneath him, flooding the bridge.

It numbed his skin where it touched him. He breathed it in before he could check himself and abruptly felt dizzy, listless.

There was an impact as the captain fell atop him. He could not turn his head to see if she was faceup or facedown.

There were footsteps on the deck plates in the corridor outside, and the navigator saw a pair of feet and lower legs. They were garbed in a civilian environment suit, something that would protect its wearer from toxic environments.

Like this one.

The navigator's eyes closed and he knew only blackness.

CHAPTER EIGHT

"I'm going to throw up." Trey sounded like he meant it, too. The walls of the passageway he and Voort walked along seemed clean enough, free of debris. The walkway was spacious, occasionally punctuated by transparisteel viewports showing the starfield outside.

But Voort knew what Trey was complaining about. The *smell* . . . It was partly loamy, partly sweet, slightly rotted, slightly chemical-sharp. It was the smell of too many passengers who'd been cooped up on small ships and then suddenly released into this space station environment. It was the smell of Hutts especially, and of the vendors scattered throughout the station, most of whom sold, as a primary or secondary product, food that appealed to Hutts. Exotic meats. Decayed fats. Live insects and rodents. Poisonous tubers.

And then, of course, there were the slime trails. Up ahead thirty meters, a Hutt, meters long, dark and slug-like, his spindly arms gesturing as he talked to the Rodian female walking beside him, left a new layer of slime as he moved. Even at this distance, Voort could occasionally hear noises emerge from beneath the Hutt, flatulent *brapps* and *blerts* as portions of the creature's underside lost or regained adhesion with the metal floor. Pushing the rolling rack on which his and Trey's luggage rested, Voort ably maneuvered the thing so that its wheels avoided the slime trail as much as possible.

Voort heaved a sigh. "We're in public." But he spoke in Gamorrean, and his throat implant was switched off, so his words emerged as a series of grunts and squeals most humans didn't understand.

"I don't get you—oh. Right." Trey mimed a smack to the side of his own head. "Sorry. One-sided conversations from now on." He glanced at the blinking sign situated at ceiling level where a cross-passageway intersected theirs at a right angle. Words flashed on the sign in a variety of languages, Basic among them. Trey read aloud. "Blueshift Passage. That's ours."

Their destination was only a hundred meters along Blueshift Passage, an innocuous double door. The sign above it blinked through a succession of languages, words reading SWEET SPOT LODGING—CORE WORLDS STYLING AT OUTER RIM RATES. Beyond the doors was a small hostel lobby, its floor being constantly trafficked by ankle-high, disk-shaped scrubbing droids.

Three minutes later, down a narrower hall lined with doors, Trey spoke his name to a door and it slid open for him.

Beyond was a tall, aristocratic-looking human man. His immaculately coiffed white hair seemed perfectly in sync with his gray Imperial Navy uniform. "You are under arrest."

"Nice." Trey grabbed his bags from the rolling rack and entered.

"No, really. Put up your hands."

Voort took his own bags, leaving the rack in the corridor, and followed. The door slid shut behind him. He activated his throat implant. "Turman?"

The Imperial officer rolled his eyes. "*Yessss.*"

"Good disguise." Voort dropped his bags on the floor beside Trey's and took a look around. This was a suite's main chamber, large by the standards of space station hostels but not commodious enough for a good-sized party, and it was blessedly free of Hutt smell. The walls, off-white, were decorated with holos of mountain and jungle nature scenes, and the floor, tiled in a similar color, was slime-free and spotless.

"If it's so good, why didn't you pause even for an *instant*? You're bad for my morale." If anything, the disguised Turman's posture improved even more with his indignation.

Trey moved up to him, peered close. "Are those your actual features when you take on human appearance?"

"No, I'm wearing a neoglith masquer." Turman reached up to tug at his nose, which stretched a full three centimeters longer before he released it and it snapped back into place. "My human features are rather bland."

Voort glanced around again. There were several piles of baggage in the chamber, but no additional people. "Where are the others?"

"Finalizing our passage. You made it just in time. We launch pretty soon."

Voort sighed. "Tell me . . . and my life may depend on your answer . . . do I have time for a sanisteam? We were on that blasted shuttle for longer than I want to think about. I don't dare sit down. I might stick."

"You have time. Make it fast."

By the time Voort emerged from his sanisteam, his green skin gleaming, the others had returned; Voort heard their voices from the refresher. He donned a fresh porter's jumpsuit and moved out to join them.

Turman's Imperial naval officer getup was gone, along

with his aristocratic face and white hair. Now, though he still appeared to be human, he was younger and dark-haired, his features inoffensive and unmemorable. Bhindi, atypically, wore a sparkly silver party frock and black leggings. She was the very image of a vacuum-brained heiress out for a good time. Jesmin, her hair red and styled in a severe bun, wore a dark visor and a sober black jumpsuit that suggested she belonged to a security detail; Trey had changed into a matching outfit. Scut wore the same round-faced human disguise he'd had on when Voort first met him; his clothes were leathery black pants, matching boots and vest, and a frilly blue shirt, suggesting that he wanted to be a smuggler but had never quite seen the real thing.

Voort gave Bhindi a look and ignored her bubble-headed mannerisms. "Do Trey and I get any sort of briefing? Mission objectives, who not to kill, that sort of thing?"

Wide-eyed, she nodded. "Uh-huh." She managed to turn that affirmative into a cute squeak.

"*Stop* that."

"Oh, all right." She dropped the party heiress mannerisms and bent to finish packing a last few items into her smallest bag. "Short form?"

"That'll do."

"In fifteen minutes we board the *Bastion Princess,* a cruise liner. It makes regular runs from Bastion, capital of the Imperial Remnant, to here and back, visiting several worlds along the way. Its passengers are mostly rich Imperial folk who want to experience some safe danger and noninfectious sleaze in Hutt space. We board, Trey does a little sabotage of ship's sensors and hyperdrive, we board an escape pod and launch undetected at a spot where Imperial vessels are known to patrol—but a comparatively *remote* spot so we're less likely to encounter a large vessel. Then we wait."

Voort felt the bristles on the back of his neck rise. "To be rescued by the Imperial Navy."

"Right."

"What if they don't show up?"

Bhindi straightened and slung the strap of her bag over her shoulder. "I've transmitted additional orders to Myri. If we don't report in, she finds a way to come get us."

"*A way.* Can't she just borrow the *Quarren Eye* from Face and come for us?"

Bhindi's expression went blank, and this time it was no act. "What's the *Quarren Eye*?"

"It's a long-range shuttle with a hypercomm. On loan to Face. It's one of our resources."

"Well, I haven't heard of it. So Myri will just have to improvise." Bhindi made an impatient gesture as if imploring the ceiling to support her argument. "And that's only if we fail. If we don't, an Imperial vessel picks us up, we thank everybody sweetly, and then we seize the thing."

Voort tried to pat down his bristles. "Just like that."

"Without ambition, a Wraith should take up, I don't know, teaching math. Everyone ready to go?"

Scut hefted his bags, immediately handed them to Voort, and was first out the door.

Despite himself, Voort was impressed by *Bastion Princess.* Though not a Star Destroyer, the ship had styling reminiscent of those vast and destructive capital ships— diamond-shaped, it looked vaguely like two Star Destroyers attached to each other, stern to stern. *Bastion Princess,* nearly a kilometer long, was painted in deep blue, its surface decorated with thousands of exterior viewports and running lights shining in all the colors of the spectrum, making it look like its own self-contained starfield.

The Wraiths presented their false identicards to cruise line officers, boarded via a shuttle running from the station to the cruise liner's belly bay, and were conducted by a spotless white protocol droid to their cabins, a row of compartments deep within the ship and well away from the outer hull.

The cabins, though small, were not claustrophobic. In place of viewports, each was equipped with four monitors—one on each wall—showing holocam views from the ship's sensors. By default, they were tuned to exterior sensors, showing the forward starfield on the forward monitor, aft starfield on the aft monitor, a distant red sun on the port monitor, and the vast, skeletal Gagrew Station on the starboard. But each could be tuned to any of scores of sensor views, including casino areas, dining halls, the viewing deck, the swimming tank with its connecting tubes to the aquatic passenger deck, and a shipboard park with grass, flowers, and trees. Turman, sharing a cabin with Voort, used the bedside controls to flip through all the views.

Then they joined the others on the viewing deck, situated topside in the ship's bow. A vast chamber fifteen meters high at its apex, it offered a view of the forward and overhead starfield through its bulkhead, an enormous curved sheet of transparisteel. Hundreds of passengers, mostly human or near-human, crowded there to watch as Gagrew Station drifted away to starboard. Then the *Bastion Princess* was under way, its acceleration so gentle that Voort could barely feel it.

"I hate to say it." Trey's voice had a grudging note to it. "It's not spectacular, but it's pretty luxurious. I could get used to this."

"Try not to show any human emotions." Jesmin herself was expressionless, but there was a note of amusement to her voice. "You're supposed to be a security man, remember?"

"Right." Trey schooled his features to absolute stillness.

Jesmin offered a brisk nod in response to his transformation. "And don't praise this ship anytime you're near Myri. She'll give you half an hour of talk about how great the *Errant Venture* is."

"Noted."

Bhindi settled on a lounging chair and stared with blank delight at the starfield above, but her words and tone were not those of a flighty heiress. "All right, we're on the chrono, and we don't have much time. Four, find the accesses to Engineering and the communications center and scope out their security. Five, you're with him—try not to kill anybody."

Scut pointed a finger at Voort. "Old School there needs to hide in his cabin or find another kind of uniform. Note that he's the only Gamorrean here, and the only porter. A butler's outfit might work."

"True." Bhindi glanced at Turman. "Two, go with Seven. See if you can buy something appropriate for a butler or valet in one of the shops. If not, I'm relying on your costuming skills."

"Done." Turman glanced at Voort. He jerked his head for the Gamorrean to follow, and headed for the nearest turbolift.

Voort followed, feeling his temperature rise. Turman's brusqueness was only playacting, of course. But Scut . . . the Yuuzhan Vong had taken less than five minutes to find a way to exile Voort, and had worked in Voort's age and inappropriateness as he had done so.

Casually. Even elegantly.

When the turbolift doors closed, sealing him and Turman away from the Wraiths and other passengers, Voort let out a rumbling growl. "I'm going to put him through a hand-cranked meat grinder."

"You should have brought one from Vandor-Three. I don't think they have any on board. Shopping deck, please." The turbolift car plunged. "Seven, he was right. You were conspicuous."

"It was the way he phrased it. He's trying to irk me."

"Clearly, he's succeeding."

"Clearly." Now he wanted to shake Turman, to add a new argument. *Don't you understand? He's Yuuzhan Vong. They came here to destroy everything we know, everything we are. Obviously some of them aren't ready to give that up.*

But the lift car stopped. Its door snapped up, revealing a broad, low chamber lined with shops. Voort tamped down his anger and switched off his throat implant, then gestured, in a polite and servile fashion, for Turman to precede him.

And he vowed to keep his eyes open for a meat grinder.

CHAPTER NINE

"It turns out to be four jobs." Trey paused to stuff a pastry, slathered in blue butter, into his mouth. He chewed briskly while the others settled in around the meal table.

It was the morning—ship's time—after the Wraiths boarded, and they were in Bhindi's cabin. Jesmin, the cabin's other occupant, had persuaded a member of the ship's crew to remove the living area furniture and substitute a large circular card table, now capped by a sheet of transparent duraplast, and six upright chairs.

Voort didn't trust the spindly-looking things. He remained standing and began to make inroads into the pastry and egg selections while the others sat.

Done chewing, Trey continued. "Job One: Selectively disengaging and reengaging passageway sensors, looping their sensor feeds so they get static images while we're doing the things we shouldn't be doing. And that means getting into the security center without being noticed, slicing into the computer there, and introducing some code that will receive a comlink-transmitted command and temporarily subvert the passageway sensors nearest the comlink's transmission point. The code's actually the hardest part. I'm only a slicer by necessity. You need to recruit us a top-notch computer slicer."

Bhindi sighed. "It's on my list. Keep going."

"Well, when Job One is done, that makes all the other steps a little easier. With our master comlink active, we can walk anywhere on the vessel and know that the security holocams and other sensors aren't picking us up. But it's still chancy because, for instance, two holocams with slightly overlapping fields of vision could end up showing very different views at the point of overlap."

Bhindi nodded. Clearly she'd heard this sort of thing many, many times before. Voort certainly had, but he listened closely anyway. He found his appreciation for and trust in Trey's abilities increasing, despite the man's too-youthful mannerisms.

Trey paused to gobble down some small, globular winefruits. "Job Two, then. Sabotaging the hyperdrive. It's not as safe to just try to inject new code *there*. One mistake and I could screw things up, sending us into hyperspace forever on our next jump."

Turman, relaxing in his true Clawdite form, remained deadpan. "Let's not do that."

"What we do instead is install what I call a disintegrating tripper at a crucial connection in the hyperdrive itself. It's an electricity-conducting form of duraplast that breaks down, basically detonates, under enough heat. And there's a tiny amount of explosive there, too. Run a microfilament wire of the same stuff off into the wall with a comlink receiver and a timer. Later, whenever you want, you issue the signal, the comlink triggers the timer, the timer activates the little explosive charge, the tripper mechanism explodes with just enough force to knock the wiring connection free. Maybe does so without damaging it, maybe does a little damage, an easy fix in any case. And there's no forensic evidence left behind except for a little powder that used to be the tripper."

Bhindi sounded uncertain. "And the comlink in the wall."

"I'm pretty good at hiding those. And the repair crew sent down to investigate why the hyperdrive isn't working have a number one priority of getting it working before the captain reams them. If they do discover the timer or other evidence, it'll be a day or days later. When it will be too late to be relevant."

"All right, I'm convinced." Bhindi snatched up the last of the blue butter pastries just before Trey managed to get his hand on it.

"Trey, I didn't ask you yesterday." Jesmin's voice was suddenly very serious. "This hyperdrive-sabotaging technique. Is it something you learned somewhere, some trick widely known in the profession?"

Trey paused, confused. "No . . . I came up with this method myself. Yesterday. Why?"

"Some of you know I spent years investigating rumors of a very big, very sophisticated black-market ring." Jesmin looked decidedly unhappy. "Of course, anywhere you have a flow of supplies, there may be crews working to divert part of it for profit. But a while back, a good friend of mine, a fellow Antarian Ranger, was murdered on Toprawa, and the evidence I found pointed toward a major black-market ring. I took a long-term leave of absence from the Rangers to look into it. Spent a couple of years under the name of Zilaash Kuh, Force-using bounty hunter and criminal for hire, trying to crack it. And failed. One of the things I kept running across was reports of Alliance naval cargo vessels being hijacked, whisked away, no sign ever emerging of their cargoes or crews, and there was a lot of speculation about Interdictor cruisers or pinpoint hyperdrive sabotage. So I was curious."

"Oh." Trey shook his head. "No, I didn't practice for

my Wraith Squadron audition by pirating naval cargo vessels. Sorry."

Bhindi cleared her throat. "One of those hijackings happened just the other day. So Five's question was relevant. But we need to focus on the task at hand. Job Three?"

"Right." Soulful-eyed, Trey stared at the still-uneaten pastry in Bhindi's hand.

She glared. "I'm your commanding officer."

"I'm a growing boy."

With an exasperated noise, she handed it over. "Job Three?"

"Job Three is choosing the lifeboat escape pod we want to use for the mission, then assembling data on every ship's sensor that could possibly detect it, and setting up a onetime sensor loop at each of those sensors to keep them from detecting its launch. Not to mention disabling that lifeboat's own alert notifications. With those three jobs done, we're good to go."

Bhindi fixed him with a stern eye. "So you'll be getting to work immediately?"

Trey froze in mid-nibble. "I was going to get some sleep. Ten or twelve hours."

"Time is wasting, Trey. There are only two really good spots along this cruise route to do this."

Trey shook his head. "I think I misspoke. *With those three jobs done, we're good to go.* Those three jobs are done. Five and I were up all day and night yesterday doing them."

"What?" For once, Bhindi looked as though she'd been taken completely off guard.

Jesmin cracked up, buried her face in her hands. "It's true, One. He's very . . . energetic."

Trey shrugged. "We're good to go. Now can I sleep?"

Bhindi stared at him, stunned. Finally she found her

voice. "Four, I apologize for being cross with you earlier. Will you marry me?"

"Uh . . ." He checked his chrono. "Sure, why not?"

"Don't do it, One." Turman's voice was low, somber. "He wakes up before dawn every day. He *exercises* constantly. He's healthy and pure."

"Sorry, engagement's off." Bhindi stood. "Our first opportunity to do this is about fifteen hours from now. Convene here in twelve hours, rested and ready. Until then, enjoy yourselves, and don't make anybody suspicious."

Pastry still in hand, Trey joined the other men heading toward the door. "Did I do something wrong?"

Voort shook his head. "In just a few hours you impressed your boss and teammates, had a *very* brief affair of the heart, and emerged with your heart unbroken. I'd say you did quite well."

In fifteen years, Voort had forgotten just how tense even the most placid and error-free Wraith activities could be.

This one took place with the same efficiency Trey had shown in setting up the event. The Wraiths began by wiping down each of their cabins with bleach and other ordinary chemicals that would destroy genetic evidence and other forensic details pointing to their true identities. Most of their baggage and clothes ended up in a waste chute destined for the burners deep within the ship.

Finally the Wraiths gathered in Bhindi's cabin, carrying one small bag each. All wore the disguises and personae in which they had boarded, including Scut in his smiling neoglith masquer.

Silent, casual, and unmemorable, they walked in pairs to the turbolift and took it down to a deck devoted to function rooms and seminar chambers. Only the ship's library was occupied, and they tiptoed past it, past the few ship's passengers who preferred the lure of texts and educational programs to drinks, formal dinner wear, bathing suits, and the company of the idle rich.

At the end of the corridor was the irising door to an emergency bay holding an escape pod. Trey checked his comlink-equipped datapad, entered a few commands, and then nodded at the others. Voort and Turman quickly disengaged all the nearby overhead glow rod assemblies, plunging that end of the corridor into near darkness.

Bhindi slapped the red panel beside the door. There was no sudden shrill of ship's alarms, no voice from a nearby speaker demanding answers. The round door simply irised open, revealing a two-step antechamber and a similarly open door into a spherical golden escape pod.

They boarded in silence. Trey, the last one in, broadcast more commands from his datapad, and both the bay door and the pod door irised closed.

Trey went through a quick, silent checklist on his datapad. Then he relaxed and leaned back. "Safe to talk. Two minutes until the hyperdrive fails."

Bhindi buckled her restraining straps. "Everybody comfortable with zero gravity?"

"Usually." Voort grimaced. "But I'm feeling a little queasy. Anybody have something to settle my stomach?"

The Wraiths looked blankly at one another as they strapped themselves in.

Voort extended his straps to their maximum length and was finally able to get them around him and buckle in. "One, we really do need a team medic."

"I know." Bhindi shrugged. "I was pressed for time, trying to put together a team as fast as Face wanted. I had a really good sniper and close combat specialist all lined up, but I couldn't track him down—too busy recruiting Scut. I had to ask Face to go after you."

"Your loss. If we go into zero gravity and I begin throwing up . . ." Voort patted his belly. "I carry a lot of ammunition."

Turman, directly opposite Voort, turned to Bhindi. "Can I trade places with you?"

"No. Seven, throw up in your bag."

More seconds passed, until there was a beep from Trey's datapad. He glanced at it and smiled. "We are out of hyperspace. Right on schedule, and ship's computers tell me we're at the right spot. You may all kiss my hand." He tapped a button. "Sequence activated."

The bay and escape pod interior lights dimmed to blackness. A blank durasteel wall centimeters beyond the rear viewport slid aside, revealing starfield. There was a lurch, like a recreation park ride first going into motion . . . and moments later the irised bay door visible through the front viewport retreated, becoming a circle of diminishing size within a dark square bay of diminishing size, itself surrounded by dark blue hull and gleaming running lights.

Voort suddenly felt a touch dizzy, off balance from the abrupt cessation of artificial gravity. But his nausea did not worsen. He focused on the *Bastion Princess* drifting away from him at the slow rate of a few meters a second.

"Why do I feel like we need to whisper?" That was Turman, whispering.

Voort glanced at him. "Because you're bad at science. Or perhaps you're just overwhelmed by the psychological effect of a kilometer-long vessel so close, our lives possibly forfeit if someone catches a glimpse of us through a viewport, our lives possibly forfeit if no naval vessel spots us and Myri cannot get to us . . ."

Turman glared at him.

Voort warmed to the torturous subject. His nausea continued to diminish. "In fact, we could scream our throats hoarse, and of course no sound would cross the vacuum between here and there, no one aboard would notice . . ."

"Not *quite* true." Jesmin's attention was on the view of the cruise liner. "If we were screaming, genuinely upset, a Force-sensitive aboard might feel it. Might even flash on a mental image of us in the escape pod. If there was a trained Jedi or Sith aboard, it would actually be pretty likely. So let's stay calm."

They did, across ten long minutes, during which they drifted nearly two kilometers away from *Bastion Princess* by Voort's calculation. Then the cruise liner surged ahead. For an instant it seemed to stretch, and then it was gone.

"Perfect." Bhindi sounded jubilant. "Well done, Trey. Well done, Jesmin."

Trey perked up. "Do I get somebody to do my laundry for a couple of weeks?"

"No."

"You said something about rewards when you recruited me."

"You got my last butter pastry, and had a one-minute window in which you could have married me. So far, you're doing great, reward-wise." Bhindi sighed. "But now we restore lights, falsify a ship's identity for this pod, turn on the emergency beacon . . . and wait."

Bhindi extended her hand and accepted the grip and the unneeded aid of the Imperial Navy lieutenant, junior grade, who stood just outside the escape pod's door.

The lieutenant was dark-skinned, doubly handsome in his gray officer's uniform, and had courtly old-fashioned manners. He had a voice to match, deep and resonant and mature beyond his evident years. "Welcome aboard the *Concussor*, Lady Sadra."

Bhindi made her voice breathless. "Oh, *my*." She allowed the lieutenant to draw her out into the vessel's belly bay, a chamber barely large enough to hold the boxy military-grade rescue shuttle, two ball-cockpit TIE/In interceptors, and lifeboat escape pod currently occupying it.

As the other Wraiths emerged, feigning weariness by blinking, yawning, and stretching, Bhindi introduced them. "My yacht crew. Fili and Dili, my security—Fili's the he one and Dili's the she one. Murt, my soon-to-be-former pilot—he's the bland one in black. The one who's all smiles is Voozy, in charge of entertainments. And the porter is Gronk."

"I am Lieutenant Phison. And I apologize for my haste, but I have to get some information and comm it to the bridge before we get you settled into quarters. Your emergency comm mentioned pirates."

Bhindi nodded, eyes opening as if she were bewildered. "We weren't yet out of the gravity field of the asteroid belt we were admiring when there they were, half a dozen starfighters that looked like they'd been slapped together from scraps and spit."

"Yes, ma'am. Uglies, in fighter pilot parlance. Did they mention their names?"

"Not individually; they didn't *introduce* themselves. But they called themselves . . . Dinner Squadron." She heard a grunt, as if caused by a minor pain spasm, from Voort. "My yacht was unarmed, unarmored. What choice did we have? We surrendered. They were actually sort of nice to us. No killing, no abusing, they took us out to a trade route and let us eject in my pod. That's sort of polite, isn't it?"

Lieutenant Phison nodded. "Very, by some standards.

Now I have to ask, is your yacht in Imperial registry, and are you Imperial citizens?"

Bhindi let an expression of disappointment cross her features. "Well, *I'd* say so. I'm from Coruscant, from when the Emperor ruled. But my family fled when those ghastly Rebels took over. We've never been back. Is that Imperial enough?"

"I certainly hope so. I'll get that information to the captain. Please come this way." He gestured toward the exit blast door.

Unbidden, Bhindi linked her arm through his and walked with him. "How many men are aboard a boat this size?"

"We're a *Burst Fire*–class Deep-Space Patrol Vessel— what we like to call a pocket corvette. We have a crew of thirty."

"Perfect! But I don't mean crew, silly. I mean *men*. Human men."

The blast doors opened for them. "I'm, uh, not sure. Sixteen? Eighteen?"

"Oh, how *wonderful*."

CHAPTER TEN

Voort kept up a litany of grunting, squealing, petty complaints in Gamorrean while Trey meticulously searched and scanned every surface, nook, niche, shelf, drawer, and furniture underside in the junior officer's cabin that had been assigned to Bhindi. It wasn't that Voort was genuinely unhappy; the noise he made would divert anybody listening in by eavesdropping device.

Finally Trey returned to the gleaming white datapad that rested on the cabin's tiny fold-down desktop. He picked the datapad up, switched it off, and snapped it shut. "That's it. No mikes in the walls or possessions. Just one innocuous datapad left behind on a shelf, set to record."

Bhindi, who'd been stretched out on the lower bunk ever since Trey had finished searching it, offered him an expression of disappointment. "The good *old* Empire would have had every one of their officers under surveillance. That's what the old-timers say, anyway. I feel let down. Call the others in, Seven."

Voort rapped three times on the aft bulkhead wall, and then moved over to repeat the knock on the forward bulkhead.

In moments the other three Wraiths entered, filling the small cabin past comfortable capacity. Trey swung himself into the upper bunk, giving himself and the others more room. "I've reassembled the component parts. We have three ugly, sort of recognizable blasters that the Imps don't know about . . . in theory. But we can't test them without making a lot of noise."

Bhindi stretched as if indifferent. "We'll just have to trust you, then. With all our lives . . ."

Trey flinched. "Stop it."

As soon as the passageway door was shut, Turman turned toward Bhindi. "That was an awful performance."

She shot him a hurt look. "I thought I did rather well."

"Oh, vocal inflections, mannerisms, your commitment to the character, they were fine. Amateur, but fine. But the character herself—stomach-turning. One-dimensional. Nothing there for an audience to connect with."

"I'll have you know that Imperial military males have a history of appreciating breathless women with the brains of a bantha." Bhindi sighed. "Everyone, listen up. The captain will have already transmitted his preliminary report on us, his new rescues, and will be awaiting orders. If my experience with the New Republic Navy is any guide, those orders will be to keep us aboard and continue with his patrol until his course takes him near a place where he can drop us off with minimal loss of time or use of resources. Which gives us maybe a day. With luck, two."

Jesmin sat at the foot of Bhindi's bunk. "We've been pretty lucky so far."

Bhindi nodded in agreement. "We've been *terrifically* lucky so far. Down to the craft that picked us up. We should be able to crew it long enough to limp somewhere we can pick up additional spacers."

"We should not have brought Piggy." That was Scut,

his tone flat, a curious contrast with his smiling expression. "All the reports of insurgency . . . someone will notice that there's always a 'Gamorrean porter.' His presence endangers us."

"Maybe." Bhindi sounded bored. "But Seven is a seasoned enough veteran not to speak someone's *name* when we're behind enemy lines. Which you, Six, and even you, Five, are not. Not yet. Not to mention, Six, that you forgot and used a name he doesn't wear anymore. And here's another reason he's along with us. Let's say the next phase of this operation goes perfectly and leaves us in possession of the *Concussor*. What's next?"

Scut shook his head. The motion made the too-large ears of his neoglith masquer wobble. "You haven't told us."

"Bad answer. Maybe a fatal answer." Now Bhindi's voice was harsh. "Let's say that in the taking of the *Concussor,* I drop dead of a heart attack. I haven't told you the rest of the plan, but you know our objectives. Six, what do we do?"

"We . . . set course for a safe port, I suppose."

Bhindi sighed. "Fail. Two?"

Turman frowned. "We *do* set course for a port where we can get what we need. Say, Parabaw Station, a smugglers' haven here in the Outer Rim."

"Fail. A slightly better fail. Four?" She reached up with her foot and prodded the bunk above with her toe.

Trey shrugged. "I'm just here to flex, fix your comlinks when they break, and look pretty."

"You're unhelpful, but correct. Five?"

Jesmin grinned over at her. "I know where this is going, so I'll pass."

"Five, you're cowardly and wise at the same time. Seven?"

"Immediate task is division of labor." Voort was surprised at how easily the planning task came back to him. "We have a military mini corvette designed for a crew of thirty now in the hands of a crew of six, so we're all going to be awake and alert around the chrono, working like Jawas high on caf, until we're fully crewed again. Four, you're Engineering, and you're going to have a hell of a time of keeping everything functioning until we make port. One, you're dead of a heart attack, so the task of crewing the bridge falls to me. Two, you're communications officer, since if we have to communicate we can't show a Gamorrean in the captain's chair. Sensors, too. Five and Six, we don't kill prisoners and we can't afford to lose a resource like that shuttle by tamping the prisoners into it, disabling its hyperdrive, and sending it away, so you two are in charge of the prisoners until we can drop them. Since they'll eventually be reporting on us, we maintain code names and false identity mannerisms until every one of them is gone. We find a drop point somewhere between here and Parabaw Station, a habitat or colony too poor to have a hypercomm and too obscure to get frequent ship visits, and drop the prisoners there. We make the shuttle dirtier and uglier because we'll be using it for the initial approach to Parabaw Station—if we show up in a gleaming new Imperial warship, they'll have abandoned the place before we can say, *No, no, we're crooks, too.* We have little operating capital, so we'll sell one of the interceptors for enough credits to hire a crew. During all this, Two will dress up as his fictitious Imperial Special Forces officer and make the recording intended to flush the general. We transmit it to Three for mysterious delivery to the general's desk. Then—"

"I think you proved my point." Bhindi glanced back at Scut. "So, Six, do we drag him along, or what?"

Scut's answer was slow in coming. "Yes, we do . . . One."

"Good boy." She swung her legs off the bunk and heaved herself to her feet. "Time for me to talk a walk around, charm the crew, and learn the geography of this place." She glanced at Jesmin. "I'll need a guard. Come along, Fili."

Jesmin stood, too. "I'm Dili."

"Oops. Clearly, I'm out of practice."

Turman sniffed. "The line is, *I'm getting too old for this*."

When Bhindi and Jesmin were gone, Voort fixed Scut with a hard stare. "Six, why did you make a face that can't stop smiling?"

"I can stop." Scut sat on the bunk where Bhindi had lain. The corners of his mouth drooped and his expression became serious. "But it requires an effort. Its natural expression is happy." The smile returned. Yet his eyes remained neutral, emotionless.

"Why make it that way?"

"Because I am happy. Almost always happy."

"Even when you're trying to poison my relationship with this unit?"

"Especially then. Because I know I'm doing my best to save the lives of the others. From the danger you pose."

"I'm not a danger to them. You are."

"I will prove otherwise. And I hope I can prove it to you first. So you will do the honorable thing and resign."

"Yeah. Good luck with that." Voort slammed his way out of Bhindi's temporary cabin and returned to his own.

Bhindi, dressed for bed in a fluttery, gauzy pink nightgown purchased in one of the *Bastion Princess*'s shops, stepped out from her cabin into the passageway. Yawning, she stretched as though there hadn't been enough room in her borrowed cabin for such an action. Then she leaned against the far wall of the passageway and arched her back, stretching those muscles, as well.

As she leaned against the wall, her left palm covered the small, almost invisible holocam lens embedded there at just above human head height.

Jesmin, watching from inside the cabin, rolled out of the top bunk and dropped to the deck, making almost no noise as she landed in a crouch. She kept her hand on the lightsaber hilt dangling from her belt, ensuring that it did not clatter against the bunk or bulkhead. She was clad head to foot in black stretch fabric, only her eyes exposed. She knew she would be virtually invisible in darkness and no more than a black silhouette in the light. Even her lightsaber hilt was now wrapped in black space tape.

She rapped on the aft bulkhead, then moved out into the passageway behind Bhindi. She turned right, toward the stern, and trotted the few steps to the next compartment door.

Not all doors in this passageway were under the scrutiny of holocams, and this was one that wasn't. Bhindi had spotted that little fact during her tours of the patrol vessel.

Jesmin waited for only a moment before that door slid open. Another black silhouette emerged—obvious as Trey only because of his distinctive musculature. The door shut.

Trey reached up to press a button on the spindly black headset fitted over his stretch hood. "Four up and running."

Jesmin did so with hers, as well. "Five here. Cam and comm check."

"Sight and sound good on both of you." It was Voort's voice.

Jesmin led the way aft.

It was the wee hours of the night, ship's time. Lieutenant Phison, giving Bhindi her first tour of the vessel, had provided a lot of information, too much for his own well-being. Such as the fact that the quietest time of the daily cycle was about two hours after midnight, when a slightly higher percentage of the crew than at other hours was getting some fitful sleep. Such as the fact that the unmarked armored door near the Engineering compartment was "the auxiliary bridge"—but the lack of a discernible Security station elsewhere on the craft marked the auxiliary bridge as probably handling that function, too.

Jesmin dropped to the deck plates and crawled a few meters, keeping beneath the eye line of another wall holocam. Trey did likewise. He made a bit more noise than she, and Jesmin winced. Bhindi had insisted that she not go on this task alone, despite Jesmin's protests.

On the far side of the holocam view, both rose.

At an intersection with a cross-passageway, Jesmin paused as she heard oncoming footsteps from around the corner to the left. She stopped, holding up a hand to warn Trey. Then she cocked that hand back to throw a blow, a breath-expelling, pain-inducing blow, if the Imperial spaceman should turn her way.

It was a woman, enlisted personnel, and she didn't spot Jesmin out of the corner of her eye. She continued along her original path, her mind clearly on other matters.

Jesmin turned to glance at Trey. His gaze snapped upward to meet hers. His eyes, the only detail of his face to be seen in all the blackness, looked guilty.

She frowned. "Were you just looking at my rear end?"

"Um . . . I'm not the actor Two is, so I'll just say . . . yes."

"Now's not the time." She turned forward again and glided across the intersection.

She barely heard his whispered reply: "So, theoretically, there would be a time."

"Quiet."

Two intersections later, as she paused at the corner, she heard voices approaching—two, male. She alerted Trey.

The voices belonged to two uniformed officers, and they both turned forward, directly toward Jesmin and Trey.

They were abreast of Jesmin before the nearest one noticed her silhouette in the dim passageway. He turned toward her, instinctively opening his mouth to speak.

Jesmin's spear-hand strike took him in the solar plexus. Only a muffled *"Uhhnn"* emerged from his mouth.

Trey was not quite so silent. He stepped forward and his fist cracked into the jaw of the second officer. The man's head snapped toward Jesmin, and he swayed backward.

Jesmin hit the first officer again, a palm strike to the temple. In the same moment, Trey lunged forward and caught his out-on-his-feet victim before the man crashed to the deck plates.

Jesmin grabbed her own target, making his collapse as silent as possible. Then she glanced over at Trey.

They couldn't just leave these victims here. Even in the middle of a dull watch like this, a naval vessel's passageways were frequently trafficked. Nor could they just look for a convenient hiding hole in their vicinity. Bhindi had plotted out some supply cabinets and ship's system accesses, but they were few, and none was nearby.

With a sigh, Trey stooped, pulled his victim over his shoulder, and straightened. He turned toward Jesmin, stooped again as she pulled her victim as far up as she could, and then Trey straightened with the second man over his other shoulder.

They continued aft. Now they moved much more slowly and Trey made more noise than before, puffing a bit, the deck plates creaking more often under his feet. Still, Jesmin thought he was doing remarkably well for a man with nearly two hundred kilos of unconscious meat hanging from his body. They made it undetected to the first of Bhindi's hiding holes, a laundry supplies storage compartment, and deposited their prisoners there. Trey bound both men with strips of cloth torn from soiled laundry while Jesmin waited with her eye at the slightly open compartment door. That task done, they continued.

They reached the aft terminus of the passageway. Behind them, just a few meters, was the last of the cross-passageways on this level. Directly ahead was a blast door marked ENGINEERING. And to their left was another blast door, this one unmarked.

Jesmin flattened herself against the wall beside the unmarked blast door. "I think this calls for a Force technique."

Trey's eyes widened. "Are you going to cut your way in with your lightsaber?"

"What are you, six years old? No, I'm not. Is there any way you can tell if there's a refresher in there?"

The stretch cloth of his hood crinkled at forehead level as he frowned. "You need to go? *Now?* Didn't you think about that before—"

"Can you or can't you?"

"I can put a mike to the wall and listen. I might hear a sink running or the refresher flushing."

"Do it."

Once Trey had the mike, a medical device, against the wall and its output leads plugged into his headset, Jesmin closed her eyes and began concentrating.

After a minute, Trey whispered again. "No water noises so far. But now *I'm* starting to need to go."

Jesmin nodded, kept her eyes closed, kept concentrating.

"Hey. Are you doing that? What are you doing?"

"Thinking of waterfalls, wine bottles pouring, faucets gushing, fountains flowing . . . and I'm putting that out through the Force."

"You *monster*. I'm . . . I'm . . ."

"Keep it together, Four. Any noises?"

"Conversation; I can't make out the words, but it's getting more urgent." A moment later: "I *understand* that urgency."

"It'll pass as soon as the door opens."

"Or as soon as I disgrace myself."

"First one out of the room is yours."

It was only a few seconds later that Jesmin heard the blast door *whoosh* open. She opened her eyes in time to see Trey, now standing just in front of the door, launch a terrific kick to the groin of the man in the officer's uniform standing there.

Foot met target and deformed it before the victim could even make a surprised face. The victim was in mid-convulsion and mid-moan when Trey grabbed him and yanked him out through the doorway.

Jesmin spun, put on a burst of Force-boosted speed, and hurtled into the chamber. It was a long, narrow room, the forward wall a blur of monitors and projected holograms, the aft wall a series of racks holding dark blobs Jesmin couldn't make out at this speed. Ahead was a semicircular desk with two chairs, one of them occupied. Jesmin hurtled to the second chair, where a fair-skinned woman in officer's uniform was in the act of reaching for a desktop button. Jesmin collided with her, knocking her hand away from the desktop. The chair had glide-plates beneath it and the two rode it, propelled by Jesmin's impact, to slam into the far wall, the undecorated starboard bulkhead.

Fetched up against the wall, Jesmin twisted, put her elbow into the officer's stomach. As the woman gagged, Jesmin caught her in a choke hold and held on.

It didn't take long. The woman flailed for a few moments, then slumped. Jesmin maintained her grip for a few moments longer, in case the woman was faking, then released her and laid her out on the floor. The woman drew in wheezing breaths but remained unconscious.

Jesmin looked up. The outer door was already closed. Trey's victim was stretched out on the deck plates and Trey stood over the desk, scanning the controls and sensors displayed there.

The blobs Jesmin had glimpsed on the back wall were trooper gear—blaster rifles, belts with blaster pistols, body armor, helmets, at least four full sets. Jesmin smiled. "Good."

Trey glanced her way. "You were right. I no longer have to pee."

"I'll notify HoloNet News." Jesmin got to her feet. "Alert the others. Tell them I'm bringing them blaster pistols. Patch any of those holocam feeds Seven wants to him. He can act as controller for the others. You'll be my controller."

"Oh, if *only*."

With holocam feeds piped to him by Trey, Voort monitored the movements of the now black-clad Scut, Turman, and Bhindi.

He kept an especially close eye on Scut's vicinity. If the Yuuzhan Vong was going to take an opportunity to betray or harm the other Wraiths, to get a message off to some Yuuzhan Vong ally, this would be a good time for it. But Scut, weird and angular in his black body stocking and hood, no longer padded out by his neoglith masquer and other disguise elements, did exactly as he was supposed to. He moved methodically up his assigned corridor, stood outside cabin doors until Voort opened them remotely, and stepped in. An instant after the door closed Scut fired off a few stun blasts with his reassembled blaster.

As Jesmin began to intersect the paths of the other Wraiths, she distributed the blasters she had taken. The others no longer had to rely just on Trey's reassembled blasters. Jesmin didn't keep one herself; she resumed stalking the passageways, using her bare hands to deal with personnel as she met them.

All the while, Trey kept up a running narrative audible over the headsets. "Ten crewmates down and counting. Zap zap, two more for Wraith Four, the galley is *ours*. Twelve and counting. Uh, I'm seeing here that there are thirty-eight sapients aboard, not thirty. Double uh, sorry, that's the six of us and thirty-*two*, I say again thirty-*two* crew—the lieutenant evidently wasn't counting the captain or ex oh. Thirteen down, Wraith Five delivers another headache."

Ten minutes later, *Concussor* was theirs.

CHAPTER ELEVEN

F ace brought his airspeeder in for a landing on the hundredth-floor visitor parking level of the Cloud Paradise residential building.

Actually, *building* was too modest a word, even by the gargantuan standards of many Coruscant constructions. Face had marveled at the Cloud Paradise edifice as soon as his closed-top black speeder had come within sight of it. Technically, it boasted only as many stories as other skytowers in this high-income residential district, but each of this building's stories was a minimum of four meters in height, allowing the ziggurat-shaped structure to tower over everything around it. Built of black granite mined from Coruscant's depths even after the world had been completely covered in city, its exterior was brightened by railings, window frames, piping, and other fixtures plated in simulated gold. No advertising marquees adorned the building's exterior, only flowing plates reading CLOUD PARADISE every fifty stories on every facing.

Even in the parking levels, the opulence continued. None of the unoccupied resident and visitor landing slots Face could see was stained with lubricants or hydraulic fluids—the building custodial staff had to be cleaning each airspeeder level regularly. The turbolifts from the parking level were enclosed in a secure area with a guard behind a desk keeping an eye on matters; the uniformed Devaronian male, all horns and teeth and bright eyes, waved a hand scanner over Face's identi-card and read every word of data that popped up on his monitor before he summoned the lift.

The hallway of the floor he entered was lined with cream-colored marble and reproductions of famous statues from Alderaanian classical antiquity, their hues as vibrant as if they were touched up every morning.

Still, Face had confronted excessive wealth before, many times. He kept his expression alert, pleasant, but not suggesting that there was anything unusual about his surroundings. Stopping at a door, he pressed the visitor button and announced himself: "Garik Loran to see Zehrinne Thaal."

There was no vocal answer, but thirty seconds later the double doors slid open. Beyond was a dim waiting room, red velvet couches to either side, and a woman.

She was no servant. Tall, nearing middle age, lean as a fashion model, her black hair in twin braids, she wore a midlength green dress that looked as though it belonged at an outdoor summertime roof party. On her feet were sandals in a matching color.

She glared at him. "You didn't tell me you were famous." Her voice was exactly the controlled alto Face had expected, low and rich.

He shrugged. "I'm not, anymore. I was famous when I was a boy."

"So the encyclopedias tell me. Come in." She gestured, then preceded him into the apartment.

Face took a look around, without seeming to, as they moved along a broad hall, lined in what smelled like real wood, with a dozen or more doors leading to one side or the other at intervals. There were blank spots on the walls where frames or monitors had once hung—someone had removed a lot of artwork from this place recently. A fine, nearly uniform layer of dust on horizontal surfaces said it had been some time since the place had been tended. At last, Zehrinne led him through a door into a broad chamber lit by natural sunlight pouring in through an oversized window; the view showed skytowers and the ceaseless airspeeder traffic of Coruscant outside. The room itself was almost devoid of furniture; there were two stuffed chairs and a low table between them, an adjustable upright chair that looked as though it normally held dental patients, an easel and canvas in front of it. That was all.

Zehrinne took one of the stuffed chairs, gestured to the other. "It's the housekeeper's day off. Her lifetime off, actually. I fired her. And the rest of the staff. Can I offer you something to drink?"

"Oh, no, thank you." Face took the other chair and looked at the canvas. It was a painting in traditional materials, a nearly holorealistic portrait of a female Naboo cliff diver, her arms spread as if in flight, in midplummet. It was not quite done; details of the bay in the background were vague around the painting's edges, and the woman's face, other than her black eyes, had not yet been detailed. The almost-featureless face was somehow a bit unsettling.

"Well, *I'm* having something. Oh, Vacuum . . ." Zehrinne stared at a side door leading from the chamber.

That door slid aside, revealing a protocol droid. He had once, perhaps even recently, been shiny gold, but his metal skin was now decorated with specks and blobs and swirls of color—paint, Face assumed, from the old-fashioned palette and brushes resting on the small table.

The protocol droid said nothing.

Zehrinne smiled. "Wine. Red. Something common." She glanced back at Face. "Nothing? Are you sure?"

"Thank you, I've just had lunch."

"Oh, well." She waved, and the droid withdrew.

Face gave her a curious look. "Vacuum is his name?"

"Sound doesn't carry in a vacuum . . . and the first thing I did with him a week ago when I bought him was disconnect his vocal synthesizers. He has to write notes or send visual messages. Oh, there's an emergency override, of course . . . but for now, blessed, blessed silence."

Face thought about it. "You know, I bet you could sell a million of those units, even aftermarket, to customers who've had long experience with protocol droids."

"I'll have to look into that. I'll need a career. I own these quarters outright . . . but I can't afford the property taxes on them."

"You were . . . unexpectedly candid about your domestic situation when we commed you. But even then it was clear that there were some things you'd only say in person." Face gave her a sympathetic look.

"I'm not paranoid . . . but he is a powerful man with his fingers in everything. I don't think he intends me any specific harm, but I'm definitely going to give him a beating, and I see no reason for him to anticipate any of it."

Face nodded.

Zehrinne burst out into laughter. "You *are* an actor."

"I beg your pardon?"

"Your face, your expression. It said, *Please go on,* and *I'm not surprised that you're going to give him a beating, he deserves it,* and *You're very attractive, but for whatever reason I'm not going to make a move at this time,* and about a dozen other things. All without words."

Face felt himself redden. "I'm not really trying to play you. It's just—"

"A lifetime of habit?"

"Something like that. Please, continue what you were telling me over the comm, and I'll try to be less . . ."

"Manipulative. Don't bother trying. You probably can't help yourself."

They were delayed by the return of Vacuum, who, silently and with a resentful stiffness unusual even for a protocol droid, placed her glass of wine on the table beside her, then withdrew.

Zehrinne sipped it while she considered her words. "Stavin and I met about thirty years ago. The New Republic had taken Coruscant five years earlier. I remember the Death Seed stories were almost all you ran across on the holonews. I was eighteen, and making my living as a model. He was thirty, a captain in the army. Not handsome exactly, but he looked great in a uniform, and he was ambitious and smart. Old-fashioned and courtly and *persistent,* and for whatever reason he decided he was going to make me fall in love with him and marry him, not necessarily in that order. And he did."

"So far, so good."

"And it was good for years. He didn't make me stop modeling, didn't ask me to, but to me it was a job, not a calling. And being the spouse of an ambitious military officer can be a job, too, and if you're good at it, you can help him do a lot better than he would do by himself. Being social, making connections, urging promotions . . . And I did get good at my job."

Face frowned. "And no trouble in all that time?"

"Plenty of trouble. But the usual husband–wife trouble. Things like, we weren't entirely compatible genetically, so we couldn't have children without major medical involvement, and he wasn't willing to do that. Or adopt." She sipped at her wine and looked out through the window. "Next week, I think I'm going to go out and adopt. Just me. No other voices in the decision."

"When you can't afford taxes on your home?" Face regretted the words as soon as he spoke them. It wasn't any of his business. But the compulsive planner in his makeup couldn't quite be silenced.

She gave him an unfriendly smile. "See, you just became a voice."

"Sorry. I'm clearly a hypocrite. I adopted my wife's daughter. So I clearly don't even know what side of your argument I'm taking."

"That's better. Where was I?"

"Mostly good years."

"Right. That brings us up to our twelve-year mark. He was Colonel Thaal then, a general's right-hand man, being groomed for promotion as much as you can be in what was mostly a peacetime army. And the best possible thing happened, from the perspective of an officer looking for advancement. The Yuuzhan Vong invaded and started killing everybody." She gave Face a carefree look.

"Now who's being manipulative?"

She raised her eyebrows. "I beg your pardon?"

"You throw out a line like that, suggesting that the most devastating war in civilized history was something to be celebrated, and give me a coy look to see how I react to it . . ."

She smiled. "I can't help it. I was born to cause trouble. For thirty years of marriage, I had to suppress that instinct. Now I'm free. Anyway . . . Stavin was his usual efficient, dependable, slightly dull self through the first half of the war . . . and then the Yuuzhan Vong started getting closer and closer to Coruscant. He packed me off to safety on Denon. When the final assault came here on Coruscant, he somehow persuaded his superiors to let him go to Vandor-Three and build a resistance cell there. Which he did pretty well. Those were his original Pop-Dogs, and he became a hero."

"Still so far so good."

"No, that was when our relationship died. I just didn't know it at the time. The war ended, Coruscant was Vongformed to more of the wilderness it used to be, evacuees started moving home, Stavin returned . . . and we weren't a couple anymore. I mean, we talked about it. He laid out his position clearly. He said he owed me a lot of his career advancement, he'd stay married to me, half of what was his was mine, he wouldn't do anything to embarrass me publicly . . . but we were done. He said it was all his fault, but he didn't want to try to fix things between us."

Face leaned forward, certain that he was getting near an answer that might be useful to him. "He never discussed the reason?"

"No. But I figured it out over time. I was still connected to his entire social life, after all." She shrugged. "He liked younger women."

"As . . . ordinary a reason as that?"

"Yes. After our unofficial split, he found a mistress, barely twenty years old. He was with her for about ten years, then set her up with a nice little home, a nice little business, a threat to take them away from her if she caused trouble, and he took a *new* mistress, age nineteen. That was five years ago. The way I figure it, she has maybe five years to go before he drops her, too."

Face blinked, considering. "Maybe less."

"Why do you say that?"

"Just a feeling I have." Face tried to sell that lie with an earnest expression. "But something has changed between you and the general more recently, correct? Which is why you're facing tax payments, why you fired his household staff?"

"He began divorce proceedings. And all his assets are

frozen, unavailable to me, until the proceedings are resolved." She waved a hand at her surroundings. "Fortunately, title in this place came to me years ago, after he moved out. If I have to, I can sell it, get a less expensive place, live on the difference. But I'd hate to do that. I love this place."

"Did he say why he was divorcing you?"

"He hinted that it was so he could marry his current girl. But I don't believe that. I think she's a short-timer just like all the women in his life are. I think it's . . ." She paused to consider her words. "One of the reasons he's such a good organizer is that he has a horror of unfinished business. Loose ends. It preys on him, makes it hard for him to sleep. I think that suddenly I became unfinished business."

"So he had to get his domestic life straightened out before . . . before what?"

"I don't know."

Face suppressed a smile. Their entire conversation had told him almost nothing—just that Stavin Thaal liked younger women and that something big would be happening soon, something that made the compulsive organizer desperate to tie off loose ends.

It wasn't a big fact, it wasn't anything that would convince a jury of anything. But it convinced Face. The *something big* could be anything, but it probably had to do with career-changing plans . . . plans that might involve an act of treason against the Alliance.

No, the conversation had told him something else, too, something he had to check into. "Can you tell me the names of his mistresses?"

"Of course. In fact . . ." She slid open a small drawer on the table's underside and withdrew a datapad. She flipped it open, typed and scrolled for a few moments, then snapped it shut again. "You'll be getting full contact information for them any second now."

"Much appreciated." He stood. "If it's any consolation, I think you're being quite generous with the general. If I had treated Dia like the general treated you, she'd borrow an X-wing, take to the skies, and burn me to a cinder."

"Tell her I like her style. Vacuum will show you out."

Back in his home, also a high-rise apartment but far more modest—and cheerful—than Zehrinne's, he sat in his study and began looking for information on the HoloNet.

Information on Cadrin Awel, now age thirty-five, originally from Vandor-3. As a teenager, she'd been a singer, winner of local talent contests, unable to make herself noticed in the much vaster market of nearby Coruscant. She and several family members and friends had camped out for two years in an unoccupied region of Vandor-3 and had eluded notice by the Yuuzhan Vong. For ten years after the war, her movements were largely unrecorded. A few years ago, just prior to the start of the Second Galactic Civil War, she had bought a large rural property on her homeworld and had set up a sort of boot camp where city folk, mostly from Coruscant, could learn nature skills. The advertising and promotional materials for Cadrin's Sanctuary mentioned her years of living off the land during the Yuuzhan Vong War but not her relationship with General Thaal. A brief news entry from two years ago indicated that she had married one of her fellow wartime survivors. Holos and stills of Cadrin showed a pretty, fair-skinned, fair-haired woman with an athlete's build.

Information on Keura Fallatte, now age twenty-four. Born on Tatooine, she excelled at engineering and mechanical work and, according to records, left home at age sixteen to live the life of a spacer. Three years later, she left her employer and moved into a trendy Coruscant hostel. After the end of the Second Galactic Civil War—and, Face noted after a cross-check, within a week of Thaal's promotion to head of the army—she relocated to the best hostel in Ackbar City, Vandor-3. But another check indicated that she was no longer there. She had left the hostel a mere week ago, checking out and leaving no forwarding information. A concierge Face spoke to, and who was more than willing to accept a HoloNet-transmitted tip, said she was happy and excited during her departure . . . but closemouthed. Face could find no trace of her current whereabouts.

Face wrote a brief account of Zehrinne's information and his preliminary investigation into the fates of the two mistresses for the Wraiths. He included no orders. The Wraiths would know what to do with the facts. He encrypted the report, installed and concealed it within a datapad game, and transmitted it.

Then he wrote another report, encrypted it, and transmitted it to the *Quarren Eye*, the yacht Borath Maddeus had supplied him with, for retransmission elsewhere.

Finally, his day's work done, he quit the study and moved out to the tiled dining area of his living chamber. His wife, Dia, and her daughter, Adra, were there already, chatting, paying occasional attention to news feeds scrolling across their datapad screens. They were so alike: green Twi'lek women, below average height but muscled like sand panthers. Dia was still in the snug blue civilian pilot's uniform of the commercial air-and-space service where she was a partner; Adra wore a jumpsuit that was a riot of green and orange stripes and zigzags.

Face's approach was so silent that neither noticed until he was almost at the table. Both turned to look at him and, seeing the expression on his face, fell silent.

He turned to Dia. "I promise I will never make you so

mad that you borrow an X-wing, take it up, and use it to burn me to a cinder."

"Smart of you." She gestured at the third chair. "Whose turn is it to cook?"

"Yours."

"We'll order something."

He sat and turned to his daughter. "And you, young lady . . . Beware of older military officers who chase you when you're a teenager. They'll just dump you when you turn thirty."

She sighed and rolled her eyes. "Dad, I hate it when you bring work home."

CHAPTER TWELVE

"You. Stupid."

Piggy looked up from his task, mopping the last portion of this corner of the station's main yard. He was surrounded by wire-mesh chairs and tables, as well as now spotless flooring of white sheet duraplast decorated at intervals with the gearlike symbol of the Empire. At this late hour the area was almost deserted. Other than Piggy, only one man was present. He was an officer, crisp and neat in his gray uniform, nursing a last cup of caf at one table.

Using his mop for leverage, Piggy scooted his bucket to within two meters of the speaker, a leathery, gray-haired man of advancing years. Piggy grunted a nonverbal interrogative.

The officer glanced at him and sighed as if despairing of being able to accomplish anything. "You understand Basic?"

Piggy nodded, grunted.

"Good. New task." The man pointed up—not at the star-filled sky, but at the top rim of wall surrounding the base. The wall was a monolithic run of permacrete, topped by an irregular layer of what looked like white gravel and powder.

But where the officer pointed, below the layer of white, a pool of darkness had oozed two meters down the wall, marring the surface's otherwise perfect cleanliness. "See that? I want that cleaned. Right now."

Piggy allowed himself a tremble. He gestured imploringly at the officer, then gestured more wildly, hands down and then rising abruptly, spreading apart, miming some great upheaval. He punctuated his move with shrill grunts.

The officer shook his head with forced patience. "No. We turn *off* the mines and their sensor triggers while you're up there. You climb Tower Three, show the guard there that you're going out on the wall. He knows what you'll be there for. He'll switch things off while you work and on again when you return."

Piggy offered up a few more mock-whimpers. Then, under the unrelenting stare of the officer, he allowed his shoulders to slump. He picked up his bucket, not allowing it or the mop to drip on his perfect floor, and walked to the door at the base of Guard Tower Three.

The officer was as true as his word. The enlisted man on duty at the tower's summit barely looked up from his bank of infrared-equipped holocam monitors when Piggy arrived. Nor did the first meter of wall explode under Piggy's feet when he stepped out on it.

Piggy situated himself above the stain and lay down on his belly, feet stretching out over the jungle beyond the walls and head protruding over the close-cropped grass within them. He got to work with his mop.

It had taken a couple of days to work out the base's security routine and come up with this approach. A frail duraplast egg and a ridiculously oversized slingshot, built and mounted on a stand in his tiny worker's quarters, had allowed him to launch a payload of fast-growing but harmless fungus against the wall top the previous evening. Now that fungus, touched by the chemicals running from Piggy's mop, sizzled, died, and dropped almost instantly off the wall, raining in sheets onto the ground.

Below and off to the left, the leathery officer appeared to be satisfied with Piggy's progress. He drained the last of his caf, stood, and began his walk back to the officers' quarters.

Piggy spent a moment fishing several items of gear from the murky fluid in his bucket. He left mop and bucket behind and headed back to the tower.

The guard on duty didn't look up as Piggy entered. "You done?"

"No, you idiot, I'm just getting started."

The guard looked at him, astonished to hear a human-like voice emerging from a Gamorrean mouth. He still wore that surprised expression when Piggy raised his compact blaster pistol and put a stun bolt into his chest.

It took only a couple of minutes to make the walk, balancing precariously, from Tower Three to Tower Two and repeat the process with the guard there.

Back at his bucket, he tore open the container that kept his rope dry. At one end was a container of quick-acting adhesive. He pressed a length of rope to the wall top and, with a small vibroblade, cut the bag. Adhesive ran down across rope and wall. The stuff began to heat up as it made contact with the oxygen in the air, cooking into a hard surface.

Piggy counted off three minutes, keeping his eyes open for anyone returning to the tables or the towers. No one did. He tossed the remainder of the length of rope down the outside of the wall. Within seconds it went taut.

A furry hand crested the wall top, then Runt pulled himself up. "You took long enough."

"The martinet with the cleanliness fetish didn't take his break until late."

Next up was Shalla, grinning with good cheer. Like Runt, she was mostly garbed in clingy black material. Piggy gave her a hand up to the top of the wall.

Runt took the rope in both hands and began hauling. It was obvious he was pulling up a tremendous weight, and Piggy winced as he heard the load occasionally rub against the wall exterior. Then a large woven basket filled with durable cloth bags came into view. He helped Shalla maneuver it as Runt pulled it the rest of the way up.

In minutes they were down at ground level, inside the base of Tower Three, each laden with a cloth bag. Runt's was largest.

While Runt peered out the window in the armored door, Shalla leaned over to whisper in Piggy's ear. "I took the promotion."

"Oh, no." Piggy let his shoulders sag. "I thought you were going to be with us forever."

"It *has* been forever. Twelve years. Next week, I become an investigative officer. No more beating people up."

"But you're so good at it."

"Aww." She gave him a kiss on the cheek. "Empire's on the verge of surrendering, Piggy. Everything's going to change anyway. I might as well take the opportunity. Start a new stage in my life."

"It won't be as much fun."

Runt glared back over his shoulder. "Will you two be quiet? This is still a mission. Oh, and there's somebody coming."

"Mine." Shalla shook as if seized in the grip of a massive shiver, but Piggy knew she was merely loosening up. Runt withdrew up the metal stairs. Piggy took a couple of steps back to the foot of the stairs and raised his hands as if surrendering.

When the door slid open, the trooper who'd activated it—dressed in an enlisted man's uniform identical to those of the guards Piggy had shot and holding a tray with half a dozen cups of steaming caf on it—stared blankly at Piggy. "Hey. What are you up to?"

Shalla stepped out of the shadows and hit him low.

Piggy didn't even bother to try to save the caf. He lunged and hit the door-closing button. The door snapped shut before the cups hit, clattering all across the floor.

By that point Shalla had thrown her second blow, unnecessary as it might have been. Runt descended, hefted the unconscious man, and carried him upstairs to deposit him beside the first.

The three Wraiths crept around the bottom of the wall and entered the scientific section. Shalla, a dozen meters in front of the others, overpowered a pair of civilian scientists, one-punched an on-duty guard at the next hallway intersection, kicked a naval captain in the throat just outside the main computer laboratory.

Piggy shook his head, baffled. "How can she give this up? She enjoys her work so." He watched as Shalla slid silently into the computer lab.

Runt nodded. "My spy agrees with you. But my family man says, how can I have a family this way? Perhaps she has a family woman in her. My pacifist says, for all the good I'm accomplishing, all I do is hurt people. Perhaps she has a pacifist in her. The self in you who is used most gets tired, Piggy. The selves of you who are used least get restless."

Shalla stuck her head out the doorway and waved them forward.

* * *

In the computer center, Piggy sat at the main console and began entering the code and command sequences Face had given him. The console obligingly transmitted them to faraway sensor facilities.

Soon enough, each of them—orbital deep-space scanners, stellar light harvesters and interpreters, comm-frequency listening posts—would begin to experience malfunctions. Some would transmit disinformation to the naval High Command Center, under Admiral Pellaeon's indirect control. Some would initiate self-destruct sequences. Some would shut down all transmissions and reposition themselves, burning all their fuel in ultimately successful efforts to fly into the nearest sun.

Yes, the war was all but over. But until it was completely over, the armed forces and New Republic Intelligence had their jobs to do.

Runt headed downstairs with his huge payload of explosives.

Piggy turned to Shalla again. "It won't be the same without you."

She gave him a sad smile. "Every time someone leaves, you say it won't be the same. But it might be if you'd figure out how to get close to the new Wraiths. Piggy, will anyone be there with you at the end?"

From a kilometer away, they watched Mulvar Sensor Station go up.

The entire station didn't blow. Runt had placed his explosives very precisely, just as Kell had taught him to. The detonation rose from meters deep in the ground, obliterated the laboratory building, collapsed one section of outer wall, and damaged the motor pool. There were probably some deaths, but as few as possible.

Shalla turned to Piggy. "Voort. Voort."

"Since when am I Voort to you?"

She reached over to shake him. "Voort."

Voort came awake gradually, realizing that he'd fallen asleep in the navigator's chair, that Bhindi was shaking him.

It was her voice, not Shalla's. "Voort."

"Sorry." He blinked at her. "I fell asleep."

"Turn on your implant—I can barely understand you."

He did. "I regret to confess that I fell asleep at my station. It is your duty to relieve me of duty and confine me to quarters."

She laughed. "You *wish*." She sat in the captain's chair. "What were you dreaming? You were twitching like a battle dog."

He looked out the forward viewport. It showed starfield rather than the blur of hyperspace. They waited, light-years from any sun, for Turman, Scut, and Jesmin to return from the smugglers' station. The captured *Concussor* crew were already cooling their heels on the habitable moon of a distant gas giant. Most of the ship's food and water stores were there with them.

Voort took a few moments to answer. "It doesn't matter what I was dreaming. It just makes me understand, the roles are always the same. Only the faces get replaced."

"I don't understand you."

"The strongman. The actor. The technician. The hand-to-hand combat expert. The explosives expert.

Sometimes the roles get broken into pieces, recombined, handed off, inherited. But they're always there, surviving the departure or disappearance or *death* of whoever embodied them."

"It's clear that it's a bad idea for you to stay awake for sixty hours straight. It turns you into a melancholy philosopher."

A blinking light on the control board drew Voort's eye. "The shuttle's transponder signal just popped up. They're back."

CHAPTER THIRTEEN

Myri nursed her first drink, a weak fizz-and-brandy, and looked around the chamber from her perch at the bar.

Things weren't really under way yet. Troopers at the army base were just now changing shift, and those with leave to go into Ackbar City were heading for the sanisteams, putting on fresh clothes, plotting their strategies for the evening. So the bar was comparatively quiet, expectant.

Here at Jokko Haning's Emporium, a grandiose name for a decidedly plain drinking and dancing establishment, the locals were planning their own strategies. Myri counted twenty locals who clearly intended to attract the eyes of troopers for the eventual purpose of marriage and escape from Vandor-3—nesters, they were called in the local parlance. Six were men, fourteen women, and Myri was dressed and in character as woman number fifteen.

Nesters were not the only locals in the taproom with predatory ambitions. Myri spotted a handful of men and women whose body language suggested they had less binding affections available for rent. A spindly droid—a converted medical droid painted the exact hue of a good dark beer—stood behind the bar washing tumblers and transparent mugs. Two cocktail servers in minimal-coverage garments—one was a Wookiee female who, Myri thought, looked decidedly odd in her serving outfit—were not yet hurrying or working hard as they kept the early-evening crowd supplied with drinks. A four-armed green-furred musician from who-knew-where, a tip jar prominently displayed atop his upright keyboard rig, cracked four sets of knuckles simultaneously. An overweight, gray-haired human man at a table by himself straightened and restraightened a short stack of colorful flimsi printouts; Myri could see the text and graphics on the top page showing lush green countryside properties.

She snorted. A land agent, anxious to sell cheap acreage to troopers foolish enough to consider staying on this planet. Perhaps he'd have some success here for the sheer audacity of offering a product so very different from the others.

A man, human, settled onto the stool next to Myri's and turned toward her. "I've seen you before." He was lean, in shape, his features almost pretty, his head capped by black curls that stirred under the flow of cool air from the vent overhead. He wore good attract-the-eye dancing clothes, black pants and a V-necked tunic that glittered with tiny white speckles, like a monochromatic starfield. He looked to be in his twenties, like most of the other nesters in the bar.

"Really?" Myri sipped her drink. She knew the answer was no, that this was just a conversational ploy. Each time she'd gone out to gather intelligence, especially to a crowded nester bar, she'd been someone different. Tonight her hair was pure white, obviously a dyed affectation, and her skin as dark as ebony.

The man nodded. "Sure. But two nights ago you had red hair and amazing freckles."

Fierfek. He *had* seen her before, and somehow he had recognized her despite her new disguise. But she affected disinterest. "I like different looks. Why are you talking to me? Nesters don't congregate. Except when it's girls looking out for one another."

He lowered his voice, tried to sound more dramatic. "Maybe I'm not a nester. Maybe I'm with Galactic Alliance Security, tracking down the Quad-Linked Militant Pacifists."

Suddenly Myri was glad for her temporary dark coloration. She was certain that she was successfully keeping surprise—and alarm—off her face. But her face felt warm.

She was *blushing,* blast it, reacting emotionally to an unexpected confrontation.

She giggled as if he'd said something silly. That gave her a second to run through a mental checklist. Hold-out blaster in its waistband holster, right at her spine under the frilly white top she wore. Vibroknife against her left calf under matching pants and white boots. The tumbler in her hand was thin transparisteel, not glass, so she couldn't shatter it and drive it into the man's neck if she needed to.

Backup . . . she had none.

She grinned conspiratorially at the man. "I'm not with them," she told him, keeping all worry from her voice. "I'm a freelancer. I lure men to their doom and leave their bodies in ridiculous poses."

"I *thought* that was you." He saw that the bartender was momentarily unoccupied and waved. "Sledgehammer, please." He turned back, extended a hand. "Kirdoff."

She shook it. His hand was soft, uncalloused. Not common for a nester male, most of whom made their livings as industrial laborers or farmers. "Rima."

"Is red and freckles your real look?"

"Nature hasn't touched my hair since I was sixteen. And my complexion is *flawless*. Sorry."

"Well, the Fey'lya Base boys love that. You'll do great." He received his drink, rolling a credcoin to the droid in return. He raised his glass to Myri in a salute. "Good luck, Rima."

"You, too."

She watched him cross the room and slide into a dimly lit booth. She tried not to show on her face the fact that her stomach was suddenly churning.

If he actually *was* some sort of investigator, leaving now was the absolute worst thing she could do. In fact, if she was suspected of something, she might be under surveillance by multiple agents, and they could trade off in shadowing her, making it fiendishly difficult to spot them.

No, she had to stay here for the evening and go through the routine of flirting, drinking, dancing, teasing, talking about army life in the hope that some useful fact would spill out during an unguarded moment . . . and then letting the dirty-minded, clean-skinned trooper boy know that she had marriage on her mind. Marriage above everything.

Then there would be a reaction. Disappointment, reinvigorated attempts at persuasion, anger, maybe even assault. The reaction she dreaded most was eager acceptance. *We can get married tonight. I know a place.*

And all this, with her stomach roiling because of what might have been nothing but a polite inquiry by a slightly atypical nester boy.

She sighed, waved down the bartender, and ordered a stomach-settling powder.

* * *

She accepted a drink invitation from the first soldier who asked her, a lean sergeant with creases at the corners of his eyes. She got him talking about his work as a drill instructor and his home on Commenor. At a crucial moment in the conversation, she asked a leading question and listened to his first couple of wistful comments about his wife and kids.

Then he realized what he'd done and looked up guiltily.

She gave him a not-unsympathetic smile. "I think we're here for different things."

He shrugged. "Same thing, I guess. I want something from you. You want something from me. So we try to get the other to offer it. We leave out facts to accomplish that. Have you told me all the strikes against you?"

"There are too many to list." She raised her glass to him, a toast. "Here's to being goal-oriented. Good night, Sergeant."

There. Anyone watching her would see that she'd been through the nester's routine of flirting, conversing, and deciding. She could leave now and not be conspicuous. She used the trooper's departure as excuse enough to escape the possible scrutiny of Kirdoff and unseen observers. But another trooper followed her out the front doors—a human man, younger and taller than the sergeant, with the Pop-Dog tooth design on his collar. His tone was matter-of-fact. "I'll walk you home." He fell in step beside her.

"I actually know the way. Forget what you've heard about local girls—some of us have more than two brain cells to rub together."

He laughed. It was a strange, artificial noise, like something just learned by a nonhuman who'd only ever heard laughter on a holodrama. "You don't understand. I wasn't *asking*." Now there was an undertone of menace to his voice.

"Ah." She forced her voice to remain steady. "Do you know who I am?"

"Not yet."

"So, as a prelude to an assault, this is basically a random one. A privileged-class serviceman who imagines that he's an alpha male seizing what he wants, preying on a local population that's been conditioned to accept this behavior."

"A university girl. I hate university girls." The dark tone in his voice grew more intense. "I think it's time for you to shut up."

Myri took her bearings. The walkway they were on was clear of other pedestrians for twenty meters ahead and behind.

She stopped at the opening to a dark, narrow gap between buildings and pointed up the walkway. "You're going that way—" She pointed into the gap. "I'm going this way. Good night, Poop-Dog." She immediately walked into the darkness.

He caught up with her after three steps, seized her arm, and swung her around to slam her into the side of a building. She couldn't see his features in the deep shadow, but his voice was suddenly full of anger. He jabbed a forefinger at her. "You do not insult the—"

She put one hand on the back of his and seized his index finger with her other hand. She bent his finger up, a sudden, all-out effort, and bones snapped.

He started to look at his stricken hand, started to make a pained noise, but she immediately drew her blaster, thumbed its side switch to make sure it was still set on stun, and fired into his stomach. The stun bolt briefly illuminated the alley and his shocked expression. Then he fell.

She looked down at him and holstered her weapon. "Sorry, Army. My heart belongs to Starfighter Command." Then she stepped over him and returned to the street.

It took her quite a while to get home. She took a circuitous route, making sure she was not being followed. In another dark alley, sure she was not being watched, she discarded her wig and outer garments, shoving them deep into a waste bin. She broke the seal on a packet, half the size of a deck of cards, that was always to be found in her footwear, and unfolded its brown polyfilm contents out into a voluminous hooded robe. She left the alley a different woman—hair black, garment brown, feet bare.

There were more trooper patrols out on the streets, joined by Pop-Dog patrols, as she traveled the rest of the way to the Wraiths' rented shop. Several of them looked at her as she passed, but none spoke to or followed her. She entered the office building sure she was in the clear.

After a quick sanisteam to remove the last traces of her disguise, she checked her datapad for messages and found one—a large file, encrypted, from Bhindi.

The text portion merely said, "This needs to get on the general's desk fast. Mysteriously."

The video file attached to it showed an elegant Imperial Navy commander, as white-haired as Myri had been an hour earlier. He looked straight into the holocam and spoke, his voice cultured, confident, and cool. "General, in the recent past you have done some excellent work in the support of certain parties. I am the new intermediary on these issues. My name is Commander Avvan Hocroft. We need to speak face-to-face. The embedded time and location coordinates are where you can find me. I'll be there with a small patrol vessel. Please try not to awe me with matériel superiority. This is a *friendly* conversation." Hocroft offered a smile that was not entirely friendly, and the message ended.

Myri pondered the message. That had to have been

Turman on the recording, but she could see no sign of the Clawdite she knew in the commander, which was a good thing.

Getting the message onto Thaal's desk would not be difficult. She'd transmit instructions to the growing legion of housekeeping droids now serving the Wraiths. Then all she had to do was get close enough to the army base's outer perimeter to throw or launch a datacard past those defenses so that one of the droids could pick it up and transport it.

Wouldn't Thaal research the Commander Hocroft name? Well, Bhindi had to have thought of that. If she, Myri, wasn't supposed to address that issue, perhaps Face was.

GALACTIC ALLIANCE NAVY COMMAND
    COMPLEX, CORUSCANT

The naval lieutenant was a Bothan. He had nearly pure-white fur, rare for his kind; that and his build, lean and muscular, had to have made him very popular on the social scene, Face thought.

But now, if Bothans could sweat, he'd be sweating. He glanced up and down the corridor, lightly trafficked by other uniformed naval personnel. "If I get caught . . ."

Face grinned at him. "You're twenty times as likely to get caught because you look like you're going to be caught than you would be if you looked like you had nothing to be caught about."

The Bothan paused before a closed door; its sign read ARCHIVE ROUTING. He frowned. "I have no idea what you just said."

"Davian, forget it. If they catch us, you tell them that I've volunteered to give you an application that scans unclassified reports for embedded language used to convey secret information to enemy spies."

"But you haven't."

"It's on my datapad. It's twenty years old . . . but the navy doesn't have it, so they won't know that."

Davian frowned, considering that, and pressed his palm to the biometrics plate beside the door. A moment later he put his left eye up to the tiny red peephole at the top of the plate. The door slid open, and both men went through. Beyond was a brightly lit, shiny-clean, impersonal office—one desk, two chairs, wall-mounted shelves sagging under the weight of stacks of flimsi.

When the door slid shut, Face sat at the computer monitor. "You have the records handy?"

"Queued up in the search box labeled TUBER SPOIL-AGE."

Face snorted. "Good choice. Not many people are going to be curious enough to give that a close look."

"Right. But first . . . your datapad. The application."

"Oh." Face drew the device from his breast pocket and slid it across the desktop. "Top menu, JABBEER SIX."

"Thanks." Davian sat at the opposite chair and fumbled in his own breast pocket for a datacard, which he slid into the appropriate slot on the datapad. He selected functions to transfer the application to his card. "We have only until my captain gets back. Less than an hour."

"I'm not going to get you in trouble." Face began flipping through on-screen records—cargo manifests from the naval cargo vessels that had disappeared during the last few years.

"I can take trouble if I have to. Thirty years back, you did my parents a big favor, and I'm happy to pay it back. I just want to keep my commission, too, if at all possible."

"Fair enough." Face reached the last manifest. "Fewer than I'd thought. Eighteen."

"Eighteen in three years, Alliance vessels. That's a fivefold increase from the three years before CivWar Two." Davian ejected his datacard and pocketed it. He shut Face's datapad. "But the cargoes themselves were pretty valuable. These pirates weren't stealing canned bantha-meat hash."

Face flipped back through the manifests more slowly, giving each a closer look. "Can I get printouts of these?"

"No, sorry."

"No matter. Your people haven't found any connections among the missing ships or their cargoes?"

"Plenty of connections. All Alliance cargo vessels. All of ship classes that require small crews for their tonnage. All traveling solo or with escort vessels only, not as part of a matériel convoy. There's always some real value in the cargo."

"But no type of matériel, or manufacturer, or receiving base common to all of them? Not every crew has a Hutt navigator from the Backstabbo family?"

Davian snorted. "No."

Face remained silent for several minutes. Then a manifest entry he didn't understand fell under his eye. "What's a *secure privacy type*?"

Davian shrugged. "I have no idea."

"One secure privacy type, origin Badfellow Station, destination Coruscant naval yards. Manufacturer, Sub-Capital Division." Face frowned. "I don't recognize that manufacturer. And isn't Badfellow Station just a cargo-routing hub?"

Davian nodded. "A civilian routing yard that does some contract warehousing and redistribution for the navy." He stood and moved to stand behind Face, staring over his shoulder. "It shouldn't be the origin of anything. Oh, look." He pointed at the on-screen field that read BADFELLOW STATION. "You see the little number one at the upper right corner of the field? That's a subfield reference number. Tap that."

Face did, and the field changed, the words in it being replaced with a new one: KUAT.

Davian smiled with the pride of a middle manager who had solved a problem no lesser person could unravel. "That happens sometimes. The idiot who put together this manifest typed the secondary data in the primary field and vice versa. The item, whatever a *secure privacy type* is, originated on Kuat and was routed through Badfellow Station, not the other way around." He returned to his chair.

Face stared at him, silent, for a few seconds. Then, troubled, he began tapping other fields on the screen. "Seems to have happened a few times here. *Secure privacy type*—aha. It's a ship's hypercomm system. *Secure privacy type* now makes sense. It has to be a one-person enclosed model, so the ship's captain or comm officer can enter it and not be observed by the rest of the bridge crew."

"That does make sense."

"And the manufacturer, Sub-Capital Division—again aha. The subfield says HyperTech Industries. Look that up for me, would you?"

Davian patted himself down, scowled, and, realizing that Face's datapad was still on the desk before him, opened it. He tapped his way through a quick search. "An Alliance military contractor based out of Kuat."

"Can you run a search on all these manifests and include all the subfields?"

"Of course."

"Can you first swap the data between the primary fields and the subfields?"

"I am the living master of the database, Face. Trade places with me."

Five minutes later they had their answer. Every Galactic Alliance Navy cargo vessel that had disappeared in the last three years had in its cargo manifest a Hyper-Tech Industries device of one sort or another, usually a hypercomm unit, sometimes a hyperdrive or a power booster.

The two men stared at each other.

Davian no longer looked nervous. Now he looked regretful. "I have to tell my superiors."

"Yes, you do. But not yet. I have friends in the field looking into this issue." Face pitched his voice to its most persuasive tones. "If you tell your superiors, and an investigation starts, the people my friends are looking at will get nervous. They'll cover their tracks. They may even turn lethal."

"But—"

"I'm not saying you have to bury this information. You just have to sit on it for a while. Until I give you the go-ahead. Then you 'discover' it and hand it over to your superiors. All credit goes to you, the investigation starts, the piracy ends, and the naval brass knows who to reward for it. But not *yet.*"

Davian winced. "How long are we talking about? A few days?"

"A few days." *Six months at most.* Face didn't add that qualifier. Davian would have to accept his restraints a bit at a time, leading him down a slippery slope of cooperation with Wraith Squadron.

"Well . . . all right. Done here?"

"I'm done here." Face pocketed his datapad. "Thanks for everything."

"I'll walk you out."

As they left the archive room, Face, last out and unseen, slipped another device from his trouser pocket—Davian's missing datapad. He left it on a shelf.

CHAPTER FOURTEEN

Face's stylish black airspeed, its viewports tinted almost to opacity, at least as seen from the outside, rose from the naval command center's landing area. It glided slowly above the field of parked speeders until it entered a traffic lane, then accelerated.

A few hundred meters away, an innocuous blue speeder, also closed-top, rose from a landing area atop a shops-and-restaurants building and entered the same traffic stream from above.

The pilot, an adult human, blond and boyish-looking, kept his eye on the black speeder ahead. "I say a kilometer."

The individual in the passenger seat beside him, a squat Sullustan, his face looking even more like sagging, melted layers of a dark dessert than was usual for his species, frowned. "Wait, wait. How soon do you sample after it goes off? Time plays a role here." He spoke in his own language. To most ears it would have been mere musical jabber, but the pilot understood and shook his head.

"Assume optimal time for maximum expansion."

"No wind?"

"For this hypothetical example, no wind."

The passenger in the rear seat, a large Aqualish covered in a cumbersome brown robe, leaned forward, thrusting his head between those of the two speakers. His tusks, his insectile eyes, and the scales of his body, which were waxed and buffed to a high sheen, gave him a ferocious aspect. He, too, spoke in his own language. "What's the bet?"

The pilot smiled. "Sit an Ortolan on top of a thermal detonator—standard yield—and set it off. How high up in the atmosphere will you then be able to detect traces of the Ortolan?"

The Aqualish turned toward him. "Traces? You mean pieces? There would be no pieces left."

"No, no. I mean chemical traces."

The Aqualish growled, a deep rumble in its chest. "Chemicals are a *myth*."

The pilot paused, considering how best to offer a negative reply to that assertion.

The Sullustan saved him from the awkwardness of his situation. "Tell him you mean *dust*."

The pilot nodded. "I mean dust."

The Aqualish seemed to accept that answer. "No wind?"

"No wind."

The Aqualish pondered. "Betting is stupid. Only way to find out for sure: get me an Ortolan and a thermal detonator."

"Well . . ."

"We do it right after we kill Face Loran."

The pilot nodded. "Good idea. I'll find us an Ortolan. *You* find us the thermal detonator."

"All right." The Aqualish settled back in his seat.

Face glanced at his control console, at the small monitor showing the rear holocam view, and continued dictating. "I pulled the old *Here, hold my recorder and speak clearly* scam. With a twist—I'd palmed his datapad, so when he needed to look something up he used mine, entering passcodes that gave my application access to the computer system. Which put me past most levels of security right there. So the Commander Hocroft references are planted and propagating. What's funny is that my cover story may have yielded useful results, too. I actually found a link between the cargoes of all Alliance Navy vessels hijacked since the end of the war. Each was carrying a large, expensive electronic component, usually a hypercomm unit, manufactured by HyperTech Industries of Kuat. Since Jesmin has been looking into that issue, you might pass that fact on to her." Face changed his voice from a narrative tone to a conversational. "Got all that?"

"Transcribed." It was a female protocol droid's voice, affected and precise.

"Good. Where was I? Oh, that was the end. No, add this." He changed back to a narrative tone. "My asset tells me that HyperTech landed its military contract well before the exposure of the Lecersen Conspiracy, so it's unlikely that this has anything to do with the general. Still, one member of the conspiracy, Haydnat Treen, was the Senator from Kuat and had a lot of influence there. She could have helped the company land that contract, so there may be some connection of some sort. I just don't know why she'd do that if all the conspirators wanted the company for was to commit acts of piracy." He paused, deciding whether he needed to add anything, and chose not to. He switched back to conversational tone. "End message. Standard closures. Encrypt and transmit it immediately."

"Yes, sir. Encrypted. Transmitted."

"How'd I do?"

"Three *you know*s, four *where was I*'s, and not a single *um* or *uh*."

"Better than usual, then. You know, the other day I met a protocol droid who wasn't allowed to talk."

"Terrible. That would be like an astromech with its mathematical functions disabled."

"Wouldn't it? So there's a protocol droid who can't talk, and I have a speeder with the brain of a droid who *can*. I think I like my way better."

"You say that, but you don't let me follow you around in your quarters."

"True. Bad for the furniture. You understand." Face cast another look at his rear holocam view. The blue speeder was still tailing him, not closing, far enough back that even some practiced eyes would miss it. "Tell me, have I backed you up lately?"

"Not in eight days."

"Commence remote backup immediately. Also, run a search and tell me the nearest high-density pedestrian zone—a walkway market, a music festival in a plaza, anything crowded and confusing."

"Which has priority?"

"The search."

"Hey." The blond human pilot frowned as the black air-speeder dropped out of its traffic lane, banked, and descended into a lane headed to the right. "Wonder if he's made us."

"Hunh." The Aqualish's noise was a grunt of disagreement. "You're too good."

"But it's clear he's not headed for home any longer."

"I don't like that." The Aqualish sounded even more disagreeable. "I want to kill the wife and daughter, too."

The pilot chose another speeder taking Face's route. He moved up close behind the vehicle, using it to obscure Face Loran's view of him until he entered the new traffic lane. "Why?"

"Those tail-things on their heads."

"Brain-tails. Or lekku, in the Twi'lek language. What about them?"

"I always wonder, if you pull on them hard enough, will they rip right off? Arms and legs do."

"Well, I tell you what. Kill Face Loran nice and neat, and you can kill one of the Twi'leks, too. Find us a thermal detonator for our experiment and you can kill both."

"You are a good man. I like working with you."

"Thank you."

"But I want more money."

The pilot sighed.

Face's speeder banked again, darting between two widely spaced apartment blocks. The blond pilot saw a bright patch ahead, what had to be a comparatively open area. He followed Face's speeder and emerged from between the buildings onto the edge of a vast plaza. The plaza's rim was gridded off into landing areas and loading zones for speeders, while the center was crammed with portable durasteel-and-duraplast stalls, brightly decorated with flashing signs and colorful banners. At this midday hour it was thick with shoppers on foot. The pilot considered what he was seeing. "A pedestrian market," the pilot said.

"I expected a market like that to be bigger on Coruscant. It should be kilometers long!" There was a note of contempt in the Aqualish's voice. "I've seen bigger on itty-bitty worlds."

"I think you mean low-population worlds. Itty-bitty worlds don't have enough gravity to hold an atmosphere. And without an atmosphere, you can't have an open-air market."

"Gravity is a *myth*."

The pilot saw Face's speeder slow, then descend vertically on repulsors to occupy a landing square. He looked around, found another one, not far from Face's, and settled into place there.

Together, the three watched as the pilot's door of the black speeder rose, wing-style. Face Loran emerged, a distracted look on his face. He had a comlink pressed to his ear and was clearly having trouble hearing over the roar of voices from the marketplace and whine of air-speeders overhead. He shouted, loud enough that the occupants of the blue speeder could hear him: "No, you idiot. *Earrings. Anniversary present.* Which booth are you?" He hurried in the direction of the nearest row of booths, his body language indicating impatience.

The blond pilot smiled. Face Loran would be comparatively easy to follow in the crowds. His clothes—black, fitted, stylish, and pretentious, matching his trim little beard and mustache—and his bald scalp made him stand out.

"It's a trick." The Sullustan's musical voice made the words sound more friendly than suspicious.

"What's the Jawa say?" the Aqualish asked.

"He says it's a trick."

"It doesn't matter."

"What's the Aqualish say?"

The pilot grinned. "He says you're a Jawa."

"*I'm not a Jawa,* and it's a trick. He spotted you, and he's lured us to this crowded, confusing place so he can lose us."

"What's the Jawa say?" the Aqualish asked.

"He says he's not a Jawa, and that you're wrong."

"He's a Jawa. An ugly Jawa. If you were as ugly as he is, you'd pretend to belong to a made-up species, too. Sullustans are a *myth.*"

"What's he say?" the Sullustan asked.

The pilot heaved a sigh. "He says you and he should chase after Face Loran and kill him while I wait here in case it is a trick and he doubles back and tries to escape you. And I agree. Get going."

The Aqualish slammed his door open and exited. "I will also keep my eyes open for a stand selling thermal detonators."

By the time the Aqualish and the Sullustan reached the first row of stalls, Face Loran was nowhere to be seen.

Standing between a booth selling toy lightsabers that made realistic sounds and extended harmless shafts of colored light, and another where the most popular candies were Corellian-brandy-flavored, the Aqualish and the Sullustan turned back and forth with the rhythm of droid gun emplacements scanning for targets.

"Don't see him." The Aqualish's voice was a grumble. He stared down at his companion. "You see his knees anywhere?"

The Sullustan spoke to him, musical words the Aqualish didn't understand.

"Hey, short stuff, I have a great idea." The Aqualish bent over, caught the Sullustan under his arms, and lifted. The Sullustan squalled and flailed as if afraid the Aqualish was going to drop him into the tentacled maw of a sarlacc. Then the Aqualish settled his short companion astride his shoulders. "Now you can see more than his knees." The Aqualish pointed at his own eyes, then at the Sullustan's eyes, then at the crowd.

The Sullustan seemed to get it. He nodded and resumed his scanning. The Aqualish set off into the crowd.

The Aqualish had spoken disparagingly of this market, but it really was his kind of environment. A buyer could see beings of every known species and find goods from all over Coruscant and around the galaxy—cheap junk, entertainments, exotic foods, sometimes good weapons. A Rodian male sidled up to the Aqualish, offering glitterstim bites—tiny quantities of the psychotropic chemical encased in lightproof, sweet carbohydrate shells—for sale. The Aqualish handed him a few credcoins for a small packet, but leaned over the seller with some advice: "If this isn't the real thing, I come back and kill you good."

"It's real, it's real." Unbidden, the seller pressed an extra bag into the Aqualish's finned hand and fled.

The Aqualish stared at the two bags, then glanced up at his rider. "Means it's real, but *weak*. We see how weak. Maybe I don't kill him."

The Sullustan jabbered in reply.

"Shut up. You know I don't speak Jawa." He handed the Sullustan the second bag of spice candy.

A minute later, the Sullustan straightened, sitting higher, and pointed off into the crowd. The Aqualish stared that way.

Thirty meters ahead along the row of stalls, Face Loran stood, retrieving a credcard from a vendor. Of all things, he had an entire mannequin under his arm. It was built along the lines of a human woman but was headless. It wore garments suited to an exotic dancer, all abbreviated bands, strips, and scarves in filmy red and pink material. Face Loran had other purchases tucked under his arm as well: folded masses of brown cloth. As the Aqualish watched, Face Loran turned away with his new prizes and moved briskly off in the other direction.

The two exchanged a look. The Sullustan jabbered something.

The Aqualish shrugged. "I bet that means the earrings were no good."

The Sullustan looked blankly at him.

The Aqualish took off after their target, his rider holding firmly on to his shoulders and head.

By the time they caught sight of Face Loran again, he was down a side row, his mannequin still clutched under his arm, but now he was towing a small cloud of large pink balloons on a string behind him.

From that point, it was comparatively easy to find him. All they had to do was watch for the cluster of pink balloons. The problem was that Face Loran kept in constant motion, trotting from one booth to the next, taking a zigzag course through the market. Sometimes their view of the balloons was blocked for long moments by a tall booth or banner.

Then, at the far edge of the market, they cornered their quarry. He was not at a booth but in a tent, the sign above it flashing with an ever-changing litany of entreaties: HOLOSTILLS! PUT YOUR FACE ON AN ATHLETE'S BODY! EMBRACE HEVANUS DREED OR KOY'TIFFIN! STAND BESIDE THE GLORIOUS CANYON OF NO RETURN! Face's string trailed out through the tent flap, the balloons wavering a few meters overhead.

The Aqualish set down the Sullustan. He gestured in accompaniment to his words. "I go in and kill him. Stab-stab-stab, understand? You wait here. *Here.*"

The Sullustan scowled and jabbered at him but moved to stand against the row of tents and booths opposite, watching the front of Face's tent.

The Aqualish slid a fin under his robe and wrapped it around the hilt of the sheathed vibroblade there. This was a knife job—quiet was better, even in this loud environment. Cautiously, he moved up to the tent, parted its flap with his free fin, and entered.

It was dark within. Directly before him was a screen, taller than a human, of flexible material stretched to tautness by a segmented duraplast frame. It was actually a flexible monitor, glowing with internal light, showing an image from nature. Even from the rear, the Aqualish could recognize a famous image, an iconic waterfall from the destroyed world of Alderaan.

Small pinpoint lights from the far side of the tent shone on the screen, and they silhouetted the Aqualish's prey. A human shape stood just on the far side of the screen, his head moving back and forth as if he were keeping time to slow music the Aqualish couldn't hear.

The Aqualish drew his vibroblade, thumbed it into humming life. Then he stabbed, his blade shearing through the screen and plunging into the back of his target's head.

It popped with a mild *bang* and disappeared.

The Aqualish stepped around the screen to look.

His victim had been the mannequin. A brown robe hung across it, concealing the flimsy dancer's garments. The remains of a pink balloon lay across one shoulder. It had been tied to the top of the mannequin, a scarf wrapped around its base to suggest a neck. Before the Aqualish popped it, it had been bobbing in a breeze flowing through the tent.

The tent was otherwise empty. A slit in the far side showed where Face Loran had gone.

This was not good. The Aqualish spun, making sure he was indeed alone, then switched off and sheathed his vibroblade. He moved back through the entry flap, alert to the possibility of attack.

The Sullustan was where the Aqualish had left him, but now he was seated on a fruit crate, leaning back against a stall's support pole, relaxed as if asleep. There was a dark stain, small but spreading, on his tunic.

The Aqualish did not move over to investigate. The Sullustan was dead, and Face Loran was doubtless nearby, prepared to launch a fatal ambush if the Aqualish moved to bend over his slain partner.

But if the Aqualish merely walked away, Face Loran

would stalk him, waiting for an ideal time to strike, and then kill him.

The Aqualish chose to outsmart his enemy. He tore off his robe, revealing belt-holstered blaster pistols and sheathed vibroblades, a grenade on a baldric strap, and more buffed, shiny body scales, and charged back toward his boss's airspeeder.

He slammed vendors and shoppers out of the way with little regard for their mass, species, gender, or age. A crowd of Bothan children flew away from impacts with his knees, shrieking in hurt and surprise. He crashed, unharmed, through a pane of clear duraplast, a replacement window, being carried by two human workers. He slammed a Gamorrean woman clear over the merchandise counter of a stall, leaving her upside down, her legs flailing, her upper body stuck in a barrel of Coruscanti subterranean whitefish.

Though shouts, curses, and calls for security followed him, in moments he could see the far row of the plaza booths just ahead. There was a gap between two of them through which he could escape.

Into the gap stepped a Jedi, a fair-skinned, robed man whose neatly trimmed mustache and beard were darker than his long, loose mane of brown hair. The Jedi's attention immediately fixed on the Aqualish and he raised his lightsaber, already in hand, thumbing it to life. Its green blade emerged with a deep, vibrating *snap-hiss*.

The Aqualish slowed his charge and grabbed for his blaster pistol.

But the Jedi, instead of charging, *threw his lightsaber*. It flew in a spin toward the Aqualish.

If he'd had the time, the Aqualish would have laughed. Instead, he tracked the incoming weapon. He reached for it . . . and nimbly caught the hilt in his fin.

Now the Jedi charged forward. He ran like a normal

man in good shape, not like a superhuman. The Aqualish swung the lightsaber. Its glowing blade plowed across the Jedi's neck.

The Jedi's body thumped into that of the Aqualish, and his head—

Stayed right where it was. There was no mark across his neck. There was no smell of burned flesh.

There *was* a pain in the Aqualish's own neck, and the Aqualish belatedly became aware that the Jedi's right arm was raised, his hand near the point where the pain began.

The Jedi, unhurt, stared into the Aqualish's face with the eyes of Face Loran. His expression was cold and implacable.

The Aqualish fell, feeling the tug as his neck slid off the vibroblade in Face Loran's hand, seeing the blade grow still as his enemy switched it off. Then blackness descended over his sight.

Just a few dozen meters away, the blond pilot witnessed the collision between Jedi and Aqualish. He saw the Aqualish collapse, the toy lightsaber in his hand falling to the ground, its harmless green beam playing across the pavestones.

He saw the Jedi turn away before any of the witnesses began to react. The Jedi moved out past the line of stalls, made an immediate right turn to be out of the sight of the shoppers in the marketplace, and whipped the hair from his head, revealing the bald scalp of Face Loran. Loran tossed the wig into the mouth of a droid trash-masher. He shed his costume cloak and robe, hurling them in with the wig. Then he made an abrupt left turn and began walking among the landed speeders.

The blond pilot shook his head in grudging admiration. In two seconds, a mysterious Jedi Knight, menace evident in his posture, had become a bald, black-clad passerby whose body language suggested ease and good cheer. Meanwhile, witnesses to the Aqualish's death surrounded the body. A couple who cautiously stepped out beyond the row of stalls looked around, saw no sign of the Jedi, and returned to stare at the body.

The pilot paid them no mind. He did watch as a security trooper ran up to take charge of the situation while Face Loran walked, unnoticed by the crowd, to his airspeeder. Loran entered his vehicle.

Well, the pilot had learned something. It appeared that Face Loran was genuinely retired or even exiled from the Intelligence community—he had summoned no backup to deal with this situation. And he clearly had some field experience.

The pilot couldn't see through the dark viewport of the airspeeder. Loran waited in his vehicle for several minutes, probably watching events unfold around the body. But finally the black airspeeder rumbled into life and rose three meters into the air.

And exploded.

Pieces of the vehicle, twisted and burning, flew in all directions, propelled by a cloud of red and orange and black. The people gathered around the Aqualish screamed. Some were knocked down by the force of the explosion. Parked speeders all around Loran's rocked and were pelted by debris. The main body of Loran's speeder dropped, only one landing space over from where it had been, onto a big, red, open-top speeder. They burned together.

The blond pilot blew out a sigh of relief. The Sullustan and the Aqualish had served their purpose—bait, distraction—and so had his explosives package. The job was done.

Well, one job, anyway. He started up his speeder and

took it skyward. Now he just needed to kill two Twi'lek women.

Maybe he could find a disgruntled Wookiee who was curious about whether those brain-tails would rip right off.

CHAPTER FIFTEEN

The new cook, a scarred, tattooed Corellian man who wore a long ponytail and no other hair—but who, Voort had to admit, could cook a fine bantha-topato stew—distributed the last cup of caf to Turman, who sat at the navigator's console.

On his way off the bridge, the cook stopped and gave Voort a perturbed look. "Will you, ah, require anything special for dinner?"

Voort also had to admit to himself that he warranted a perturbed look or two. He was dressed in the remnants of the gray uniform once owned by *Concussor*'s captain. Their seams had burst rather than let out, so the garments hung in tatters on him, held in place only by the elaborate array of gun belts and weapons bandoliers with which Voort had draped himself.

Too, across the last couple of days the other Wraiths, in their various disguises, had told many stories about "Gronk." How his favorite meals involved human meat. How one should never gamble with him, because he couldn't read cards and always lost . . . which inevitably meant death for the other players. How the ends of his tusks and fingernails were coated with invisible slow-acting poison—it was death just to scrap with him. Even for smugglers and pirates anxious to earn a credit by any means possible, the sheer volume of the stories was alarming.

A pity the other Wraiths hadn't told Voort they were telling these stories. He only discovered the fact after all the new crew members began shying away from him.

He was pondering his answer—the cook understood Gamorrean—when Jesmin, at the sensor officer's console, still in her security operative identity's wig and makeup but wearing an Imperial lieutenant's uniform and insignia, looked up. "Contact. At the limits of sensor range. They're transmitting . . . It's the priority code we've been waiting for."

Bhindi, now in an Imperial uniform, slouching in the captain's chair, snapped upright. "Command crew only. Everyone else clear the bridge."

The cook dashed out. As soon as the door was shut and sealed behind him, Voort activated his throat implant. "It's about time." He strode to the navigator's station as Turman abandoned it.

Bhindi stood up from the captain's chair but hit the intercom button on its arm. "Four, Six, we're on. Report readiness."

Voices spoke from the chair arm, Trey's first: "Four here. Engineering clear except for me, and sealed. All power and engines are optimal." Then Scut responded: "Six in security. Ready."

Voort shed a belt and a bandolier; they made it hard to sit. He took Turman's seat and bent over the navigation controls. "Transferring pilot controls to my station. Complete."

"Transferring communications controls to my station." Jesmin sounded as cool and unworried as Bhindi and Voort had. "Complete. Sensors now indicate the contact is a small warship, probably corvette, probably twice our mass and weaponry. But not huge. They're approaching at cruise speed."

From the corner of his eye, Voort glimpsed Turman performing a high-speed identity change. The man threw his tunic into a corner; from an emergency equipment locker in the bulkhead, he pulled the white-haired, aristocratic-featured neoglith masquer Scut had made for him. He donned it in seconds, then slipped into clothes from the same locker, a tidy gray uniform with a lieutenant commander's rank insignia on the breast.

Voort nodded, satisfied. In years past, he'd seen Face do it faster, but Face had never had to deal with a neoglith masquer. Voort rated Turman's effort as a tie with Face's.

Turman, now Lieutenant Commander Hocroft, took the captain's chair. "Ready." His voice bore the clipped accent that was natural to upper-class Coruscant citizens and affected by many Imperial officers.

Bhindi moved to sit at the station between Jesmin and Voort. "Weapons and deflectors down but ready to raise. Comm, are they hailing?"

Jesmin nodded. "Just now. Alliance corvette *Starhook,* Captain Evlen commanding."

Bhindi considered. "Voyce Evlen. Just promoted to captain. This is her first command. I'm sorry to hear she might be mixed up with Thaal. I know her family. Her mother is Admiral Biana Drayce."

Turman cleared his throat. "Go?"

"One second. Sensors, make *sure* Voort's not in the holocam view."

Jesmin clicked a couple of switches and looked at one of her auxiliary monitors. "All clear."

"Go."

Turman faced the center of the viewport directly ahead. "Put her on, Lieutenant."

The forward viewport darkened to opacity, and a new

image glowed into life there. It was another ship's bridge, its furnishings and consoles showing more blue than white, its captain in the background and a trio of bridge officers in the foreground, a virtual double of the arrangement Bhindi had set up. The officers wore Galactic Alliance naval blues. The captain was a human woman, her brown hair in a bun, her skin a reddish tan.

Turman gave the other officer a pleasant nod. "Captain Evlen. Congratulations on your recent promotion. Your mother must be quite proud."

Evlen raised an eyebrow. "You know my mother?"

"I've met her. But I was not in this uniform at the time. Or in any uniform. She probably wouldn't remember me."

While Turman spoke, Bhindi began typing, innocuously, at her console. The forward port-side viewport blanked, and then text began to appear on it. BIANA HIDES RECURRENT TACYODERMITIS FROM COMMAND.

Turman continued without a break, "I hope her twitching has finally cleared up."

Evlen paused, then offered a chilly smile. "Certainly. It was mysterious, but at least it was brief. And how is your knee? Better, I hope?"

Voort almost cheered. Not only had Face gotten to the naval archives, but someone had accessed them in a search for Hocroft's name. The searchers would have found only one report, an addendum to an operation by Alliance commandos during the Second Galactic Civil War, mentioning their encounter with an Avvan Hocroft and his recent knee injury.

The last exchange between Evlen and Turman would cement in the captain's mind the notion that Hocroft was a black-ops Imperial operative with extensive connections in and knowledge of the Alliance military.

Voort returned his attention to the navigation board and his elation evaporated.

Unpleasantries concluded, Turman got to the subject. "By the way—I *was* expecting the general."

Evlen nodded. "He's been notified. We made good time by taking a couple of cross-jumps off the major routes, so our arrival caught him a little off guard. He'll be here momentarily."

Voort began typing, and his words appeared beneath Bhindi's. ONCOMING CORVETTE HAS SIDESLIPPED IN APPROACH. DIRECTLY AHEAD. IF WE NEED TO GO TO HYPERSPACE, MUST MANEUVER AND EXPOSE FLANK. He saw the gaze of the others flick over to that screen and take in its message.

Bhindi typed back, STAY CHILLY.

Turman offered a slight shrug. "While we wait, care for a game of virtual sabacc?"

Evlen frowned. "I've never heard of it."

"It's also called Excess. I shuffle a deck of cards in my mind, as you do in yours. We each deal a hand. Of course, since it's a mental exercise, we have the ultimate power to cheat, as if we had decks entirely composed of skifters. Since we could each choose the most valuable hand possible, the first trick each of us faces is to choose a hand that will win but not be absolutely unbeatable. That wins the hand, but the real trick, the one that wins the entire game, is to lose by the narrowest cumulative margin across the entire series of hands."

"That's preposterous."

"It's all the rage. Experience shows us that losing by the narrowest possible margin until almost the end is often the way to win a lengthy war."

"And when have you ever done that?"

Jesmin began typing. PASSING OUT OF EXTREME WEAPONS RANGE INTO EFFECTIVE WEAPONS RANGE. JUST SAYING.

Evlen glanced off to her right as if she, too, were reading something outside the holocam view. She returned her attention to Turman. "Well, I suspect we'll have plenty of time to discuss our respective philosophies of war."

"How so?"

"Because—"

Jesmin hit a button on her console. "Deflectors!" Her bellow was loud enough to startle Voort.

Bhindi reflexively brought up the ship's deflectors.

On-screen, Evlen did not immediately react to what was going on aboard *Concussor*. "—seizing your vessel. Heave to and prepare—" Then alarm notes began blaring on the corvette's bridge and Evlen's words cut off. The screen blanked and became a starfield again. In the distance, the glow of *Starhook*'s deflectors going live made the ship suddenly visible.

Yet Bhindi's voice remained cool. "Sound general quarters. Two, trade with me." While swapping chairs with the ersatz Imperial officer, she glanced at Jesmin. "You felt something in the Force?"

Jesmin nodded, most of her attention on her console. "Four new contacts. They've dropped out of hyperspace at *Starhook*'s original distance. They're coming on at flank speed."

"Seven, bring us about, then all ahead full, then plot us a hyperspace jump out of here."

"Coming about." Voort sent *Concussor* into a spin rather than a bank—he fired forward starboard maneuvering thrusters and the stern port maneuvering thrusters. The vessel began to spin in place. "Exit jump already plotted."

"You love math."

"I *love* math."

Impatient, Turman, now at the weapons console, looked back at Bhindi. "Orders?"

"Stand by. We don't want to provoke them."

"They're already provoked, One."

She glowered at him. "Don't worry about weapons. Put all discretionary power into whatever deflectors are facing the enemy; constantly update as we turn."

"Already being done—" Turman's acknowledgment was cut off as the *Concussor* shuddered and the ship's lights dimmed for a moment.

Not everything dimmed. New lights began blinking or glowing steadily on Jesmin's console.

She glanced at Bhindi. "Engines damaged. Losing power. We're at seventy percent. Hyperdrive appears to be reinitializing."

Turman interrupted. "Permission to return fire."

"Denied." Bhindi hit her intercom. "Four, report."

There was no answer.

"Four, *report*."

"Sorry, Leader." Trey's voice sounded harried. "Engines damaged, but I'm holding them together. Brief air-pressure drop here, but I got a plate of durasteel over the leak."

Bhindi breathed a sigh of relief.

Trey's voice came back: "Orders, Leader?"

"Stand by, Four." Bhindi leaned back. "Six?"

"Here."

"Execute command *Pollinate*. It's on your top menu."

"Yes, Leader." Scut sounded confused.

Voort kept his eye on his controls. He discontinued the maneuvering thrusters. But as he prepared to fire their opposite numbers, which would decelerate *Concussor* from its spin, Bhindi interrupted. "Don't complete the maneuver, Seven. Leave us spinning."

"What? I mean, yes, One."

Bhindi glanced at Jesmin. "Signal to the crew *Abandon ship*."

CHAPTER SIXTEEN

"Very surgical, Lieutenant." Captain Evlen studied the image on the screen ahead. Magnified so that it appeared much closer than it was, the enemy patrol vessel, an Imperial-styled triangle narrowed at the base to the proportions of an ancient arrowhead, slowly spun in place. Sheets of sparks resembling flame jetted from its stern section. In mid-spin, its thrusters still on full, the vessel was maneuvering in an ever-widening spiral pattern, clearly out of control. Its shields were still up, but it offered no return fire. "I think they're helpless."

The communications officer, a gray-skinned Duros with large, emotionless eyes, turned her way. "They're hailing us."

"Put him on."

The image that replaced the view of the vessel suggested that things were at least as bad as Evlen had anticipated. The other vessel's bridge was dim with smoke. No bridge crew members remained other than Hocroft, who stood at the communications officer's station. He had sustained a minor injury; a rivulet of blood trickled down from his scalp at his hairline and smeared his right cheek.

His voice was icy. "Well, *that* was unpleasant."

"As I was saying, heave to and prepare to be boarded."

"I *can't*, you karking idiot. My engines were hit. They're on runaway. My engineering crew is all dead. *I can't stop.* Which, I take it, will be justification enough for you to continue firing until we're all dead." His voice turned bitter. "All those boys and girls . . . was this really necessary?"

"Drop your deflectors and I'll hold my fire until you figure out a way to heave to . . . or we decide to shut down your runaway engines by destroying them completely. But if your deflectors come up, if just one of your weapons systems begins to track us, if you resume a level course without immediately coming to a full stop, there won't be enough of your craft left to fill a refresher stall."

"Understood." Hocroft stepped to the center console and hit a couple of buttons.

Evlen's sensor officer nodded at her and made a lowering-hand gesture, indicating that the enemy's deflectors were down.

"I'm going aft." Hocroft blotted his scalp wound with his sleeve. "I can initiate a compartmental self-destruct that will destroy the engines safely. Then I'll be back here to use the maneuvering thrusters to stop us. Give me ten minutes."

"Five."

Hocroft glared. Without bothering to shut off the holocam view, he turned and strode from the bridge. The bridge doors snapped open for him, snapped closed behind him, leaving Evlen with her view of the smoke-filled bridge.

Evlen glanced at her communications officer. "Instruct the others to hold back. We'll pace the target and stay close. We'll signal when we want the others to close. Tell *Shieldbreaker* to stand by to pick up prisoners. And tell our boarding shuttle to stand by to launch."

"Aye aye."

Evlen paused. "Have any of you ever heard of a *compartmental self-destruct*?"

She got only silence and the shaking of heads in reply.

Heading aft to *Concussor*'s belly bay, Bhindi answered Turman's latest question. "The *Pollinate* command did a bunch of things. Locked down the shuttle bay so crewmates couldn't enter. Slaved the escape pods' launch ability to our comlinks. Disabled their comm systems." She, Turman, Jesmin, and Voort passed one emergency pod bay. Its exterior door and the pod door within were both closed, sealed. The Wraiths could see crew members within pounding frantically on the doors and viewport. As the Wraiths passed, the crew redoubled their efforts and shouted words the Wraiths could not hear.

Bhindi went on. "So when Five issued the *Abandon ship* order, the crewmates packed into the pods, which sealed them in tight, trapping them inside pending our issuing the launch command."

Jesmin sounded suspicious. "Which we are going to do, yes?"

"Yes."

"They think they're about to die." Turman's voice held a note of sympathy. It was at odds with his Commander Hocroft disguise.

"They're not."

The Wraiths reached the shuttle bay doors, which stood open. Trey was visible through the shuttle's forward viewports, clearly going through a preflight checklist.

Bhindi ran up the shuttle's boarding ramp, the footsteps of the other Wraiths clanging up behind her. Scut was not in the passenger compartment. Bhindi went forward to the cockpit. "Where's Six?"

Trey glanced at her. "Fuel at max. Um, he's staying in

the aux bridge until the last possible second. He says that if he patches everything through to our cockpit, he can't be sure it will all work."

Bhindi sat in the copilot's seat and strapped herself in. "Two, we need you to come up and pretend to fly this thing in case they get a holocam image of the bridge."

Movement on the other side of the bay drew her eye. Voort, awkward, had climbed on top of the one remaining interceptor and raised its topside boarding hatch. He was now clambering down into the cockpit. "What's he doing?"

Trey shrugged. "Saving us a resource? Checklist complete, by the way."

Turman came forward and took the pilot's chair. "Saving us a resource and providing us cover."

Bhindi reached for her comlink, then thought better of it. Any commed message at this point might be overheard by the *Starhook*. She couldn't order Voort to the shuttle, so she'd have to trust his judgment.

Blast it.

Trey went aft into the nearly empty trooper compartment. "Hey, lady. Mind if I sit here?"

Bhindi opened the ship's intercom to the auxiliary bridge. Since it was not a broadcast link, it could not be overheard by *Starhook*. "Six, execute these actions. Activate self-destruct, five-minute timer. Shut down engines. Set a one-minute timer to re-enable all escape pod functions and execute all commands that their occupants have entered since boarding. Transfer all bay controls to me. Also, kill the artificial gravity. Then—one guess what your last order is."

"On my way."

"Their engines have shut down. Still no sign of activity from their weapons or deflectors."

"Good." Her attention mostly on the view of the crippled enemy, Evlen nodded.

Then her eyes grew wide as gouts of thruster fire heralded multiple small-craft launches from the patrol vessel's hull.

Her sensor officer was quick. "I mark five, six, seven launches. Ball-shaped craft, they look like escape pods. Something else—thrust emissions from the underside, some other type of craft launching, but we don't have a visual."

"Incoming signal!"

"Put it on, Comm."

The view of the distant ship didn't change; this signal was voice only. Hocroft's voice: "Rather bad news, Captain. There was damage to the computer. Turns out there's no such thing as a compartmental self-destruct, so I had to activate the usual sort."

"I knew it." Evlen's angry words were spoken in a low tone, one the bridge mike would not pick up.

"Looks like we're done for. I've ordered abandon ship, as you can see."

Evlen caught her communications officer's eye, then made a throat-cutting gesture that meant *Cease transmission*. When he nodded, she spoke aloud. "Launch boarding shuttle."

"Aye aye. Launching."

"Tell them to steer well clear of the patrol vessel and be ready to engage a fleeing shuttle."

With minute adjustments of his maneuvering thrusters and repulsors, Voort kept his interceptor close to the *Concussor*'s underside. The shuttle, ahead of him, was coming up to speed on its outbound course, keeping the *Concussor* directly between it and the *Starhook*.

Voort kept another part of his attention on his console

timer. The Wraiths were now two and a half minutes into the self-destruct sequence. It would be very nice to be clear of the ball of explosive force the ship was about to become. Voort's hands twitched on the interceptor's yoke.

There was movement on his sensor board. Something was launching from *Starhook*'s underside. The signal suggested a shuttle similar in size to the one Bhindi was piloting.

The enemy shuttle vectored to pass the *Concussor* from a safe distance to port. *Starhook* was accelerating now, vectoring to pass from a safe distance starboard. The corvette would accelerate more slowly than the pursuing shuttle.

Delicately, Voort rotated his interceptor's nose toward port and kept his eye on the sensors.

And the chrono continued its countdown. Two minutes fifteen left. Two minutes. One minute forty-five.

As the pursuit shuttle came into view a bare two kilometers off to port, Voort lined up his shot at first by sight alone—weapons sensors would alert the target. He tracked his target, made sure his lasers were at full power.

The shuttle's deflectors were up . . . all energy forward, toward the Wraiths' shuttle. Voort almost smiled. He clicked his weapons sensors on, paused only the split second it took to adjust his aim to the center of the new bracket that had appeared as a heads-up display on his forward viewport, and fired.

Green bolts leapt from the leading edges of his solar collection wings and converged on the shuttle's stern. They chewed their way across its hindquarters, blackening its gray paint, carving metal debris free.

The shuttle's deflectors readjusted, strengthening at the stern. The shuttle veered away from Voort, sparks erupting from its aft thrusters.

A stern shot for a stern shot, thrusters for thrusters. Voort didn't bother with a taunt over the comm board. He just brought his own deflectors up to full power. He hit his thrusters and vectored in the direction of the Wraiths' shuttle, putting his interceptor through a series of tiny, erratically timed maneuvers designed to make life hard for the gunnery officers back on *Starhook*.

Parallel rows of light flashed past his interceptor, bright enough to be alarming, not close enough to interact with his deflectors.

The chrono clicked down to one minute.

The *Starhook* shuttle stayed on its escape vector. The crew had to be evaluating the damage Voort had done, deciding whether to resume pursuing and reengage. Every second they delayed took that decision further out of their hands. The Wraiths' shuttle was now up to speed and might have its hyperspace jump plotted. Voort began to overtake it. It grew large enough that he could distinguish it by eye, not just on his sensors. *Starhook*'s laser pulses flashed near it, too, but at this distance the gunners' chances of success were poor.

Voort received a low-strength transmission on the Wraiths' frequency—voice and data, encrypted and compressed. He decrypted it.

Bhindi's voice: "Our new course. Check my math, would you?"

He snorted, amused, then ran numbers through his head while absently juking and jinking to keep the distant lasers from making too easy a target of him. Then he replied: "My numbers agree with yours to three significant digits. Discrepancies my fault, rounding errors. Have a safe jump."

The shuttle ahead seemed to stretch and then was gone.

Voort activated his own hyperdrive and leapt into hyperspace after it.

* * *

Captain Evlen watched the distant targets vanish. She sighed and looked to her navigator. "Plot likely destinations along their course. Prioritize for planets and stations with strong Imperial Remnant sympathies. Communications, signal for a pickup of the escape pods. And *somebody* tell me what the hell this actually was all about."

CHAPTER SEVENTEEN

   29 ABY (15 Years Ago)

Piggy sat on a hilltop, watched over the vista of forest patches and fields of green ankle-high drymoss, felt cool breezes from the north as they tickled his cheek and caused the scrub bushes around him to sway.

And he clamped down on his rebelling gut. Absently, he glanced over the readouts on his blaster rifle—a bulky model with a scope and a built-in underbarrel grenade launcher—for the sixtieth time since setting up his observation nest.

The natural beauty down below was doomed. The Yuuzhan Vong held this world, and when they chose to devote the resources, they'd Vongform this lovely planet, transforming it into a likeness of their long-lost homeworld. Then it would be a vista of eerie, menacing plants and animals and who-knew-whats. The communities here would be destroyed, their populations penned, brutalized, taught the ways of the Yuuzhan Vong until their past was a dim and meaningless memory.

Perhaps he, Piggy, was doomed as well. Perhaps the other Wraiths on this operation, somewhere between his position and the Yuuzhan Vong shapers' nest set up a dozen kilometers to the south, were doomed.

Perhaps everything he knew was doomed.

Piggy caught sight of motion a few hundred meters to the south. Colors so like those everywhere in the landscape, but not part of it, moved over the rolling terrain.

Piggy crawled forward across an angled flat rock at the hill's summit. It supported his weight; he'd tested it earlier. His head protruding over empty air, he brought his macrobinoculars to his eyes.

This was a highly computerized set of macrobinoculars. They stabilized his view, compensating for slight motions of his hands, compensating for his breathing. They subtracted the least movement, such as plant stalks bending in the wind, from his vision. What was left was what was really moving.

In moments he had it. Two figures covered neck to feet in camouflage-pattern clothing and gear.

Estoric Sandskimmer and Runt Ekwesh. The sandy-haired human carried a gray, conical cylinder, dull and featureless. He cradled it in his arms as he ran. There was a dark spot on Estoric's side, not a part of the camouflage pattern—blood. Runt seemed unhurt. Both were traveling fast, straight for Piggy's position.

It took Piggy a moment to realize what was missing from the picture. Neither Estoric nor Runt carried a pack or blaster rifle. They must have been forced to abandon that gear in order to increase their speed.

Missing gear, blood on Estoric—the two had encountered Yuuzhan Vong warriors. But they had the cylinder. They'd succeeded in their mission, at least so far.

Piggy set the macrobinoculars aside and brought up his blaster rifle. He trained it on his friends, focused through the scope, and tracked south from where Estoric and Runt were.

Yes, only about fifty meters behind, three Yuuzhan

Vong warriors came at a full run, not slowed by the organic vonduun crab armor they wore. The armor, glistening like the inside lining of some seashells, covered their torsos. Accessory pieces acted as helmets, greaves, bracers. They were living things, those pieces, no two identical, and were so durable that a breastplate could deflect a badly struck blow from a lightsaber or an angled shot from a blaster rifle.

Piggy froze for a moment. He was a good shot, but not good enough to take out fast-moving targets at this range. If he waited until the warriors caught up with his friends, they'd be too close to Estoric and Runt for Piggy to snipe safely. And he couldn't open up a comm channel to Bhindi in the gunship, not if what New Republic Intelligence believed about the shapers' nest on this world was true.

There was no good answer. There was no mathematically perfect response.

The three warriors held amphistaffs, deadly serpent-like life-forms that could be stiff blunt-force weapons one moment, pliant whiplike entanglers with poisonous heads the next. But now they transferred the amphistaffs to their off-hands. Each reached into a pouch, withdrew something, and threw.

Piggy winced. Thud bugs, it had to be. Flying insects that distorted gravity, they could become far heavier just at the moment of impact, unloading lethal amounts of kinetic energy against whatever they hit.

At this range, Piggy couldn't see the thud bugs themselves. He saw Runt's stride continue unbroken. That meant Runt's jammer had to be functioning—a late development from Intelligence's research-and-development department, the jammers confounded thud bug senses in a limited area, making them less accurate.

But Estoric arched forward as if he'd been hit by a

catapult stone at waist level. He went down hard, tumbling, the gray cylinder rolling away from him.

Coldness gripped Piggy's insides. He heard himself murmuring, "No, no, no," as if the words might somehow convince the impending tragedy to seek other victims.

He flipped the selector on his blaster over to grenades. He sighted in on Estoric and marked the range to the man. It was 153 meters. Piggy knew Runt would not abandon Estoric, and that meant the fight would take place right there.

The three warriors slowed in their approach. The biggest one had the most ornate, most gleaming armor, and his helmet made him seem as tall as Runt. The next largest was the size of an average human man, the smallest slightly shorter. The smallest also had the least impressive armor—he was probably a juvenile.

Runt stopped beside Estoric. He turned toward the warrior, a vibroblade, long and wicked, in his right hand. His left fist was closed around something Piggy couldn't see. Estoric, clearly in pain, clawed for his own blaster pistol, struggling to get it free of its holster.

Then the warriors reached them.

The biggest one held back, standing atop a small rise, directing the smallest forward.

Piggy ground his teeth. The Yuuzhan Vong leader was making this a training exercise. But the biggest warrior was now stationary. Piggy sighted in on him, did not bother reading the numbers on his scope display. Mentally he calculated the warrior's distance from Estoric: 10.3 meters. There was a two-meter difference in Estoric's and the warrior's respective altitudes. Winds from the north-northwest, eight knots. No heat shimmer to factor in. Piggy elevated his barrel to the correct angle for the grenade launch and squeezed the trigger. With the blast, the weapon's stock thumped back into his shoulder. He would have a second before the grenade hit.

Piggy sighted in on the second largest warrior.

That one charged at Runt, swinging his amphistaff. The smallest charged Estoric.

Runt's arm came up—his left arm. His hand opened. A cloud of glittering dust erupted from it, blanketing the smallest warrior, enveloping his head.

"No, no, no . . ." Piggy knew it was a tactical mistake. Runt was trying to protect Estoric.

The second warrior's amphistaff cracked across Runt's midsection, hurtling him to the green-covered ground.

The biggest warrior was abruptly replaced by a cloud of black and red smoke. Piggy forced himself not to look at the explosion. But the second warrior did. The smallest warrior staggered back from Estoric, flailing to clear the dust from his face.

The sound of the grenade explosion reached Piggy, a distant *crack-boom*. Piggy's sighting brackets settled on the second warrior's back; he elevated his aim a touch, finding the bottom of the back of the warrior's helmet.

The warrior turned to look for the source of the grenade. The movement brought his neck into view in the scope brackets. Piggy squeezed the trigger. The scope view flared with light from his blaster bolt, and the pale Yuuzhan Vong skin blackened. The warrior staggered back and fell.

Piggy reoriented, took in the whole situation.

The biggest warrior was on his back, his upper body scorched. His entire head was gone.

The second warrior was down, not moving. Piggy was sure of the kill.

The smallest warrior stood over Estoric. The tail end of his amphistaff was a third of a meter deep in Estoric's chest, right where the heart was. Estoric's body was in mid-convulsion, stiffening. The warrior's head was turning as though he was scanning for sound. Runt's dust had to have blinded him, and yet he'd found and killed Estoric.

Runt, up on his feet, slammed into the last Yuuzhan Vong warrior. They went to the ground together. Runt's right hand came up and down, stabbing again and again with the vibroblade. The blade ran black with the alien warrior's blood.

And suddenly nobody down there was moving.

Though he seemed to have no breath, Piggy ran, his blaster rifle in his hands, down his hill slope and then up the slight rise to where the fight had taken place.

In moments he reached the five combatants. Four lay still. Runt was alive, his chest heaving, his features twisted in pain. His movements were weak.

Runt looked up as Piggy reached him. His jaw worked. "Am . . . phi—"

Only then did Piggy hear it, the rustle slightly louder than the wind, from just a couple of steps to his right. He spun, aimed.

One of the amphistaffs, now mobile, glided toward him through the moss with a sidewinder motion. Piggy fired. The heavy rifle blast caught the amphistaff, picked it up, hurtled it meters away. Even that didn't kill the beast. The amphistaff landed, charred along the mid-section, and slithered away.

Piggy looked around. The smallest warrior's staff was also in retreat, and the biggest warrior's staff was not in evidence.

He knelt beside Runt and slung his rifle on its strap. "Hold on. I'll get you out of here."

"Ampi . . . staff . . . hits. I'm bitten, Piggy." Runt's lips, where his fur did not cover them, and his upper palate inside his mouth were already pale. Runt panted as if superheating from the inside.

Piggy shook his head, denying the evidence of his eyes. "Your metabolism's not like ours. You're fighting it, Runt." He pulled Runt up to a sitting position and then partly across one shoulder. He prepared to stand.

Runt tapped Piggy's sides, his touch barely strong enough to be felt. "Let me down."

Piggy hesitated. He felt his face twist against the fact he had to face. Gently, he lowered Runt back to the moss.

His old friend looked up at him, sympathy mixing with the pain he clearly was experiencing. "More . . . warriors. One, two kilo . . . meters back. The grenade . . . will bring them. You can get away with the . . . commbuzzer. Or you can die with me."

"I'll stay. I can't leave you like this."

"No. Nothing would be worse . . . than if they had an . . . antidote."

Piggy looked at his friend's face, saw the thoughts that were crossing behind Runt's eyes. An antidote to the amphistaff's venom, even a temporary one, meant minutes, maybe hours of suffering. Suffering, interrogation, horror.

Now there was only one escape for Runt.

Piggy felt tears flood his eyes, but he drew his blaster pistol. "Forgive me."

"I . . . forgive . . ."

Piggy put the barrel beneath his friend's chin and pulled the trigger. Runt's body jerked and the smell of burned hair mixed with the odors of smoke and burned Yuuzhan Vong skin.

Piggy rose, shaking, and holstered his pistol. He gave his friend one last look.

Hohass "Runt" Ekwesh, poisoned and burned in

death. His body would not be sent back to his home-world for proper rituals. This was . . . wrong.

Piggy caught up the gray cylinder. Its contents buzzed, angry.

Commbuzzers. New Republic Intelligence had heard rumors of a new insect species created by the shapers of the Yuuzhan Vong. It was said these insects sensed comm traffic. They were infuriated by it. They would track it to its source. If the source was intermittent, they would fly while it was active, swarm when it ceased, resume their search when it became active again. With enough time, even a comm unit sending brief-burst data packets at intervals could be traced.

Chashima was the planet where they were being developed.

If Runt and Estoric had done their work right, the tremendous load of explosives Runt had carried would now be situated in, under, and around the shapers' nest where the commbuzzers were being developed. The prototype insects, their creators, everything related to that project except the living examples in this cylinder would—

There was a distant rumble, followed by a succession of additional rumbles, and a pillar of black smoke rose into the sky to the south.

Piggy turned with his box full of bugs and ran.

"I know you don't want to hear this." Face's manner and voice both demonstrated his sympathy, the sense of loss he himself must be feeling. "Despite our losses, you did something important down there."

Piggy slammed his large hand down on his superior's desk. In the tiny office cabin aboard the frigate that was the Wraiths' temporary headquarters, the noise was especially loud. "This was a *nothing* assignment. Two good men died for nothing."

"Yes, the war's almost done. We have the Yuuzhan Vong on the ropes. But they're so inventive."

"Those bugs wouldn't have turned the tide of the war."

"Maybe not. But they could have led to the discovery and elimination of countless resistance and insurgency cells, countless commando and intelligence units. How many men and women would have died? A thousand? Just two hundred? Piggy, tell me that Runt or Estoric would stand in front of me and say, *I won't die for just a hundred men, I don't want to go.*"

Piggy sagged back in his chair. "Face . . . I don't care. I'm done."

"You weren't done yesterday. Get some rest, take some leave, say your good-byes. You'll come back in a few days ready for another fight."

Piggy shook his head. "I don't have another fight in me."

"Piggy—"

"And don't call me Piggy. I'm Voort. I left Piggy back with Runt."

CHAPTER EIGHTEEN

They filed into the office building of Toozler's Speeder Repair and Maintenance, six bone-weary Wraiths.

Myri breathed a sigh of relief, holstered her blaster, and stepped out from the shadowy nook behind the stairs where she'd taken cover. "You didn't comm me from the spaceport."

"Refresher's mine." Jesmin dropped her bag against a wall. She stopped to give Myri a quick hug, then trotted upstairs.

"Blasted Jedi-like reflexes." Trey put on an expression of irritation. "I thought for sure, this time the refresher would be *mine*." He and the others set down their bags.

Myri gave them all a second look. "And you're all sunburned." It was true. Jesmin had borne the patchy redness of a new sunburn on fair skin, and everyone else showed signs of time spent outdoors under a hot sun—even the neoglith masquer Scut wore.

Bhindi fluttered her hands as though suddenly transformed into a dewy-eyed lady whose brain waves didn't quite budge the needle. "Tatooine is so lovely this time of year." Her voice and manner turned back to normal.

"On the other hand, we got a good sale price on the second interceptor—we now have a budget for ongoing operations—and we have a hastily redecorated military shuttle in a hangar at the spaceport. As for not comming you, we didn't know how long it would take us to scan and secure the hangar. How long you'd have to wait. So we just hired someone to speed us out here." She took the chair behind the computer setup. "I'm starting to hate travel."

Myri leaned over the counter toward her. "Your message didn't tell me much. I take it the rendezvous was . . . unproductive."

Bhindi snorted in wry amusement. "Turns out the general did the full-blown innocent thing and sent someone to capture us."

Turman took a chair, stretched out his legs before it. "If Thaal turns out to be innocent, I'll never forgive him."

"So." Bhindi put on a bright, cheerful face. "What's *your* good news?"

Myri tried to decelerate from the sinking feeling she'd been experiencing for the days the other Wraiths had been incommunicado, in transit. "Face Loran is missing and presumed dead. So is his family."

"What?"

"His airspeeder was blown up at an open-air market on Coruscant. A market where, at about the same time, two mercenaries—and suspected assassins—were found dead. Face's body wasn't found, but security detected genetic material, confirmed as his, in the wreckage. His wife and daughter are just missing. No trace. He hasn't responded to messages sent to any of the back routes I know. Jezzie's folks and other friends of the family can't reach him."

All the air seemed to go out of the other Wraiths. They stood in silence and stared at Myri.

Voort leaned heavily against a wall. When he spoke, his true voice was raspy and somber, at odds with the pleasant tone of the Basic words rising above it. "I hope it's a ploy on Face's part. I hope he's in hiding somewhere, hunkered down. But we can't deal with his disappearance right now. We have an objective, and it just got harder because we no longer have Face Loran as a resource. We can no longer ask him to swoop in and prove we've been doing things at the request of the head of Galactic Alliance Security. Face insulated us from him, which means we're on our own at this point."

"Agreed." Bhindi sounded as weary as Voort did.

Voort looked at Bhindi before continuing. "Before I get to what's really been occupying my mind, I want to say, one veteran to another, that I didn't like what happened on the *Concussor*. Not so much the outcome as the fact that we didn't have a plan to fight Thaal's representative if we had needed to. It's clear your plan was to break and run if anything went sour. We had no tricks up our sleeve to deal with them in an aggressive fashion if we'd needed to, no combat option."

"That's correct. We didn't."

"Why?"

"My decision, Voort." Bhindi turned a hard stare on him. "You can ask me my reasoning if I retire and you take over as commander of the unit. Not before."

"That's not a good answer."

"It's all you're getting. Now, you said something about what's really been bothering you."

Voort turned his head to stare at the blank wall opposite him. "I've been thinking about the *Starhook* and the other ships showing up with nothing but capturing us on their mind. I've been thinking about it during our whole time on Tatooine and the trip back. We've been talking as if Thaal's decision to send that command to get us was the action of an innocent man, or at least had that appearance. Now I say it didn't. Thaal's decision was that of a guilty man trying to appear incompetent. It means he's guilty. And I hope he puts up a fight when we come for him, so I can vape him myself."

Bhindi seemed to welcome this chance not to think about Face. "What's your reasoning? I don't follow."

They were interrupted by a metallic screech from overhead—the distinctive sound of their sanisteam stall's malfunctioning compressor being activated.

Voort waited a few moments until the sound subsided. He scratched his cheek and his tone turned thoughtful. "Thaal did not act as a good senior officer should unless there are some odd influences at work. An offer made by an officer of a distant power to a major political force of the Alliance should pique the interest of anyone whose job is rooting out enemy spies. Meaning Galactic Alliance Security. If Thaal had reported the attempt to suborn him along official channels, it would have gone straight to General Maddeus. And I have a hard time imagining that Maddeus wouldn't have put Thaal on a ship, sent him out to meet Hocroft, and had him play along. To give security more information about the effort to flip him. So Maddeus wasn't notified. What happened instead was the most awkward and ineffective 'innocent' response possible. For it to have happened, Thaal had to have bypassed security completely. He had to have gone to an ambitious friend or acquaintance *in another service* and said, 'You want to stay on the fast track to promotion? Here's a spymaster you can catch.'"

Scut's smiling human face frowned, an odd study in contrasts. "Which he would do only if he is stupid, or a really bad tactician—"

Bhindi nodded. "Which we know he isn't."

"—or because he wanted to make a big public show of being innocent, and is not worried about the harm the *stupid* tag might do to his reputation." Scut looked thoughtful.

"It's the last part that I find especially unlikely. If Thaal doesn't mind people thinking he's stupid—especially with a new Chief of State in office!—then he doesn't care if he remains Chief of the Army. An ambitious officer who gets to the very top rung of his profession and then doesn't care if he stays there."

Bhindi caught the eye of each of the others in turn, Voort excepted. "That's today's lesson, children, except it's from Math Boy instead of me. Be *sure* how smart your mark is. Be *sure* what his tactics should be. Then, when he deviates from them, you know you're on to something."

Scut reached up to pull off his neoglith masquer. "Sorry. I have to scratch." He did, furiously scratching behind one ear. "But I see. The general does not care about being thought stupid, does not care about offending Maddeus of security by bypassing him, because he has no interest in protecting his current position. Because he knows he is leaving it. Leaving it for his new identity."

"Thank you, Voort." Bhindi sounded thoughtful. "This makes me feel a lot better. We didn't lose the *Concussor* for nothing. We lost it to confirm, in a way that is inadmissible in court but I'm happy with, that Thaal is guilty. He's our man."

"I have some good news, too." Myri tried to put on a hopeful expression. "It came up while you were in transit."

Bhindi brightened. "Show me."

Myri sat down beside Bhindi at the computer, brought up a planetary map, and began scrolling westward from Ackbar City.

Trey moved around behind her. "We really need a holoprojector. One, can I buy one?"

"Yes."

"Great! Ummm . . . we need a mansion?"

"No."

Myri's scrolling and zooming filled the monitor screen with an ever-closer satellite map view of foothills graduating to mountains at the bottom of the screen, a village in the lower right corner, an irregular oval-shaped patch of what looked like indigenous scrub foliage dominating the left side, and grain fields everywhere else. "I also have a lot more information about procedures and schedules at the army base. And by the way, Pop-Dogs are much more grabby than normal soldiers, and I suspect there's a warrant out for my arrest—well, me with white hair and dark skin—but none of that may be relevant anymore. The good news is that two more of Trey's battery droids went active . . . and one of them is nowhere near Fey'lya Army Base." She pointed at the monitor screen, toward the top of the natural-landscape oval. Under her fingernail was a small black square. "Last night, the new droid started transmitting from here. Right at that square."

Bhindi leaned closer to peer. "What's there?"

"The Javat Caridan Environment and the Javat Caridan Children's Animal Habitat. It's a preserve for endangered animal species—endangered because they're from Carida and most were wiped out when that system was destroyed. Just after the Yuuzhan Vong War, one of the original Pop-Dogs, Captain Jam Javat, bought this property and turned it into a preserve. He retired a major a few years back and moved out of the Coruscant system. The property operates under a trust now. No business relationship at all to General Thaal, in theory. Anyway, over the years Javat assembled breeding populations of several Caridan species, including real pop-dogs, and let them adapt."

Voort moved to stand by Trey. "No business relation to Thaal."

"None. So it doesn't show up on any searches of Thaal's business connections anywhere. He's never even contributed to the charity fund that operates it." Myri hit a few keys. Abruptly there was a design superimposed on the map, a wire frame representing some sort of structure, narrow, a few hundred meters in length. "Parasite Droid Twelve sent us a few floor-level views of a dark bunk room with army-style beds and no occupants. Apparently the only droid it's managed to subvert runs on nonvisual sensors, so I don't have any pictures from it to offer you. Just distance measurements from its movements, which I've turned into this schematic. This is a subterranean complex, ranging from one to four vertical levels depending on where you are, with working turbolifts, including one to the surface. Right where that black square is. At maximum magnification, the square looks like an old equipment barn, a good-sized one." She pointed to a white square at the top of the property. "That's the children's habitat. Not that they keep children there. Children visit to pet the pop-dogs and the dwarf banthas, and to learn about the bluehair spiders and walking cephalopods."

Bhindi stared off into the distance, past the walls. "Fruit crates."

Turman glanced at Scut. "I'll admit it: I did not know she was going to say that."

"I, either."

Bhindi snapped back to reality. "Trey, new shopping list."

Trey scrambled to bring out his datapad and opened it. "Recording."

"We need a big load, several bushels, of fruit in crates. Local produce. Some carpentry tools and some heavy-duty flexiplast sheeting. Rope. Small winches capable of hauling any of us up or down. Ambience suits for all of us, but don't be surprised if you can't get one for Voort, even from Coruscant. An ambience shroud. Make sure everyone has a blaster pistol and a vibroblade. Macro-binoculars or goggles with night-sight functions. Packs and gear belts in black." She thought it over. "Various types of detonators, and lots and *lots* of explosives. Estimates?"

Trey thought it over. "Two days."

"Get started. Take all the boys with you. You can sanisteam when you get back." She gave them a little shooing gesture.

Scut pulled his mask back on, and the men left.

Overhead, the sanisteam screeched as it was shut off.

Bhindi returned her attention to Myri. "I don't know how close they actually are, but Jesmin's known Face all her life."

Myri nodded. "He's basically an uncle to her. Not so much to her brother Doran. Jezzie and Doran weren't raised that much together."

"And Jesmin's known you a long time. I don't normally ask this sort of thing . . . but would you tell her? About Face?"

"Yes, ma'am." Suddenly Myri began experiencing that sinking feeling again, worse than before.

It was not a thing of beauty, the wooden framework Trey and Turman built atop the cargo bed of their landspeeder, but it would do the job.

It started with Vandor-3 yellow spotmelons. The spotmelons filled numerous wooden crates, which the carpenters fitted to a wooden rack affixed with quick-release bolts to the upper rim of the speeder bed. The crates covered the rack's top so that it looked as though the bed was loaded with them, but the space beneath the rack was open, with a layer of insulating foam laid in place for the comfort of passengers there. When it was done, the landspeeder looked like many such vehicles destined for a growers' market. But the space beneath the rack was large enough to comfortably hold four normal-sized humans.

Voort studied the design, then went inside to talk to Bhindi. "Three in the cab and four in the bed, then."

She sat in the midst of a riot of purchases, doing a quick check on the battery packs supplied with the ambience suits. She smiled up at him. "Yes."

"We're taking all seven of us on this operation."

"Again, yes."

"Shouldn't this be a one-or-two-Wraith job? Minimum presence, maximum speed?"

She shook her head. "Maximum mutual support."

"Which makes sense if we know the environment we're going into, or know that it's going to be a firefight. If we take seven operatives in, we're more likely to be detected."

Her expression became thoughtful, as if Voort were imparting wisdom. "In which case we know there's going to be a firefight."

"Bhindi—"

"That was a joke, Voort. But you're partly right. You'll remain with the speeder. You'll be the armored cavalry if things go bad. Scut will stay topside, too, since he has no insertion skills to speak of."

"Leaving five going in. Still twice as many as we want for an initial reconnaissance."

"I know it's not the way we used to do it." She returned her attention to the power packs. "Things change, Voort."

* * *

The next afternoon, they loaded up—Bhindi, Turman, and Voort in the pilot's compartment, the rest reclining in the bed—and the Wraiths began the long haul to the village of Kreedle, the community nearest the mystery installation. They arrived just before nightfall, Vandor's setting sun casting and then lengthening the shadows of the mountain foothills south of them. In the landing area of a wooden general store shaped like a truncated cone, Voort and Bhindi stretched their legs while Turman went in to shop for refreshments and snoop for information.

A crate of spotmelons spoke up. "Leader, I need to go to the refresher." The crate had Trey's voice.

Bhindi grinned. "Not here. We'll be back in the air in a few minutes and we'll find you a tree. Are you finding anything in local news or tourism archives?"

The spotmelon's voice became deeper, smoother, Trey impersonating Turman's announcer voice. " 'The most famous sites in Kreedle Precinct are Sachet Springs, a popular water park known for its natural beauty, water-sport facilities, and campsites; the Javat Caridan Environment and the Javat Caridan Children's Animal Habitat, a preserve for endangered Caridan species, with a petting area for children'—it says something here about not petting the bluehair spiders, because though they are not aggressive their hair-bristles conduct a rash-inducing toxin—and 'Mount Lyss Meteorological Station, a long-abandoned government facility used during the Yuuzhan Vong War as a hideout by freedom fighters.' Tours apparently not available, as the place was abandoned again after the war and is in an ongoing state of decay."

Another crate of melons, this one with Myri's voice, spoke up. "I say we bag the mission and go to the water park." There was a general murmur of agreement from the rest of the crates.

"Good try, Three, you almost convinced me." Then

Bhindi frowned. "How do they keep the toxic spiders from spreading all over Vandor-Three?"

Voort heard key clicks from under the crates, and then Trey answered. "A series of three one-meter-high perimeter barriers that transmit low-intensity tones, supersonic and subsonic, that send the spiders and other nonindigenous species into retreat."

Bhindi laughed. "That'll be where their perimeter sensors will be, as well."

Turman returned, with no new information except that the locals seemed to be suspicious only of people who spent no money at the store. He carried two bags of refreshments, one for the passengers in the pilot's compartment and one for those in the bed. Then the Wraiths boarded the speeder once again and lifted off.

The route to the Javat Caridan habitat was marked by a paved ground-vehicle road used by heavy haulers taking crops to processor plants or market. Trey's downloaded data showed that the road went all the way to the children's animal habitat and beyond. When the Wraiths, traveling just above that road, came within a few kilometers of the preserve, sturdy, low Vandor-3 scrub trees bordered the road, blocking ground-level views of the preserve all the way to the children's habitat building.

Darkness had fallen by the time they reached the preserve. Two hundred meters from the children's animal habitat, Voort could still not see it ahead; the road curved, blocking his view.

At the speeder's controls, Turman brought the vehicle to a slow landing off the pavement, as close to the scrub trees as was feasible. Voort, out first, retried the ambience shroud from the very back of the speeder bed.

The shroud looked like a green awning of thick flexible material, a telescoping pole at each of its four corners. Hastily, Voort situated each pole just beyond a corner of the speeder and triggered a button at the pole's bottom. Each trigger deployed a spike that punched its way into the ground, giving it an instant, firm foundation in the soil. In moments the awning's cloth top was taut, waving slightly in the mild summer breeze.

Voort activated the power pack nestled against the awning's underside. In moments it would compensate for heat rising from organisms and vehicle engines beneath it, making it difficult for infrared sensors in satellites and airspeeders to detect the speeder.

Voort wrote a note in big letters on a sheet of flimsi—REPULSORS FAILED, RETURNING ON FOOT TO KREEDLE, PLEASE DON'T STEAL OUR MELONS—and affixed it to the front window. Meanwhile, the other Wraiths struggled into their ambience suits. Made of black elastic cloth a centimeter thick, the suits operated on the same principle as the ambience shroud. A web of temperature sensors throughout the suits sent data on interior and exterior temperatures to a tiny processor. The processor adjusted the power sent to thousands of fluid-filled capillaries embedded in the material, cooling or heating different areas in turn. The result was a material that cooled its wearer's skin and maintained its own external surface at the temperature of the surrounding air—again, making the wearer almost invisible to infrared holocams. The suits included long-sleeved body stockings stretching from neck to ankle, gloves, shoes, and hoods that bared only the wearer's eyes.

In minutes they stood ready as a unit. Scut carried a blaster rifle; the others wore holstered blaster pistols. All had black packs. Others had tools of individual preference clipped to belts: glow rods, pouches, vibroblades, comlinks.

Bhindi turned back to Voort. "If you hear alarms go off, don't wait for us to signal. Come roaring in, purge anyone shooting at us, and get us out of the danger zone."

Voort nodded. "Sure you don't want to reconsider?"

"I'm sure."

Once the black-clad Wraiths had vanished into the line of scrub trees, Voort took his blaster rifle and walked a few dozen meters into the trees. He sat down to wait.

CHAPTER NINETEEN

The Wraiths waited in a little hollow, a depression in the ground twenty meters from the outermost sensor ring.

A few hundred meters north, by the ground-vehicle road, was the children's building, a low, long yellow structure with glow rods up on poles all around it. A paved landing zone surrounded the building, with a few landspeeders parked on it. Lights glowed behind curtains in the viewports, but there were no people to be seen around the building. The Wraiths had looked over the building from a distance for a few minutes, then had moved on to this location.

A few hundred meters to the south lay the building that was supposed to be the surface access for the mystery installation below. Myri stayed at the depression's upper rim, her macrobinoculars trained on the building. She had a good view of it. Square-shaped, it was constructed along the lines of corrugated sheet-metal businesses in Ackbar City. In her macrobinoculars' infrared filter, the building was a sieve for internal heat. Warm air poured out of a number of gaps and seams all along the angled metal roof, from a tall rolling door on the east face, from various vents, and from what looked like popped rivets along the north and east facings.

Myri set down her macrobinoculars and slid a couple of meters down into the depression, joining Scut, Turman, and Bhindi. "It doesn't match the satellite view."

Bhindi pulled at the eye opening of her hood and peeled the hood off her face, exposing her features and giving herself some fresh air. "What do you mean?"

"The whole place is bigger than that image shows, at least thirty meters on a side and ten high. And it's surrounded by a permacrete lot. None of that's on the satellite image."

"Meaning . . ." Bhindi pondered that. "Meaning they have to have sliced a constant image into what the satellites see—either an old scan or a computer-generated image. I'll bet Four would call that some tricky coding. Speaking of Four . . ."

Myri shrugged. "He's up at the sensor wall, checking it out. I lost track of Five when she got about a third of the way around the perimeter."

There was a faint scrabbling sound from above, then Trey's head crested the rim of the depression from above. He elbow-crawled over the lip and slid down to the bottom. He, too, pulled his hood's eye-gap so his head could emerge. "Good news and bad news."

Bhindi gave him a chilly *isn't it always that way?* smile. "Start with the bad."

"That sensor wall is a continuous belt that broadcasts supersonic and subsonic audio tones, just like the tourist notes said. It also has continuous belts of listening sensors and short-range motion detectors—by short-range I mean a meter or less. It's going to be difficult to get over without an airspeeder. And I'm detecting sensors from the building that become viable at an altitude of about three meters."

Bhindi sighed. "And the good news?"

"Well, we were presuming sound imaging, too, and

there isn't any. And it looks to me like the two inner-perimeter fences are set up identically."

Bhindi, judging by what could be seen of her face in the moonlight, didn't look happy. "Well, maybe Five will have better news for us."

Five did. Half an hour later, Jesmin slithered over the lip of the depression and down to join the others. She didn't bare her face.

She sketched out a diagram by dragging a finger through the soil. Under Trey's glow rod, switched to minimum power, it showed the square building, three concentric sensor rings, the distant children's animal habitat, and a straight line from the square building to the children's habitat. "This line is a rut in the soil. The local grasses and shrubs don't grow there. The rut looks like it was blown, abraded, by the constant passage of heavy-duty airspeeders. Cargo speeders. The repulsor wash has undermined the soil at the base of the sensor fence, at least on the outermost ring. It looks to me like someone has replaced the dirt there, packed it in, but they haven't done anything to address the problem, like pouring a permacrete base for the fence."

Scut frowned. Myri felt a twinge of sympathy for him. He was wearing his neoglith masquer face and gloves with the ambience suit over them; perhaps he wasn't overheating, but Myri decided she'd be on the verge of claustrophobic panic in such a rig.

Scut touched the points where the line representing the rut crossed the curves representing the sensor fences. "Can we dig through deep enough to crawl under?"

"I think so. And quietly. Deep enough for me, One, Two, and Three certainly. I don't know about you and Four. You're kind of thick-chested."

Trey snorted. "Thank you for not saying thick-headed."

"I thought about it."

Bhindi began to tug her hood back into place. "Let's do it. Hands only for the digging, no tools. And no talking. That means *you*, Two. Let's go."

Turman sniffed as if offended, but he did not reply.

They set their blasters and other hard equipment aside and dug as quietly as they could, slowly, painstakingly deepening and widening the loose soil packed around the fence base. They did not worry about being seen by unaugmented eyes. In deep shadow in their black ambience suits, against a black permacrete wall with a black metal mesh sensor layer on top, they were invisible to anything short of special light-gathering sensors.

Jesmin was quietest, as befitted an Antarian Ranger with extensive wilderness experience. Turman remembered not to practice soliloquies. The task seemed to take forever; the stars wheeled by overhead as the Wraiths dug. Myri could see artificial objects up there with them—capital ships, illuminated by the system's sun, approaching or departing the atmosphere, space stations in their orbits, all of them tiny shapes.

Eventually the gap under the meter-high sensor fence became large enough for even Trey to slither through. Permitting themselves no noise-increasing haste, they crawled under, transferred their bags and blaster rifles across, and moved on.

They elbow-crawled along the repulsor rut, taking advantage of the slight visual cover it offered, until they were at the second sensor wall. This time things went a bit faster; their experience with the first wall had developed their stealthy digging technique. This wall took only half an hour to dig beneath.

They were halfway between it and the inner wall when the landspeeder appeared.

Scut, in the rear, was first to notice. He rapped on

Myri's leg and pointed back. Just turning off the ground-vehicle road into the landing area of the children's habi-tat was a long, sturdy landspeeder, one optimized for cargo hauling. Its running lights were not on; it became visible only when it passed under the pole-top glow rods around the long yellow building. Myri could now hear its repulsors humming.

The Wraiths froze where they were.

Bhindi kept her voice a whisper. "I'll bet Four's left arm they're running with infrared sensors on, and that they're coming this way—yes." The landspeeder floated across the landing lot and then onto the rut. "Everyone do exactly as I do." She resumed her elbows-and-knees crawl toward the inner fence, moving faster now.

By the time the landspeeder floated over the middle fence, the Wraiths were beside the innermost fence. They lay motionless in the rut, arrayed in two ranks of three. Myri, on the left of the front rank, kept her atten-tion on Bhindi in the middle. Jesmin, on the other side, did the same.

The hum of the oncoming landspeeder grew into a low roar—and then Myri felt sudden pressure from the repulsors passing above her. It started at her feet and ankles, moved quickly up her body. She imagined the sensation to be like having a rancor-sized baker try to flatten her with a giant rolling pin.

Then it was past, just barely past, and Bhindi sprang to her feet only centimeters behind the landspeeder's rear panel. Myri and Jesmin scrambled up. Together the three women leapt over the sensor wall, hit the ground in a roll, and then went flat again. There were more im-pacts as Trey, Turman, and Scut hit the ground behind them, and one of them—Myri thought it was Turman—went flat with half his body weight across Myri's legs.

They lay still and silent while the landspeeder contin-ued on toward the square building. Myri heard a metallic rolling and scraping noise from the east face of the building, probably the door being opened. The landspeeder made the turn to the east wall of the building and floated out of Myri's sight.

The repulsor noise began to echo and diminish. The scraping-rolling noise resumed and continued for quite a while. Then, finally, all became silent.

Myri turned her head to see who had fallen on her. But half a meter away was a spider. A ten-legged arachnid, it was as large in diameter as a Wookiee's open hand and almost as hairy. As Myri stared, wide-eyed, it raised its front four legs skyward in a threat display.

Myri cringed and didn't move.

The spider's forelegs wavered, but otherwise the creature remained still.

Myri tugged her face mask away from her mouth and blew, a steady stream of breath that flowed across the arachnid, causing its hair to stir. Myri hoped the action would be a deterrent, not an invitation to leap on her face.

It was. The arachnid's forelegs wavered again, and then the creature turned around and ran away from the rut.

The Wraiths waited a dozen meters away while Jesmin finished her reconnaissance around the square building's exterior. Then she appeared at the northwest corner and waved them forward. Myri and the others joined her at the west—back—wall. They huddled midway along the wall, where Jesmin showed them a sheet of wall metal with most of the rivets torn out, probably from years of being flexed by winds. Jesmin pulled the metal sheet a few centimeters to one side, and light streamed out.

Through the gap they could see that the interior was a single chamber, thirty meters on a side, dominated in the center by the darkened top of a cargo lift shaft, itself twenty meters on a side.

Jesmin pointed at a spot directly above the east-side door, and at locations about six meters up on the north and south walls as well. In each place, a bracket bolted to the wall held a good-sized holocam unit, its lens pointed out through a round hole cut in the sheet metal of the wall, aimed outside. She kept her voice so low that Myri could barely hear her. "I think there's one overhead, too."

Trey eased her out of the way and trained his macro-binoculars at each of the three holocams in turn, flipping between several filters and enhancement options as he did so. Then he lowered the device. "Infrared. We're covered. And I don't see any cams monitoring the interior."

There were no people, either military or civilian, to be seen. Bhindi nodded. "Six, pull back twenty meters and prepare to offer us warning or covering fire. And you don't need tissue samples from the spiders. Everyone else, we're going in."

Inside, the chamber was eerily silent. Only a few metallic clanks and the waver of distant voices, too faint to be understood, floated up from the lift shaft. Myri crept up to its edge. The permacrete all around was curiously clean and was marked with holes, two to three centimeters in diameter, whose edges were even cleaner— almost white.

Trey edged up beside her, looking at the same holes. "Something was bolted down all over the floor until recently. I'm guessing it was flooring, maybe concealing the lift. The holes are deep for strength."

Jesmin leaned over the shaft. From her pack she withdrew one of the winches Trey had bought. About the size and shape of a human shoe, it consisted of a coil of industrial-strength cord a hundred meters long, high-torque gripping rollers, and a power pack, with simple controls on one surface. The trailing end of the black cord had a black grappling hook attached. She leaned over the shaft edge with the hook in hand, attached it to something underneath, and clipped the winch to her belt. "Ready."

In moments all five of them, one by one swung themselves over the edge, into the darkness. Far below a square of light showed them their destination.

As she descended, Myri decided that it would have been a serious misstatement to refer to the shaft as part of a turbolift. *Turbo* did not enter its description at any point. Myri had occasionally seen lifts like this, on back-rocket worlds and in industrial complexes. At the four corners of the square shaft were durasteel tracks, something like gigantic chains with regular sprocket holes. Presumably, far below, there would be a large, square lift car, probably open-top, with motors at each corner driving gears that spun slowly and engaged the sprockets. Ascending or descending might take one minute or several, but the lift could haul tremendous weights.

As the square of light below grew larger, what lay within it resolved into objects Myri could recognize. The lift car had reached bottom and the late-arriving landspeeder was still upon it. Men and women in brown moved on the lift-car floor, hauling cylinders—half a meter high, perhaps the same in diameter, black at the ends and pink in the middle—and stacked them in the landspeeder's lengthy bed. Myri saw a total of six workers doing the loading. None of them looked up. When she drew closer, she could see the stylized tooth design of the Pop-Dogs on the workers' collars.

When Myri was about twenty-five meters above the landspeeder, Jesmin, five meters below her, stopped her descent. Myri could only see her eyes as Jesmin looked up at the other Wraiths. Moments later Myri reached her level and switched off her winch. As they arrived, the other three Wraiths did likewise.

Jesmin pointed toward the side of the shaft directly ahead. Peering, squinting, Myri could barely see that there was some sort of horizontal gap there. She drew out her macrobinoculars and looked through them, cycling through different light-amplification modes.

Ahead was a railed metal balcony. It would be beyond the edge of the lift car when it rose or descended. On the other side of the balcony were doors at intervals—open doors with blackness beyond. Myri put her macrobinoculars away.

Jesmin reached for her, and Myri caught her hand. Awkward, unable to brace herself, Myri swung Jesmin forward. Jesmin swung free and came within a couple of hand spans of the metal rail. When she swung back, Myri pushed her again, and this time Jesmin caught the rail.

In two minutes, all five Wraiths were at and over the rail. Jesmin and Trey disappeared through the nearest door. Myri and the others waited at the rail, watching below.

It looked as though the lift car was at the floor of a chamber much larger than the lift shaft; sturdy square durasteel columns took the lift's tracks all the way to the floor, but Myri could see open space beyond them in all four directions. Open space, and the noses or tails of vehicles. Some were very large; others seemed to be ordinary airspeeders. It looked as though a metal trench, deeper than the floor by at least a meter, ran north and south from the lift shaft. Myri thought that the trench might meet in the middle, directly beneath the lift car. When Myri spotted the rails along either side of the trench, she knew what it was for, had seen its like in some old cities: it was a slot to guide vehicles that traveled laterally along it, probably also hauling cargo.

The stacks of pink-and-black cylinders grew higher. When the first of them protruded well above the landspeeder's cargo bed, the Pop-Dogs threw a blanket across it, then tied the stack firmly in place.

Jesmin and Trey returned from their scouting run. Jesmin leaned close to Bhindi to whisper in her ear. Trey did the same with Myri. "It's a residential floor. Empty. Stripped of furnishings. Air ducts closed down and power off."

"How long ago?"

"Some dust on the floor, but not thick. A few weeks?"

Bhindi drew another twenty meters of cord from her winch, then clipped the end of the cord. She tied it off to the metal rail so it would be loose but not dangle into the shaft. She gestured for the others to do as she did.

Finally the loading of the landspeeder was done; blankets secured and concealed four stacks of cylinders. The Pop-Dogs talked among themselves until a seventh individual, a human man in civilian dress, stepped onto the lift car from a spot out of the Wraiths' view. He spoke briefly to one of the Pop-Dogs and climbed into the cockpit of the speeder. The Pop-Dogs stepped off the lift car and moved to the side, out of Myri's view.

Bhindi waved the Wraiths back through the doors. Before they were quite through the doors, the lift was in motion, rising slowly and noisily.

In the darkness of the abandoned residential level, Myri breathed a little more easily. "This is some sort of distribution center."

"The cylinders are military casks for bacta." Jesmin sounded grim. "A hot commodity on the black market."

"I think this will be the proof we need." Bhindi sounded happy. "If we prove that Thaal is in an operation trading military bacta to the black market, he'll be ruined, dishonorably discharged, imprisoned, and investigated from his scalp to his soles. It'll be so thorough that there's no way he'll be able to keep an association with the Lecersen Conspiracy secret. Record everything you see here . . . and I think we've won."

The lift car rose clanking past their level. The noise gradually declined as the car climbed.

CHAPTER TWENTY

Two minutes later, the Wraiths rode their winches down their lines to the floor, landing silently at the edge of the loading area. Jesmin was first, landing in the shadow of one of the track columns, and she took a few moments to scan her surroundings before waving the others down. Coming to rest on the permacrete floor, Myri also scanned their surroundings.

It was a large chamber, a motor pool by the looks of it. Most of it was a broad permacrete shelf with that gash of a metal trench running down its middle, dividing it in half. The trench continued north and south along the center of a broad, high, arch-topped corridor lit by ancient glow rod fixtures, many of them flickering with age and lack of maintenance. The corridor extended to the limits of Myri's vision in this gloom, and she could see doors, some human-scale and some six or seven meters high and wide, dotting the walls every twenty to thirty meters. She also thought she glimpsed cross-corridors in either direction.

The vehicles around her—she saw full-sized plasma artillery batteries, modern units that rode easily on repulsorlifts. There were hauler landspeeders, expensive personal airspeeders, speeder bikes, and armored personnel speeders.

There were no people to be seen, and the place was eerily quiet. The only noise came from the lift car now reaching the top of the shaft.

The Wraiths tied their cords off to metal rings at the base of one of the columns, then gathered in the deepest shadows, which were on the wall beneath the abandoned residential level.

Bhindi looked around at the bounty of the motor pool and shrugged. "We've won."

"We're not out of here yet." Myri didn't know whether or not to be appalled at Bhindi's assumption of victory.

"True. But look. Artillery units. I'll give you hundred-to-one odds that they were reported destroyed in field exercises. Now they're going to the black market. All that bacta."

"Why is it so empty?" Though his whisper could not carry much emotion, Trey sounded distracted, bothered. "Why was the top-side floor pulled out?"

"We'll find out. Orders." She pointed to Turman. "He gets all the explosives with comm-based detonators. The simple ones. Four, check him out on them to make sure he knows how not to blow himself up. Two, you'll stay here in this chamber and put charges beneath the repulsor motivators on as many of these vehicles as you can—military vehicles first. As we leave, we'll set them off so they can't fly the evidence away on short notice. Then, Four, you and Three check out everything interesting to the south while Five and I do the same to the north. Record everything. Don't get caught. We'll muster back here in an hour. Clear?"

Myri nodded. "Clear." But her confirmation did nothing to diminish the unease she felt.

* * *

Myri crept with Trey a few dozen meters down the south corridor. They peered into the first doorway, an open rectangle of black, and within it saw only a storeroom whose shelves held crates of food—cereal products, dried fruits, sweeteners, powders meant to be mixed with drinks.

"I need to check this out." Trey turned his back on the storage room and moved in a crouch over to the trench. He slipped down into it, disappearing from Myri's view.

She followed, landing beside him in the shadowy gap. "I told you, I know what it's for."

"Yes, you did, and you were right." Trey gave her an enigmatic look—enigmatic only because she couldn't see his face and interpret his whole expression. "But do you know *everything* it's for?"

He pointed to the trench side, which was beneath an overhang perhaps ten centimeters deep. He flicked on the glow rod in his hand, illuminating a section of metal trench wall. "See those bolts? They're securing a panel a meter wide, a meter tall."

Myri nodded. "Sure."

"A panel to an access tunnel. Under the permacrete floor. Probably a lot of them. Some will handle drainage, some will give access to infrastructure machinery. As empty as this place is, I bet many of them aren't ever looked in. When we pull out, we ought to leave one of us behind to continue surveillance. Our evidence will be a lot stronger if we do."

"Tell Leader."

"I will." He crawled southward, keeping well below the trench lip above.

Myri followed, occasionally peeking up above the rim to see her surroundings. "My father was on the Death Star Trench Run. You know, the famous one. Me, I get the General's Basement Trench Crawl."

Myri couldn't see his face, but Trey's shoulders seemed

to stiffen. "I know who your father is. *Everyone* knows who your father is."

"I beg your pardon?" She looked at him, startled.

"Some of us don't have famous relatives to admire. Or nonfamous relatives to admire."

"I didn't mean it that way. It was a joke."

"All right."

Jesmin and Bhindi kept to the shadows along the wall when they were deep enough, switching to the trench when they were not. The two worked their way northward. In short order, they passed a succession of doors into darkened areas on either wall.

"So quiet." Bhindi raised her head a little from the trench and looked around before ducking again. "I hear distant voices and music. Recorded music, I think. Echoing."

Jesmin peered under the lip of the trench edge. With one gloved hand, she reached for the lump she saw adhering there and tugged at it, levering it free of the metal above. It came loose with a faint ripping noise, and she presented it to Bhindi.

It was an irregular mass, centimeters thick, of some material Bhindi obviously couldn't at first make out—layers of different colors, white and tan and gray and black. Bhindi peered more closely at it.

"Paint." Jesmin squeezed it in her hand, causing the edges to buckle, warp, and peel away. "Scores or hundreds of layers." She sniffed at it, detected the dim smell of solvents and durasteel treatments. "This complex is very old."

Bhindi's eyebrows rose, disappearing under her hood. "I know what this place is."

"Enlighten me."

"A Tech Raiders base. The black marketeers from

long ago. Thaal and his original Pop-Dogs hid out in one of their bases near the city of Vangard to do their guerrilla activities against the Yuuzhan Vong. While I was flitting all over the galaxy with your dad and Piggy and the other Wraiths, Thaal was squatting in a place like this and harming the enemy his own way. But not from *this* base. This one doesn't appear in his history anywhere." Bhindi blinked, considering. "That would explain why he had Fey'lya Base built so far from Vangard and the old clone trooper facilities. He wanted to be conveniently near here—his own black-market staging area."

Jesmin offered her a nearly silent whistle. "He found more than one base and never reported it. He's been corrupt ever since the end of the Yuuzhan Vong War."

"At least. I wonder . . ." Bhindi shifted as she thought. "Maybe there were still some old Tech Raiders here when he arrived. They might have helped him learn the lay of the land, taught him smuggler stealth techniques . . . and convinced him to become one of them. Maybe his Pop-Dogs are the Tech Raiders of a new generation."

Jesmin nodded. "And maybe Thaal is just the man to put them through a massive expansion. Make them a galactic-class crime syndicate."

The first two chambers Jesmin and Bhindi examined turned out to be dormitories, each occupied by a dozen bunk beds now shrouded in transparent flexiplast. Dust collected in a thin layer on all surfaces.

The third chamber, on the far side of the trench, was free of dust. Bhindi slid the corridor door shut behind her and switched the door-side control panel so that the glow rods overhead would stay shut off even though there were people in the room. Then the two women moved from shelving rack to shelving rack, navigating by the light from their glow rods, looking at what was warehoused there.

High-grade, military-specification electronics parts, repair and replacement components for comm systems, sensor systems, and power generators. Opaque black transport cases marked only with the dates they were sealed; the planet of origin on each was shown as Kessel. Bhindi actually seemed to pale in the light from Jesmin's glow rod. "Glitterstim cases," she told Jesmin.

Several shelves held bacta—lots of bacta, black-and-pink cylinders identical to those loaded on the landspeeder. Each cask of the miracle healing drug was clearly marked with the name of a military base. Most numerous were those marked FEY'LYA ARMY BASE, VANDOR-3. And on nearby shelves were crimson casks marked VRADIUM and AMBORI.

Suddenly tired, Jesmin rested her forehead against one shelf.

Bhindi moved closer. "Five, you look like you want to cry."

"I do." Jesmin drew a couple of ragged breaths, trying to get control of herself.

Bhindi frowned. "I'm not familiar with—what are they? Vradium and ambori."

"Mix them together and they offer up the chemical cues that tests use to determine if a fluid contains bacta. Mix them with an inert pink fluid medium, and they *look* just like bacta. And so those two drugs are part of what is referred to as the Bacta Three-Way, or the Bacta Triangle Scam."

Bhindi shook her head. "I haven't heard of that one."

"Pretty much confined to the black market. It's a triangle because it's a three-component scam. You need new bacta, and bacta nearing the end of its useful life, and quantities of these two chemicals. Say you're the receiving officer for supplies at a hospital or military base. New bacta comes in. You take the new bacta and pour it all into containers marked as something else. Then you sneak them out of storage and sell them on the black market. You take the old bacta and put it in the new bacta containers. And you put the vradium-ambori-inert-compound mix in the containers that are supposed to hold old bacta. When those containers go through their periodic tests, one test confirms that they're bacta, but a second test indicates that they're past their effectiveness and should be destroyed."

"Oh."

"And it's worse even than just stealing a hospital's bacta. Because anywhere this scam is run, the medics requisition a cask of new bacta. It's sent up, used on a patient—or, in a crisis, like the aftermath of a battle, a bunch of patients—and the patient sickens or dies, because in the meantime that batch, which is actually old bacta, has gone bad. People die." Jesmin turned away for a moment so Bhindi would not see her face. "My fi . . . friend . . . was murdered while looking into an instance of that exact scam. During the last war."

"I'm sorry."

The door slid open. Jesmin looked in that direction. A Pop-Dog, a datapad in his hand, walked in.

The man, a Twi'lek, his skin blue and his brain-tails hanging loose, approached the aisle where the Wraiths stood. He did not look their way at first.

Then the door slid shut, plunging the chamber into blackness.

"*Stang.*" There was a clank as the Pop-Dog, probably turning back toward the door, hit a metal shelf. A dura-plast object clattered on the floor.

Jesmin fixed the scene, everything she had seen just before the room went black, in her mind. She darted up the aisle, brushing past Bhindi, and turned where she thought the intersection to the Twi'lek's aisle was.

She was right. She dashed forward, unimpeded.

Then she ran into him. He seemed to have grown shorter in three seconds—he barely came up to her waist and she tripped over him, crashing headfirst down on the hard floor. The thick ambience suit hood cushioned the impact, but she still saw little pinpoints of light dance around in the darkness like embers drifting up off a fire.

"Who's that? Who's there?" The Twi'lek moved forward, stumbled across Jesmin in turn, and slammed down on top of her.

She grabbed at him, found his neck, tried to catch him in a choke hold. But one of his brain-tails impeded her.

A shaft of light blinded Jesmin. Then there was a familiar sound, a blaster being fired. The entire chamber illuminated for a moment, blue light flickering across the Twi'lek's chest, Bhindi silhouetted by light from her own shot. Then the Twi'lek went limp and the chamber went dark again.

Jesmin froze, listening.

All she heard was Bhindi's breathing. Then, Bhindi's voice: "Five?"

"Here." She rolled the Twi'lek off her and rose. By memory, she moved to the door. It opened at her approach, allowing light to pour in; cautious, she leaned out, looked both ways.

There was no one in sight.

She withdrew, and when the door closed, she adjusted the wall switch to disable the door's proximity sensor.

She turned back toward Bhindi, who now stood in the light cast by her own glow rod. "I'm sorry."

"Not your fault."

"Yes, it was. I got emotional. Clouded my ability to sense others. My fault." She moved to grab the unconscious Pop-Dog and drag him to the back of the chamber. "I'll tie him up. You record everything."

In a darkened warehouse chamber toward the southern end of the installation, Myri stared at the shelves full of blaster rifle cases, power pack cases, grenade crates. For someone like Myri, who liked her mayhem occasional but loud, the chamber was a playroom of unrealized promise.

Then she noticed that Trey had stopped talking. Instead, he was leaning forward, his forehead pressed against a heavy-duty, locking transparisteel cabinet.

Myri moved until she could see his face. "Four? You suddenly look like you want to cry."

"I do." He stepped back from the cabinet and shone his glow rod on its contents.

The cabinet had two shelves, themselves transparisteel. On the top shelf were two silvery bowl-like stands, and in each rested a globe larger than a balled human fist—a globe with dials and a depressible button.

Myri stared at them for a moment, then clamped her hand over her mouth to suppress a gasp. "Thermal detonators."

"Two of them." Trey's voice was almost rapturous. "Two, I have to steal these."

"Is there security on that cabinet?"

"It looks like . . . Yes. Really good security, too." Trey peered at the locking mechanism, which was made of durasteel and not transparent. He crouched to give it a good look.

"You just want them for yourself."

He stood up, put a finger to his lips, and walked as quietly as possible to join her. He turned her toward the exit door and preceded her there. He slid the door open manually—they'd taken a moment to disengage its proximity sensor—scanned the main corridor beyond, and led her out. Only when the door was shut again did he speak. "There was a listening device in the case's security system."

Myri felt a chill pass through her. "So base security is already on to us—"

"I don't think so. That type of device isn't very sophisticated. I bet it just noted that someone was talking in the vicinity of the case and broadcast that fact to the central security computer. It dropped a flag saying, *That was a little odd.*"

Myri blew out a breath of relief. "But not until enough flags are dropped around the base—"

"—does the computer say, *Things are getting stranger. I'd better wake everybody up.*"

"Let's not drop any more flags."

"Good idea, Three."

Continuing on, they found more warehouses, both of them empty and dusty, and a dormitory block—two large chambers for men, one for women, both dark but sparsely occupied. Myri could hear the regular breathing of sleepers within. One door farther on led to a communal refresher. Myri could hear the hiss and feel the flow of moist air from an old-fashioned water sprayer; the old base had nothing so modern as a sanisteam. She and Trey crept past, not alerting whatever soldier was within.

In the last cross-corridor before the main hall ended, they discovered the cell block.

It wasn't a big tunnel, only three meters wide and three tall, lined with metal doors. Each door had a metal crossbeam at waist height and a metal mesh grate, through which some air and light could pass, at head height. Only one door, the one farthest from the main corridor, was lit from within.

Trey checked his chrono. "Almost time to rendezvous.

And we have the proof we need. Private ownership of thermal detonators is kind of illegal. Suggests terroristic impulses."

"Look, all our recordings can't explain why we've only had to duck two Pop-Dogs while exploring this whole wing. Why we keep finding sealed-off, empty dormitories and officers' quarters. The farther we get away from the central shaft, the emptier the place is. Why?"

"Because nobody wants to live close to a pair of thermal detonators?"

"Nice answer, but I want some confirmation. The kind of confirmation only a willing witness can give us. Like a *prisoner*."

Trey sighed. "Let's make this fast."

They moved silently up the corridor and paused outside the door that showed light from the room beyond. Both took long moments examining the door exterior, the surrounding walls for holocams and audio pickups, but there were none. In fact, the entire arrangement here looked primitive—doorway carved by long-ago lasers out of living stone, doors and fittings made from heavy, armor-quality durasteel.

While Trey looked over the door's locking mechanism—a large metal lock, crude but effective, it clamped down over the center of the metal crossbar that held the door in place—Myri stood on tiptoes to peer through the metal grate. Yes, the chamber was lit inside, and Myri could see two stuffed chairs, a low table between them, a gridded game board on the table. In each chair sat a man, both Duros males with large black eyes and gray features.

One of them glanced up to look at the door just as Myri caught sight of him.

She ducked down again.

A voice, thin but musical, floated out through the grate. "Who's out there?"

Trey glared up at Myri. "Stealth not being one of your skills."

"Four, I notice you never go on intrusions with the same member of the team twice. Diplomacy not being one of *your* skills." Myri stretched on tiptoes again and brought her mouth close to the grate. Her reply was a whisper: "Be quiet if you want to live."

"Very well."

Trey made a faint noise of disgust. "These guys make me sick. The jailers, I mean. This is a low-tech nightmare. No electronic security on it at all. The lock and the end caps keep the bar from being moved. The keyhole is for a huge, simple metal key. Ordinary lock picks won't budge the mechanism. And if I *can* get it unlocked, the bar's got to weigh a hundred and fifty kilos. The Pop-Dogs must use a lifter droid to move it."

Myri put some sweet-sounding mockery into her voice. "Big, strong man like you, you can clean-and-jerk a hundred and fifty."

"Of *course* I can. But I was thinking about someone of more average abilities. You, for instance."

"Ooh, you'll pay for that."

"If I had Five's lightsaber, I could cut through this in sixty seconds."

"Just unlock the door, Four."

"Yeah, yeah." Trey thought about it for a moment, then pulled his vibroblade out of a waist sheath. "Give me your blade."

"You've got yours."

"I need both. To disassemble."

"Oh." She drew her weapon from its sheath and handed it to him.

While Myri watched both him and the surrounding corridor, Trey took apart the vibroblades, separating the metal blade components, which could still stab and cut with reduced efficiency even if the weapon's ultrasonic augmenter or battery failed, from the electronics. He slid both blades into the key aperture and began prying and twisting with them.

Two minutes later there was a *clunk*, too loud by far for Myri's taste, and Trey withdrew the blades, which were now bent and scarred, their edges ruined. He dropped them into his pack and flipped up the main body of the lock so that it no longer held the bar.

He stood and bent to grip the metal bar, both his hands cupped along its underside. He straightened with a grunt, heaving the bar clear of its brackets, and carried it a few meters along the wall. With similar care, he set it down again, making less noise than the lock had.

Myri drew her blaster. She waited until Trey had done the same. Then, cautious, she pulled the cell door open.

Bright glow rod light poured out. Her quick glimpse showed social room furnishings, side tables loaded with computer equipment. The chairs, their occupants, and the game table had not changed. The Duros men stared at Myri with their big, dark, alien eyes, their faces schooled into expressionlessness.

Myri entered the chamber. From her new vantage point, she could see side doors that probably led to auxiliary chambers.

Trey entered behind her, pulled the door shut, and pressed his face against the grate to keep an eye on the exterior.

Myri lowered her blaster just enough that she was not pointing directly at either Duros. The men wore orange-and-yellow-striped jumpsuits, easy to see in any environment, suitable for prisoners.

Myri knew a little about Duros physiology, enough at least to distinguish age. She turned to the older man, recognizable as such by the extra wrinkling of his face, his slightly more sallow complexion. "Who are you?"

"My name is Usan Joyl. Who are *you*?"

Myri felt her jaw drop. "Usan Joyl?"

The Duros shook his head. "No, that's *me*."

Trey glanced back in their direction. "Who's Usan Joyl?"

"I am."

"He's . . . He's . . ." Myri felt herself on the verge of stammering. She tried to clamp down on her emotions. She'd grown up surrounded by famous people, but most of them weren't *artists*. "He's a master of false identity preparation. Maybe the most famous one alive. Though we didn't know for sure that he *was* alive. He disappeared years ago. We assumed he'd made himself a new identity and retired."

The Duros kept his voice pleasant. "I'll never retire. I'll die before I retire. But I'm only famous within certain societies. Who are *you*?"

"I'm . . . I'm a protégée of Booster Terrik. I was named for his daughter. I own six fleecing records on the *Errant Venture*."

"Ah." Usan Joyl at last sounded satisfied. He stood, bowed, sat again. "Allow me to present my grandson, Dashan. He is as adept as I was when I was four."

The younger Duros snapped his head around to stare at the older. Myri thought he was glaring. But he merely said, "You'd been to jail twice by the time you were my age. My record is clean."

"Things were different then, child." Usan turned back to Myri. "Can we offer you some caf?"

"No. I assume you're a prisoner of General Thaal. Can I offer you some escape?"

CHAPTER TWENTY-ONE

Flanked by two clusters of patchy, waist-high grasses, Scut sat staring at the square building thirty meters away. He kept very still, blaster rifle across his lap, macrobinoculars to his eyes, moving only to sweep his field of enhanced vision across the terrain before him.

Wheet.

That was a whistling noise, not the wind, not human, coming from well past the building.

A response came from the north: *Whooo.*

Wheet.

Whooo.

Scut frowned. He hadn't heard these noises before. He slowly scanned leftward, looking for their source.

Wheet.

Whooo.

He didn't worry about the bluehair spiders creeping up on him while he was concentrating on events farther away. They already had. Twice now while he was aware of it, perhaps more times when he wasn't, spiders had walked cautiously up to him, had begun to step up on him . . . and then had apparently decided they didn't like the feel of the ambience suit cloth. They had turned and wandered away at an unconcerned pace.

Wheet.

Whooo.

There, motion—something had moved, closer than his depth of field. Scut adjusted his optics, bringing his point of focus back toward him twenty meters. But there was nothing to be seen on that patch of ground, though Scut was sure he'd found the correct place.

He remained motionless.

From a dark spot on the ground, right at the center of his macrobinocular view, a creature rose into place. It was furred, rodent-like, with long incisors and stubby arms that ended in paws like spindly hands. It was perhaps thirty centimeters long, and it sat up out of a hole in the ground as though it had been raised by a tiny turbolift.

It opened its mouth, and that noise emerged: *Wheet.*

A call came in response from off to the south: *Whooo.*

Scut grinned. It had to be a pop-dog, the original variety. Was that a mating call, an all-clear, a *We're fine here, how are you* cry to a distant nest? And could he, Scut, get a tissue sample before they left?

The pop-dog lowered itself into its hole.

From behind, a huge, heavy hand came down and clamped onto Scut's right shoulder.

Myri, Trey, and the Joyls kept to the rail trench all the way back to the motor pool chamber. It was slow going—Usan Joyl was not a young man, and his knees did not permit fast passage—but they moved steadily.

When the motor pool chamber was visible ahead, Trey, in front, waved to stop the others. He peered at the trench ahead, clearly troubled.

Myri, in back, scooted up to join him. "What is it?"

He pointed to a spot on the trench's right side. There, a circular metal hole a centimeter in diameter could be seen. He tugged his right glove down and held his bared wrist over the hole. Then he withdrew and gestured for Myri to do the same.

When she did, she felt cool air on her skin.

Trey groped around on the floor. "All four bolts holding that panel to the trench side are gone. I swear, there was no panel undogged like that when we came this way."

"Are you sure?"

"Not absolutely sure, no." Trey drew his blaster pistol from its holster.

Myri did likewise, and moved a few meters back to have a better angle on Trey and the panel.

With his free hand, Trey gripped the top of the panel and tugged. The panel leaned open, revealing a black, open space beyond.

Trey aimed, clearly saw nothing, and relaxed. He carefully pushed the metal panel until it fit snugly where it had been before.

Troubled, he holstered his weapon. "Sorry." He resumed his crawl, leading the others on toward the motor pool.

They reached the near edge of that chamber without incident. Myri glimpsed movement in the trench ahead, though it was hard to make out because of the dimness of the glow rods. Two figures, nearly flat against the trench floor, worked their way toward Myri and Trey. After a moment she recognized them: Jesmin and Bhindi.

Myri raised her head to look beneath the parked landspeeders and other vehicles nearby. She saw no sign of Turman. Perhaps he'd finished and concealed himself.

Jesmin and Bhindi crawled the last few meters to reach them. They stared past Trey at the Duros men. Bhindi glanced at Myri. "Report?"

"Leader, meet the witnesses. Witnesses, meet Leader."

The Joyls offered low-energy waves of their hands.

Bhindi nodded. "Good. We have some, too. Not living. We're going to cook the general in his own juices. Where's Two?"

Myri shrugged. "Unknown."

"If that long-winded attention magnet delays our extraction—"

"See, here's another one." Trey sounded irked. He pointed to the side panel to Bhindi's left. "I *know* there were dog-bolts in that one before."

Jesmin disappeared. Myri saw the blur of motion suggesting that the woman had leapt straight up from a crawling position, but she vanished so suddenly she could have been a hologram image suddenly terminated.

The same instant, the panel Trey was pointing at fell over, slamming into Bhindi, knocking her sideways. It clanked to the permacrete floor; the noise echoed off distant walls. Two black-clad human men rolled out from the tunnel it had concealed.

One was lean, angular, and fair-haired; he covered Bhindi with his blaster pistol. The other was more muscular and lithe, his hair dark and curly; he covered Myri with his own weapon.

The fair-haired man glowered but kept his voice low. "Don't move!" He whispered the words, but it was a high-volume whisper, like steam escaping from a faulty caf brewer.

Then Jesmin leaned down from overhead and pressed her own pistol barrel to the top of the fair-haired man's skull. "You, either."

Bhindi stared at the man. Her eyes widened. "Sharr?"

The fair-haired man stared back at her. "Bhindi?"

Myri looked at the man covering her. "Kirdoff!"

He peered back at her, just as bewildered. "Rima? Is *this* your natural color?"

"Blasters down, everybody, before somebody fouls up irretrievably." Bhindi glared in all directions.

The man she'd called Sharr nodded. "Do it." Everyone holstered blaster pistols.

"Five, incoming?" Bhindi asked.

Jesmin rolled back over the lip and dropped silently into the trench. "No one coming yet. But that clank . . ."

Sharr glared at Bhindi. "This is a Wraith operation."

Bhindi nodded. "You guessed right. So you and your little friend—"

"Guessed, hell. This is a Wraith operation, and you're about to foul it up."

Irritated, Bhindi gestured at Trey, Myri, and Jesmin. "It's a Wraith operation, and here are the Wraiths. You need to get your—"

Sharr's glare was no less forbidding than hers. "No, *we're* the Wraiths, and you—"

"Both of you, *shut up*." Myri didn't raise her voice, but she put a threat into her tone. She pointed at Sharr. "Who recruited you for this?"

He paused, considering his answer.

Myri felt herself getting more annoyed. "Now's not the time to give me the silent treatment. If you're Sharr, you're Sharr *Latt,* and you used to be a Wraith. I'm Myri Antilles, and my father *founded* the Wraiths. So answer me. Who recruited you?"

Sharr's eyebrows rose. "Myri Antilles. I met you when you were a little girl. You probably don't remember—"

"*Who?*"

"Face Loran."

Myri turned to look at Bhindi. "We've got two teams here. Both being played."

Bhindi looked baffled. "But why?"

Myri turned toward Trey. "You said you thought we were good on flags. But what if there are two teams here dropping them?"

He shrugged and looked apologetic. "We could be in trouble."

A noise, a combination of clanging and keening wail, filled the air.

Bhindi glared at Sharr. "Do you have our Clawdite?" She had to raise her voice to be heard over the alarm. She straightened so that her eyes were above the lip of the trench. She looked northward, then southward.

"Oh, he's *yours*. That explains the ambience suit." Sharr maneuvered himself into a crouch and took a top-side look as well. "My medic darted him. Would have used a different drug if he'd known it was a Clawdite. As it is, your guy has just become dopey and amiable instead of unconscious." He turned toward the tunnel he'd rolled out of. "Everyone out, we're extracting!"

"Was it before or after he sabotaged all these vehicles?" Bhindi growled.

"His explosives bag was pretty full."

Bhindi clawed at the air above as if trying to punish some greater power for letting her down.

Now there were shouts from north and south, but no Pop-Dogs came immediately into view. A great creaking and rumbling sounded from overhead as the lift began a slow descent.

A third person rolled out of the trench tunnel. A dark-skinned human male, probably in his twenties, he was clad, like Sharr, top to bottom in black, but he also wore a black hip-cloak that would have looked good on any fashion icon. He held a long rifle, almost spindly compared to a mil-spec blaster rifle, in both hands. From his prone position he flexed his back and was suddenly on his feet, crouching beside Bhindi.

Bhindi looked at him. "That's Wran Narcassan. Sharr, you stole my sniper."

"He's *my* sniper."

Narcassan didn't look at either of them. "I'm open to offers. But let's leave first." His voice was mellow and unperturbed.

"We all need to be at the balcony one floor up before the lift gets to it." Jesmin glanced at Bhindi for confirmation. "Otherwise we won't be able to winch all the way up."

Bhindi nodded. "Go."

Jesmin led the way, leaping effortlessly up to floor level and darting between landspeeders as she raced to the column where they'd tied off their cords.

Sharr added, "Two, back her up."

"Two's our Clawdite." Myri gave Sharr a confused look, but it was Wran who leapt up to floor level. "Oh, your Two, not our Two."

Bhindi raised her voice almost to a shriek. "This is not going to end well, this is not going to end well, this is not going to end well."

A blaster bolt from the south plowed into the metal of the trench lip a meter from Bhindi's head. She flinched, then returned fire. Myri thought it was more suppression fire than an attempt to hit the enemy; the enemy was not in sight. The Joyls flattened themselves on the trench floor.

To the north, a figure in the distance moved from left to right, crossing from one side of the main corridor to the other, leaping the trench. Sharr took a shot at the figure, missed him by several meters.

Now another man crawled out of the access tunnel. He was a Devaronian, red-skinned and bald, with horns protruding from his brow and sharp, sharp teeth in his mouth. He got to his knees, spun, reached back in the hole, and dragged out yet another man—Turman, bound hand and foot, his hood off, an improvised cloth gag holding wadded cloth in his mouth. He was now in Clawdite form, his human appearance abandoned or unavailable to him.

Bhindi yanked the gag down off his mouth and pulled the wadding out. "Two, did you plant the charges?"

Turman looked blearily at her and cleared his throat. "So it has come to this. Perhaps a Rodian and a Bothan should never have wed, and yet we did. And now our union is as dead as Shacobi there. Yet can we not preserve one last happy memory of our years together?"

Bhindi paused, studying him. Then she shoved the wadding back in place and yanked the gag back up.

Myri chanced a look southward. Figures were moving there, too, Pop-Dogs in uniform, no armor, but rifles in their hands. One of them, too, darted toward the far wall, preparing to leap the trench.

Myri aimed straight along and above the trench and fired. Her shot took the Pop-Dog as he jumped. He fell, limp, smacking into the permacrete on the far side of the trench with a bone-breaking impact. Myri frowned. "Leader, in a minute they'll figure out they can jump into the trench and shoot at us, and the trench walls will channel the bolts right into our bodies. Now that we're all together—"

"Yes, Three. Let's go." Bhindi scrambled up out of the trench and ducked behind a red, open-top landspeeder.

In moments they were all up and charging toward the column with the tied-off cords. Trey had Turman over his shoulder. Sharr and Bhindi held back, moving up more slowly, providing covering fire, Bhindi north and Sharr south.

Myri saw Jesmin and Wran begin their ascent, both on the same rope, Wran holding on to Jesmin. She guessed that the second team of Wraiths didn't have winches of their own.

Reaching the column, Myri untied the next cord. "Kirdoff, with me. Four, our Four I mean, carry Usan." In seconds, she hooked up her winch to her belt and the cord.

"I'll get the other Duros topside." The Devaronian

slapped Dashan's arm, gestured toward a far corner of the back wall where the Wraiths had convened earlier, and went running.

"Where's he going?" Myri gestured for the curly-haired man to wrap his arms around her neck.

He did. "Emergency-escape stairwell. Standard on underground bases that might be damaged by bombing. Except *our* bomb's in there now, and Drikall will set it off when they're past it."

Myri entangled their legs, then hit the winch button.

"By the way, it's not actually Kirdoff. Fodrick, Thaymes Fodrick. Nice to meet you."

"I'm Three. Just Three."

"Awww. You can trust me. I'm a Wraith."

"A Wraith in an enemy facility, vacuum-brain."

She and Thaymes reached the rail of the darkened residential level. Jesmin, standing there, tossed the trailing end of her ascent cord and Thaymes caught it. Jesmin hauled them in. Wran now stood against the side wall and was methodically firing into the thrusters of all the airspeeders within line of sight, crippling them. His laser rifle was eerily silent compared with blasters.

Thaymes kept talking as they climbed over the rail. "One of the leaders should really be up here, directing. I mean, the orders you were barking out were fine, but—"

"I think they have unresolved issues." Myri glanced overhead. The lift car was halfway down. "If the Pop-Dogs had any sense, they'd lock that car down where it is right now and trap us here."

Thaymes trained his blaster pistol at the scene below. Sharr and Bhindi were now in sight, backing the last few meters toward the column. Trey began his ascent, slow because of his and Usan's combined weight. No Pop-Dogs were yet in sight below, but a constant rain of blaster bolts slammed into parked speeders all around the Wraiths. Myri estimated that at least eight Pop-Dogs were firing, and their numbers seemed to be growing.

Thaymes grinned. It was a charming expression, completely out of place in this environment. "They can't lock the lift. I can take control of it at any time. When it gets right below this level, *I'll* lock it. Which will last a minute or two, until they figure out how we did it."

"Well, that's . . . clever, I guess. But there may be forces on the lift car itself when it passes us."

Down below, Bhindi and Sharr were both in the process of hooking up winches. Myri guessed that Sharr was using Turman's; the actor, now unbound and ungagged, sat with his back to the column, apparently singing to himself.

A Pop-Dog, a female trooper, appeared, creeping out from under cover just beyond the lift shaft's northwest support column. She drew a bead on Bhindi or Sharr. Wran didn't have line of sight on her, but the others did. Thaymes got off a quick shot, missing the woman but causing her to flinch. Stun bolts from Myri and Jesmin struck her, sending her unconscious to the floor.

And Thaymes kept talking throughout. "No. Our Wookiee has taken care of all the Pop-Dogs at the big building."

"You have a Wookiee? *We* don't have a Wookiee." Myri knew she sounded hurt.

"*We* don't have a Clawdite."

Below, more Pop-Dogs were creeping in toward the leaders and Turman. The Wraiths at the rail stepped up their fire, forcing the Pop-Dogs to keep down and behind cover.

Sharr picked up Turman, a strain for him, and started his ascent. Bhindi unloaded blasterfire, ill aimed but furious, at the enemy.

"Wait a second. Your Wookiee. Female? Cream-brown fur?"

"Yes."

"I think she served me a fizz-and-brandy the other night." Myri crouched, taking better cover behind the rail, as the Pop-Dogs below began returning fire.

Wran, his shoulder braced against the wall to the right, fired. His rifle discharged with a quiet hum. The bright bolt that emerged hit just below the visor of a helmeted Pop-Dog. He fell.

Myri winced.

Trey and Usan reached the residential deck level and stopped his ascent, hanging a few meters ahead. Myri flipped him the trailing end of her cord. Usan flailed but caught it. Myri hauled them in and helped them over the rail.

Thaymes left off his semi-inaccurate covering fire. From a waist pocket he drew a comlink, pressed a button. The lift, now just a few meters overhead, ground to a halt.

All the Wraiths poured covering fire down on the Pop-Dogs, keeping them from targeting Bhindi as she ascended. The Wraith leader made a bad target anyway, a black shape rising on a black cord into a black shaft, but the blaster bolts themselves provided some illumination.

Bhindi reached the rail at the same time as Sharr and Turman. None of them had taken a hit. Myri helped them over. Thaymes started the lift car down again. It passed them, empty but for an unconscious Pop-Dog. Once it was at their level, the sound of alarms from below muted.

Thaymes stopped the car right there. He hopped the rail and dashed over to take possession of the Pop-Dog's blaster rifle and gear while the others began their staged ascent up the shaft, Trey and Usan first.

Bhindi brought out her comlink. "Sharr, what's your extraction vehicle?"

Ruefully, Sharr pointed downward. "We came in earlier this evening on a ground transport we'd boarded. We were going to take it out, too. Until *someone* triggered the alarms."

"You, probably. I guess you'll want a lift, then."

"If it wouldn't be inconvenient."

She activated her comlink. "Seven, come get us. Prepare for seven additional passengers."

CHAPTER TWENTY-TWO

Voort scrambled to the fruit-laden landspeeder. He undogged the bolts holding the wooden rack to the bed and gave the whole rig a tremendous shove. The rack with all the crates of spotmelons slid backward until almost half of it was out over empty air.

He got behind the pilot's controls and had the vehicle in the air before its console diagnostics even admitted that the vehicle was awake. He roared out from under the ambience shroud awning and accelerated all the way to the turnoff onto the children's habitat landing lot. He slewed leftward across the lot.

There were people in the way.

There were at least a dozen men and women in the lot, most wearing sleepwear but carrying blaster rifles or pistols. Some were on foot, running toward the building that had been Bhindi's target. Others were climbing onto speeder bikes or into airspeeders.

Voort triggered his running lights, shining brightness into the eyes of the enemy, and cranked his repulsorlifts to maximum. The hauler seemed to bounce as it gained another meter of altitude—Trey had done quite a job in rebuilding the old machinery. Voort shoved the thrusters up to full power and headed straight for the line of speeders now being boarded.

The pilots tried to scatter. Some got clear. Most did not. Voort roared over the line of vehicles, his repulsors hammering them down, knocking the speeder bikes flat, slamming pilots down into their seats or onto the pavement.

Some of the men and women on foot hit the ground. Others turned and fired. Voort heard and felt an impact as one rifle shot struck home.

He slewed a little to the left so that he would not hit the shooters full-on. Instead he grazed them, slamming them into the side of the children's habitat building as he passed.

Seconds later he reached the building. He made the turn onto its eastern facing, decelerating and dropping to boarding altitude in just a few meters. Now he could hear, muffled and distant, a sound of alarms. The building's sliding door was shut.

Somewhere, during all that maneuvering, he had lost the rack of fruit crates. He hoped it had landed on some of the enemy speeders.

He picked up his blaster rifle and hit the control to open the passenger-side door. He tried to keep his attention simultaneously on the console's holocam monitors and on the viewports all around him.

The building's main door slammed open, not a normal thing for a door of those dimensions to do, and dropped off its metal railings. It fell to the ground, barely missing the speeder's rear panel. The individual who had slammed it open from within—a Wookiee, fur a light brown in the overhead light, wearing a weapons bandolier with a bowcaster hung from it, glowered at Voort.

Voort kept his grip on the rifle, ready to aim.

But then Scut ran out of the building, past the Wookiee, and hurtled into the landspeeder's bed. Neither he nor the Wookiee reacted to the other.

Voort slid open the rear viewport of the pilot's compartment. "Be ready to return fire from the other building."

Scut nodded, scrambled to the rear of the bed, and readied his rifle.

Jesmin, emerging from the building, trotted past the Wookiee as though she hadn't seen it. She leapt onto the speeder bed and took up position beside Scut.

Wraiths and strangers began cresting the lip of a square gap that dominated the building's floor. They ran to the speeder, most of them piling into the bed. Trey carried Turman, whose hand motions suggested he thought he was directing an orchestra. Trey saw the blaster damage to the speeder's front panel; he shot Voort a hurt look before boarding. Voort saw a curly-haired human man, a dark-skinned man with a late-model sniper rifle and a hip-cloak, a male Duros he did not know. All boarded the speeder.

Bhindi and an angular, light-haired man emerged. They clambered into the pilot's compartment, the man in the center seat, Bhindi on the far side. She shut the boarding door. And still the Wookiee waited where it stood.

Voort looked at Bhindi. "Go?"

"Not yet."

"Piggy!" That was the angular man. He sounded surprised.

Voort stared at him. "Sharr?"

His onetime teammate smiled. "How did she recruit you? I thought you'd *never* come back. I didn't even think to try."

"It's Voort now, not Piggy."

"Right now it's *Seven*," Bhindi spoke through clenched teeth as she stared back past the Wookiee into the building's interior. "Come on, come on. . . ."

Behind Voort, someone opened fire with a rifle. Obviously targets were in range and in view.

Finally, out from the doorway came two more men, a Devaronian and a Duros. They were drenched with sweat and staggering from exhaustion. The Wookiee went into action, helping them to the speeder, lifting them into the bed. Then the Wookiee jumped on just behind the cab, facing forward.

Bhindi nodded, satisfied. "Now." Her head snapped back as Voort hit the thrusters. There was no tremendous thump from behind; the Wookiee must have known to hang on tight.

Voort steered them out over scrubby terrain, not yet heading back toward the road. "Where to, Leader?" He had to raise his voice to be heard over the sound of the suddenly straining thrusters and repulsors.

Bhindi and Sharr both started talking at once, then glowered at each other.

Voort tried again. "Bhindi? Destination? There *will* be pursuit from the other building. I can't have wrecked all the speeders there."

"And from below when they get the lift topside with vehicles we didn't wreck." Bhindi sounded disgusted. "I'm thinking, I'm thinking. We're probably under satellite observation now. We need to get somewhere we can mix with crowds and traffic . . . really fast."

"Really fast." Voort glanced at his sensor board. It didn't show any pursuit yet. "You're talking about over a hundred kilometers. We're in the boondocks, Bhindi."

"What's the next broken terrain?"

"Foothills start nearby. Real mountains a little farther on."

Bhindi made an unhappy face. "That might work, but we don't know those mountains. Unless"—she fixed Sharr with a stare—"you do."

He shook his head. "We haven't had time to scope them out."

There was a beep from the sensor console. Voort saw two blips, then a third, back near the roadside building. There was another blip far ahead, from the vicinity of the village. "We have pursuit and one incoming from ahead."

"All right. Mission objective first. We get the data to the authorities now. If Thaal knows it's all over for him, he may decide not to add killing us to the list of charges." She craned her neck to look back through the viewport. "Four! Transmit all our recorded data. All comm channels, maximum strength, so they can't possibly contain it."

Sharr added, shouting, "Three—*my* Three—do the same. In fact, you two patch your files together. Give them a big data dump."

Bhindi, still looking backward, craned her neck. "I see them. The pursuit. Two airspeeders, one swoop. We can take them."

Voort shook his head. "See how they're hanging back? Their job is to pace us, not let us out of their sight. So we can't duck into a ravine somewhere and be gone by the time the real pursuit arrives. Which it will."

Sharr kept his eye on the sensor board. "Bhindi, we need to set down, scatter, and hide out until the broadcast brings the authorities in."

"Comm frequencies are being jammed!" That was someone in the bed. Voort didn't recognize his voice. He thought it was the young man with curly hair.

Sharr gritted his teeth. "Never mind."

Now the distant pursuers began shooting—blasterfire flashed across night-black fields and stands of trees, hitting soil or plant life near the landspeeder. The shooters seemed to have little accuracy, but Voort began a series of minor course corrections to throw them off.

Nor were the Wraiths and passengers having much more luck returning fire. They were obviously being bounced around too much to get an accurate aim on any of the pursuers.

Bhindi looked back. "Four! What was that historical site again?"

Trey left off firing, turned to shout forward. "Mount Lyss Meteorological Station."

"Defensible?"

"Deep under stone at the mountain's summit. I'm guessing it's defensible for a while. Maybe."

Myri left off firing, too. She pivoted and clambered her way forward. She gripped the viewport's rim with both hands to stabilize herself and leaned in past the Wookiee's furry legs. "If things are hopeless, I have an idea."

Sharr nodded. "Definitely hopeless."

Bhindi glared at him but answered Myri. "That's more than I have! What is it?"

"Get us behind cover and slow down just for a second. I'll drop off and hide. If I can get clear of the jamming, I can transmit a call for help from one of my personal assets. I'm talking about a full-strength extraction force. I think it'll get here pretty fast—a few hours at most."

"We'll do it. You get clear and send your message. If your asset can't help or doesn't reply, then transmit all our evidence data instead and we'll hope that it does some good."

"Done."

Bhindi pulled out her datapad, opened it, brought up a map. "Here's where we are. Here's Mount Lyss. Let me switch to topological view . . . there." She pondered for a few moments. "All right, Voort. Up ahead is a drop-off. Make for it. Once we get on the other side, we'll be out of their direct sight for a few seconds. Slow down so we can drop off a unit. As soon as they've deployed, turn to course three-one-five and make for Mount Lyss."

"Understood."

Bhindi turned to Myri. "You take Five. She'll get you through. Sharr, on your team, who's best with rough terrain?"

"Huhunna. That's our Wookiee. Kinetic artist with first-rate wilderness skills. Who's going with her?"

"I am."

"The hell you are."

"I have a plan, so shut up. Give Huhunna the order."

Sharr scowled, then stuck his head out the viewport. "Huhunna! Prepare to jump when we slow down. You're Bhindi's wingmate."

Voort heard an answering rumble. The Wookiee didn't sound happy.

Voort wasn't happy, either. "Bhindi, you're a planner. A trainer. You need an infantryman for this. I've done it before; I should go."

"No back talk, Voort. This is woman's work. Time?"

"Thirty seconds until the ridge. This is not a good plan."

She merely looked back through the viewport. "Somebody pass me a rifle!"

One came forward. Myri handed it to her.

"Ten seconds." Voort kept his eyes on the sensors, saw the ground ahead simply end. He raised his voice in a bellow: "Hang on!" Then they crested the ridge.

The landspeeder was canted downward. It was a steep slope, forty or forty-five degrees off horizontal. Voort let off the thrusters. He disengaged the automatic levelers on the repulsors, revving the port-side repulsors and reducing power to those on the starboard. As the landspeeder began to tilt to starboard, he slewed into a rightward turn. The repulsor thrust kicked up a tremendous cloud of loose stones and dirt, driving it before them as if the speeder were a giant broom. The landspeeder half flew, half skidded down the slope, its left side now its leading edge as it slid. The speeder's bed remained almost perfectly horizontal.

They hit the bottom of the slope and slid leftward another few dozen meters, but had no forward thrust left. Voort adjusted the repulsors, brought them level again.

The rear thrusters began to put the speeder in forward motion again.

Voort's second bellow was as loud as the first: "Jump, jump, jump!"

Bhindi went out the starboard passenger door and was lost to sight in the darkness. Voort felt the speeder's load lighten as three in the back also bailed. Then the vehicle began to get up to speed again.

Sharr scooted rightward, grabbed the door, and yanked it shut. Then he grinned over at Voort. "You're still pretty deft at the controls, aren't you?"

Voort glanced at his sensor board. "More contacts. Some big ones, from the installation. What did they have down there?"

"Artillery."

"Stang. Navigate us to this meteorological station, would you?"

As the landspeeder roared off to the southeast, Bhindi sprinted southwest along the ridgeline, Huhunna lumbering along behind. Bhindi could hear the footsteps, punctuated by clattering rocks, of Jesmin and Myri running northeast along the ridgeline, directly away from them.

Bhindi could also hear oncoming speeder thrusters. She didn't turn to look—a single misstep on this rough terrain could leave her with a broken leg. She simply shouted. "As soon as they crest the ridge, we separate. When they spot our speeder, they'll turn to follow, and will present their flanks to us."

Bhindi's command of the Wookiee language was not impressive, but she understood Huhunna's rumble of agreement.

It took only thirty seconds. Then the roar of pursuit became very loud. Bhindi took up position behind a line of knee-high stones. Huhunna, faster when not hampered by a human, got up to full running speed and was thirty meters ahead, behind an outcropping of boulders, when the first pursuing landspeeder crested the ridge.

Bhindi braced her rifle on the rock before her and tracked the speeder, a white closed-top model with at least two rifle bearers inside. It roared down the slope, kicking up its own cloud of dust and pebbles. Just before the ground leveled off, it began a rightward turn in pursuit of the Wraiths. Its maneuver had none of the grace of Voort's, but the speeder remained upright through its turn. Behind it, a red speeder bike piloted by a stocky blond man in rumpled white clothes topped the slope and roared down in the speeder's wake.

Bhindi switched her aim to target the speeder bike, leaving the landspeeder to Huhunna. She tracked the speeder bike, led it, and squeezed the trigger.

Her bright blaster bolt hit the vehicle's rear thruster array. Bhindi saw the speeder bike's tail end slew toward the left; then the pilot lost control. The speeder rolled down the slope, its front strut hitting stone, and the vehicle began to come apart while still moving at better than two hundred klicks an hour.

There was a loud report behind Bhindi. She turned in time to see the lead landspeeder slew to the left, a gaping hole spilling black smoke low on the vehicle's right side. Huhunna had made her bowcaster shot count; the landspeeder did not crash, but it was definitely down for the count. Bhindi watched as its pilot managed to slow it expertly and bring it in for a skidding, slewing, yet successful landing.

There was still more noise coming. Bhindi swung around and aimed at the spot on the ridge where the previous two vehicles had crossed.

The next speeder, a silver-gray open-air model, crested the ridge about thirty meters north of that spot. Bhindi lowered her rifle's aim to compensate and fired, but her shot plowed into the stone of the ridge. Then she tracked the speeder as it descended and began a gentle arc to the right. She glimpsed three humans in it, two in the front, one in the rear, and saw the rear passenger turn his own rifle barrel toward Bhindi. He fired. His bolt went high, flashing over the ridge crest.

As the speeder reached the bottom of the slope and banked rightward, both passengers began to fire at Bhindi, rapid and badly aimed shots that still converged on her position. Closer, closer, too close—she went flat. Sharp stones dug into her chest and ribs, and she was grateful for the padding offered by the ambience suit. Two shots flashed over her body and hit the slope just above her.

There was a minor explosion from that vehicle. Daring, Bhindi raised her head to look. The gray speeder was slowing to land, a hole suited to a bowcaster in the right flank. Its pilot and passengers, two men and a woman in civilian dress, rolled out over its top edge, landing on the ground on the vehicle's far side. They took shelter behind it and continued returning fire.

Bhindi hissed to herself. It was good news, bad news—the constant state of life in Wraith Squadron. Her plan had succeeded brilliantly so far. All three vehicles were stopped and the other Wraiths should make it to Mount Lyss. But there were now five—no, six: she now saw that there had been three people in the white speeder—

Pop-Dogs arrayed against two Wraiths, and more were on the way.

There—a man from the gray speeder sprinting north, toward the slope to Bhindi's left. It was the enemy's first attempt to flank the Wraiths.

Bhindi shot him. She wasn't sure where her bolt took him—in the ribs, she thought. She was sure that the runner fell and stayed down. Five Pop-Dogs to go.

There was a scream from the white speeder. Bhindi glanced that way, saw that the speeder was smaller than it had been before. Huhunna appeared to be taking it apart with methodical bowcaster fire. A man sprawled behind, on his back, smoke rising from his chest. Four to go.

But now more roaring was audible, both from the west and the northeast. In the latter direction, in the distance ahead, Bhindi could see a brown airspeeder cruising at an altitude of about two hundred meters. It wasn't headed her way, but off at an angle toward the right . . . toward Voort's even more distant speeder. And the noises from the west were mixed, shrill speeder repulsors and a deeper rumble. Something big was approaching.

Another shooter behind the gray speeder opened up on Bhindi, firing rapidly, carelessly. Bhindi crawled a few meters to her left, and the shots did not track her; they continued hammering on the stones near her original position. She peered through a gap in the stones. The female trooper from the same vehicle ran in the direction the first had taken.

Bhindi fired at the runner, once, twice. Her second shot took the runner in the thigh, throwing the woman to the ground. Three to go—fewer, if Huhunna had managed to tag any of the other Pop-Dogs behind the white speeder.

Bhindi ducked as the sniper offering covering fire from

the gray speeder targeted her new position. His shots slapped into stones, superheating them, only centimeters from where she lay.

Then the enemy fire stopped. Things fell almost silent as Huhunna stopped shooting, too. Now there were only the repulsor whines and rumbles from oncoming vehicles.

Bhindi raised her head to peer over the stones. She could hear little gasps of breath from the woman she'd shot. But nothing moved.

Nothing but a pebble, clattering down toward her from above.

Bhindi rolled onto her back, brought up her rifle. Meters above her, at the top of the ridge, stood the silhouette of a man with a rifle.

He fired.

She fired. Simultaneous with the kick of the rifle against her shoulder was a kick to her gut.

She saw her enemy fold up around his rifle. He collapsed and fell, rolling down the slope. He fetched up against stones only two meters away from her.

Bhindi looked down at herself. Steam rose from a hole in her midriff. Funny that it wouldn't hurt. . . . and then it did. Pain shoved its way through her like a hydraulic ram, forcing a moan from her throat.

She tried to call Huhunna's name, but all that emerged was a low wail.

CHAPTER TWENTY-THREE

Voort's sensor board showed a growing number of probable enemies. Two blips now sped toward them from Kreedle, one close. Two big blips and four small ones were en route from the underground installation. All the small blips were significantly faster than Voort's speeder. And Trey reported that the comm jamming was as strong as before.

Voort glanced at Sharr. "Sixty seconds to Mount Lyss."

Sharr nodded. He turned to face back into the bed. "You, uh, Four. Where's the station access?"

Trey didn't consult his datapad. He answered instantly. "Cable car. Northeast at plains level. Or stairs if you want the exercise. North face."

Sharr turned forward again. "Another joker."

"Tell me you don't have a single joker on your team and I'll buy you a bottle of sixty-year-old Corellian brandy."

"I don't have a joker on my team."

"But it has to be the *truth*."

Sharr offered an annoyed sigh and said nothing more.

* * *

When they reached the site—not truly a mountain, despite its name, it was a hill a couple of hundred meters high protruding from comparatively level ground surrounded by grain fields—what must have been the cable car building was a decades-old ruin, no cabling still strung from it. Voort swung around westward. In moments, Sharr, with his macrobinoculars up, pointed to the spot where permacrete stairs and tube-metal rails led from ground level to the summit.

Voort set the speeder down near the base of the stairs. The Wraiths scattered from the speeder and started up.

The Devaronian peered up the slope. His words came out as a moan. "*Not. . . . more . . . stairs.* Kill me now." Then he began climbing.

Voort, who'd chosen the role of rear guard, stayed behind for a moment. So did Wran, the man in the hip-cloak, who braced himself against an outcropping one step from the stairs and sighted in with his rifle scope on a distant target Voort could barely see, a set of tiny running lights well off the ground.

Voort squinted at the target. "Speeder from the village?"

"Uh-huh. And they'll get here before we're halfway up the slope."

Voort took up position behind another slab of stone. He switched his rifle over to grenade mode. "I'm your wingmate."

"Thanks. But they're running in a straight line. Morons . . ." Still as a rusted droid with only one digit still functioning, Wran squeezed the trigger.

The bright light from the rifle dazzled Voort's eyes. When they cleared, he saw the distant target coming to ground at a steep angle.

It didn't level off. It hit the grain field. Moments later,

Voort heard the *crump* of its impact. "You shot out the repulsors?"

"I killed the pilot." Wran turned and began the climb.

Puffing, his chest heaving, Voort reach the top of the stairs. The landing at the top led through a gap in a waist-high wall partly cut from natural stone and partly made of textured permacrete. Behind it was a walkway, twenty meters long and four meters deep, with a natural stone overhang three meters above. The walkway fronted the north wall of the station, also cut from living stone; one doorway and two broad windows, empty of glass or transparisteel, led into a dark chamber beyond.

As Voort reached the walkway, the first four speeders were reaching the hill. One landed three hundred meters away. The others split up, circling the hill.

The Wraiths and the two Duros stood on the walkway, Sharr issuing orders. "We are now the distraction for Myri and the others down there. Our job is to prevent the Pop-Dogs from killing us while the ladies do their business. I want three teams. Shooters on the wall here." He pointed at Voort, Trey, Wran, and Scut. "Explorers, you scope out every centimeter of this base and report resources, weak spots, possible escape routes to me." He pointed to Thaymes and the Devaronian. "Civilians and the . . . injured." He pointed at the Joyls and Turman. The Clawdite, whom Trey had set down on the walkway, seemed to be fast asleep. "And dispense with the number designations, they'll drive us crazy until we get the two teams sorted out. Break. Go." He clapped his hands.

The Wraiths scattered. Voort picked a spot on the wall and peered out into the night.

Trey had his macrobinoculars up and was surveying the situation. "Two big things, I won't call them speeders, just crossed the ridge. Artillery of some sort. The Pop-Dogs down in the fields are spreading out, but they're not aiming their rifles."

"Containing us." Voort peered through his scope. He could see one landspeeder, a small sporty model, with one human woman, hard and military by the look of her, in its main compartment.

Wran sat down, his back to the wall. He glanced at Voort. "Wran Narcassan."

"Voort saBinring. Narcassan—are you any relation to a woman named Shalla?"

"My aunt. Her sister, Vula, is my mother. But my father was kind of a waste of breathable air, so I took my grandfather's family name. You're the math-genius pilot guy, aren't you?"

"That's me." Voort glanced at him. Wran was relaxing, not bothering to sight in on any enemies. "You could probably pick off one or two before they catch on to you."

"I could! But I don't think they realize we have a long-range weapon yet. I brought down that speeder, but I don't think its crew survived or that anyone else was close enough to see that a laser did it."

"Ah . . . so you're saving up for a valuable target."

Wran smiled, showing lots of white teeth. "You guessed it."

Trey lowered his optics and knelt behind the wall. "By the way, this is the Weather Walk. That's what the diagram in the tourist information said. The Weather Walk on Apex Level. The room through there is the Observatory, which was actually not an observatory but a lounge. Stairs go down into the equipment and computer chambers, the quarters, the top of the cable car run, and so on."

Sharr sat on the wall top as if daring distant snipers to fire on him. "The artillery won't stay."

Voort frowned. "How do you mean?"

"They're stolen. We ran their identifier numbers while we were down there. Reported destroyed in military exercises. Thaal probably uses the same wreckage over and over again, across a span of years, setting the junk out for the inspectors to see while hiding and selling the stolen ones. There were four down there, though." Sharr frowned, too. "That's a *lot*."

"He's stepping up his black-market activities." Trey sounded sure of his statement. "He's stolen *thermal detonators*. He must know thefts like that, as bold as that, have to be detected soon. It can't be long before he bolts."

"About that . . ." Voort looked at Sharr. "By the way, what the hell?"

Sharr smiled. "You mean, why are there two Wraith teams, both investigating General Stavin Thaal?"

"That's what I mean."

"I have no idea. Bhindi and I exchanged short forms of our mission objectives. Our stories were almost identical. Face recruited us, told neither one of us about the other. I think we almost met a few days ago—my comm and computer guy, Thaymes, spotted Myri a couple of times, flirted with her in a bar, but thought she was just an unusually adventuresome nester."

A blaster bolt hit the exterior surface of the overhang. Two meters lower and it would have hit Sharr instead. Pretending not to notice, he slid off the wall top and sat behind it. "I'm sorry we screwed up each other's insertions. But Voort, it's good to see you."

"Likewise."

Across the next hour, Voort met the other strangers as they came up to report to Sharr.

There was the Devaronian medic Drikall Bessarah,

who had darted Turman. "Don't call me Doctor. You only get that honorific if you're licensed to practice medicine."

The curly-haired man was Thaymes Fodrick, a Corellian who said he'd decided not to follow the family tradition of becoming a perpetual student. "I got well known for slicing into secure computer systems for fun. Got caught by a security consultant named Garik Loran, who shook a finger at me and let me go. Two years later, Sharr recruits me."

Huhunna, the Wookiee, wasn't on hand to introduce herself. Sharr told Voort, "I heard about this Wookiee aerialist who'd been on Kashyyyk when Jacen Solo tried to burn the planet up. Since then, just as a civilian, she's brought down a couple of military officers who abuse their privileges, which makes her very unpopular in certain circles. But when Face told me about Thaal, I thought she'd be . . . motivated."

In that same hour, a total of four blaster artillery units arrived, setting up at four cardinal points around the hill. Numerous airspeeders and landspeeders joined them, all bearing Pop-Dogs. None approached closer than two hundred meters, but now they set up a slow, steady barrage of blasterfire.

And more than that. From two kilometers out, the artillery units began beating on the hilltop and slopes. Every few minutes, a plasma pulse, large enough to look fiery rather than like a bolt of coherent light, would launch from one of the units. It would make a noise as if it were ripping the sky open as it flew, then would crash onto nearby stone, detonating. The impacts shook the hilltop, causing stone chips, tiles, and pieces of plaster to break off ancient, decaying walls and ceilings.

The Observatory chamber was shaped like an X—two long, relatively narrow chambers that intersected in the middle. The north, south, east, and west extensions ended in balconies with windows looking out over plains, with the north extension connecting with the Weather Walk. The tiled floor was littered with years of debris and even rodent nests, and stairs led down from the intersection. But there were no furnishings, no water fixtures. There was no power, and Usan thoughtfully lit the chamber intersection with Turman's glow rod.

And all the while, the comm jamming continued.

Voort switched off his comlink and the hiss that was the only noise it offered. "Let's assume that not every Pop-Dog is in on Thaal's secrets. They may all be arrogant bullies with a sense of entitlement, but a secret spread too far never stays a secret, so we can assume there's an inner core of trusted Pop-Dogs. They operate places like that installation, which Thaal uses as staging areas for black-market operations."

Sharr nodded. "Reasonable."

"What we're facing right now is that inner core. They're as treasonable as Thaal is, just not as powerful or important. I have no sympathy for them. But Thaal using them here works in our favor. He can't have an infinite number of them, and he won't bring them all to bear against us. He'll be calling in more to that installation to empty it. Clear out all evidence that it was a black-market warehouse. Thaal will do that so if there is any investigation for any reason, there's no proof of his activities at that site. At this point, he can't absolutely count on no evidence getting out."

Sharr thought that over. "I really envy you getting rescue vehicle duty last night. It means you got to wear comfortable clothes. These stretch things my team has on are uncomfortable and make me self-conscious. Those ambience suits your guys have—when the power packs run out, they'll be in hell."

"Tell me you're not drifting off into dementia."

"No. That came up by way of association. Intrusion.

The installation. Mostly empty. It'll be fast to empty, because Thaal was almost there anyway. Your man Trey thinks they even removed a false floor topside to make moving goods faster. He'll get it done by morning, I'm sure."

Wran looked over at them, frowning. "So it's important to them to get those artillery units away from here—so they won't be found and identified as stolen."

Voort nodded. "Yes. Why?"

"Thinking. Thinking."

Sharr leaned over to Voort, and his voice became a conversational whisper. "Wran's a deep thinker. And even better with hands and feet than with that rifle."

"I'm not surprised. I remember Shalla in the field. And she said her sister—Wran's mother—was even better."

"My backup plan is to have Wran go down to ground level and just kill everybody. If he can clean a wide enough gap in the enemy lines before they get him, we can sneak out."

"I heard that." Then Wran considered. "Though I am at least that good."

Sharr leaned back. "Blast it, Piggy—I'm sorry, I mean Voort—we *had* him. General Thaal. Recordings of stolen goods. But now . . . the longer we're pinned here, the more our evidence evaporates."

"That's actually why I hope Myri *doesn't* broadcast the evidence. That would cause Thaal to flee, and we might not catch him. I don't just want him out of business, I want him punished, made an example of. But if he thinks there is no evidence and we can get away, we might have another chance to bag him."

The sky-ripping noise came again, this time from the east. Voort hunkered down, bracing himself.

The eastern slope of the hill thundered. More stones rained down from above. Then the moment was past.

"You want to cause the general some grief? Maybe

leave some more evidence?" Wran had his rifle up again, staring through the scope at the northern artillery unit.

"I'd love to." Sharr sounded enthusiastic. "How?"

"It's a long shot, both literally and figuratively. But we've been giving them return fire only from the blasters. They've got the mobile artillery piece out there at two klicks, and they're not running the deflectors because they think we're out of their range. In fact, they've got some side panels open so the power plants will run cooler."

Voort raised his head to look. Though his own scope, he could see that Wran was correct. "Can you make that shot?"

Wran shrugged. "I give it one chance in three."

"Would it increase your odds to have a spotter?"

Wran glanced at him. "You're trained in that?"

"Don't teach your grandfather to root tubers, son."

Wran grinned. "Two chances in three."

Voort used his macrobinoculars for his tasks. The distant artillery unit had landed at an angle, its front and left side both visible to the Wraiths. Venting panels were propped open. Through one of them Voort could see components that Trey explained to him—main capacitor, capacitor charger, cooling for the capacitance system. He calculated range with the macrobinocular rangefinder, double-checked it with his blaster rifle scope, returned to the macrobinoculars. "Range to the main capacitor is two point oh oh three four seven klicks at the left edge of the unit, two point oh oh five four four to the right."

Wran, his eye to his own scope, didn't move, but he did blink. "Oh oh three four *seven*? How do you get centimeter readings on that?"

"Measuring by eye. I take an average of the heights of

the Pop-Dogs in the immediate vicinity, compare that with the average heights of military men of their respective species—"

"Which you've memorized?"

"Which I remember—and compare that to my readings. Then I calculate distances from those Pop-Dogs to the target and adjust for the difference."

"Will you do my taxes?"

"Wind—wait. You're firing a laser. You don't need wind or angle, do you?"

"No." Wran's voice became quieter, even silky. "Ready for nonlethal ranging shot."

"Fire away."

Though Voort's macrobinoculars were not as good as Wran's scope, they gave him a broader and taller view of the target than the scope did. Voort heard Wran breathe out, becoming as silent as space . . . and then make a tiny noise, a *click* as his trigger reached the end of its arc.

A small red dot appeared on the target ahead of the open panel. It lasted for just a second. No one down at the artillery unit reacted to it.

Wran remained quieter than a teen returning home after curfew to dark, silent quarters. "I didn't see that."

"One point six two meters left, *your* left, of the forward edge of the main capacitor. And six centimeters high."

"I read. Compensating." Wran reached up to adjust dials at the rear of his scope, minute adjustments. Then: "Reacquiring . . . going live . . . locking it down." Again, he breathed out slowly and smoothly, then began easing the trigger back.

Click.

The rifle hummed and its laser discharge flashed instantly from Wran to the distant target.

Voort saw the curved side of the capacitor indent as if

hit by a tiny meteorite. Pop-Dogs around the artillery unit turned to look at the open panel. They stared in confusion.

One Pop-Dog shouted. Suddenly he and all those around him were running away from the artillery unit.

They had time to get thirty, forty meters away. Some of them were in the act of throwing themselves to the ground when the unit exploded. Others were caught by the concussive force of the explosion. Fire and smoke roiled up from the artillery piece, propelling much of the top one-third of the vehicle ahead of it.

The instant the visual flash of the explosion occurred, Voort began counting seconds. Just short of six seconds, the *boom* of the blast reached his ears.

He nodded. "That's about right." He turned to Wran. "Great shot." Then he ducked behind the wall.

"Thank you."

"Now everyone get under cover." Sharr did so, turning away from the tableau.

"Hmm?" Wran looked at him. "Why?"

"Because experience shows that military personnel, honest or crooked, become cranky when their toys are taken away, and if it's from enemy action, they may retaliate."

"Ah." Wran settled down behind the wall.

A rain of blasterfire began hammering into the wall.

They endured a stepped-up artillery barrage that lasted an hour. Then it tapered off.

The two Duros endured the siege pretty well. They sat at the center of the Observatory chamber, their backs to the sturdiest stone wall, near the stairwell in case they felt the need to flee downstairs. Turman, lying against the wall nearby, rolled over in restless sleep. Voort spent some time there and decided that the pounding was comparatively endurable at that spot, and the Joyls demonstrated no fear.

They did have questions, Usan especially. "Can they batter their way through the mountain with their weapons?"

Voort shook his head. "Not those weapons, not in the time frame we have to concern ourselves with. They may be trying to beat us up psychologically so we'll surrender. But they really just need to keep us here a few days. We'd die of thirst."

"Ah. Far more pleasant."

"Myri, in her investigations, found out that they have some skyhoppers over at the army base, but if they loft any air support against us, the planetary government and Starfighter Command will notice them and get curious. Which Thaal doesn't want. And so on. No, their plan is just to wait us out."

"Ah." Usan nodded. "You fill me with hope."

Turman sat up and gestured at Usan like a Sith from a bygone age rousing a dragon to action. "The virtues of irony are only evident when irony itself is. Those who know not the face of Duros grasp not your meaning."

Voort frowned at him. "Turman, that was almost comprehensible. Are you back with us?"

"I am. Wherever and whoever *us* is. But I do not wish to stand." He did still look wobbly.

"Stay where you are. Keep recovering."

"So, how did your Wraiths find that installation?" Voort kept his face pressed to the small vertical gap in the wall but spoke to Sharr.

They were a level down from the Observatory, in the rubble-strewn cable car receiving chamber. The wreckage of a cable car rested on the floor. What had once been a lifting door of solid stone in the outside wall was now permanently closed, but it had jammed shut with a gap eight centimeters high at the bottom, and it was out through that gap that Voort stared. The chamber was almost as black as a cave now, and Voort's eyes had adjusted, giving him a good view of the distant Pop-Dogs and artillery emplacements.

Sharr, propped against the wall by the doorway out of the chamber, offered a half cough, half laugh. "We wondered if Thaal was comprehensively crooked, top to bottom. Which would mean stealing everything he could get his hands on. Thaymes worked up some transponders embedded in transparent flexiplast, sticky on one side. We broke into an army receiving warehouse on Coruscant and attached them to bacta casks, among other things. We tracked the signal to several locations where they were supposed to go, including Fey'lya Base . . . but then we saw signs that too many had been diverted to Ackbar City."

"Which is why you went there."

"Which is why we *didn't* go there, initially. I'm guessing now that he gave us the order to stay away from Ackbar City because he didn't want us to bump into you. But when he vanished, we decided to check that lead out. Found a warehouse in Ackbar Base they were staging stolen stuff through. Earlier today we managed to get in there and conceal ourselves in a hauler delivering food and fuel to a mystery destination—that underground site. And thus tonight's dream date with your Wraiths."

"They're good men and women, Sharr."

"I'm sure they are. How'd *you* get there?"

"Trey ran a variation on Lara Notsil's King of the Drlids scam. He didn't even know about Lara."

"Punk."

"Yeah." Voort pulled back from the gap and looked in the direction of Sharr, though he couldn't see the man in the darkness. "Come on, you're the master of psychological warfare. Face Loran, two Wraith Squadrons—*why*?"

"Not because it would be more efficient this way, obviously." He sighed. "I can't believe he'd deliberately set us up for failure. But he didn't make our lives any easier, and because of that, we're here. You make sense of it, I'll call *you* the master of psychological warfare." Noises suggested that he was standing up. "Come on. Back to the wall."

CHAPTER TWENTY-FOUR

A tap on Voort's shoulder awakened him. He looked around. He was stretched out on one section of the walkway behind the Weather Walk, his head on Trey's backpack.

He could dimly make out the features of Trey above him. "Anything new?"

"Signs of dawn in the east. Which makes it your shift."

"I meant wake me at dawn in a couple of days."

"Good try."

Voort sat up.

Thaymes, to Voort's right, looked his way. "Good news or bad news?"

"Good news."

"The Pop-Dogs aren't moving any closer."

"Bad news?"

"This makes it harder to shoot them."

A bolt of energy from below hit the rocky ceiling directly above Thaymes. It expired in a loud *bang-crack*. Stone chips dislodged from the point of impact, superheated, rained down on Thaymes. He yelped and rolled, getting clear of the white-hot debris.

Wran, on the other side of Thaymes, dissolved into silent laughter.

Voort heaved himself partway over the wall. "They've crept up to the base of the hill . . ." He let his eyes and brow show over the wall as he scanned the slope below.

Near the bottom of the stairs, behind the same rock Wran had used to brace his shot against an oncoming speeder, shone a light. It was a glow rod, held to shine up into a face—a Wookiee face, staring up at Voort.

"Huhunna?" Voort pulled back, then looked at Wran. "Your Wookiee's down there."

Wran leaned into a gap in the wall at knee height, a hole just larger than his head. He peered down the rocky slope and scanned. "There she is, waving. She's with what's-her-name, your commander."

"Bhindi." Voort peered downward again. His eyes evidently weren't as good as Wran's, but he could see a plate-sized palm waving up at them.

"They're both behind cover." Wran paused. "She made it back here through the grain field, but she won't have enough visual cover climbing the stairs to rejoin us. I'll bet she wants some covering fire. Can't tell us on comlinks because of the jamming." He withdrew from the gap and looked at Voort. "I don't think Bhindi's moving. Huhunna's just waiting there."

Voort dropped back down and turned toward the doorway into the Observatory. "All guns to the wall!"

Sharr sounded hurt. "I'm supposed to say that."

"Well, say it."

"Never mind."

Voort waited while the Wraiths abandoned their stony beds or explorations of the station's remote tunnels. They assembled, groggy and hollow-eyed, on the wall. During that time, distant Pop-Dogs began peppering Huhunna's surroundings with opportunistic blaster-fire.

Voort addressed the Wraiths. "In a moment, we're going to begin providing covering fire. Huhunna and

Bhindi are going to come up and join us. *Our* job is to identify Pop-Dogs firing on *them* and send them running—or send them to another life. This means not returning fire on those firing at us. Except Wran and me—that's our job."

Wran, Thaymes, and Drikall glanced toward Sharr for confirmation. He nodded.

Voort waited until they were all arrayed along the full span of the wall. Then he rose, leaned over the wall, and waved Huhunna up.

Blasterfire began to hit the wall, converging on Voort. He crouched and returned fire. He could no longer see Huhunna, but he could spot emplacements firing on her. So could the other Wraiths, and they rained blasterfire against those sites.

Voort went through the steps again and again. Acquire a target. Check the rangefinder in the scope. Look around the target, gauging the movement of the grain stalks to estimate wind direction and speed. Reacquire the target. Settle, calm, become as still as the stone, breathe out.

Squeeeeeeeze . . .

The other Wraiths fired more often. Voort hit more often. A mixed blessing—he wasted few shots, diminished the numbers of the enemy more rapidly.

But he was killing people, not just making them duck.

He had counted up six kills when Huhunna reached the top of the stairs, carrying Bhindi in her arms like a sleeping child. She hustled through the gap in the wall, moved to the side to be out of the Pop-Dogs' line of sight, and knelt. She raised her voice in a Wookiee rumble that rose to a high-pitched peak.

Voort did not speak Wookiee, but, like many individuals with wide travel or wartime experience, he knew curse words in a startling number of languages. Curses, requests for food and drink, demands for or offers of surrender, and the word Huhunna had roared: *"Medic!"*

The smell of burned flesh and incinerated cloth was already forcing its way down Voort's nostrils.

The Devaronian, Drikall, holstered his blaster pistol and, scrambling on hands and knees, followed Huhunna through the door into the Observatory.

"Everyone else, stay here." Voort scrambled after the medic. "Wran, direct them, rotate their fire."

Unbidden, Sharr and Scut followed him, Sharr igniting his glow rod and holding it high so the others could act within its pool of light.

Drikall, standing, peeled off his black tunic, revealing a black undershirt. He wadded the tunic up and set it down on the tile floor, then nodded at Huhunna. She laid Bhindi there, head on the tunic. Bhindi's eyes were closed.

Drikall knelt beside her and unclipped his medpac from his belt. He spoke as if to a recorder: "Patient is a female human apparently in good physical condition, age forty-five or fifty. We have an abdominal blaster wound, rifle intensity by the look of it." He glanced up at Huhunna for confirmation, received her nod, and returned his attention to the patient.

With a pair of small shears from the bag, he carefully cut Bhindi's ambience suit hood away from her face and pressed a small object to the side of her neck. Voort recognized it as a field-grade vital signs monitor. Flexible like a bandage, the size of a large credcoin, it adhered to her skin. Its surface was mostly translucent red flexiplast, and it began to pulse with a glow at the center in the rhythm of Bhindi's heartbeat—a rhythm that was too slow by far to offer Voort any reassurance.

Bhindi's ambience suit top was already unsealed. With precision and delicacy, the Devaronian used the shears to cut away the lower portions of her tunic. The action revealed that a portion of her abdomen, to the right of her navel, was covered with a bandage patch; the center of the patch was brown with crusted blood, and the skin around it alternated between healthy pink and burned brown-black. Drikall began a quick but gentle removal of the patch.

Once the patch was set aside, Voort, even with his minimal first-aid skills, could see that the wound was bad—it was broad and black and deep. Though it had been mostly cauterized by the energy discharge of the blaster bolt that had done the damage, there were places where it was still welling with blood. The smell of burned flesh became more intense.

Despite himself and his profession, Drikall winced. "We'll start with a pain suppressor and a shock blocker. They should . . . help." One after another, he pressed two micro-injectors against her neck.

Then he looked up, glancing between Sharr and Voort. "If you want her to survive . . . we're going to have to surrender and turn her over to them. Right now. Only a full medlab can do the job. The wound's too severe."

Voort and Sharr looked at each other.

"I . . . *heard* . . . that." Bhindi's voice was faint and her eyes were still closed, but she was clearly conscious. "You will not do that."

Voort approached, knelt beside her. "Bhindi . . ."

"Those are my orders. We know Thaal's dirty. They know we know. Surrender to save me, and every one of you is dead. Not just me." Her eyes fluttered open and she looked up at the medic. "What's your name?"

"Drikall. Drikall Bessarah."

"That anesthetic is good stuff. I actually don't feel too bad." She returned her attention to Voort and Sharr. "Get these kids home safe. I'm transferring command . . ."

She stopped talking; she just stared into empty air between Sharr and Voort. The monitor on her neck ceased pulsing.

"Bhindi?" Voort fell tears well up. "Bhindi?"

"She's gone." Drikall reached up to close her eyes. "I'm sorry."

Huhunna stared up at the ceiling and offered a low, almost musical moan.

"*Kark* it." Voort slammed his fist against the floor hard enough to hurt himself. He ignored the pain and stood. He felt himself shaking so badly, he wondered if he could articulate clearly enough for his implant to translate his words.

"Drikall . . ." Sharr's voice was raspy, as though his throat had become coated with sand. "Step outside and find out if anyone has any sort of cover, a survival blanket or something. To cover her."

The Devaronian nodded, walked out into the darkness.

"We need to elect a new leader." That was Scut. His voice was subdued, even pained.

Those words jarred Voort, forcing him from the nest of his own misery. Images of the other Wraiths ran before his eyes like numbers.

Sharr will be elected. Sharr's strength is mounting slow, meticulous capers that cause people to doubt their own sanity or their trust in others. Everyone else is too young, too green. Elect any of them to deal with this situation and everybody dies.

Voort found his voice. He turned to stare at Scut, but spoke to everyone. "To hell with that. I'm taking command."

Scut stared back at the Gamorrean. If ever there had been a time when the preposterous smile on his face did not match his eyes, now was it—from the nose up, he was all sorrow and anger. "No, you are not. Perhaps

Sharr will lead. If not, we must elect. Sharr was leader of his team, as Bhindi was of ours. You are just a member. And not fit to lead."

"War leaders aren't elected, idiot." Voort looked at Sharr. "I'm assuming command. You want to take it from me?" Though he had worked with Sharr through much of the Yuuzhan Vong War, though he counted the man as a friend, his tone was now one of pure menace.

Sharr shook his head. "You're senior in years of experience. And mass."

"You've got that right."

Drikall returned, Wran's cloak in his hands. He spread it over Bhindi, covering her from waist to head.

Voort continued. "Everyone, back to what you were doing before. Except you, Scut. You come with me." Stiff-legged, he turned and marched to the stairs.

Voort entered the cable car receiving room and waited only until Scut stepped through the doorway. Then Voort spun, grabbed Scut by the shoulders, slammed him into the wall, and held him there. "I have had *enough*."

Scut's voice was a little hoarse, but his tone stayed defiant. "I don't think you have."

Voort gave him a final shove, then let go, but he did not retreat a centimeter. "Take off that idiotic face. Let me look at your true self. Your Yuuzhan Vong self."

Scut reached under his ambience suit collar and peeled his merry face away, revealing the hard, angular features and glaring eyes of a Yuuzhan Vong.

Voort enunciated very clearly. "This is a direct order. I want it all. Everything you don't like about me. Every reason you think I'm not fit to lead. I want every one of those maggots of complaint to spill out of your mouth, and I'm going to crush them under my boots. Start."

"First, you are a quitter. You quit the Wraiths before. Too sad to continue. Bhindi told me that story. She should never have invited you back. Now she is dead, you will be sad again; you will quit. *Again.*

"Second, you are an illogical fool."

"Strange words to hear from a Yuuzhan Vong mouth—your kind has no idea what logic is."

"There. There!" Scut's voice rose. "I am Yuuzhan Vong like you are Gamorrean. *In part.* I have human family, too."

"Adopted. You had plenty of years before they came along to become twisted, a sociopath."

"Oh. Well, if I am all Yuuzhan Vong despite how I was reared, you are all Gamorrean. Lazy, stupid, fat, amoral, coarse. Grunt for me, pig-man."

"Is that the best you have? No, you're not done yet. Keep going. I'll know when we've gotten to the truth. If there's any truth in you."

"Very well." Scut returned his voice to normal pitch and volume. If being pressed against the wall by Voort, being physically intimidated, was making him uncomfortable, he did not show it. "I knew of you, you personally, from when I was a child. From when I first met my human parents."

"How?"

"Not important yet. But I knew about the Wraiths. Heroes! They outwit those who enslave and destroy. You think I lie? You lie. Tell me, did you become a teacher because you love it?"

"Because I love it. Yes. Because I needed to turn to the next phase of my life. All Wraiths do that eventually. The ones who survive, anyway."

"I have met teachers who love teaching. Tell me now, the whole truth like you want from me. When you are through with your students, do they go forth, engines roaring, filled with a love of numbers that you have taught them?"

"Not . . . many." Thoughtful, Voort finally took a half step backward.

"Because you have no love to bestow on them. You teach because it doesn't remind you of what you quit. You teach because it's a painless way to die."

Voort felt his fist clench. But he forced it to relax. Somewhere, buried in Scut's words, there was a kernel of truth. Unlike other instructors, he never had prize students. He never seemed to infect his pupils with the love of the art of numbers.

What *did* that mean?

Scut continued, relentless. "You are not a fit teammate, much less a leader, because every day you show us that you have let down every teammate who ever worked with you, especially those who died serving with you, and you will let us down the same way."

"Explain."

"Because you are not full of life, idiot! You saved, you preserved. My own human father among them. And now, when you are reminded of times gone by, you do nothing but grieve. The ones who have fallen, would they smile to know that all you do is grieve and count your losses? That you dress yourself in their burial shrouds?" Scut took a deep breath. "Bhindi just died at your side. And now you will never speak her name again, any more than you speak the names of those who fell before. Bhindi died knowing that you will not tell happy stories of her, or use her example to inspire. Just like your numbers, you cannot impart love of us."

Voort felt his anger ebbing. The change was probably more due to adrenaline fading than to Scut's argument. He injected a little mockery into his next words; his implant, trained to interpret certain vocal traits, did add the appropriate sarcasm to his tone. "I am so very, very sorry I didn't live up to your expectations."

"I think you are lying."

"You mentioned your human father before. We helped him?"

"Long ago. The Joyls' situation reminds me of how my father met the Wraiths, including you. You saved him. Like Usan Joyl, he was kidnapped by a powerful officer for his skills. The Wraiths rescued him. In an unguarded moment, they spoke frankly to him. He learned some of their names. He learned the name Wraith Squadron."

Voort snorted. "That wasn't an unguarded moment. Face Loran used to make a snap judgment about someone the Wraiths had helped. He'd spill a few secrets. Only when that someone had skills or resources the Wraiths might be able to call on later."

"Oh." Scut pondered that. "So in an instant, Face understood that my father was trustworthy and useful."

"Clearly, Face didn't grasp how faulty your father's judgment was on certain things."

Scut let the insult pass. "And Face knew that, over time, stories of the Wraiths would filter out into the wider military and intelligence community. And even elsewhere."

"Including to smugglers and pirates. Having a fearsome reputation can win battles before they're fought."

"Wise." Scut looked thoughtful. "But more calculating than I would have guessed."

"And that's how Face knew about you? He recommended Bhindi recruit you?"

Scut nodded.

"Your father is a xenobiologist, correct?"

"No, that is my mother. My father is a multidisciplinary scientist. Inorganic chemistry, mineralogy, gemology, physics."

That triggered a distant memory in Voort. He looked more intently at Scut. "His name isn't Gorsat, then."

"Gorsat is a Yuuzhan Vong name, one I chose. It is a name not of the class I was born into, so it angers the older warriors to hear it. My father is named Mulus—"

"—Cheems. Of course." Voort nodded and let his memories float back three decades. "I remember him. I *was* on that mission. So were Jesmin's father and Wran's aunt." Voort let his voice become more dispassionate. "And so was my best friend. I had no other family, and we were like brothers. He was always playing pranks on me. I always said that I'd get him back, but I never did." He paused, forcing himself through the quagmire of the next memory. "Sixteen years later, I put a blaster under his chin and burned his brains out."

Scut's expression did not change. "I know the story. It was a mercy killing."

"Yes. But the instant I pulled that trigger, and for the next fifteen years—and still today—there's been a little voice in the back of my head whispering, *You finally got him back*. I hate that voice. And since I was stupid enough to let Face recruit me again, there hasn't been a moment when the presence of the new Wraiths hasn't reminded me of that instant. So you might think about that the next time you're tempted to preach to me about finding joy in life and telling funny stories about dead people."

"You have just admitted you are irrational." Scut's stare did not soften. "*That* was the last maggot of complaint. You have not begun to crush them."

"I can't . . . crush them all." Oddly, that admission did not disturb Voort as much as he'd thought it would.

"Then you must resign as leader. *You cannot lead.*"

Voort smiled at him. It was a teeth-baring, tusk-displaying warrior's expression. "Watch me."

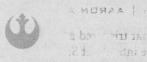

CHAPTER TWENTY-FIVE

Just past dawn, four more artillery units arrived and settled in to add their strength to the siege. The pounding of the hilltop became more intense.

Trey finished his explorations into the hill's lower levels. He returned with word of food and supply storage chambers, now empty. He had found corridors that led to chambers that had once held power machinery but did so no longer, and corridors that led nowhere. He had found circular doors in permacrete plugs blocking the way to natural caves; the doors were not locked but the caves did not lead to the mountain slope or some distant exit hole.

Trey had used a rangefinder to gauge the mountain's exterior dimensions and superimpose a wire frame of that roughly conical shape over the map of the chambers below. In the former cable car chamber, on Trey's datapad, Voort studied the results.

He pointed at one spot on the mountain's south slope. "It looks like we have a natural cave here that comes pretty close to the surface."

Sharr, one of the Wraiths gathered for the meeting, shrugged. "So?"

"So . . . we came away from the intrusion with a bag full of explosives. Enough, maybe, to breach the cave's outer wall, creating a hole we could leave through? If we could manage some distraction on the north slope, blow our south exit innocuously . . ."

Trey gave him a dubious look. "The phrase *high explosives* and the word *innocuously* don't really get along. It would be more likely if we had a really experienced explosives expert and a really good geologist. Plus, the measurements we get from a blaster scope rangefinder to build this diagram are a little chancy."

Voort fixed him with a stare. "And if I ordered you to do it and make it work?"

"I'd make it work . . . or die trying. I'd put my credits on *die trying*."

Voort made an exasperated noise. "Well, that becomes our backup plan, then."

Wran frowned. "What's our primary plan?"

"Wait for Myri to save us."

"Oh. How reassuring."

Voort closed Trey's datapad and returned it to him. "I *am* reassured. Has anybody on the wall noticed anything to suggest she and Jesmin have been grabbed? Pop-Dogs congregating at a spot out where there's no soldier emplacement or artillery unit?"

They all shook their heads.

"So she may still be our best chance for relief. Plus, we have two more resources we're unfamiliar with."

Trey frowned. "What are they?"

Voort sighed. "Back to the bad-student corner, Trey. The Joyls. Send them in."

Usan and Dashan joined them, sitting, like the others, on the litter-strewn floor.

Voort spent no time on pleasantries. "Do you two have anything to get us out of here alive?"

Usan shrugged. "Oh, dear. When they ask the hapless for help, it means the helpful have become hapless . . . Probably not. I don't know much about this area."

"But you know Thaal better than any of us." Voort tried to look approving. That was a sentiment difficult for a Gamorrean to convey facially. "I guess we'll need you to tell us all you can."

Dashan was heard to murmur, "In case you die and they get away, they need their facts to survive."

"Easy, child." Usan kept his tone calm and melodic. "That human girl who went off on her own mission? The daughter of Wedge Antilles. I doubt these people are of a mind to sacrifice us to lighten their load and just take our knowledge away."

Dashan's reply was a sniff.

Usan returned his attention to Voort. "What do you want to know?"

"I understand that you were forging new identity records for Thaal. What is that new identity? Where's the new him supposed to be from?"

Usan shook his head. "It's not as easy as that—neither part of your question. I was doing more than creating a file of data to be plugged into some distant records computer. I was creating a new type of new identity, comprehensive, more elaborate perhaps than has ever been done before."

Thaymes's eyes gleamed. "How?"

"Multiple stages, multiple levels of deception. False birth, education, and business records, the basics, yes—of course."

Thaymes, if anything, seemed more delighted. "But handprints, palm prints, retinal identification—"

"Skin prints do grow back, in humans anyway, if abraded away. But what happens if you change relevant genes, a full course of gene therapy, and *then* abrade them away?"

Thaymes's eyebrows shot up. "They grow back different?"

Usan nodded. He waited as a series of explosions

sounded from outside and shook more pebbles from the ceiling—the latest sweep of artillery hits—then continued. "As for eyes. More problematic. Treat the pupils with special dye to alter the color. And subject each eye, in a series of laser operations, to, well, what I call a retexturing sequence. Each eye undergoes four operations—"

"Stop." Even in the glow from Voort's glow rod, space-taped to the wreckage of the cable car, Sharr was beginning to pale. "Just stop. We get it."

Thaymes chortled. "Sharr? *You?* Master of psychological warfare—squeamish about eye penetration?"

"Don't even say those words." Sharr glared at him. "I've only ever strangled a man to death once, but I was very, very successful at it."

"Thaymes." Voort kept his tone light. "Whatever Sharr throws up, you clean up. Please go on, Usan."

"Also surgeries to eliminate or add distinguishing features, to alter old bone breaks and his dental profile. A comprehensive series of treatments. For speed's sake, as I was under duress, I integrated dozens of techniques introduced by colleagues or more legitimate medical scientists, and created an entire program for Thaal to experience. But I was never privy to the precise details of the identities Thaal and his loyal soldiers were to experience."

"*And his soldiers.*" Voort frowned, puzzled. "How many alternative identities will he be generating?"

"I do not know. I was never privy to that information, either. As many as he wants. He only trusts his Pop-Dogs and a few others, all military or former military."

"Interesting." Voort glanced at Trey. "His mistress wasn't military. Do you remember her name?"

"I ran searches on her." Trey frowned, thinking back. "Keura something."

"Keura Fallatte." Dashan's voice was raised barely

above a whisper. "She was in a cell near ours. For a while. Nice girl. Confused by her imprisonment. Said the general referred to her as *a loose end*." Dashan finally met Voort's eyes. "The general killed her. Shot her himself, in front of us. He told us, 'This is what I'll do to someone I love. I did it to attain my objective. Imagine what I might do to someone I find inconvenient.'"

Voort struggled for an answer, but could not come up with one. Finally he returned to the original subject. "So the instant Thaal disappears, he'll begin this transition to his new identity. Will he need you? If we drop hints that you're where he could find you, would he come for you?"

Usan shook his head. "He'll send someone to kill me. He already has his experts, his medics, everyone he needs to alter his identity."

"Commonality." The one word was spoken by Thaymes.

They waited while another series of explosions rocked the west face of the mountain. Then Voort brushed some pebbles and plaster from his head. "Explain that, Thaymes."

"He's changing lots of identities, not just his own. There have to be points in common between some of them, if not all of them. That's his weakness. If I had to forge, say, forty identicards, and I'm pretty good at that—maybe not as good as Usan here—there would be common elements to their backgrounds."

Voort looked back at the older Duros. "How about that?"

"He is correct. And, at least in a vague way, there is a profile I established for Thaal's new identity that he could have used as a template for all the Pop-Dogs."

"Let's hear it."

Usan paused a moment, staring at the wall above and behind Voort. Then he returned his attention to the

Gamorrean. "First, the planet the false identity is from will be one that has had a significant catastrophe or disruption in the past. The person's date of birth will be from the time of the catastrophe or before it. For instance, Coruscant, conquered and transformed by the Yuuzhan Vong less than twenty years ago. Thaal's own world of Carida. Alderaan, destroyed nearly forty-five years ago. And so on."

Voort nodded. "The disruption in question accounting for a limited number of records and a limited number of people who might be expected to have known the person. In other words, this identity is set up to withstand more than casual investigation."

"Correct." Usan sounded approving. "It will hold up to the most rigorous investigation. Second, the government bureau or other agency that recorded the birth and any other details must not maintain noneditable records or archives. This also goes for academic records, sports achievements, and so on."

Thaymes brightened. "Meaning that you're confident that you can crack the security on the editable records . . . but if those records are backed up in some noneditable way, anyone going back through the archives could spot the discrepancy. So you prevent any discrepancy by choosing only those records that can be altered, no matter how difficult that alteration is."

"Very good." Usan looked at his grandson. "Clearly, we have fallen in with scoundrels."

Dashan nodded. "I feel very comfortable with them. I'd be more comfortable if we weren't being bombarded."

"You are wise beyond your years. Third, I told you that the individual receiving the new identity experienced a genetic therapy treatment that resulted in some genetic alteration. Enough to give him a unique genetic numerical identifier, enough to 'prove' that he is not who he was before. But it's still possible for a comprehensive set of laboratory tests, performed on new tissue samples compared with old tissue samples, to establish a link. Therefore all old, pre-change tissue samples must be stolen, destroyed. To prevent such a laboratory comparison."

Voort considered that. "So if you've been hospitalized for an injury, and tissue samples were taken—"

Usan nodded. "They must be eliminated."

"So tissue-bank thefts or sabotage at various hospitals suggest that they were storing samples from people who later went through the transformation process." Voort scratched his cheek. "That helps tell us who's part of the conspiracy . . . at this end. But not where they go after the change."

"Wait a moment." Turman's eyes widened as if he'd just been splashed with cold water. "Aren't your family members a type of genetic tissue sample that can be matched to yours? Their own gene structures could be compared with the person who's received the transformation."

"Yessss." Usan hissed out the word. "So you will see a specific set of results from that fact. Pop-Dogs who have no children or other immediate family are more likely to be in the clear. Those who do have blood relations will either take those family members with them into disappearance, if they trust them utterly . . . or see to it that those family members disappear. Thaal has no immediate family members."

Turman's face lost all expression. "And his mistress?"

"She had family."

"So . . ." Voort shook his head, unable to arrive at a complete answer. "We might be able to figure out who's part of his conspiracy by comparing these characteristics of people, especially Pop-Dogs and their family members. But how do we find them, once they've fled?

Scattered all over the galaxy? And how do we pinpoint which one is Thaal?"

The others fell silent. The walls began to shake from a new artillery pounding. Plaster and stone chips descended upon them from above. Then the pounding ended.

Turman spoke, and his voice was deeper, rougher than usual. "You idiots clearly have no idea what you're dealing with."

The others looked at him. Voort leaned toward him. "What?"

Suddenly Turman was on his feet, pacing. His walk was now wrong for his lithe build; he looked as though he were abruptly carrying an extra twenty or thirty kilos of body weight. "I'm not just going to retire, you know. I've commanded for decades. I've decided whether men and women live or *die*. You just don't give that up."

Trey opened his mouth to respond, but Voort waved him quiet. He gestured for everyone to remain still.

"I will never abandon my leadership role. All my good boys and girls. We'll build an empire, a financial empire." Turman looked thoughtful and stared at the near wall as if viewing distant stars through it. "I already have its beginnings, my fleet. I wasn't just stealing those vessels for their cargo, you know. The vessels, they're the most valuable part. Why have none of them turned up on the black market, in pirate hands? Because they're *mine*. I'm still operating them. My fleet . . ."

Voort felt bristles rising on the back of his neck. He smoothed them down and spoke directly to Turman. "What about the Empire?"

"For me, it was never about the Empire. It was about me. My fortune. My boys and girls. I've been taking ships since the conspiracy started, before there was any chance of it being uncovered."

"That's crazy." Voort forced a little contempt into his

voice. "Senator Treen of Kuat was an Empire loyalist. She would never have helped you set up HyperTech just to steal cargo vessels."

"She thought I was doing something else. She thought . . . She thought . . ." Turman wavered. He passed a hand over his eyes, then straightened. He turned an apologetic look on Voort. "I'm sorry. I've lost the character."

"No, no, you did great." Voort heaved himself to his feet. "It makes sense. They *aren't* scattering across the galaxy. Thaal would lose most of his power if they did. They're going to set up as a unit together somewhere. To run their fleet, maybe as pirates, maybe as legitimate shippers."

Sharr cleared his throat. "Turman, it's not necessarily such a good idea to get that deep in the enemy's mind. Take it from one who knows."

"But what . . ." Voort looked among the others. "What was HyperTech doing? Do we have to relocate to Kuat and raid them next?"

"No." Thaymes's face lit up. "I know what they were doing."

They were interrupted by a shout from above, Drikall's voice. "Something's happening!"

CHAPTER TWENTY-SIX

Voort reached the top of the stairs at Apex Level and trotted out to the Weather Walk. Most of the other Wraiths were out there already, heads low, peering out across the grain fields. Voort moved beside Scut and knelt.

Out in the fields, a different artillery unit had taken position beside the burned wreckage that Wran had caused. It fired just as Voort looked at it, and moments later an explosion sounded on the mountain slope dozens of meters above Voort's head. Stones, some of them the size of airspeeders, rained down past the Weather Walk. Pop-Dog snipers continued to fire occasionally from behind airspeeders, their blasters braced against the vehicles' sides.

But some of the Pop-Dogs were standing, looking off to the east.

Once the last of the boulders clattered past, Voort heard what the Pop-Dogs had to be hearing: a distant, thunderlike rumble, deep and constant.

Wran, to Voort's immediate right, gave him a curious look.

"Incoming craft." Voort leaned farther forward so he could stare to the east. There was nothing to be seen yet.

"Not airspeeders. That's a lot of thrust, but they're moving subsonic. I suspect atmospheric fighters."

Wran sighed. "Probably some of those Tee-sixteen skyhoppers the Pop-Dogs use."

Voort nodded. "Those are definitely Incom four-jay-fours. We are in for a pasting."

Then he saw them. They must have been traveling at just a few meters above the ground, but now they vectored skyward, two of them, black silhouettes with their wings in a split-X configuration.

Voort yanked himself back and looked at Trey. "Do the Pop-Dogs have X-wings at Fey'lya?"

Trey shook his head. "I don't think so. Skyhoppers here and at most of their bases, E-wings at a couple of their bases."

Voort raised his voice so everyone on the walk could hear. "Pack up, we're about to move out." He bounced up and down on the balls of his feet. "We're going to do it, Bhindi. We're going to get out of here."

The black X-wings rose to a few hundred meters, leveled off, began a new descent, and opened fire with their quad-linked laser cannons. Red lances of light spattered down on the artillery unit on the field below.

The lead X-wing struck the target with its first salvo, only a handful of laser bursts missing the artillery piece. The unit detonated, leaping into the air, bending in the middle like a quadruped attempting to buck off a rider. Pop-Dogs all around were slammed to the ground by the detonation. Those nearest the artillery unit caught fire, as did the yellow-white grain for meters in every direction.

The wingmate's salvos were less concentrated. They sprayed along the line of smaller vehicles, chewing through airspeeders, vaporizing speeder bikes. Voort didn't think a single vehicle along a two-hundred-meter stretch escaped being hit.

The X-wings flashed by, black profiles at almost exactly the altitude of the Weather Walk. Then they were diminishing dots off to the west, banking to the left for a new strafing run.

Voort forced himself to stop bouncing. "Myri came through. Those are StealthXs."

Scut shot him a confused look. "Jedi stealth X-wings? But we heard them coming."

Sharr, rising, kept his voice patient. "The pilots are running at full throttle and with baffles off. They're doing it to panic the enemy. Psychological warfare."

Voort caught sight of a third flying craft off to the east, a *Lambda*-class shuttle with its wings down and locked. It was white, but there was a large irregular blotch of sky blue along its port fuselage, doubtless obscuring its registry number and other identifiable details. "A hundred credits says that's our extraction vehicle. Trey, gather up every gram of explosives we have. When that's done, Sharr, you lead the others down to the plain. Keep your eyes open for Pop-Dogs hiding in the grain. Trey, rig up a deadman switch, a detonator for the explosives. Then you and Scut come with me."

The StealthX fighters looped around Mount Lyss again and again. The artillery units were all gone by the end of their first orbit—Voort heard each of them detonate. Subsequent passes eliminated every speeder on the ground and scattered Pop-Dogs in every direction. Scores of fires burned brightly and began spreading across the grain fields.

A kilometer out from the line of destruction, Myri and Jesmin—rumpled, dirty, and flecked with bits of grain—stood.

Myri glanced at her comlink-equipped datapad. "Jamming's stopped. Call the shuttle to our location, would you?"

"I'm on it."

Myri triggered her own comlink. "Three to Leader, Three to Leader. I'm pinging you our location. We're extracting here."

Thaymes's voice came back. "*I'm* Three. And message received. We're on our way. Who the hell did you call for help, anyway?"

Myri paused while the StealthXs screamed by overhead and a succession of laser hits blanketed all other noise. Then she smiled and answered, a considerable quantity of little girl in her voice. "I called Daddy." She flipped the datapad shut and looked at Jesmin. "When you've lost everything else, you can always count on Daddy."

Jesmin nodded. "I know that."

Then Myri frowned. "Why didn't Bhindi answer?"

Up in the Observatory, Voort knelt beside Bhindi and carefully drew the cloak off her. He stared down into her lifeless face.

His true voice was hoarse. His throat implant ignored the fact, and the Basic words that emerged from his mouth were in an incongruously pleasant tone. "Bhindi, I have to ask one last favor of you. I don't know where we're going from here. Taking you along might lead to some of the Wraiths being captured. Leaving you here will mean you'll be identified and all our identities will eventually be known. Our families would be endangered. I know you understand. I just wish it didn't have to be this way."

Voort waited a moment, as if for an answer, but there was none. He rubbed a tear from his eye and looked up at Scut. "Put it on her."

Scut, features expressionless, leaned over and carefully fitted his smiling neoglith masquer onto Bhindi's head, tucking her hair up beneath it. He straightened when he was done. Bhindi was now a study in contrasts—a human with a fleshy man's face and a slender woman's body, eyes closed as if in sleep but lips upturned in an active smile.

Voort turned his attention to Trey. "Your turn."

Trey knelt on the other side of the body from Voort. He held a black backpack in both hands. His improvised deadman switch was wired atop it. "This is set for one second."

Voort nodded.

"My point is, this is kind of chancy. One slip and this whole mountaintop goes up *way* prematurely. I think you two had better head on downhill while I finish here."

Voort shook his head. "Scut can go if he wants."

"I do not."

Trey depressed the activator button on the deadman switch and held it down with his thumb. "We're armed. Please lift her."

Carefully, even tenderly, Voort took Bhindi by both shoulders and lifted, bringing her back up off the floor.

Trey slid the pack beneath her. "Lower her."

Voort did, releasing her completely only when her full weight was on the floor, the pack, and Trey's hands.

Trey slowly, carefully slid one hand and then the other from beneath Bhindi. He raised both as if surrendering.

Voort stood and carefully spread Wran's cloak once again over the upper half of Bhindi's body. Then he looked at Trey and Scut. "Let's go."

The shuttle, its wings rising to their vertical locked position, and the lead X-wing, its S-foils closing, descended to land mere meters apart. The wingmate's fighter stayed circling at altitude.

The lead X-wing's pilot popped his canopy, nimbly climbed out of the cockpit, and swung over the edge to drop to the ground. Myri rushed over to embrace him. "You came *fast*."

Retired general Wedge Antilles, veteran of both Galactic civil wars and every New Republic or Galactic Alliance war in between, pulled his helmet free and returned the embrace. A lean man, not tall, he had graying hair just slightly shaggier than a military cut. Instead of a traditional orange jumpsuit with black-and-white accessories, he wore an all-black pilot's suit more appropriate for these X-wings.

He smiled down into his daughter's face. "It felt like forever. *You* try borrowing two war machines, a shuttle, and two crazy pilots on short notice. I had to cash in some serious markers."

She beamed up at him. "It's not that hard. *I* just did it."

"Braggart." He kissed her, then donned the helmet again and snapped its visor down into place. "I've got to get airborne again. Can't leave Tycho up there all by himself. He gets lonely."

Myri's voice turned wistful. "I'll see you soon."

Wedge gripped the lip of his cockpit, pulled, and sprang up onto the S-foil, then rapidly climbed back in. "Write your mother."

Voort, arriving on the heels of Trey and Scut at the extraction site, was twenty meters from the StealthX and the shuttle when he recognized who the departing pilot was. He threw an informal salute. He got an answering wave; then the starfighter's canopy came down and the fighter began its rise into the air.

Voort lumbered up the boarding ramp of the shuttle behind Scut. He was the last Wraith to board. The others were already strapping themselves into seats. The faces of Jesmin and Myri were rigid with shock. Obviously they'd just learned about Bhindi.

From his seat, Sharr caught Voort's eye. "I don't know our pilot."

"If Wedge Antilles chose him, I'm sure he's fine, if not great." But Voort headed forward to the cockpit.

The cockpit door was open, and there was a little patch of red hair to be glimpsed just above the back of the pilot's seat. No one sat in the copilot's seat.

"Captain, I'm Voort, and I'm rated on these shuttles." He leaned over the back of the copilot's seat and turned to look at the pilot. "So if you need any cockpit help . . ."

The woman who turned toward him was fine-boned, with delicate features that had been beautiful, as Voort understood human beauty, nearly forty years before and were beautiful still. In fact, laugh lines humanized looks that had once been a little chilly and impersonal. She wore her hair long, with one swaying curl that half obscured her left eye. "Piggy, get your rear end in that seat and strap down."

"Kirney!" Voort scrambled to comply.

Kirney Slane flipped a switch, and the cockpit and passenger cabin were filled with the whine of the boarding ramp rising. "If you're on Corellia and you want the best shuttles, the best pilots, and the best prices, who do you comm?"

Voort's reply was automatic—he'd seen those advertisements. "Donoslane Excursions."

"Kriffing right you do. We're lifting without a full preflight, so keep one eye on the diagnostics readouts and the other on the sensor board. Tell me about anything incoming." She increased power to the repulsors. There was a sudden lurch and they were airborne, the shuttle's wings gracefully lowering into flight position. "You put the team back together."

"I didn't. But . . . yes. It was done."

"I saw faces back there I recognize, young faces." Kirney smoothly transitioned every bit of power toward the thrusters and tilted the shuttle's nose spaceward. "Piggy, you will *not* recruit from my children."

Voort saw the sensor board light up with activity. "Four blips incoming. Sensor returns and speed suggest starfighters or atmospheric fighters. Our escorts are turning to meet them."

"Skyhoppers out of Fey'lya Base." Kirney sniffed, a noise of contempt. "What did I just tell you?"

"I do *not* recruit from your children. This cockpit smells like fur."

"Shut up. What did I tell you?"

"I do *not* recruit from your children. How's Myn?" On the sensor board, the four incoming fighters closed with Wedge and Tycho and suddenly became two.

"Grinning from ear to ear. You know why? Because we have a very profitable business and *all our children are alive*. What did I tell you?"

"I do *not*—"

General Stavin Thaal—burly, his hair in a military cut and durasteel gray, his skin burned brown by a lifetime of exposure to summertime drill yards under myriad suns, his blue uniform pressed and crisp—leaned over his field coordinator's chair, staring over her shoulder at the bank of monitors before her. He sensed her tensing at his proximity—her brown-clad shoulders and the Pop-Dog collar of her shirt rose half a centimeter.

Some monitors showed the ruined fields before Mount Lyss and its meteorological station, fires still burning, artillery units still burning, bodies draped in improvised shrouds. Other monitors, their images bouncing because they were receiving helmet holocam views, showed the points of view of Pop-Dogs ascending the mountain's stairs.

Thaal spoke into his officer's ear. "Reorder these views by proximity to the station."

"Yes, sir." She hesitated a moment, then blanked one monitor, replacing its images with text. With a series of commands, she brought up the planetary positioning system, then brought up the comlink-transmitted positions of everyone within a klick of the mountain, arranging those names and ranks into a list. She fed in the exact location of the station and sorted the list by proximity to those coordinates. Then she flicked the top twelve results to the right hand of the screen; as she did so, a corresponding holocam view appeared on a different monitor screen.

Thaal nodded. "Not bad. But not perfect. Now figure out how to make the system constantly update the views, reordering them as new signals get closer than old ones."

"Yes, sir. Shall I subtract overlapping views? So you don't end up with twelve angles on the same location as troopers congregate there?"

"Good thinking, Lieutenant. Not this time, I want multiple views of where those insurgents were holed up, but figure out how to do it either way."

Thaal felt some of the tension leave the lieutenant's shoulders.

On the lead views, the topmost row of monitors, Thaal could see troopers reaching a stony walkway that looked out over the burning plain. They approached a doorway cut into natural stone. A moment later they were through, into a narrow, long chamber, its floor littered with debris doubtless shaken from the ceiling during the artillery pounding.

There was also a body on the floor, slender, its upper portions concealed under a black hip-cloak that would have looked good on General Lando Calrissian.

Several holocam views approached the body. Flicking his attention from monitor to monitor, Thaal could see that six troopers now half surrounded it, five with their rifles trained on it, one reaching to remove the cloak.

This revealed the face of a human man, eyes closed, mouth upturned in a cheerful smile.

Something about that smile sent a chill down Thaal's spine. He jabbed a finger toward one of the monitors. "Patch me through to that sergeant."

The lieutenant reached for her keyboard. One of the troopers at the scene prodded the smiling man's body with a toe, rocking it to one side.

"I have him—" Then the lieutenant fell silent as all twelve monitor views went to static.

Quiet settled on the command center. Officers at nearby consoles stopped what they were doing to look over at the main bank of monitors.

A second later, one by one, the monitor images began to be replaced by new ones, points of view from troopers farther down the mountainside and some down on the plain.

All those holocams were now turned toward the meteorological station, which was obscured by massive clouds of black, red, orange, and yellow, a massive explosion venting from every possible gap in the stone.

And then the rock slides began to hit the leading edge of troopers climbing the stairs. Their points of view suddenly became confused swirls of stone, flesh, and blood. Some of those views winked out as comlinks were destroyed. The surviving views, some of them just showing the blackness viewed by corpses buried in stone, marched toward the top row of monitors and were replaced by views from surviving troopers farther away.

Thaal felt that chill in his spine creep through his entire body.

Aware of the eyes of the Pop-Dog officers in the command center trained on him, he forced himself to speak. "Lieutenant, get more medical resources out there. Rossin, I want that telemetry on the shuttle and the X-wings *now*. Argast, get me an update on the cosmetic work at Glitterby." It was hard to talk. A lump had formed in his throat. All those brave, loyal boys and girls . . .

He received a chorus of *Yes, sirs* in reply.

Her task done, the lieutenant spoke. "Sir? What are we facing here?"

By rote, the general turned the answer into another exercise. "What do you *think* we're facing?"

"I think . . . that the Quad-Linked Militant Pacifists are a front. A cover story of some sort. For these people."

"Good. Go on."

"They have insertion skills. Combat skills. We don't know yet if those X-wings were actually StealthXs or regular X-wings dressed up to look that way. Their activities in Glitterby Base were . . . weirdly undisciplined. I think we're looking at Jedi or Sith."

"An interesting conclusion. And it matches some of the evidence. But, no." Stavin shook his head. "They're commandos. Intelligence field agents. They're called Wraith Squadron. Their leader, a man named Loran, is dead. Their field leader, now in charge, is someone we thought for more than thirty years was dead. His name is Ton Phanan." He looked at another officer, a male captain. "You get that, Rossin?"

"Yes, sir."

"Put all your covert ops resources toward finding Ton Phanan and Wraith Squadron. And kill every last one of them."

"Yes, *sir*."

CHAPTER TWENTY-SEVEN

Myri stepped aside, pressing herself more firmly into Turman's side to let the two green-uniformed inspectors pass. Their booted feet thudded up the boxy shuttle's boarding ramp.

The droid who had been addressing Myri resumed his speech. With limbs like sticks, and head, hands, and feet that swelled into balloon-shaped extremities, the droid looked like he had been designed to be comforting to small children, and the wide, childlike optical sensors that served him as eyes reinforced that impression. "It's important to understand that, though there are Alliance military bases here, Kuratooine is not a member of the Galactic Alliance. Outside those bases and the embassy, local laws apply. In fact, it's rumored that with certain of our judges, the phrase *You can't do that to me, I'm an Alliance citizen* earns an extra three months of imprisonment."

Myri sighed as if vexed. She spun in place and threw her arms around Turman's neck, but she continued speaking to the droid. "We're on our honeymoon tour, silly. Does anyone ever commit a crime on a honeymoon?"

"Frequently, madame. Usually very thoughtless and foolish crimes. And these honeymooners raise an extra share of public sympathy while being arrested, tried, convicted, and imprisoned."

Myri tilted her head back and kissed Turman. He wore an especially kissable face now; his features were human and holodrama-handsome, his hair thick and dark. She tried not to think about the fact that what she was kissing was not his actual face but an organic mask. The thought of it twitching under her lips or opening an eye somewhere caused her to shudder.

She spun again. Turman wrapped his arms around her waist in husbandly fashion. Myri appreciated the contact; this bay, like most chambers separated from the vacuum of space only by an atmosphere barrier of projected energy, was chilly. She faced the droid. "Are they going to take long?"

"As long as it takes, madame. Would you care for a datachip about local history, regulations, and tourist attractions?"

"Give it to Bubbo." With a tilt of her head, she indicated the Gamorrean porter waiting restlessly on the other side of the boarding ramp. Bubbo shot her a dirty look.

They were in the Arrivals and Customs Bay of Skifter Station, a classic, huge ring-and-spoke satellite orbiting far above the planet of Kuratooine. Fully one-quarter of the outermost ring was devoted to customs and other civilian planetary government functions. Like other ring stations, it did not use artificial gravity—spin imparted a semblance of gravity to the outer edge of the ring. The floor of this bay, gridded off into countless landing and inspection berths, curved gently, bending upward in the distance in either direction like a reverse horizon.

The customs inspectors eventually emerged from the shuttle and presented a tablet, all screen, to Myri and

Turman. The taller of the inspectors, a Mon Calamari female whose night-black skin was stippled with old scarring, gave them what was clearly meant to be a friendly look. "All clear. Thank you for not smuggling. Palm print, please."

Turman placed his palm on the tablet and waited while a light within the device flashed. Myri tried not to appear concerned . . . and the device faded to blackness. There was no sudden blinking of red text reading, *He's wearing fake skin with a fake print, arrest at once.*

The inspector continued, "As soon as we receive payment for your visas, you'll be clear to go planetside. Welcome to Kuratooine." With little half bows, she and the human male beside her turned to leave, heading to the next spacecraft in line, an unlikely looking Y-wing of considerable antiquity. The child-friendly droid followed.

Myri let out a slow breath. "I hate that part."

"But you're good at it." Turman released her.

"What I like is the gambling. I can smell the cards from here."

Voort joined them. "You cannot. And, by the way— *Bubbo*?"

Myri grinned. "You look like a Bubbo."

"It's not the name on my identicard."

"It could be a nickname."

Voort moved over to peer out the nearest viewport. Large, with curved corners, it showed Kuratooine, a large disk of blue water and mossy green continents, white at the polar caps and sandy brown at the equator.

Myri joined him. "Very, very pretty. Too pretty for a reptile like the general to be allowed to settle here."

"We don't know for certain that this is his destination." Turman breathed the words into her ear, like an ardent husband whispering sweet nothings. "It's just our number one choice."

Myri's datapad beeped. She pulled it from her pocket and looked at the messages on the screen. "Scut's portable lab has cleared customs. He's arranging to get it planetside. Sharr says there are no reports from Vandor-Three of the general going on a long trip, disappearing, anything like that—obviously, he's pretty confident. And our payment has been confirmed. We're clear to go down ourselves."

The Wraiths arrived in twos and threes at their new temporary headquarters, a cluster of old office prefabs on the cliffside overlooking a played-out rock quarry. Situated only twenty klicks from the northeastern edge of Kura City, the property was remote enough to conceal Wraith movements; a deep stand of trees surrounding the cluster of buildings on three sides improved the site's privacy. The property was also close enough to the city and the army base beyond to be convenient.

Myri, Turman, and Voort were first to arrive, Myri piloting the *Concussor*'s shuttle, now painted a stylish silver with gold trim. They immediately performed a quick inspection of the site, making sure that it corresponded to the materials they'd been transmitted by the Kuratooine company that managed it.

Scut and Trey were delivered by a commercial airspeeder that also hauled the crate, large as a Wookiee's coffin, that held Scut's organic tissue samples and laboratory equipment.

Sharr and Huhunna arrived in a rented airspeeder, a long, black, closed-top vehicle that looked like it had been intended to transport celebrities inconspicuously. Under the rear hatch, its cargo area was filled with food and other supplies they'd bought in a marketplace in Kura City. Trey immediately got to work disassembling and upgrading the vehicle's thrusters and repulsors.

Thaymes and Drikall arrived on rented speeder bikes. They didn't immediately come to the cluster of buildings when they arrived. Instead, they roared down into the quarry and chased each other across rough terrain while Voort watched from the clifftop and pondered possible expenses incurred by wrecked swoops and broken bones. But both men and their vehicles reached the buildings intact.

Jesmin and Wran were last, arriving in a large, boxy gray delivery speeder they had purchased. In its spacious rear compartment it carried the "hot box," the dirty white duraplast shipping crate that had had to be coddled all the way from Corellia, its travels made smooth by the paying of bribes at every transfer and inspection station. Within it were some of Scut's tissue samples that would displease or even terrify local health authorities, plus a variety of weapons, including Wran's sniper rifle, that would have caused any peace officers to issue an arrest warrant.

Scut, in his new face—a tall, angular human face with a flat-top hairstyle and an enigmatic little smile—set up his lab in one of the outlying prefabs. Thaymes, assuming computer and comm duties for the team, brought in a compact holoprojector of local manufacture and set it up against one wall of the largest building's main room, the operations center. Thaymes also set up an elaborate computer-and-communications array in a corner of the same chamber.

Trey, in charge of equipment fabrication and maintenance, took possession of a prefab adjacent to Scut's lab. When not fine-tuning the vehicles, he also set up an exercise floor in one end of the same building. Huhunna rigged a hammock high in the trees near the buildings and then helped Jesmin hide sensors at critical spots in foliage around the property. Drikall set up a small medical ward, as well as his own quarters, in one of the smaller prefabs, and the others chose rooms in the same building as the ops center for their individual quarters.

By nightfall they were done unpacking and arranging. They gathered in the operations center.

Myri looked around, annoyed. "I know what we forgot. Cookware for the kitchen."

Jesmin sagged into one of the chairs left behind by the property's previous operators. "Tomorrow. We can survive on field rations tonight."

Voort moved along the exterior walls, sliding shutters closed. "This place actually feels weirdly like home."

Jesmin shook her head. "We haven't yet put explosives under all the floors to blow the place up when we leave. *Then* it becomes like home."

Voort slid the last viewport shut. "You *are* your father's daughter." He turned to Thaymes. "All right. Give me the planetary view."

Thaymes sat at his computer array and began pressing keys. The holoprojector hummed into life. A glowing image appeared in midair at the center of the room, a globe showing Kuratooine's continents. Tiny dots orbited above the globe, representing Skifter Station and other artificial satellites. More distantly, two spheres smaller than Kuratooine, the planet's moons, orbited, sometimes disappearing into an ops center wall and then emerging minutes later from another.

"So we have here a very pretty location where our target may have set up a nest. A nest where he'll take refuge when he abandons his real identity. Or maybe it's not here. That's what we have to find out." Voort indicated a darker patch on the planet's surface a bit north of the equator near the center of one of the northern-hemisphere continents. The patch lay between mountains to the immediate west and an enormous lake immediately to the east. "Kura City, which was once just Kura, a mining colony. There were precious metals and gems to be dug out of those nearby mountains, including Black Crest Mountain, just at the city's western edge, though the original veins were pretty much played out as of fifty years ago. When planets started to fall during the Yuuzhan Vong War, most members of the Kura family died, and the one survivor was right here on Kuratooine. In contrast with a lot of planetary leaders, she put out word immediately that refugees were welcome to settle here. Kuratooine was outside the control of the New Republic, the Empire, and any other planetary alliance, so Dame Kura could get away with imposing some indentured-servitude restrictions on the new settlers . . . but she was smart, too, giving every settler a fair buyout price after three years of indenture. Immigrants would work hard for three years, save every extra credit they could, get to know the environment, buy out their contracts . . . and Dame Kura would immediately loan them back their buyout funds so they could buy land."

Sharr looked impressed. "I get it. So what you end up with is a population of hard workers with long-term financial ties to, and even gratitude toward, the planetary leaders."

"Correct." Voort reached down into the bag of field rations and other supplies Huhunna had deposited on the floor. He fetched out a small packet—a self-heating dessert—and tossed it to Sharr. "So today we have a revitalized mining industry, thriving trade, slow but continued immigration, and a growing tourism business. Including Skifter Station and lots of other gambling emporiums groundside."

"That doesn't explain the military bases." Myri dragged one of the newly purchased pillow chairs to a spot against the wall and seated herself.

"Thaymes, give us a closer look at Kura City and its surroundings." Voort waited until the floating globe transformed itself into a flat map showing just the city, plus a few kilometers of mountains and lake. Now the division between Kura City and the army base just south of it was obvious—the military base's roads and buildings were arrayed in neat grids compared with the organic sprawl of the civilian city.

Sharr frowned. "We're in the field now. Shouldn't it be Three instead of Thaymes?"

Thaymes looked confused. "Am I still Three? Or is Myri Three? Sorry, I meant Other-Three."

Voort growled. "All right. Obviously, renumbering so soon after we all got numbers established in the first place isn't working. And saying something like *Team One, Wraith Four* won't work. So we'll do it the way Jesmin's father used to." He pointed a finger at himself. "Leader, or Math Boy." He gestured at Sharr. "Mind Boy. Myri, you're Gamble Girl."

It took a couple of minutes. Turman was content with Stage Boy, and Thaymes with Comm Boy. Jesmin and Huhunna both wanted Tree Girl, but Jesmin yielded and accepted Ranger Girl instead. Trey argued that Muscle Boy was too confining, not showing him in comprehensive light, but Myri's suggestion of Pretty Boy caused him to shut up. Voort assigned the very neutral tag of Lab Boy to Scut, and Drug Boy to Drikall. Wran accepted Gun Boy pending a better suggestion.

"*Now.*" Voort wiped imaginary sweat from his brow. "Where was I?"

His reward dessert half consumed, Sharr looked up. "How the military bases relate to Doomed Boy."

"That's right." Voort gestured at the army base on the map. "That was old Dame Kura again. She offered the armed services of the Alliance long-term leases on large land grants for a century for the princely sum of one credit. Plus, she or her heirs get to keep any nonmovable improvements when the military forces leave. The armed forces were anxious to accept because Kuratooine is well situated, not a tremendous distance from the Imperial Remnant border, and Dame Kura might make the same offer to the Remnant if the Alliance declined. You'll recall that the Remnant was doing pretty well at the end of the Yuuzhan Vong War. So we have Rimsaw Station in orbit, shared by the Alliance Navy and Starfighter Command."

Myri smirked. "So it's a place of calmness and cooperation, a model of how interservice relations should be conducted."

Voort gave her a disapproving look. "You're too young to be such a cynic, Gamble Girl. That's my job. And then there's the new army base next to Kura City. Blow it up, Comm Boy."

Thaymes looked at him, blank-eyed. "Explosives aren't really my—"

"Expand the *image*."

"Sorry." Thaymes manipulated his controls and the holomap altered again, its lower center stretching to dominate the whole image. Now the base appeared in greater detail, training yards and walkways clearly visible, barracks distinguishable from office and motor pool buildings. Square structures along the perimeter were revealed to be defense and observation towers.

Voort's gesture took in the entire map. "This is Chakham Army Base. An infantry battalion is stationed here, the Eighty-ninth—five companies of Pop-Dogs, a fact that brought this planet to our attention. The base was built after General Thaal assumed command of the army, another warning flag for us. It's named for a General Chakham who was one of Thaal's boosters after he defected from the Empire, but it may be noteworthy that General Chakham's daughter, Norena, was one of the original Pop-Dogs and is a newly minted general herself. Chakham Base is a test site for new weapons systems being evaluated for possible deployment. The Pop-Dogs there also have starfighters, a small unit of E-wings that are theoretically for training, a fact that annoys Starfighter Command greatly."

Voort moved a step away from the hologram. "So we started looking at Chakham Base. What did we find? A lot of personal attention from General Thaal. Several original Pop-Dogs were here for the groundbreaking and dedication a few years ago. And if we assume that he uses consistent tactics in his illegal activities, well, right next to the base, between it and the city, is a peak called Black Crest Mountain, which has extensive played-out mines beneath it. Old maps show that some of those tunnels reach as far as the new base south and into the city north."

Wran looked thoughtful. "Extensive mine works offering a lot of room to store stolen goods intended for the black market."

Voort reached into the bag for another dessert and tossed it to Wran. "Exactly. The more we look at Kuratooine, the more suspicious it becomes. Then there's Usan Joyl's new-identity profile. This world has a lot of settlers from destroyed or badly disrupted worlds. It's a tourist world, so the local government is used to bending regulations and looking the other way when enough credits are handed around. Local people are used to seeing unfamiliar faces. Comm Boy has verified that planetary government records here are replicated across a standard number of archival machines but are theoretically editable."

Sharr frowned. "How about HyperTech? Any connection with HyperTech Industries of Kuat?"

Voort shrugged. "We have no way of knowing if any of the armed forces sites here have HyperTech equipment installed. The odds say probably so."

Sharr frowned. "I wish . . ." He selected a folding

chair for himself and pulled it out of its wrappings. He unfolded it and sat on it backward, leaning forward against its backrest. "I wish we knew whether the situation with HyperTech was connected with this whole mess."

"We do." Voort nodded toward Thaymes. "Comm Boy figured it out just minutes before we left Vandor-Three. Things were confused during the extraction so he told me about it afterward, once we were on Corellia. Comm Boy, give me the graphic I asked for."

The view of Chakham Base faded, replaced by a three-dimensional rendering of the HyperTech corporate logo, a black field with the company's name made up of what looked like stars being stretched horizontally, an artistic interpretation of what bridge crews saw when jumping to lightspeed. "It wouldn't make sense for every HyperTech hypercomm unit to have ended up on a hijacked cargo vessel." Voort went on. "The 'coincidence' would have been noted a lot sooner. Which means that other units, plenty of them, have been manufactured, bought, and sent safely to buyers, including our armed forces. And when did this start?"

"We know they won the military contract before the Lecersen Conspiracy was detected." Sharr's frown deepened. "Before there was any *hint* the conspiracy would ever be detected. So if HyperTech is connected with the conspiracy, it was set up to achieve the conspiracy's goals, not Thaal's personal goals."

"Correct." Voort seemed to be in full professorial form now, pacing back and forth, making eye contact with one Wraith after another as if imparting a mathematics lesson. "We have to assume that they set the company up with one goal, which wouldn't logically have involved hijacking cargo vessels, and that Thaal somehow subverted the company for his own goals— with hijacking cargo vessels definitely consistent with his black-market operations. But what was the original use of the company? Remember, it had to involve helping the conspirators fold the Alliance into the Empire as a subject state. Remember, too, they underbid other military contractors supplying hypercomm units of a certain size. They may be running the company at a loss to do so."

"Oh. *Oh!*" Excited, Myri began bouncing in her chair. "I know. The hypercomm units are sabotaged."

Voort reached into the bag and came up with another dessert, but he held on to it. "Sabotaged how?"

Myri frowned. "Not to fail at a critical time. Not enough units are HyperTech, so a failure like that wouldn't cripple Alliance communications . . ." Then she smiled. "They're sampling all transmissions. Compacting, encrypting, transmitting them to a central location. Put enough analysts on all that traffic, and you get an ever-improving view of Alliance defenses, fleet movements, secret operations . . ."

Voort threw her the dessert. "That's it exactly. It would have to be very, very subtle sabotage. Probably not mechanical defects. Instead, we'd be talking about built-in coding that works with the specific architecture of HyperTech's computer hardware. Put the same special coding in other hardware, nothing bad happens. Nothing to detect."

Sharr's eyes widened. "This would have given the conspiracy a critical military weakness to exploit. And it still gives Thaal something very valuable he can sell. Maybe not to Imperial Head of State Reige, but there are a lot of Moffs who would pay for it. Other enemies of the Alliance might as well—crime cartels, for example."

"He'd make a fortune." Trey sounded awed. "V—Math Boy, this is more important than just General Thaal's corruption. We have to report it *right now*."

Voort shook his head. "We'll report it later. We're going to bag HyperTech *and* General Thaal."

"Not if we all get killed." Trey didn't keep the dismay out of his voice. "Not if we end up like . . . like One."

"Even if we do." Voort turned to Myri. "Gamble Girl, I have a file with all the pertinent information and speculation we have on HyperTech. I want you to get it to your father by the same back-channel methods you used to call him to Vandor-Three. If we stop communicating, he's to get the data into the right hands."

Myri nodded. "For that, I get an extra dessert."

"Done."

"Thank you, Dessert Boy. Now all we have to do is not die."

Voort finally sat, settling in on one of the older chairs near Jesmin. "What we're here for is to find out if this is the place Thaal intends to disappear to. We're under time pressure, though we don't know quite what our deadline is. At any moment, because of triggers we can't yet guess at, Thaal might decide to disappear, begin the identity transformation process, and head to his new home. If he does, if we don't find him before he's gone through the process, we'll have a very hard time proving that his new identity is General Stavin Thaal. We still don't have a good idea of why he hasn't done it yet."

Wran caught his eye. "His wife. Their divorce proceedings. She's a loose end."

Voort shook his head. "I think, to him, that loose end is tied up. He shut off her ability to get at those assets, so he can take whatever he wants and disappear. The divorce proceedings will conclude in his absence. No loose ends." He frowned, staring off into nothingness. "Why hasn't he begun the transformation? It will be hell to prove . . ." His voice trailed off. "Hell to prove . . ."

The others stared at him.

"Math Boy?" Myri tried to keep worry out of her voice.

But Voort didn't reply.

"Math Boy? Leader? *Voort?*" Myri stood and moved up to Voort. "Are you all right?"

He looked up at her, his motion so sudden, his expression so savage that she jumped back.

He stood again, and it seemed that he'd gained centimeters in height during his brief mental lapse. "Why not yet. Of *course*. Hell to prove. Of *course*."

Sharr turned to stare accusingly at Drikall. "You didn't dart him, did you?"

The Devaronian shook his head. "I was hoping you'd say he did this sort of thing all the time."

"Never in the years I worked with him."

Voort spun in place, his gaze falling on each Wraith in turn. His movement was almost balletic. "Thaal has given us a superweapon."

"Good . . ." Myri tried not to sound dubious.

Voort ended his spin looking at her. "It doesn't matter if Kuratooine was his intended destination. We need to bring him here, right now. And here we'll point his superweapon at him and pull the trigger. *Boom!*" He threw up his arms, enhancing his shout. Myri stepped away from him.

Voort ignored her. "Orders. Scut."

Turman offered him a stage whisper: "Lab Boy."

"*Lab Boy.* I need a neoglith masquer simulating Thaal's face. And something I suspect will be much harder. A full-body neoglith suit for Turman."

Scut frowned and his new human face lost its smile. "What species?"

"A *new* species! Relate it genetically to an indigenous Kuratooine life-form if you can; otherwise something from a nearby system. I want examiners to poke him, prod him, scan him, and say *This is new.*"

"Understood." Scut didn't sound like he understood a bit of it.

"And . . . gems. Do you think your father would be willing to do us a favor, no questions asked?"

Scut nodded. "I know he would."

"I'll tell you later. Witnesses! We'll need witnesses. And . . . an air skirmish, draw them in. Who's the best pilot among you?"

The other Wraiths looked at one another. Myri, Sharr, and Jesmin raised their hands. Jesmin saw Myri's hand up; she lowered her own.

Sharr looked Myri's way. "I think this one is mine. I've been piloting since Gamble Girl was seven."

Her return smile was deceptively sweet. "*I've* been piloting since I was seven. I'm not as good as Daddy or my sister Syal . . . but I'll vape you."

Sharr rolled his eyes. "We'll let the simulators settle it."

"No." Voort pointed at Myri. "Gambler will be my wingmate. Mind Boy, I need you to go back to Coruscant."

"I just got here!"

"Pack light. You'll be coming right back." Voort looked around. "Comm Boy, find out if the mine under Black Crest Mountain is his black-market base. If it's not, find out where that base is. And where its topside exit is. Drug Boy, they'll send Pop-Dogs. I want something debilitating for them, like a tear gas. Some sort of precipitating dust would be better than gas—it'd be better if the wind didn't immediately blow it all over our witnesses. Muscle Boy, fabricate us some explosives. We can always use explosives, we're the *Wraiths*. Oh, and we need starfighters. Make it X-wings. Everybody, work together to figure out if he has a local mistress." Voort looked among them and took a deep breath. "And smile. We have him. We have General Thaal."

CHAPTER TWENTY-EIGHT

Turman's handsome-husband face wore an expression of mild curiosity. "What do you think? Buy them or steal them?"

He, Voort, Myri, Trey, and Thaymes stood on one landing field of the broad, mostly outdoor business just north of Kuat City, not far from their quarry. This particular lot was thick with decommissioned military vehicles. Some were early-production-run vehicles that had failed to impress the soldiers testing them—proof-of-concept repulsortanks, armored personnel carriers with side armor panels that now looked like they'd been chewed to pieces by insects, airspeeders with slots in the beds for modular systems that never made the grade.

And there were starfighters from the orbital base. Some were old and so worn that their lift wings drooped. Others, though, belonged to designs that were simply being phased out over time, such as the four classic Incom T-65 X-wings the Wraiths stood beside.

Voort looked at Trey, who had his head in an open panel on the side of the fuselage. "Muscle Boy. You're sure about these two?"

"Huh?" Trey withdrew his head to look at Voort. "Oh. Yes." He pulled the panel shut. "They need lots of work but are in good shape. Lasers and deflectors functional. Proton torpedo tubes removed, of course, since civilians can't own proton torpedoes. Yes, I can get these two combat-ready in short order. The others, too . . . but I'd need six months and a beautiful Twi'lek assistant to fix *them*."

Voort thought it over. "I'd like to steal them . . ."

Myri brightened.

"But that would be one caper too many, I think. Our resources are stretched thin as it is. And this would be something the local authorities would look into. We can't afford to drop too many flags." Voort put additional meaning into those words. The others nodded.

A few meters away, the salesman who had conducted them here brightened at the Wraiths' suddenly affirmative body language. He was a rotund Besalisk dressed in an expensive suit and a ruffled silk bib, and his upper left arm and lower right arm old-fashioned mechanical prosthetics. Now he turned a smile that was both friendly and excessively confident on the Wraiths.

Voort clapped Turman's back. "Go get him."

"And what do I use for credits?"

"The *Concussor* shuttle."

Myri offered an obviously fake pout. "Aww. My honeymoon shuttle?"

Voort shrugged. "In exchange for two X-wings."

Myri clapped her ersatz husband on the back. "Go get him."

Turman walked off to begin the struggle with his new opponent.

Voort turned his attention to Thaymes. "All right, you. You've been grinning like one of Lab Boy's masquers since we left the ops center. Out with it."

Thaymes gave the others a conspiratorial look. "Admire me, praise me. I've just confirmed that Kuratooine is Thaal's intended getaway home. And I know his new identity. Thadley Biolan."

Voort frowned; not that anyone but Myri could really interpret the expression. "Haven't I heard that name since we've been here?"

Thaymes nodded. "One of about a thousand entrepreneurs who show up in business reports and investor profiles. He leases cargo vessel berths on Ruby Habitat up in orbit. Like a lot of rich people who don't want to get their children kidnapped, he avoids the press, and there aren't many stills or recordings of him, but I found a few." He opened his datapad, whose screen already showed a still image.

It was a man, very solidly built in shape but with a frame that looked like fat would settle on him quickly if he took to idleness. His skin was yellow, his eyes black, his forehead unlined. Thick hair and a black beard and mustache made it hard to guess what his shaven features would look like, but Voort could easily picture Thaal's face under all that hair.

Voort rubbed his chin. "So his altered genetic profile will include genes for yellow skin. Which would be much less painless than getting a full-body tattoo job."

Myri shuddered, doubtless contemplating the pain induced by a tattooing effort like that. "Was this still taken on Kuratooine?"

"No." Thaymes sounded confident. "Unless it was three years ago when they broke ground for the new base, I don't think he's ever been here."

She stared at him. "Then why do you think here's his destination? I bet he's leased or bought properties all over the galaxy."

"It was Face's report on the mistresses. I ran data on them and his wife Zehrinne through some heavy-duty comparison programs, and I got what they had in common." Thaymes swept his finger across the screen, and the image changed to that of a woman's face.

From Trey's intake of breath, Voort concluded that she was a stunner. A red-skinned Twi'lek woman, head tilted a little down as she faced the holocam, she seemed to stare right at Voort. There was the faintest curve of a smile to her lips, and her eyes promised passion and maybe danger. The top of a deeply V-necked white tunic could be glimpsed at the bottom of the still image.

Trey shook his head. "Even her *earlobes* are beautiful. Who is she?"

"Koy'tiffin. Twi'lek actress born about sixty years ago. Early in her career she did the usual range of beautiful-Twi'lek holodrama roles—slave dancers, hopeful young entertainers, fatal females. Later she concentrated more on stage work. Still acts. Now look. Here's Zehrinne Thaal at age twenty." He flipped to a new still.

It showed the former model as a very young woman, her hair long and unstyled, her eyes guileless. Her facial resemblance to Koy'tiffin was startling. "And here again, Cadrin Awel and Keura Fallatte." He flipped to two more stills, one of an outdoorsy blond human woman and one of a dark-skinned human girl wearing a mischievous grin. Both had cheekbones, lips, eye shape and spacing that resembled those of the Twi'lek star. "Thaal is one of those men who falls in love with an image and selects only women who match it . . . and only for as long as they match it."

Myri sniffed. "And throws them away when the resemblance is no longer as sharp."

"So I ran an image search for women, apparent age eighteen to twenty-five, whose facial structure was like Koy'tiffin's. I prioritized by places Thaal had personally visited in recent years and by the planets we suspected of being his destination. And here was my number one hit." He flipped past Keura Fallatte.

The new image was motion, not still, and showed a lovely long-haired brunette woman, human and apparently in her late teens, garbed in a sparkly sleeveless party gown, incongruously holding a stringed acoustic instrument and concentrating as she played what looked like an intricate instrumental piece. Her surroundings suggested she was onstage under nighttime skies. No sound emerged from the datapad to tell Voort what the musical piece was.

"Her name is Ledina Chott. From here on Kuratooine, a local celebrity. Age eighteen. She's a singer of popular music. Gossip reporters on Kuratooine's news feeds say that in the last few months she's been receiving a lot of presents and communications from a wealthy shipping tycoon, a mystery man she's never met in person. That's when I began concentrating on shipping tycoons with local interests, and the facial profiler partially matched Thaal with Thadley Biolan."

"Good work." Voort studied the image of Ledina Chott. The clip started over. "We need to be sure. Muscle Boy, you and Ranger Girl need to break into her quarters, find and copy any transmissions 'Thadley' has sent her. We'll study them. Get to know this new identity a little better."

Trey grinned, the expression broad.

"But you can't leave behind any holocams to spy on her."

"Oh." Trey sobered.

Turman rejoined them. "He wants to see the shuttle."

Late that evening, after the sun had gone down and the moons were in ascension, shining down on Kuratooine's surface, after most of the Wraiths had retired for the evening to individual pursuits, Voort rapped on the door to Scut's lab.

"Come." Scut's voice was as neutral as usual.

Voort entered, the top step of the small set of duraplast-and-wood stairs creaking under his feet. Beyond the door was a small, deceptively innocent social room, and the door beyond that led into the laboratory. Voort walked through.

The lab occupied most of the building. Side shelves held transparisteel containers, large and small, holding tissue samples, and bins on two of the three large tables bubbled and slurped with chunks of what looked like skin or meat floating in fast-growth liquid environments. The place smelled as appetizing as the Hutt space station Voort had recently visited.

Scut, not wearing his human disguise, stood beside the third table. On it lay a body that looked like a corpse that had been hollowed out and allowed to deflate. The skin was reddish brown with short, spiky extrusions that did not look particularly sharp but did seem to have a defensive function. The elbows, the kneecaps, and the knuckles on hands and feet had sharper spurs projecting from them. The forehead featured hornlike extrusions that looked dangerous.

The face—Voort had never seen its like. Two eye sockets were set deep under a massive supraorbital ridge. There was no nose; directly beneath the eyes was the lower jaw, broad and massive, with lips that were segmented plates. Toothlike ridges of blood red were visible behind them. The head looked just large enough to contain a human-sized skull.

Voort looked the body up and down. "This is the final form of the suit?"

Scut tugged at the thing's chest. It split open along a vertical seam that had been impossible to see before. It ran from the creature's neck to where the navel would be on a human. The seam opened with a moist noise.

Not looking at Voort, Scut leaned down, his head entering the empty chest cavity. He looked back and forth. His voice was hollow inside the cavity as he answered. "Not quite the final version. It conforms to Turman's dimensions, but I'm having trouble stabilizing its life cycle. This one will live only two days or so. If you must have a week, I must make more modifications." He withdrew and finally looked at Voort. "It shares thirty-eight percent of its genes with one of Kuratooine's ocean crustaceans. Genes I haven't worked with before. It's tricky."

"I believe you."

"I have been here all afternoon and evening. What news is there?"

"Muscle Boy and Ranger Girl got back with the Thadley Biolan recordings. They're studying those. Thaymes has found out a few things about Biolan. Supposed to have been a citizen of Alderaan, but grew up shipboard and built his own fleet of cargo vessels plying Rim space and the Unknown Regions. A good fit for Usan's new-identity profile."

"Ah." Scut released the creature's body. The seam began to close, starting at the bottom and working its way up, as if the gap were a quickly regenerating wound. "You are not here to talk about the suit."

"No, I'm here to talk about our upcoming action. About you causing the deaths of all the Wraiths."

Scut looked skyward, a *here we go again* gesture. "Because I am Yuuzhan Vong. Because we are all destroyers, ravagers, and monsters."

"No, actually. Because you don't support me as Wraith Leader." Voort looked around for a chair, saw none. He leaned against a wall and tried to look nonchalant. "You think I'm unfit to lead. Meaning that you'll be questioning every one of my orders in the field. Which can result in a mistake in our very complicated timing, or a miscommunication of new orders, or a last-second decision to refuse to do part of your job."

"I cannot just set aside my own judgment." Scut returned his attention to the neoglith masquer suit, watching it seal itself.

"So you think your judgment may be superior to mine."

Scut shrugged. "I *know* it is."

"And the fact that your father arrives in two days is kicking your protective instinct up to maximum power. Scut, I've got to prove to you that I'm right and you're wrong. If I don't, the probability that you'll do something that gets some of us killed increases exponentially."

Scut stood silent, staring at Voort with his blank features and black Yuuzhan Vong eyes. "I will admit, this sounds different from your usual ravings."

"It *is* different. But here, just to make you feel more at home, I'll throw in something familiar to you. You were correct on Vandor-Three. I hate your kind."

"I know." Scut moved to another table. There a white metal tub held a quantity of reddish liquid. Scut dipped his hands into the stuff, spread it liberally on his bare arms up to his elbows. It did not flow or drip off his skin. "This is a neutralizing agent. It cancels the digestive juices that coat the inside of the Embass prototype."

"The inside where Turman would be?"

"Yes. Another problem I am working on. Figuring out how to modify the design so Turman will not be digested."

Voort snorted. "Back to the subject. When you were still with the Yuuzhan Vong, when you were a Shamed One, were you afraid for your kind? Afraid that they would become extinct?"

"No."

"And when you were with the Cheems family?"

"No . . ." Scut's voice sounded thoughtful. "They kept me away from much of the war news. I simply studied. And I have seen your hatred of my kind before. My parents lost many friends when they adopted me."

"Scut, I was *in* the war. Not on the front lines—often behind them. Sometimes breaking into the Yuuzhan Vong's weird complexes. Seeing how they dealt with captured populations. Seeing how they twisted the worlds they conquered. Then I'd get back to safety, just beyond the front lines, and see all that fear and resoluteness and pain on the faces of the people of the New Republic. People who *did* think not only that they were going to die, soon, in agony, but that their whole civilization would die. That not only would they, individually, not be remembered, but that *nothing* would—nothing they grew up with, nothing they loved and admired. All gone forever."

Scut began peeling the gel off his arms. It came off like two gloves. He held them over a silver cylinder; its top surface irised open, then closed once he'd dropped the gloves within. "After the war, I learned from my parents that they had those feelings. They insulated me and their other children, my human brother and sisters, from them."

Voort nodded. "So that was five years of my life. Years in which I lost friends and watched the universe I knew being eaten away as if by a cancer. The only being I really ever acknowledged as my family died during that time."

"This was the one called Runt?"

Voort nodded. "So is it any wonder that when I think of the Yuuzhan Vong, I find myself in the middle of all those thoughts, those memories?"

"No. No wonder. I do not judge you for that. But you are irrational. And irrationality kills people in this trade.

So Bhindi told me, and so I have heard from many stories."

"Ah." Voort stood away from the wall. "Good. Which gets us to what I wanted to talk about. You would follow Bhindi but not me. Correct?"

"Correct."

"Despite the fact that her own irrationality got someone killed in the time since you joined the Wraiths?"

Scut frowned. The Yuuzhan Vong brow was already a brooding type; when he frowned, he looked like a judge ready to issue a death sentence. "You think she somehow caused Face Loran's death?"

"No. Her own."

"This is—what does Sharr call it? Transference. In your mind, you transfer your own bad trait to another."

"Bhindi was my friend." Even though the human voice issued by the throat implant remained pleasant, Voort's true voice, under it, turned heavy. "I loved and respected her. But I've been thinking about this since you and I talked on Vandor-Three, and it's clear that she made a series of bad, irrational mistakes that led to her death. She would have doomed the mission here on Kuratooine the same way . . . and you're not experienced enough to understand that."

"I want fresh air." Scut moved past him and headed to the door. "Convince me."

Outside, they took a walk along the treeless strip of land immediately around the buildings. Far overhead, just moving away from the face of the larger moon, a tiny spoke-and-ring shape, Skifter Station, drifted serenely.

Voort watched it as he walked. "You see her mistakes in several of her decisions. The *Concussor*. We could have prepared a dozen different offenses that would have given us a fighting chance if we chose or needed to fight. Sure, we didn't want to kill any innocent Alliance military personnel. But it could have been a Pop-Dog transport coming after us. It could have been Thaal, admitting guilt and just begging for a missile strike. We weren't prepared for any aggressive action. We were prepared only to cut and run. Why?"

Scut shook his head. "I don't know."

"The answer was in one of the last things she said. Here, I'll try again. All six of you going into that Pop-Dog base on Vandor-Three. That was a mission for Jesmin and Trey alone. Or Jesmin and Turman. Instead, five Wraiths went down into the installation. Which, as Trey puts it, dropped more security flags, which eventually tipped off the Pop-Dogs and sent us running. Why did Bhindi do that?"

"I still don't know." But Scut now sounded curious.

"Fleeing toward Mount Lyss, we had an improvised plan. Jesmin conducted Myri out of the comm-jamming zone so she could get us some backup. Good idea, ultimately successful. Bhindi went with Huhunna to take out the closest pursuit and provide an ongoing distraction. Was Bhindi the best choice to be on that action?"

"No." Scut frowned. "But she couldn't necessarily know who would be best because she didn't know Sharr's Wraiths. So, like you asking who is the best pilot, she should have asked who is best in fieldwork. It should have been Wran. Or you, with your experience. Bhindi was perhaps the worst choice." He sounded startled with the realization.

Voort changed direction, turning them so they would not walk to the very edge of the cliff overlook. "So. What was Bhindi's irrationality?"

It took Scut a few moments to answer. "Almost her dying words. *Get these kids home safe.*"

"Good. Correct. Sometime in the last few years she must have lost something, some objectivity about putting people at risk, especially the young. I bet she jumped at the chance to put Wraith Squadron together again. It was a chance to get back in the game. To, I don't know, prove that the unit should never have been disbanded. But the new team she assembled, most of its members so young, tripped that overprotective instinct. *Kids.* She was unwilling to put kids in harm's way, and when there was no other choice, she put *herself* in harm's way instead. And died."

"I . . . think you may be correct."

"And I'm the only one both experienced and objective enough to have seen it." Voort heaved a sigh. "And even I didn't see it in time. I was too out of practice, too far removed from the mind-set."

"Can you put the *kids* in harm's way? As Bhindi could not?"

"I almost wish the answer was no. But it's yes. I can. We have a job to do. We have to take Thaal down. It's another mercy killing. We're going to kill what Thaal has become so he can't kill others with his betrayal."

"Very well." Scut nodded. He stopped where he was and peered into the black gulf that was the rock quarry in shadow. "I will . . . give you a chance. I will support you as leader."

Voort stopped, too. "Thank you."

"But understand something." Scut kicked a pebble. It flew out over the cliff edge. Two seconds passed before it clattered on stones far below. "I have heard my father's story of his meeting with the Wraiths since childhood. He knew their objective was the destruction of an admiral and a biological warfare facility. They used my father to achieve it . . . but saved him in so doing. They did not have to. Perhaps it cost them extra effort to do it that way."

"It did."

"And still they saved him. That was on my mind as I grew up. I never met anyone who had been on that operation. Then I was recruited by Bhindi and heard that I would finally meet one, the Gamorrean-who-talks." He stopped speaking for a moment, evidently sorting his thoughts. "I am offtrack. What I mean is, I will hold you to the standards of those Wraiths."

"Fair enough." Then Voort felt a wave of something like dizziness as bits of Scut's speech broke apart, forming up in his mind like columns of numbers. They added together into a sum he could understand.

. . . heard . . . story of . . . Wraiths since childhood . . .
. . . on my mind as I grew up . . .
. . . never met . . . the Gamorrean-who-talks . . .

Voort's stomach lurched. He bent over, put his hands on his knees, drew in a couple of shaky breaths.

"Voort?"

"It's nothing."

Voort remembered Scut's eyes from every time the Yuuzhan Vong had stared at Voort. They had been hard and flat and full of hatred. Voort had seen them as a Yuuzhan Vong's eyes. But in the fifteen years after that war had ended, he had seen eyes like those many, many times, not on Yuuzhan Vong.

Students. Defiant, resentful, eloquently stating with their stares, *You don't have the* right *to keep me here and tell me what to do.*

Scut had joined the Wraiths to be like the heroes of his childhood stories and even meet them.

Voort had been one of his *heroes.*

Voort had been a *hero* to somebody.

And Voort had looked Scut straight in the eye and told him he was a monster.

"Voort?"

"It's nothing. Just one of the side effects of getting older." Voort straightened. "Thanks for your support, Scut."

"You are welcome."

"And, Scut?"

"Yes?"

Voort held out his hand. "Welcome to Wraith Squadron."

CHAPTER TWENTY-NINE

Well before the two X-wings reached Tildin, Kuratooine's smaller and more desolate moon, the
enemy starfighters overtook them.

First they were distant blips on the sensor board, moving along the flight path of the X-wings, mere hundreds
of kilometers behind. Then they crept near enough for
the sensors to identify them by class. Finally they were
close enough, only a few klicks back, that the astromechs' visual sensors could capture images to show
Myri and Voort.

Myri glanced at the image on her screen. The
starfighter creeping up behind her looked very much like
what would result if an X-wing with strike foils open in
attack position mysteriously lost its top two foils. What
was left was a nose assembly and fuselage very much
like an X-wing's, with only two wings in open and down
locked position.

It was an E-wing. It was painted brown and had a
distinctive set of stylized triangular teeth painted across
the nose in white.

Pretending she had just noticed her follower for the
first time, Myri clicked her comm board. "Hey, sweet-
heart, it looks like we have company."

Voort's implant voice responded. His Gamorrean

grunts were not audible beneath it. "We could use some recordings of our practice runs. Let's ask them if they'll help."

Then Myri's comm board popped and a male voice, louder than Voort's only because the other pilot was almost bellowing, came across it. "Unknown flight approaching Tildin, identify yourself at once."

"*Unknown?*" Myri let her voice climb into an angry squeak. "We filed a flight plan with Rimsaw Station and Kura City Flight Control. And we had to fill out different forms for each one!"

"But you didn't file with us. I say again, identify yourself. We have a lock on you." It was true; Myri's sensor board showed that her pursuer had a sensor lock, suitable to launch either laser or missile attack, on her X-wing.

Voort was next, sounding ridiculously meek. "Maybe we'd better do what they say, dear."

"Oh, *all right*. Bully." Myri switched to internal comm and spoke to her R2 unit, a flaking gray thing barely brought back to functionality by Trey. "Fuzzy, transmit Packet One to Sith-for-brains back there." Then she switched back to a broadcast channel and her sweeter voice. "I'm Rima Farstar and the fellow behind me in the silly costume is Matran Farstar, and we're doing some practice run on your moon for a holodrama I intend to make when the rest of the backers give me the money they *promised* but haven't yet transferred. We've been here for days and days, but the money still isn't here yet, my actors are bored—"

"Say again. Did you say costume?"

"Did I? Oh, yes. Matran's costume. He can barely see out of the head! He's going to crash into the side of a crater because he can't see, I swear."

"Maintain your course and speed. I'm coming up for a visual."

Myri smiled. "A visual *what*? *Visual* is an adjective, you know. It can't just float around by itself like an asteroid. It needs a what-do-you-call-it, a noun. I know this because I had to learn all about adjectives and nouns so I could write the script."

"Maintain comm silence."

Myri suspected that the pilot wanted to add, *Or I'll kill you.* But that would not have been a suitable threat. It might be recorded and presented at a complaint hearing. Apparently, even a Pop-Dog knew better than to utter it.

The lead E-wing rapidly closed the distance between the two flights. It came up behind Voort's X-wing, positioning itself behind and above in classic dogfight laser-attack position. It maintained that position for about thirty seconds, then accelerated and repeated the process with Myri.

She loosened her seat restraints, twisted around so she could look back at the E-wing pilot, waved, and blew him a kiss.

"Rima Farstar." The pilot sounded pained. "Confirm that there is a Gamorrean piloting the second X-wing."

"I don't have to maintain comm silence anymore?"

"No! Confirm . . . species of your wingmate."

"Oh, he's human. That's his costume. I'm surprised I forgot to mention his costume. He can barely see out through the eyeholes in the mask, you know." Myri faced forward again and tightened her straps. "It's a heavy, sweaty, gross costume. Don't you know the Legend of the Flying Pig? That's also the name of my script."

"Negative."

"Negative. Oooh, I love that word. I'll have to use it. No, this was from a long, long time ago. In the war against the Empire. People started seeing a Gamorrean pilot. What a great story! So I thought, this needs to be a holodrama. Or a holocomedy. I'm still not sure which. I've written it both ways. What do *you* think?"

"You're clear to continue." The E-wing abruptly banked, a hard maneuver for such a peaceful situation. His wingmate banked to join him on the return flight to Kuratooine.

Myri watched them depart, her smile replaced by a hard stare. She switched her comm board to transmit on very low power on a little-used frequency, encrypted. "Did you hear all that? They have no jurisdiction in this area; it's a Starfighter Command issue. They didn't even *identify* themselves. They had no right. They *are* rodents, just like they're named for!"

"Keep your mind on the exercise, Gambler." Voort's voice was now matter-of-fact.

"I just want to smash them. They shouldn't have licenses to pilot a hovering snack stand."

Tildin was entirely devoid of other spacecraft when they arrived. There was a sensor station on the side facing Kuratooine, but at Voort's direction Myri led the way to the far side. It was half in shadow and half in sunlight.

Voort chose a stretch of lunar surface several hundred kilometers long in the sunlight. "This exercise will be all terrain-following mode. We're going to need to be very good at that for the Skifter Station run."

"And what do I get if I'm better than you?"

"Enough cute talk, Gambler. This is deadly serious." Myri sobered. "Yes, sir."

"But good work scamming those Pop-Dogs."

"Thank you, sir."

Planetside, on a low hard-rock mountain at the western edge of where Chakham Base bordered on Kura City's south end, two Pop-Dog troopers, one human and one

Quarren, both female, examined the small hypercomm antenna inset into a patch of stony, treeless ground. The antenna, a durasteel-mesh bowl ten meters across, was now decorated with a fallen tree. Small by the standards of the forest verge surrounding the antenna, this tree had evidently been uprooted by one stiff wind too many. The dead tree lay half in, half out of the depression.

A maintenance droid, barely waist-high to a human, its head a round vertical plate with a single optical sensor, lay under the tree trunk just where it touched the stone rim around the antenna. Pinned, the droid flailed, its metal arms clanking against the stone. A series of musical notes that might have been pleas for help or droid curses emerged from its vocal synthesizer.

The Quarren trooper laughed. The sound, filtered through the nest of tentacles over her mouth, was muted and rubbery. "That explains the interference."

The human trooper shook her head, clearly saddened by the futility of dealing with droids. She stooped, getting her arms under the tree trunk, and lifted. The tree rose only half a meter, but the droid was able to scramble free. He stood, pointed accusingly at the tree, and continued his harangue.

The Quarren gestured to catch the droid's attention. "What happened?"

The droid put his hands where hips would be on a human and turned his harangue on the Quarren.

"What do you mean, you don't know?" she asked.

The human assumed an expression of disbelief. "What does he mean, he doesn't know?"

The Quarren shrugged. "He says he was headed up here from the droid access tunnel. He was still fifty or sixty meters downslope when he experienced an emergency shutdown. He woke up under the tree."

The human rolled her eyes. "Here's what probably happened. He came up here, the tree fell on him, and he reinitialized. When he was online again, his memories were cross-linked or corrupted."

"That's probably it."

"Come on, give me a hand. The tree's still too heavy for the droid."

Together, they dragged the tree completely clear of the antenna depression. Throughout, the droid offered counterproductive advice and complaints about the troopers' interpretation of events.

Then the Pop-Dogs left, the droid stomping along behind them, all three crushing fallen leaves underfoot with the stealth and grace of drunken banthas.

Two minutes passed, then Jesmin stood, letting the synthcloth blanket and the leaves spread across it slip to the ground.

Huhunna, beside her, also rose. She offered a single word: "*Kreekkraakkruump.*" The word was onomatopoeia, the Wookiee sound of someone falling through a succession of tree branches before hitting the ground—hence, a klutz.

Jesmin, whose own command of Wookiee was pretty good, grinned and responded in the same language. "Yes. Kind of like listening to a construction droid learning to tiptoe."

"But you were right." Huhunna's words, echoing softly off tree trunks, would sound to most people like a distant animal growl of warning.

Jesmin nodded. "Abandoned mines closed for safety reasons don't usually have hypercomms, droid workers, or Pop-Dog guards. This is the place." She looked northeast. Through the trees, some of Kura City's few skytowers could be glimpsed in the distance. "Over there somewhere will be the old entrance to the mine. Probably not as sealed off as people think." She turned to the southeast. Chakham Base lay in that direction, though it could not be seen for the trees. "And I'm betting there's another entrance down there."

Huhunna rumbled her reply: "Let's finish this operation and get off this world of spindly little trees."

"They're not *that* spindly. Come on."

CHAPTER THIRTY

Voort and Myri brought their starfighters in on a slow, tediously lethal approach to the Wraiths' base of operations. They descended on repulsors to land in the quarry. It took a few minutes to extract their astromechs, Fuzzy and the dented black R5 unit Voort called Dustbin, and cover the starfighters with large sheets of tan flexiplast. They loaded themselves and the droids onto the railed open-air turbolift that had been original equipment when the quarry was a going concern. It rose, clanking, to clifftop level.

The two Wraiths, still clad in orange-and-white X-wing pilots' gear, their helmets in hand, walked into the main building—and a storm of activity.

Overhead in the ops room was a hologram of the Kura City–Chakham Base boundary. Huhunna had her hand up in the image as if grasping a low mountain at the western edge of the boundary.

Jesmin looked up as Voort and Myri entered. "That's their base. We're working on the accesses."

Voort nodded. "Excellent. Muscle Boy, kiss their hands."

Trey, sprawled in a puffed chair, ignored him. "You'll need a case for the jewels."

Voort waved his comment away. "I want a crystal

case. Not your department. I want you up on Skifter Station as soon as possible to plant the sensor disruptors on the exterior. And what about proton torpedoes?"

Trey shook his head. "Not likely. But I can attach new hardpoints to the S-foils and put together some rocketry for them."

"That'll have to do." Voort caught sight of Drikall. "Drug Boy! Can you mess up Turman's vital signs?"

"Of course." The medic smiled, showing an impressive array of sharp teeth. "What would you like? Tachycardia a specialty."

Turman looked up from his own chair, his expression alarmed. "Wait a minute—"

"Don't worry about it." Thaymes looked back and forth from his monitor screen to the hologram Huhunna continued to poke at. "I've recoded a child's noisemaker. Tack it to the inside of the Embass suit and it'll make Turman sound like he has two heartbeats. You want three? I can give him three heartbeats."

Drikall looked betrayed.

From the adjoining room, the combined kitchen and dining space that Wran had dubbed the Catastrophic Mess, came Scut's voice: "Do not drug the Clawdite. No good can come of it."

Then someone emerged from the Mess—not Scut, but a lean human man now in the shadowy halfway zone between middle age and old age. His hair was white but not yet thin, and his suit, silver-gray and in a contemporary Coruscant style, was well fitted and clean. He emerged holding out a hand toward Voort. "Professor. So good to see you again."

"Doctor Cheems." Voort shook his hand. "How was your shuttle flight?"

"Tedious, thank you. And call me Mulus. Please."

"I'm Voort. Are you all settled in?"

"And on the job. Come, I'll show you." Mulus led the way back to the Mess.

The dining table was almost covered in diagrams, machinery halfway through fabrication, various hand and blaster weapons. At one end rested a device that could have been a pistol-grip soldering iron if the barrel were a heating element instead of a tiny transparent dish. Beside it were several small duraplast boxes filled with what looked like precious and semiprecious stones, some cut and faceted, some rough.

Mulus seated himself beside the pistol-grip tool. Voort took the chair next to him, and the other Wraiths gathered around, some standing.

"So." Mulus held up one box of uncut stones. "Assorted samples of Kuratooine stones that Viull acquired for me."

"Viull . . ." Voort frowned. "Oh, you mean Scut."

Mulus glared at his Yuuzhan Vong son. "You know your mother hates that nickname."

Scut shrugged, smiled. It was an odd expression on a Yuuzhan Vong face.

"Anyway." Mulus set the box down. "Standard distribution of gemstones for a world of this type. Kuratooine sapphires are especially appreciated. Though I really like the amber found here."

Voort shook his head. "Amber won't work for us. It's organic. We need mined, inorganic stones."

"Pity. I'll have to take some amber home." Mulus set the box down. "But, to the point, if you're going to convince people—what did you call them?" He looked at Scut.

"The marks."

"If you're going to convince the *marks* that they're seeing gems mined and crafted in absolute isolation, hitherto completely unknown, you have two basic approaches. You need either a material they've never seen before or a crafting technique they've never seen before. To have both would be even more convincing, of course. Materials they've never seen before are tricky, because either you have to have actually *found* materials no one has ever seen before . . ." His voice trailed off and he waited for a response.

The Wraiths shook their heads.

"Blast. I was hoping you'd thrill me. Or you use something created in a laboratory. And that's tricky, too. Such a material would have to have been developed in secret. No published descriptions of the stuff to thrill fellow gemologists or justify the government grant money. You can see how that would be rare. As you probably know, scientists in a specific field tend to know what others are doing. Clearly, what we need to overcome this problem is more startlingly rich mad scientists, and I'd like to apply for that job."

"Father." Scut sounded impatient. "Few of us have much more than a century to live, and you're off on one of your tangents."

"Oh. Sorry. And even if you had a helpful mad scientist, some artificial gem production techniques reveal themselves under the microscope."

"So the other approach—" Trey looked like he was struggling to remember. "You said, crafting techniques no one's seen before."

"Correct. There I think I can help you. Over the years, I've developed several sonic devices whose purpose is cutting gems. In the right hands, they're better than cutting them physically. In the wrong hands, you end up with a small pile of pretty but valueless gemstone chips."

Voort frowned. "These devices are commercially available?"

"Oh, yes. In fact, sales of and training on the Cheems Sonic Chisels are paying for a lot of my in-name-only retirement."

"My point is, they're well known and won't fool anybody."

Cheems smiled. "But they're not the only sonic gem-shaping technology I've invented. There's another that I'm still fooling around with. I don't know if there'll be a market for the results. You take a sonic chisel apparatus with micrometer positioning control and a fractal mathematical set for guidance and let them loose on a gemstone. Here, I'll show you." He opened another box, removed from it a small object wrapped in black velvet, and extracted the object. "Does anyone but my boy here know anything about gems?"

Myri raised a hand. "I can spot lots of kinds of fakes." At Voort's confused look, she explained. "Any gambling environment, people try to pass off fake jewelry as valuable. So they can stay in a game or pay off debts."

Cheems passed the object to her. He also handed her an optical device, a small single-eye scanner.

She held the first item up so it was fully in the light from the overhead glow rods. It looked to Voort like a sprig from a bush. There was a main stem two centimeters long, with tiny branchlike extrusions radiating from it at random intervals and in random directions. It was red, a creamy hue.

"It looks and weighs kind of like coral." Myri sounded thoughtful.

Cheems shook his head. "Ah, but it's a Hapan form of ruby."

"And it looks *organic,* like coral." Myri held it under Cheems's optic. "Interesting. Under magnification, you can see the facets. Thousands and thousands of them." She handed the two objects to Jesmin, sitting beside her. "I really haven't seen anything like it."

Cheems beamed. "No one has. Except Viull, and my wife, who has several pieces. But she's helping orchestrate my grand debut of the technique by keeping them to herself, never wearing them in public, until I'm ready to have a showing. The beauty of the technique is that flawed stones yield results as beautiful as flawless. Cracks and imperfections become part of the final design . . ."

Voort watched the gem as it was handed around the table. "Scut, the Embass suit. Could it incorporate some of those pieces as decoration? As if the Embass people practiced self-modification like the Yuuzhan Vong."

Scut considered. "That would be beautiful. And yes. I can do that."

"It's not your top priority. Keeping the suit from digesting Turman is still number one."

Turman jerked up from looking at the gem. "What?"

"And the Thaal masquer—also more important."

Scut nodded. "Decorations will be priority three, then."

"*Digest* me?"

Voort returned his attention to Cheems. "This is definitely what we want. You can perform the technique with what we have here?"

"With what I brought with me. Though anyone working with me will need total isolation ear protection."

"We'll get it. Mulus, thanks for coming. You may end up helping save a lot of lives."

Cheems beamed. "Just paying back a favor."

A day later, they had more answers.

Thaymes, digging through old, off-line geological surveys made before the planet had a name, found sonic interpretation maps of caves below the Chakham Base property. Some were deep and seemed to have no access to the surface. Others, closer to ground level, had openings at base level. A few of those entrances were located in stands of woods well away from the base's buildings.

Trey, tracing some of the cave and tunnel passage-ways on Thaymes's monitor with his finger, nodded. "Since it doesn't have to be a very big explosives pack-age, I think we can get it pretty deep."

Voort looked between him and the map. "Not so deep the base seismographs won't detect it."

"Oh, they'll detect it."

"The crawler has to be the very first thing ready, then."

Trey nodded. "Boom."

"And the Thadley Biolan recorded messages to Ledina Chott—you've been studying them? Can you do it?"

Off duty after a day of serving drinks at a bar frequented by Pop-Dogs, Turman sat, weary, in an operations cen-ter chair beside Voort's.

Voort didn't look up. He continued studying the dia-grams Jesmin had given him earlier in the day. They showed a large building housing water pumps. Jesmin had said the building was in the northwest quadrant of Chakham Base, on the lowest slope of Black Crest Mountain. One diagram, which Jesmin had admitted was partly theoretical, showed a concealed turbolift shaft that supposedly descended to the old mine works beneath the mountain and its surroundings. "Stage Boy. How's that all-liquid diet working for you?"

Turman groaned. The sound went on awhile. He paused for a breath. "I'm not here to talk about that. It's Ledina Chott."

"Thaal's next mistress, unless we get to him first. What about her?"

"Just recently the Pop-Dogs have received orders, un-official orders, about her. She's off-limits. Word has fil-tered down to the rank and file that the Pop-Dogs, to a man and woman, are supposed to be respectful and very, very hands-off if they ever encounter her. It's also considered good luck to scare off anyone else showing interest in her. This is as of just a few weeks ago."

"Soon, soon, soon . . . He'll be abandoning Thaal and becoming Thadley very soon now." Voort sounded almost smug.

"Thaal's operating procedures are changing. He killed his last mistress just to make a point. What if he approaches Ledina Chott and she refuses him?" Turman looked distressed. "Is she safe?"

"I don't know." Voort set the diagrams aside. "We can't cover every eventuality with eleven Wraiths. You can't be there to protect her. You're more important somewhere else."

"I know." Turman rose. "I just wanted someone to complain to."

The next morning, Huhunna and Jesmin delivered a package to within ten meters of the army base's forest-side sensor fence.

Behind a tree, they removed the package's contents from the bag that held it.

It was a droid of sorts. A lozenge half a meter long, it was fitted with a score of articulated durasteel legs radiating from all along its body and in all directions. There were green globes housing optical sensors at either end of the body.

Jesmin twisted one of the optical sensors until it clicked into place. The droid went active, standing up on a few of its limbs. It oriented itself, facing its distant destination. Unfortunately, there was a tree only centimeters away, blocking its path.

It looked the tree up and down, then turned to the left and began what, to Jesmin, looked like the slowest walk in history toward the sensor fence.

Huhunna heaved a sigh, then spoke in Wookiee. "Too slow. Nothing will want to eat something that smells like that, but something may come along and want to play with it. And will wreck it. It needs to move faster."

"No, any faster and the motion detectors would pick it up. At this speed, it looks like static display on the sensor screens. And once it's ten meters past the fence, it can pick up speed."

Huhunna just stared after it, shaking her head, her expression sorrowful.

Back in the operations center, Trey watched the occasional burst-transmitted holocam images from the slow-moving droid. Occasionally he'd run through the entire visual recording at high speed, which made it look like the droid was moving at a normal rate while windblown leaves and insects flashed past at supersonic speed.

Long after Jesmin and Huhunna returned, the image showed the droid entering a surface-level cleft in a small hillside. The holocam view cycled unsuccessfully through standard optical mode, infrared mode, and light-gathering mode, then clicked on and stayed on motion-detector mode. Now detection of air movements allowed the droid to build up a three-dimensional diagram of the series of cracks, caves, and tunnels it was navigating.

Eventually Trey stopped receiving new signals. "It's too deep for the comm signals to get through." He rose and began assembling his pack. "So it's Skifter Station and more sabotage for me. How are you going to get Stage Boy on base?"

Jesmin glanced at Huhunna. "We put Stage Boy in a bag to prevent him picking up any forensic evidence. Then we go through the trees, bridging gaps with an old-fashioned cord-and-grapnel rig, which Huhunna is a genius at using, until we're past the perimeter defenses. I break trail, and Huhunna does the heavy lifting."

Trey hefted his pack. "Tell Turman you heard that the shellfish the suit's based on adapts for survival by modifying itself to digest new food types introduced into its environment."

Jesmin grinned. "That's the dark side of the Force talking through you."

"I suspect the dark side is more fun. 'Night."

"Good luck."

Voort and Turman stared down at the body Turman was about to wear. The Embass suit, the final version of the full-sized neoglith masquer, lay on Scut's laboratory table, the vertical slit in its chest and the emptiness beyond the eye sockets indicating that it was not truly alive.

Except that it was. Voort was certain he could see it breathing. He offered Turman a sympathetic look. The Clawdite was about to crawl into a liner bag of living tissue that had been engineered from a crustacean's stomach. And he was going to live there for days.

Turman turned to Voort. "I once swore—*swore*—I would never again play ridiculous-looking monsters while wearing cumbersome full-body suits."

Voort snorted. "Just remembered that, did you?"

"Just made it up. I'm still looking for a way out of this."

"Get in, Stage Boy, and you get one year of me telling all the ladies that you're the bravest man I ever met."

Turman's expression graduated from tension to resignation. He nodded. "You've discovered my weakness. Every actor needs validation. And reviews." He took a deep breath, then stepped up on the crate Scut had set beside the table to facilitate his climb.

He wore only a kilt, of a material Scut swore would not irritate the masquer's stomach lining—undyed suede leather. As Scut held the edges of the suit's chest cavity open, Turman stepped up on the table, then, a brief flicker of distaste crossing his features, put his foot into the suit.

It took several minutes and help from both Scut and Voort. Turman had to sit in the chest cavity and gradually ease his legs into the suit's leg channels, stretching the fleshy suit lining to conform to his body contours as he did. Then he leaned back, unenthusiastic, and repeated the process with the arms.

Scut grabbed the suit's jaw and pulled, firmly and steadily. After a few seconds, with a slurping, ripping noise, the head split open, seams appearing that ran from behind the jaw and up to the temples. The action opened the head cavity.

Turman leaned back, lowering his head inside. "Ever since I stepped into this thing, every second of my life has been more disgusting than the last."

Scut smiled. "And you are not even done yet." From opposite sides of the table, he and Voort shoved the chest seam closed. "How is it?"

Turman grimaced. "Like putting on an ambience suit that someone has poured warm butter into. But it occurs to me that if you could add a vibrator function, you could sell three trillion of these."

"I will consider that. Hands?"

Turman raised the Embass suit's hands. He flexed its fingers. Then he did it again, making the gestures seem spastic, jerky, insectile. "Its own muscles are helping."

"You will want those muscles for walking." Scut checked along the entire length of the chest seam, making sure it was correctly aligned and once again invisible. "Otherwise you will tire fast. And remember, in about two days the masquer will start to die. That might take two more days, or four. The enzymes used to accelerate its growth to this stage can't be neutralized, and its body mass doesn't carry enough nutrients to keep it alive for long."

"I know, I know. And spray it down frequently with water, and keep it out of direct sunlight." Turman sounded miserable.

Voort moved up to the head. He fitted a compact headset to Turman's true head, carefully positioning the earplugs, affixing the mike to the corner of Turman's lip with a dab of sticky gel. He looked at Scut. "Turman's skin needs oxygen, right? The masquer provides that?"

"Oxygen?" Scut looked stricken. "I forgot that part."

Voort and Turman both looked at him.

"Kidding. Yes, the lining brings oxygen—the surrounding atmosphere, actually—to his skin and carries toxins away from it. *Instead* of digesting him." Scut took hold of the suit's open skull. "Ready?"

"No."

Scut lowered the skull into place.

This version of the Embass suit's head was somewhat different from the previous one Voort had seen. The eye sockets were a trifle smaller, fitted more precisely to Turman's facial dimensions, and a film of red tissue covered them, transforming Turman's eyes into reddish orbs. More red film crept into place across Turman's lips and jawline, transforming them into what looked like odd inner-mouth organs of indeterminate function.

Two horns of Mulus's fractal-coral ruby protruded from the forehead, decorative but menacing.

Turman spoke. "It's clinging to my jaw." As he spoke, the suit's mouth moved realistically. "And my eyeballs— that red coating is *touching* them."

Scut smiled again. "Good. Everything is working correctly."

Voort tried to make his voice soothing. "The effect is very realistic."

"I think I'm going to throw up."

Scut's good cheer did not falter. "You can! The mouth will admit whatever you decide to purge. But you've been on a liquid diet for days, so it won't be very interesting."

Voort put his hand under Turman's back, preparing to lift. "While he decides how to tell us he hates us, let's get him on his feet."

They did. Turman spent a few minutes adapting the body language he'd been developing for the last week— an extension of the movements of his hands, it was jerky and twitchy, definitely non-mammalian—to the limitations imposed by the suit. He also tottered a bit until he mastered the art of balancing on alien feet.

Finally he turned to Voort and Scut. "I am more panicky, claustrophobic, and revolted than I have ever been in my life. But I'm *ready*."

CHAPTER THIRTY-ONE

"Boring detail." The Pop-Dog corporal, a dark-skinned human, stopped at the fork in the forest trail and looked in both directions. He could see little but the hard-packed soil trail; the trees met overhead, permitting only slivers of moonlight to reach the ground. He raised his blaster rifle to his shoulder and repeated his scan, this time peering through its scope. His augmented vision showed everything ahead in shades of gray, but there was still nothing interesting to see, only tree trunks, tree roots, stones. "They ought to import some regular army pukes to pull details like this."

"Oyah." The private, redheaded, freckled, rawboned, looked exactly like what he was, a rube from a back-rocket planet trying, and failing, to acquire a veneer of experience and sophistication while serving in the army. "Better, even. Convicts." He mimicked the corporal's action, scanning the surroundings through his blaster scope. As his barrel aim swung across the corporal, the corporal ducked.

Once the barrel was past, the corporal rose. "Let me get this straight. You'd put blasters in the hands of convicts so *they* could do the dirty work of the base."

"Oyah. They'd suffer more than they do lying around in jail all day, living off my taxes."

The corporal's jaw worked. No words emerged.

He was saved from answering. A crackling noise from down the right fork in the trail drew his attention—feet walking on dried leaves. "Come on."

Quiet compared with their quarry, the two trotted along the trail, slowing every twenty or thirty meters to get a better estimate of the walker's location. After three such stops, the corporal pointed the private toward a tree, then concealed himself behind another. He put his finger on the button that would activate the glow rod located under his rifle barrel—it would shine where the barrel was pointed, blinking a prospective target in light conditions like these.

The crunching noise approached, resolved itself into heavy footsteps as well as crackling leaves.

Then a shape, bulky, its body language strange even in this darkness, stepped out on the trail.

The corporal aimed and triggered his light. "Don't move!"

In the glow stood a . . . thing. Taller than a normal human, shorter than an average Wookiee, it had rough, reddish brown skin that looked rigid, massive jaws, eyes that gleamed with an evil redness. Red, too, were the small, strangely delicate horns that protruded from its brow. In its left hand it carried a square object, glittering. Its right hand was raised and open, palm toward the corporal, in what the corporal hoped was a gesture of peace. The creature wore no garments.

Then the private's light came on, shining right into the corporal's eyes. "Don't move!"

"Blast it, shut that off!"

"Oyah. Sorry, Corporal." The light went out again.

The reddish creature still stood in the corporal's light, unmoving.

"State your name and your purpose!"

"Me, Corporal?"

"You, *shut up*." The corporal felt his blood pressure rise to a dangerous level. He returned his attention to the creature. "State your name and your purpose."

Finally it answered, its voice shrill, garbled, alien. *"Stayte joor nayme mand joor pyurpose."*

The corporal breathed just a touch easier. Whatever it was, it didn't seem hostile and was trying to communicate. Maybe it was just an Outer Rim visitor who'd gotten drunk and decided to wander around nude on the army base. He'd call in the situation. In half an hour this wouldn't be his problem anymore.

He wondered if he could give the private to the base police and keep the alien as his partner.

He hit his comlink with his thumb. "Patrol Six to command, we have a situation."

Colonel Gidders, a Bothan whose fur was gradually shifting from a gray of youth to the gray of age, stared unblinkingly at the hologram of General Thaal. Around the colonel were the light-and-sound dampening wall and ceiling tiles of a dedicated holocomm chamber. "I've had a team of specialists working with it, on it, all this time."

General Thaal, shown standing before a galactic map with blinking situation lights at several star systems, looked like he felt much less weary than the colonel. It was morning, Fey'lya Base time. "What are your findings?"

"It allowed us to obtain some tissue samples with our micro-extractors, so we've done some preliminary genetic work on what we obtained. It's definitely related, distantly, to a local aquatic species, but it's unprecedented in the planetary fossil record. The creature is very intelligent and has learned three or four hundred Basic words in just the hours it's been here. It can string

simple sentences together. Our xenolinguistics expert
has worked with it to make some determinations of its
role and mission."

"Which are?"

"To act as ambassador—it likes the term *embassy
who climbs*—with the new species here, us. It says its
kind sleeps in the deep caves but will awaken soon. It
awoke because of some sort of fault-line slippage we
detected fifteen hours ago. The creature brought a present for our king-warlord, whom I have explained is
you."

"Yes." Now Thaal showed additional interest. "I've
looked at the scans you sent of the gems in that casket.
Interesting."

"The casket itself seems to have been shaped by the
same technique, but it's only rock crystal."

"All right. Show him in."

Colonel Gidders gestured. The door at the back of the
chamber slid open. The creature, flanked by two Pop-
Dog sergeants, entered, his walk jerky and spasmodic.

The colonel gestured between the creature and the
general. "King-Warlord Stavin the First, I present
Embassy-Who-Climbs."

The general bowed. "I am honored." His words
sounded more perfunctory than anything else.

Embassy-Who-Climbs walked, twitching, past the
colonel to the general's image. He reached for it, his
hand passing within the hologram. "Glitter." His voice
was less shrill than it had been hours earlier, but it still
sent a chill up the colonel's spine.

"Yes." The colonel resigned himself to another slow
struggle to communicate. "A glittering image. The king-
warlord sees and hears you through the glitter."

The creature withdrew a step. "We sleep. Stavin-First
spawn come. We wake. Share or eat?"

Thaal looked blankly at the colonel.

"He means we've settled on their world while they hibernated belowground. What do we do now—share the world and its bounty, or eat one another? Meaning wage war."

"Oh." Thaal didn't bother to restrain a brief chortle. "What do they taste like?"

"Sir . . ."

Thaal looked at the creature. "Share, of course. Peace is what we want above all. Peace and mutual respect."

The creature rocked forward and backward, a crude simulation of a human nod. "Share. Arrrrrt." It turned back toward the door. Past the two sergeants, just in the doorway, a dark-haired woman in medical whites waited. At the creature's look, she moved forward and handed Embassy-Who-Climbs a crystalline case, twenty centimeters long, ten wide and deep.

The creature held up the case and lifted its lid. It opened as if hinged; the colonel could see, and again admire, the intricacy of the slots and projections along one edge that fitted into each other, allowing the lid to behave like a hinged component.

The creature displayed the organic-looking gems, red and blue and green, within. "Arrrrrt. For king-warlord. More below to share."

Thaal's eyes widened just a little. "How much more?"

The creature paused. Its head twitched from side to side, its jaw vibrating. Then it answered. "Cave. This cave."

Thaal looked blank again.

The colonel cleared his throat. "I think he means he could fill a cave the size of the holocomm chamber with the gems."

The creature listened to the colonel's words. "Ten of ten cave."

The colonel's eyebrows rose. "Twenty caves this size?"

"Ten of ten! Ten of ten!"

The woman who'd brought the case interrupted. "He means one hundred, Colonel. Ten times ten. Or perhaps several hundred. We're still working on the concept of plurals. I think he indicates them with body twitches, but we're not there yet."

"*Hundreds* of caves this size full of art." Thaal looked as though he were struggling to shake off the effects of a stun bolt.

"Ten of ten for king-warlord. More not for king-warlord. What arrrrrt for me and me-spawn?"

"Oh. Yes, of course." Thaal clearly had to switch mental gears. "For you we have spice and sweetblossom. Brandy. Dancing pit droids and the most sordid Hutt melodramas. We'll let you sample a thousand arts and tell us what you like best, and we'll give you that and more."

Embassy-Who-Climbs performed his nod again. "Must not glitter. Must smell to share."

Thaal looked at the linguist.

She shrugged. "Trade talks must be conducted in person."

The creature rocked in affirmation. "Yesssss. Smell to share. Embassy-Who-Climbs and King-Warlord Staaaaavin-First."

"How inconvenient." Thaal took a deep breath. "Colonel, prepare for a surprise inspection by the Chief of the Army."

"Yes, King-Warlord."

Thaal grinned. "King-Warlord will smell you soon, Embassy-Who-Climbs. Soon."

"Sooooon."

After the sergeants and linguist escorted the creature away, Thaal became businesslike. "You think the underground slippage you mentioned will wake others of his kind?"

"He indicated so, yes. My scientists speculate that the slippage may somehow have been part of a life-cycle event. He wakes up first, emerges as a scout. Then the others begin to awake. *Tens of tens of tens of tens* is what he told me."

"Tens of thousands." Stavin rubbed his chin, thinking. "Well, maybe we can drop some barrels of targeted toxin down in their caves. Wipe them all out cleanly. Get your people to work on that."

"Yes, sir."

"I'll see you in a couple of days."

Trey had invented it, the game of Backstop, and tonight the Wraiths played it on a patch of grassy soil down in the quarry. Each wore a stretchy black nightsuit and carried a toy laser pistol that fired a harmless beam of light.

Trey was the first Controller. He held a large screen-only datapad and used the on-screen controls to command a floating droid. Round and glowing, the size of a human head, it drifted up to chest height in the middle of the wide circle the Wraiths formed.

Trey set the timer for sixty seconds. He put his finger on the floating ball controller, knowing that the first twitch that set the ball into motion would also start the countdown. "Ready . . . go." He sent the ball into flight.

As he maneuvered the ball, guiding it through a spinning, diving, zigzagging route that still stayed within the circle of Wraiths, they began to fire. Tally-marks began to appear beside names listed along the right side of the datapad screen.

Each time a Wraith's shot hit the ball, the ball made a noise, a musical *thunk*. Other hits, badly aimed ones, yielded a different sound, a musical *thoooo* that sounded like a droid, suddenly depowered, sitting down for an unexpected nap.

The last second counted down. The ball stopped glowing and came to a dead stop. Trey raised his voice. "Round One done. Your results . . ." He scanned the list of names, which was sorted by score. "Wran, you disgust me. Ten shots, eight hits, no tragedies. Voort and Myri tie for second place with twelve shots, four hits, no mistakes each. Drikall and Scut, you each had three hits on the ball and none against your fellows, but Drikall, you shot thirteen times and Scut ten, so Scut wins the tiebreaker . . . Jesmin, one shot, one hit on the ball, none on any of us. Are you not feeling well?"

There was no answer from the darkness.

"Jesmin?"

"One shot, one kill." Jesmin's response was a whisper breathed in Trey's right ear. "That's the Ranger way."

Trey jumped with her first word. "Not funny. Well, maybe a little funny. Thaymes, you make us all proud: sixteen shots, no hits on the ball, and you killed me, Drikall, and Jesmin, and Voort *twice,* for a total score of negative ten."

Thaymes's voice floated out of the darkness. "Thank you all. I couldn't have done it without you."

Trey handed the datapad to Jesmin. "Your round."

But the screen blanked, showing a sensor view of the quarry and a kilometer around it. A blinking green dot approached the quarry property.

Voort stepped up to take a look, then checked his chrono. "That'll be Sharr . . . probably. Everybody get topside."

Sharr paid the driver, took his bag, and waited until the speeder had lifted off and gotten half a klick away before he mounted the short step to the main building and the ops center.

The main room was empty of Wraiths. He shut the outer door and stood in the doorway, puzzled.

"It's him." The voice was Trey's but muffled, and it came from a blank spot on the floor. A square of flooring a meter on a side, its seam invisible, lifted and tilted back on hinges. Trey stood up out of the hole beneath.

The door into the Catastrophic Mess slid up and the Wraiths filed out. All wore nightsuits. Voort spoke first. "Welcome back. Don't unpack: you're going to Chiss space."

Sharr sagged. "Tell me you're joking."

"I'm joking. Sit. Eat. Drink. Report."

Sharr settled into a chair, pointed to where Trey was stepping out of the hidey-hole. "That's new."

Trey shut the hatch. Again it became an innocuous part of the floor. "I can't leave any device, vehicle, or construction unchanged. You know that." He and the others took seats.

Sharr rubbed his face as if to scrub a thick layer of tiredness away. "You want the good news or the bad news?"

Voort snorted. "You know our traditions. Lead off with the bad."

"General Thaal knows it's Wraith Squadron."

All the others leaned forward.

Voort's eyes widened. "Say again?"

"While I was on Coruscant acquiring the package, I did a little sniffing around. You know, checking into how much of a trail we might have left without meaning to. And I found out that, quietly but very persistently, General Thaal is looking for Wraith Squadron. I was actually queried, a comm message sent to my home. An army investigator asked, politely, if I'd had any contact with certain individuals since the unit was dissolved three years ago. He apparently bought into the notion that I was indeed retired and making my living writing the 'What's Wrong With You?' quizzes."

"So if he didn't suspect *you* . . ." Voort rubbed his jaw. "He was only looking for Bhindi's team."

"Not even that." Now Sharr let a bewildered smile cross his face. "When I dug into it, I found out that they're looking . . . for a *third* Wraith unit."

Thaymes put his face in his hand. "My head hurts. Please hammer a nail into my skull. To release the pressure."

Voort kept his tone light and pleasant. "Ah. And who is *in* this third Wraith unit?"

"Well, there's a Defel named Queevar."

Voort shook his head. "I've never heard of—him? Her?"

"Her. Female name. Then there was a manumitted destroyer droid, pre–Clone Wars era, named Impaler."

Scut jerked, surprised. "That's a freakish coincidence." He frowned. "When I was first taken in by my human parents, they gave me something to help me get over my fear of machinery. It was a toy droid in the form of a destroyer. It chased stinging insects out of my room. And it would impale bits of litter on its claw-spikes and take them to the waste bin. I called it Impaler."

Voort's expression grew blank. "Sharr, if this is a joke . . ."

"No joke. Jokes around here usually involve stealing your clothes. You're still dressed. No, there's a real, ongoing investigation by the army, and a big one. Anyway, also in this Wraith Squadron, there's a bounty hunter named Zilaash Kuh."

"*Wait* a minute." Jesmin looked as startled as Scut had. "*I'm* Zilaash Kuh. Or I was, for a couple of years. It's a cover identity."

"Well, this cover identity is supposed to be a woman

who trained as a Jedi until she was kicked out because they discovered she was only masquerading as a human. She was Anzati."

Jesmin looked appalled. "A *brain eater*?" Then her expression cleared. "Actually, that would explain a lot. That's a good addition to her background."

"But the kicker . . ." Sharr returned his attention to Voort. ". . . is the unit's leader. A man thought dead for decades. Now more machine than man. Doctor Ton Phanan."

"Not possible." Voort shook his head vehemently. "Ton Phanan *is* dead."

"Who?" Thaymes looked as though he were falling behind in the day's school lesson and beginning to panic.

Voort explained. "One of the original Wraiths, back when we were with Starfighter Command. Back when Myri's dad was still in charge. Ton was our first medic. He died on a mission."

Sharr shrugged. "Did you see him die, Voort? Did you see his body?"

"No, only Face did."

"*Could* he still be alive?"

"Sure. If Face lied to us all those years ago. If he maintained the ruse all this time to preserve Ton as—as an asset of some sort." Voort shook his head. "Or this could be a ruse on Thaal's part, an effort to draw out Scut or Jesmin by using details only they would react to. Or some other sort of disinformation. Maybe we can use it ourselves."

"Well, that's all my bad news." Sharr pointed skyward. "The package is installed at Skifter Station."

Trey nodded. "I know, I installed it myself."

"Not your package. My package from Coruscant. And she wants to help. And . . . what was the last thing? Oh, yes. General Thaal's here. His troop transport docked at the naval station as I was coming in to Skifter Station."

"That was fast." Voort whistled appreciatively. "He must really want those gems."

"What's been happening here while I've been gone? In addition to Trey making a very nice hole in the floor."

Trey glowered. "I got us three droids today. Really banged up, just as ordered. I'm working on fixing two of them now. The third one's a loss."

"Turman's in position." Voort gestured at Jesmin. "Huhunna's on watch duty now. Jesmin will be relieving her in an hour."

"Jesmin and I found the civilian exit from the Black Crest Mountain mines." Thaymes sounded pleased with himself. "It wasn't at the site of the old mine exit, which really is all sealed over. It's a few hundred meters farther into the city, in an army-surplus business and warehouse. It's on the plaza surrounding Old Kura Courthouse Square."

"Plaza." Sharr raised an eyebrow. "That's . . . actually good, isn't it?"

Voort nodded. "When it comes time for witnesses, we'll have them by the hundreds. And there's room in the plaza and on the courthouse lawn to land the starfighters. Sharr, our number one goal is accomplished—getting all the elements into place."

"Good." Sharr smiled. "Now we just have to live through triggering all of them."

CHAPTER THIRTY-TWO

General Thaal suppressed the impulse to grimace as he shook the alien's hand. They hadn't told him that the creature ... smelled. From its mouth issued a faint but inescapable odor—sweetness, rotting. Thaal just gulped down a touch of nausea and continued speaking. "I hear you have made remarkable strides with our language just in the time I've been traveling."

"It is ... my gift." Embassy-Who-Climbs shook the general's hand. "An Embassy is spawned with that gift. A Render is spawned with savage claws and jaws. A Tapper has spikes that cut stone."

"*Your* jaws aren't savage?"

"Mine—small."

Thaal kept himself from shuddering. "Well. Formalities are called for. As King-Warlord of the Galaxy, I accept you as ambassador of all your race, and wish prosperity and peace on your kind. Speaking of prosperity ..." He held out a hand. An aide placed a rolled piece of flimsi in it. Thaal presented it to Embassy-Who-Climbs. "This is the deed to the world of Bastion, one of my many worlds, for your own king-warlord. He may find it to be a charming world to visit. I hear its cavern systems are lovely. He may reshape it to please himself and find many colonies there for his own glory."

Embassy-Who-Climbs bowed. "I will convey it to him when the first Lifters come with his gifts for you."

As he left the negotiations room, the alien's crystalline box of jewels in his hands, Thaal smiled. He kept his voice low so that only his aide could hear him. "Pretty good day so far."

"Pretty good, General."

"Wouldn't Head of State Reige be startled if he ever found I just gave away his capital?"

The aide kept his face straight. "Yes, General." But Thaal suspected that he heard the man snicker.

TIARA RIDGE ESTATES,
    NORTHWEST OF KURA CITY

She let the door slide closed behind her, shutting out everything that did not belong in the sanctuary of her new home.

Ledina Chott leaned back against the outer door and looked down at herself. The white dress she wore, which had been crisp and almost incandescent this morning, now drooped a bit. A day's worth of public appearances had left the cloth sagging like her energy, and the garment bore purple-blue smears where an overenthusiastic little girl had hugged her with food-stained hands.

But Ledina smiled and kicked off her shoes. After two short years of fame and wealth, she still wasn't used to them yet. She hoped she never would be. Or ever too jaded to delight a small child with food-stained hands.

She moved forward through her entry hall toward the social room. "Twelve-String? What's for dinner?"

Her droid house manager did not answer.

She moved into the social room. Two stories high and

larger than the house where she'd spent her entire childhood, it was filled with expensive furniture. Its walls were decorated with holos from some of her concerts. She'd have preferred holos of some of the singers and actors *she* liked, but her publicist had wanted it this way, so visitors to her home would be reminded of nothing but Ledina Chott.

"Hello, Ledina." The voice was not Twelve-String's—it was deep, raspy, male.

Startled, Ledina whipped around. Her visitor stood in the hallway leading to the bedrooms. Burly, with yellow skin and dark hair and beard, he leaned against one stone wall with a nonchalance that suggested he was in his own home. He wore casual clothes in white and tan that would be appropriate to a day sailing; Ledina recognized the maker's mark on the breast and knew that this one ensemble was worth a new speeder bike.

She thought about turning, bolting for the front door . . . but then she recognized her visitor. "Oh! Thadley Biolan. In person. You *startled* me."

"I'm so sorry." He moved forward, extended a hand. "Your droid let me in. I'm so delighted to meet you at last."

She gave him her hand, expecting him to shake it, but he leaned over and kissed it like an old-fashioned courtier. She withdrew it, hoping she hadn't actually snatched it back. "I'm the one who should be sorry. You've caught me right after a day of publicity. I'm a mess."

"Nonsense. You're . . . *beautiful*."

"Let me get you a drink. *Twelve-String*."

"He said something about power fluctuations. Perhaps he's having them diagnosed."

"She."

"Yes, I meant she." Thadley turned away, surveying the room. He smiled as he saw the crystalline glow rod housing, all flowing bars in different colors, atop one end table. "Ah! I see you enjoyed the moodsetter enough to display it."

"I've appreciated all your gifts. Thank you so much." Ledina forced a note of gratitude into her voice. She had appreciated the gifts and the messages of praise for her music. But meeting him in person was not turning out to be what she had expected. She was . . . unsettled. "I need to find Twelve-String. Give her a talking-to about not being on hand."

"No, no." He spun to face her again, the smile never leaving his face. "I've traveled thousands of light-years to see you. Just arrived earlier today. Please, talk with me for five minutes. I have a business proposition for you."

"*Business.*" She felt a touch of relief. "Of course. But I should get my manager on the comm to listen in. So you won't have to repeat anything to her later."

"Oh, it's so simple, there'll be no problem remembering the terms I'm offering." He shrugged. "I want you to sign a personal services contract with me. Five standard years, renewable by me if I wish. Salary, whatever I choose to give you."

Hoping she was as innocuous as she'd been taught to be, Ledina used her thumb to depress the band inset in the ring she wore on her right hand. Then she spun and ran for the door.

The door ahead snapped open before she was close enough to trigger its sensor. In the doorway stood two men, their uniforms brown, their collars decorated with stylized teeth.

She turned rightward and dashed toward the hallway Thadley had emerged from.

Another uniformed man, stepping out from the shadowy interior of her music room, caught her around the waist and lifted her. He ignored her kicks and ineffectual blows, carrying her back to Thadley.

Thadley sighed. "Clearly, negotiations are going to take a while." He scratched at his beard. "And *blast* this thing." Irritated, he tugged at his sideburn, then peeled the beard and mustache entirely away from his face, revealing tanned skin, the color of Ledina's own, beneath. Thin streamers of transparent adhesive stretched between beard and skin; he began rubbing them away.

Ledina stared at him, confusion crowding out the fear for just a second. "You're that general. You were on the news today." Then she felt a sting, as if from an angry insect, in her left shoulder. She twisted in time to see a uniformed woman with muddy brown hair and dull eyes withdraw an injector from her arm.

"*No!*" Ledina kicked at the man holding her, lashed out at the woman with the injector. She connected, but the strength was already fading from her limbs. Dizziness swept over her, followed by a murky darkness.

One Pop-Dog trooper struggled to hoist Ledina onto his shoulder.

Thaal offered the man a mildly disapproving stare. "Careful, Lieutenant. She's delicate. She's an artist." He finished rubbing the adhesive from his face and handed the false beard to another trooper. "Her ring is an emergency beacon. Switch it off. Let's go." He led the way to the door and out into the night.

Two hours later, the man with the yellow skin, dark hair, and beard sat in the rear seat of the expensive airspeeder while his driver walked the half block back from Ledina Chott's home. There, Kura City Guard speeders were situated with their lights flashing all around the home, and cordons had been strung so no one could step onto the property without the guards' leave. The man with the beard felt a stab of worry. This was not good.

His driver returned and slid behind the controls. "She's been taken."

"*Taken?* Who took her?"

"Unknown. I dropped some credits and think I got some real answers, but they know very little. It happened a few hours ago. The housekeeper droid apparently took a scrambler hit and saw nothing. There's no sign of violence and there was no ransom note left behind. She broadcast a brief panic signal, but it went out after less than a minute."

The man with the beard sat back, stunned. "Back to the base. We have to figure out what's happened here."

CHAPTER THIRTY-THREE

Midmorning the next day, Voort, dressed again in his orange X-wing fighter pilot jumpsuit, began dispatching Wraiths from their operations center.

He heard Huhunna roar off on the larger swoop. She'd be joining Jesmin, forming Team Shellfish. The two of them would be making their last insertion into Chakham Base.

There was a metallic slam as Scut finished loading the delivery speeder. In moments the Yuuzhan Vong appeared in the doorway, then nimbly navigated among all the remaining Wraiths as they packed their bags, donned disguises, checked the charges on their blaster rifles and pistols.

Scut stood before Voort. "What's our motto?"

"*What do we blow up first?*"

"The other one. *Good news and bad news.*"

"Stang." Partway through sealing up his too-tight black boots, Voort slumped. "Bad news first."

"I just heard from the commercial managers of the courthouse plaza. There was a mistake and the space for our tent was rented to someone else. A souvenir seller."

"A mistake?"

"Clearly, the mistake was that the souvenir seller came to them with more money than what we paid. The plaza managers have refunded our money with insincere apologies. But the souvenir booth is already set up."

Voort sighed. "Can we get any other spot in the plaza this late?"

"Yes. I secured us a spot at the edge. But the first bad news leads to more bad news."

Irritated, Voort resumed sealing up his second boot. "Spill it."

"Our scapedroid reported early to the location I gave it yesterday. It didn't realize that the souvenir stand was not us. The stand operator told it that its services were not needed. So it returned to its dispatcher and was given another assignment."

Voort growled and stood. "And how about securing us another scapedroid?"

"None available."

"*Blast* it. I'm going to strafe that souvenir stand." This was indeed bad news. A scapedroid, in this case a Model V37 Ambassador, was a humanoid droid whose entire torso and head area was replaced by a large monitor or holoprojector. Skittish negotiators would send scapedroids to a parley site and speak to one another through the safe telepresence functions offered by the droids. The Wraiths needed their scapedroid to foster an illusion and escape with their identities intact.

Voort got to work donning his other gear. "Well, we're just going to have to improvise. Get us a new scapedroid."

"I have tried. There is none closer than orbit, and all are engaged. This is a small world. There are only three onplanet."

"Scut—I'm about to go get shot at. You have to fix this."

Scut threw up his hands. "I am not complaining. I am

not shirking duty. But I have to manage the changing booth. Timing there is very complicated."

"I'll take the changing booth." Mulus Cheems, the only island of calm in the room, rose from his chair. "I know your equipment, son. I know your procedures."

"*No*, Father. This is dangerous work."

"Oh, yes. I should let my son run off to do dangerous work while I sit here watching holodramas." Mulus moved up to stand beside Scut and Voort. "Viull, I think I would very much like to pay back the debt I owe the Wraiths."

"That's what *I'm* doing!"

Mulus smiled but shook his head. "You can help them all you want and it will never diminish my debt. Wait until you've incurred a debt of your own. Then you'll know what I'm talking about." He looked at Voort. "Sign me up, Professor."

Voort considered, then nodded. "Scut will show you what goes with who. The first sign of trouble you see or hear, you lie down on the ground and stay there."

"*Father . . .*" Scut leaned forward, pleading.

Mulus leaned forward, too, and touched his forehead to his son's. "At a certain point, Viull, you'll learn that you just can't keep protecting your parents from themselves. Parents are wild, hormone-addled, uncontrollable creatures. As you'll understand someday when you're a parent."

Voort was struck by the two men's identical poses. In age, height, mass, and skin color they were different, but their postures were identical.

Scut finally lowered his eyes and nodded.

Voort waved to get their attention. "Scut. The good news? There *was* some, correct?"

"Team Oversight is ready."

"Then get going." Voort watched as Scut, Mulus,

Thaymes, and Wran—now in burgundy clothes and a new hip-cloak—left.

Drikall, wearing a Pop-Dog sergeant's uniform, watched them go. "I hate last-minute changes."

"Get used to them." That was Trey, standing beside him, in a blue Galactic Alliance Army general's uniform, a headset on his head instead of a hat. "How's the package?"

Drikall looked baffled. "Your package on Skifter Station, Sharr's package on Skifter Station, or our package here?"

"Here."

"Fine. In the speeder. The repulsor cart's loaded in back."

Trey turned to Voort. "Leader, we have to come up with better 'package' designations."

"Agreed. Next time."

Trey took off his headset and put it in a pocket. He hefted his neoglith masquer. "Speaking of which, Mind Boy reports he and *his* package are boarding to leave the station."

"I hear you." Voort hefted his helmet.

Trey donned the neoglith masquer. Drikall helped him fit it and shove its trailing edges down under the uniform's collar. When they were done, Trey was an identical image of General Stavin Thaal.

General Thaal picked up and donned his hat. "Team Enemy Mine ready."

"Get going. Good luck."

When the two of them were gone and the sound of their airspeeder had retreated in the distance, comparative silence descended over the operations center. Only Voort and Myri were left, both in X-wing pilots' gear. Myri's hair was now a virtual match in color for Mulus's coral-cut sapphires.

Myri lifted her helmet. "Team Rage ready."

"Let's get 'em, Antilles."

She grinned.

But once they were down in the quarry, standing beside their X-wings, Myri hesitated. "We don't *know* that they're inner-core Pop-Dogs."

Voort finished with the portable frame and winch he'd used to lower his astromech into position behind the cockpit. Myri's was already in place. "Meaning that we're about to go up and shoot at people who might not know that they're serving a traitor."

Myri nodded, her eyes miserable.

Voort wheeled the frame away. "Well, now you're at that point. A point your father doubtless hit when he was younger than you, just joining the Rebel Alliance. The point where you ask yourself, *Can I kill someone I'm not sure is guilty?*"

"You've been waiting for this, haven't you?"

Voort nodded. "Ever since I realized how meticulous you were about making sure your blaster was always set on stun. And now you're stuck with lasers and missiles, and they *can't* be set on stun."

She leaned heavily against the S-foil of her X-wing. "Maybe you could have warned me."

"Maybe thinking about it for days would have made you neurotic." Voort moved to the nose of his starfighter, patted it as if it were a riding animal. "Myri, I might be able to do this mission myself. Odds are kind of long, but I might be able to. Or we could summon Sharr back, rusty as he is behind the controls, and let Mulus tend his package. But I think you can do this, because you're your father's daughter, and because you've grown up knowing that a warrior like your dad sometimes has to face an honorable enemy. An enemy whose only fault is that he's working at cross-purposes with you, and if you don't fight him until he falls, very bad things will result. Which is the situation here."

"I guess it is."

"You have to keep this in mind: you have to win."

She gave him a slow, miserable nod.

"So?"

She sighed and put on her helmet. She snapped the visor down over her eyes and added the helmet's final, nonregulation element, a veil of black, clinging synthsilk over her lower face.

"Good." Voort donned his own helmet and veil. Then, awkward, he climbed onto the strike foil and into his cockpit.

They lifted off, crested the quarry clifftop, and headed southward over the property at an altitude of two meters.

They observed local speed regulations. Other speeder pilots, less conscientious, passing them at higher speeds, pointed at the two beautifully restored antique X-wings with hand-built missiles bolted onto their strike foils, and at the two veiled pilots.

Voort and Myri stayed in the main airspeeder lanes all the way into Kura City's south side, creating no sensor blip that would cause a suspicious traffic warden to challenge them. But then they were at the city limits again and pointed toward Chakham Base.

Voort clicked his comm board over to the main Wraith channel. "Rage One to Team Enemy Mine, Team Shellfish. We are a go. I say again, we are a go."

Trey was clearly in character when he answered. He spoke in General Thaal's gravelly tones. "Enemy Mine, understood. Go get 'em, soldier."

Jesmin replied in a whisper. "Shellfish here. Understood."

Voort switched back to the subfrequency he and Myri shared. "Rage One to Rage Two. We're going in."

* * *

Lying prone on his cot in the room he had been given, Turman heard the distinctive triple click over his headset. Then it came again.

He sat upright and stood. The nurse, a male Chadra-Fan, looked over in concern. "Are you all right?"

"Sunlight. Embassy-Who-Climbs needs sunlight." Turman's throat was hoarse from performing the rough Embassy-Who-Climbs voice for days.

"No, no. You said sunlight would hurt you." The nurse rose, tilting back to stare up at his much taller patient.

"Before, yes. Now, need sun. Life cycle demands."

"I need to comm the front office for permission."

Turman raised his hand as if pointing at Kuratooine's star. "Sun!" Then he brought his fist down on the Chadra-Fan's head. The durable exoskeleton of his hand cracked down on the small humanoid's skull with a meaty thump. The man collapsed to the floor, his comlink clattering down beside him.

Turman grimaced. Getting on his feet, swinging that blow had been difficult. The neoglith suit was weaker, much weaker. The thing was dying.

He waited a second to see if Pop-Dogs would come bursting in through the door.

None did. That was great news. It meant that, as they had across the last couple of days, the soldiers believed in Embassy-Who-Climbs's passiveness and cooperativeness. They didn't always have a guard in front of his door, relying on the nurse to warn them of trouble.

That, and one other thing. The door didn't open for Turman as he approached it. But he punched the keypad with one oversized, hard-shelled finger, using the nurse's code, which he had spent considerable time and effort to observe while pretending to be asleep. The door slid aside.

In a back hall of a minor function building well away from the main base facilities, Embassy-Who-Climbs went tiptoeing toward the building's rear door.

"I wish Muscle Boy were here." Jesmin, aggrieved, bent over the building's rear door handle, a bar meant to be depressed. There was clearly security on the door—multiple contact points of metal extended from the frame to touch others on the door. The security was more extensive than Jesmin was comfortable with.

Beside her, keeping watch all around, Huhunna rumbled a reply in Wookiee. "Let's just blast it."

"What?" Jesmin looked at her.

Huhunna gestured all around. To their right, southward, were empty drill yards. Leftward, more of the same. Ten meters behind them was the start of the closest thick stand of trees. There was no one to be seen. The voices of Pop-Dogs practicing close-order marching drills sounded far away.

Huhunna hefted her bowcaster and gave Jesmin a significant look.

"Oh, all right." Jesmin pocketed her electronics bypass tool and took a couple of steps back. "Go ahead."

Huhunna fired. The bowcaster bolt hit the door beside the lock and detonated, charring the door metal. The lock and the left portion of the opening bar disintegrated. Huhunna grabbed the door well away from the superheated portion and shoved it open.

Embassy-Who-Climbs stood there. He put his hands on his hips as if indignant. "Klutz."

The building alarm sounded.

They sprinted—tottered very quickly, in Turman's

case—into the woods as other alarms on the base began wailing.

They got only deep enough into the trees that the building was no longer in sight. Then Turman stopped. He reached up and ripped open his alien mask so the others could see his real face, which was flushed red and sweating. He yanked at his chest, splitting it open, and tore himself free from the suit's interior. As he emerged, so did a sweet, sickly odor of rotting sea life. Jesmin and Huhunna took several steps back.

Shaking himself free of the suit's legs, Turman advanced on them. His body glistened from sweat and whatever the suit's interior had secreted on him. His eyes were wild, and his words emerged in a scream: "Get me to a sanisteam!"

"Time to leave, Stage Boy. This way." Jesmin pointed northward and led the way, trying to keep well ahead of the funk that surrounded Turman.

"A pool. A waterfall. An acid bath! Sandpaper! *Get me clean!*"

Drikall unloaded the folding hover cart from the back of the speeder, set it up, and activated it. Then he carried the unconscious Ledina Chott from the backseat and stretched her out atop the cart. He shook a blanket over her, covering her from head to foot.

Only then did Trey, imperious in his General Thaal garb, exit the vehicle. "Did you switch on her ring?"

"I remembered."

The main doors into the building were several meters away, directly under the sign that read MAJOR SAVING'S ARMY SURPLUS. But Trey marched to an unmarked side door made of transparisteel. Through it he could see a small office, a hallway leading from it deeper into the building, a muscular young man with close-cut brown hair lounging in a desk chair.

Trey schooled his features—Thaal's features—into an expression of disapproval. He hammered on the door. The man behind the desk looked over, then stood so fast it looked as though he came up off the floor.

He opened the door. "General!"

"It's bad, son, very bad." Trey waved Drikall forward. The Devaronian came forward, pushing the hover cart. "That body—do you know Private Zizbisterling?" Trey stood in the doorway, keeping it open, as Drikall pushed the cart through.

"No, sir."

"Well, she's dead now, so you're never going to. You hear the alarms?"

The man cocked his head. Though not loud at this distance, the wailing alerts from the base were indeed audible. The man's face went blank. "Sir, are we under attack?"

"Hell, yes. Take us down *immediately*."

"Yes, sir!" The ostensible clerk half saluted, remembered that this was not the right protocol, and dashed into the hallway. Trey and Drikall followed.

As they moved along a back corridor flanked by storerooms, well behind the clerk, Drikall leaned forward to stage-whisper to Trey, "Nice improvisation on the alarm thing."

"There weren't supposed to be sirens yet. I didn't know what else to say."

"No, I meant it. Nice improv."

The false clerk led them into a side room that was far too large and empty for its evident purpose—an unmanned comm center with one large computer-communications unit and a single chair. As soon as the door was closed, the clerk hammered on the undecorated back wall. It was a distinctive series of taps.

The wall slid aside, revealing a chamber of similar size. But this one had durasteel-mesh walls showing rock walls and steel support pillars beyond. It was a freight lift car.

They moved onto the car. Trey turned to the clerk. "I need you to come with us."

Baffled, the clerk joined them. He hit a button on the front wall control panel, and the wall-door closed. He hit another and they began their descent. "General, if I may ask—"

The body on the hover cart moaned and stirred.

The clerk looked at her blanket-shrouded body, his eyes wide.

Trey opened his own eyes wide, as well. "A miracle! Sergeant, you know what to do."

Drikall drew his blaster and shot the clerk at point-blank range. The stun bolt took the man in the chest. He slammed back into the metal-mesh wall and slumped.

Trey turned to the controls. "Long way down. We have a few seconds." He whipped the blanket off Ledina, revealing her to be wearing the same dress in which she'd been kidnapped. Her eyes were closed but she was fitful, her head now turning as she struggled to awaken. "How much time, Drug Boy?"

"A few minutes. I can give her a stimulant."

"No, don't worry about it." Trey looked up and noted the location of the lift car's roof access hatch.

Two seconds later the lift came to a stop. The shaft's back wall and the car's rear metal-mesh wall rose.

Just beyond them was a stony tunnel that ran off into dimness in the distance. Along its floor ran a metal rail. The stone ceiling had wires stretched along it, with glow rod coils every five meters. Standing right at the door was a dark-furred Bothan woman in a Pop-Dog corporal's uniform. Her eyes widened and she saluted. "General!"

Drikall shot her.

CHAPTER THIRTY-FOUR

"Captain?"

The officer of the day, a human whose burly body and bald head suggested that he might be a missile in disguise, looked to the officer at the sensor board. "What is it?"

"We have two new transponder signals. A kilometer out and closing. The craft themselves are not on the sensors. I think they're at ground level. They're now sending standard starfighter transponder data. Their designations are Phanan One and Phanan Two."

"Phanan—sound a general alert."

"We're *already* on general alert, sir."

It was true—the alarms had begun when the building confining Embassy-Who-Climbs had been breached. The wails continued even now. The base was already in turmoil.

"Alert the wall towers—"

Two X-wing starfighters, painted in classic gray, roared past the command center's south-facing viewport. The officer of the day caught a glimpse of white helmets with black veils concealing the pilots' features.

Voort checked his sensor board, made sure he was correctly oriented toward their first target.

There it was, straight ahead. Just past the first stand of trees was the small-craft spacefield, one good-sized hangar in brown and a paved landing square. Arrayed on the square were two rows of four E-wings in Pop-Dog colors and a military shuttle. Men and women ran toward the starfighters on the ground.

"One to Two. I'm to starboard."

"Rage Two, aye."

Voort drifted rightward and triggered his lasers. Red beams slashed down into the right-hand row of starfighters, riddling them, punching through canopies and fuselages. One exploded less than a second after Voort passed it. Pop-Dogs turned to run the other way.

Voort heard Myri's laserfire and the distinctive sound of lasers chewing up metal. Then the two X-wings were past and out over more trees.

Voort banked and came around again. Myri stayed on his wing. Once the landing field was directly ahead, Voort could see that all four of his targets were now burning wreckage. So were the shuttle and one of Myri's E-wing targets.

"Two, we need to pick off one more. If I miss, it's yours."

"Yes, sir."

Voort lined up a careful shot on the E-wing nearest the shuttle and fired a burst at it. He saw the beams converge on its fuselage. The craft seemed to implode, then exploded.

"Confirmed kill, One."

"Second target, then." Voort banked and headed for the distant north end of the base.

Distant to one traveling on foot, that was. The water-pumping station, screened on three sides by trees and on the fourth by a mountain slope, was in view within moments.

Voort sent his starfighter into a climb. It started out steep, then went vertical. He rolled axially so his belly now faced west, his canopy east, and Black Crest Mountain to the north was off his right S-foils. On his sensor board he saw Myri hanging tight just to port. "Fall in behind, Two. I'm breaking trail; you're dropping the first load."

"Two here is Two obeying."

"You're fired." At a couple of kilometers' altitude, Voort sent his starfighter into a loop. In moments he was headed straight down, pointed at the pumping station. Myri continued her climb for the moment, getting a few seconds' separation between herself and Voort.

Voort fired. His lasers hit the pumping station and all around it, a wild scattering of shots compared with the precision he'd demonstrated against the E-wings. He continued firing as the ground and pumping station grew larger with startling speed.

There was a purpose to his sloppiness. Pop-Dogs, three of them, ran out of the increasingly riddled pumping station.

Voort pulled out at two hundred meters and checked his sensors. There seemed to be nothing in the air that hadn't been there before—normal airspeeder traffic off in the civilian lanes.

He watched Myri descend. She came down at the same vertical angle he had chosen. Voort tensed—not from worry over Myri's skill as a pilot, but from worry about the barely tested rocketry bolted to her wings.

At half a klick, she fired. A gout of flame lanced down

from her starboard wing. A fraction of a second later she fired again, and her port-side rocket launched. Both devices flashed down to ground level on columns of fire.

The first rocket hit the station's roof and detonated. The second shot through the center of the fireball. The fireball got bigger.

Voort took a recon pass over the target. He couldn't see anything through the smoke cloud, but his sensors showed that the hole in the pumping station went a long way down—a hundred meters at least.

He sent his starfighter into another climb. "Direct hit, Two. And the shaft is open. I'm going to drop my load for luck."

"I'm covering you."

At two klicks up, he started his second loop and began one last descent, straight toward the smoke cloud. Sensors still showed a deep hole ahead. His targeting bracket locked on the shaft's bottom and he launched both rockets. Then he leveled off.

Myri swung into position off his port wing. She waited until the sound of the twin detonation reached them before she spoke. "I think they'll be taking the stairs from now on."

"I think you're right. Next stop, Skifter Station. Not too fast, now."

They sent their X-wings into a steep climb.

The technician from the security firm waved unnecessarily as the two Kura City Guard speeders crested the old courthouse building, descended, and came in for a landing in the lot just outside Major Saving's Army Surplus. City guards piled out of the two vehicles—two investigators in civilian dress, two uniformed troopers in riot gear.

The investigators, a Mon Calamari man and a human

woman, stepped forward. The senior of the two, the Mon Cal, looked the security technician over. "You're Yinkle?"

"Yes, sir. I—"

"Funny name, Yinkle."

Yinkle tried not to grit his teeth. "I know. I've heard that all my life. I—"

The Mon Cal indicated himself. "Detective Sergeant Husin." He gestured at his partner. "Detective Biller."

"Yes. Hello." Impatient, Yinkle held up his datapad, which showed a map of this sector of the city with a line transcribed on it. "The client's rescue transmitter was activated when she was grabbed last night, but it switched off right away. Then it went live again just a few minutes ago. Right here where I'm standing. The track of its movements says it went right in that door."

The Mon Cal gave him a hard, emotionless stare. "This had better not be a mistake."

"It's not." Yinkle was diverted by the distant sound of explosions to the south, clearly audible over the ongoing wail of alarms. Moments later everyone in the lot could see smoke climbing above Black Crest Mountain—and two X-wing starfighters, climbing much faster, headed for space. "Interesting day we're having."

"Army business. Not our problem. Come on." The Mon Cal led the way to the door into the army-surplus store.

There was no one in the open office area beyond the door, but a short, burly woman arrived at a full run in response to the Mon Cal's hammering knock. Frowning, she looked harassed. Her eyes opened even wider as she saw the uniformed troopers. "Can I, uh, help you?"

The Mon Cal displayed his identicard, emblazoned with the seal of the city guard. "We have no search warrant. But we're invoking act thirteen, paragraph six of the Uniform Planetary Code. We have compelling reason to believe that there is a crime in progress and lives are in danger."

"Stay here. Let me call my supervisor." The woman reached for the door controls.

The Mon Cal stepped into the doorway.

The door shut anyway, slamming him into the jamb. Yinkle saw that the man was pinned, helpless, and under his arm could see the woman run to the office desk and reach into a drawer.

The human detective, stooping to see between the Mon Cal's legs, aimed a blaster pistol and fired. Her shot, not a stun bolt, took the woman in the ribs. She collapsed, a hold-out blaster dropping from her nerveless fingers.

The Mon Cal grunted, grabbed the doorjamb with big finny hands, and heaved. The door mechanism whined; then flames erupted from the very top and bottom of the door, where actuators would be located. The door slammed open and stayed that way.

The Mon Cal glanced at his partner. "I owe you a drink. Call in for an ambulance and backup. Yinkle, I'm willing to concede that something may be wrong here."

"*Thank* you."

Tracing the line on the datapad map, Yinkle led them down the hall from which the woman had emerged. At the end were double doors; the transparent panels in them showed warehouse beyond. But Yinkle indicated a door to the left just before that point.

The door opened into a spacious, empty computer center.

The Mon Cal gave Yinkle a dubious look. "Your map may be off."

"No, sir."

The back wall of the room, seemingly ordinary and featureless, shot up. Beyond it was a lift car with metal-mesh walls, rough stone visible beyond them.

On the floor of the lift car lay two bodies, a man and a woman in the uniforms of Pop-Dogs from the base, and on a hover cart lay a third body—Ledina Chott.

The Mon Cal looked at Yinkle again. "That your client?"

"Yes."

"Well done." He looked at the Pop-Dogs and sighed. "I hate making big discoveries. They don't usually end well."

Ledina came to full consciousness, her body jerking in fear reaction, but the man leaning over her looked thin and harmless, not military at all. Above his head was a sound-dampening ceiling.

Groggy, Ledina looked at him. "Where am I?"

"You're in a store. Your captors brought you here. My name is Kadd Yinkle. I've *saved* you."

"Yinkle?" She frowned, trying to think. "That's a funny name."

He sighed and put his head in his hands. "Anyway, the others have gone down to scope out whatever's below us. All the city guards you'll ever want to see are headed this way, so you're safe." He looked up and gave her a reassuring stare. "No more unpleasant surprises for you."

The back wall of the room shot up, revealing rough-walled lift shaft . . . and no lift. Ledina and Yinkle stared at it.

From a point above the door, two figures swung down and landed on the floor just inside the room. Both were men clad head to toe in black stretch material. Their hoods concealed their features, but the bigger one looked human, and the shape of the other one's head, horns protruding through the stretch cloth, suggested he was Devaronian.

Yinkle moved around to stand between Ledina and the intruders. "I'm putting you two under citizen's arrest."

They hurried forward, flanked him, passed by him on either side, and rushed out the door.

Yinkle looked down at Ledina. "Well, I *could* have tackled them, of course. But my primary mission here is to protect *you*."

Out in the speeder, Trey discarded his hood, replaced his headset, and pulled on a gold-and-black jacket. Now, from the waist up, no longer clad in a skintight nightsuit, he would look normal to anyone viewing him through the vehicle's viewports.

Off in the distance to the east he could see oncoming airspeeders in city guard colors, blue and red. He put his own speeder into motion, cruising slowly away from the vicinity of the storefront, putting the large redstone courthouse between him and the oncoming guards.

Drikall pulled his own hood free and donned blue medical scrubs. "You realize we're already here. At the plaza. We can't afford to get too far away."

"But we have to break line of sight between us and anyone who might connect us with the surplus business. We do that as many times as is feasible before we get to our second station. Didn't you know that?"

"Well, I'm kind of new to all this. Mostly, I drug people. It's what I'm good at. Which is why I'm confused as to why, when we're about to prove that Thaal is guilty of so much, we also had to frame him for a crime he *didn't* commit. The kidnapping of Ledina Chott."

Trey guided the speeder down a side landspeeder lane, then turned to circle the block. "We don't care if he's convicted for the kidnapping, and he probably won't be. But, first, given what he did to his last mistress, and the fact that he was showing a lot of interest in Ledina, by us kidnapping her, we may have prevented *him* from kidnapping her. Or worse."

"A preemptive felony."

"There you go. And in kidnapping a celebrity with some interplanetary fame, we have ensured that the civilian news will hear about Thaal and that civilian authorities will launch their own investigations. Not to mention the musicians' union. You don't want to mess with the musicians' union."

"Really?"

"No, I'm kidding. What are they going to do, serenade you to death?"

A few hundred meters away, Huhunna, Jesmin, and Turman—now wrapped in a simple gray robe and wearing sandals—boarded the Wraiths' delivery speeder.

The tall cargo compartment was now divided into two sections, forward and rear, by a thick black curtain. Thaymes sat in the forward section in a side-mounted seat with computer and comm gear packed tightly around him, a headset on his head. He looked relieved when they entered. "You're late."

Jesmin smirked. "We had to run Turman through an airspeeder wash. Without benefit of airspeeder. He was a biohazard."

Thaymes glanced back at the curtain shielding the rear compartment. "Well, at least I don't have to wear that new masquer, which I would have if you'd been a minute later."

Turman's hands came up as if he intended to strangle Thaymes. Huhunna wrapped an arm around him, held him still.

Jesmin moved back to the side door. "What do I need to know before I go out there?"

"Lots of city guards on hand. The relays are working fine—the enemy would need a comm genius, like me, to track these broadcasts. Lab Boy's still setting up the replacement for the scapedroid at the confrontation point. Muscle Boy reports, 'Kidnapping is thwarted.' There are two E-wings closing in on Leader and Gambler, intending to kill them. And Stage Boy needs to get into his next outfit *right now.*"

Jesmin nodded. "Sounds like business as usual."

Several hundred kilometers up, in her cramped personal quarters in the Starfighter Command portion of Rimsaw Station, Colonel Kadana Sorrel heard the medium-priority tone sound on her intercom. She brushed a lock of brown hair out of her eyes and set down the object in her hands—an actual bound book, one of her few personal indulgences. She activated the intercom. "Sorrel here."

"Colonel, we have a sort of strange transmission standing by for you . . . if you want to take it." The speaker, her on-duty communications officer, sounded more puzzled than he usually did. "It's a civilian who won't identify himself, says he's going to shake the armed services here until they crack, but it's nothing personal."

"It's not my husband again, another of his jokes?"

"Not . . . this time."

"Sure. Put him on. I could use a laugh." She turned toward the monitor on her wall. "Face mode, please."

The holocam in her monitor buzzed as it adjusted depth of field. Now her caller would see only her face and not realize that she was lounging in her bunk, out of uniform.

An image materialized on her monitor. It, too, showed only a face. A man's face, lean and angular. The entire left half of his head was covered by a durasteel-gray shell, and his whole jaw was a prosthetic in an identical color. A gold mechanical eye gleamed in the left side of his face and his right eye was blue. His hair was a solid white and his expression registered somber intensity. "Colonel Sorrel?"

"I am. And you are?"

"You wouldn't know my name. I've been dead longer than you've been alive. But I'm comming you with a warning."

"A threat, you mean."

"No, a warning. I'm trying to help you. I'd send a warning to General Thaal, too, if I could. But he's already dead."

The colonel leaned forward. "All right. Let's hear it."

CHAPTER THIRTY-FIVE

Voort kept his eye on the sensor board. Skifter Station was close ahead, visible to the naked eye, its independently spinning concentric rings glowing in traditional white against the backdrop of space. Also nearby were two E-wings, coming up fast from behind. There was constant chatter on the comm frequencies, civilian and military authorities demanding that Phanan One and Phanan Two take up orbit well away from any other craft and wait for the authorities to arrive.

"Second act, Two. You ready?"

"I'm doing my hair."

"I'll take that as a yes." The first laser blast from the pursuers flashed past Voort, then past Skifter Station ahead. "Idiots!"

"We need to vape them *fast,* One."

Voort put a bit more effort into his evasive maneuvering. "Stand by to break."

Their pursuers drew close and began unloading short, disciplined bursts of laserfire at the two Wraiths. But as they neared Skifter Station, as their greater proximity made it more likely that any missed shot might hit the habitat, they left off firing.

Voort and Myri shot through the large gaps between rings and spokes. Voort broke to starboard, Myri to port. One E-wing followed each of them. Now they edged even closer.

Seeing an opportunity, Voort threw all discretionary power into reverse thrust and dropped about fifty meters of relative altitude. His enemy, caught off guard, rocketed past. With no space station in the background, Voort took his shot, but the E-wing pilot was canny enough to go evasive the instant he passed the Wraith. The burst of laserfire went wide.

Voort began a tight loop back toward the station. On his sensors, he saw Myri doing the same, headed toward the far side of the habitat. Her E-wing enemy remained on her tail.

Voort approached the outermost ring of the station and oriented himself so that its outer edge was beneath him, as though he were performing terrain-following flying just over the surface of a very small moon. Without gravity to pull at him, it was a tricky maneuver, contrary to pilots' instincts, like constantly following a planetary surface as it dropped away ahead. On the opposite side of the ring, Myri was doing the same . . . and heading straight for Voort.

Voort's enemy swung into line right behind him, at a higher relative altitude.

Voort almost smiled. There it was, pilot's training and instincts—and the Wraiths playing them like a musical instrument. A combat pilot in a close dogfight preferred to be above and behind his target, utilizing the visual and psychological advantage that position offered. With most starfighter designs, the enemy couldn't shoot backward. But now, for just one confused moment, there was no way the Pop-Dog could fire on Voort. Any miss would plow into the civilian space station. Any hit might send the X-wing into that habitat.

The sensor board showed the energies of Myri's and her pursuer's thrusters on an incoming arc. Now it was up to Trey—the work Trey had done days earlier, planting a sensor jammer up here on the station's surface. "Activate Snowfall!"

His R5 unit, Dustbin, tweetled an affirmative.

The main sensor screen fuzzed and went to static. Now all four starfighter pilots were flying blind—blind except for their own eyes.

Numbers, fractions of a second, spun down in Voort's head. "Two—*now!*"

Ahead, the incoming E-wing crested the false horizon of the station ring, visible before Myri's X-wing was in sight because of its greater relative altitude. Voort fired and yanked the control yoke to port.

At the same moment, Myri, unseen beyond the curve of the ring but able to see Voort's pursuer, fired and yanked her control yoke.

The two X-wing laser blasts, angled upward, could not hit the station ring. But they did hit their intended targets. Voort glimpsed the bright flash of vehicle-grade metal composites being incinerated by quad-linked lasers. "Vape one."

"Vape two, Leader."

"Well done." Voort banked toward Kuratooine's surface and Myri slid into place off his wing.

As they cleared the zone of Trey's jamming, Voort's sensors resolved back into crisp images. Skifter Station spun serenely, undamaged. Two small masses hurled away from it on straight-line courses, one of them expanding as a cloud of debris, the other in one piece but apparently out of control. That E-wing, Voort's target, suddenly became two objects as the pilot ejected. There was no survivor from Myri's target.

"You all right, Two?"

"Holding it together with space tape and spit, One."

* * *

The woman in the piloting compartment of the general's speeder was probably a starfighter jockey with limited chauffeuring experience. Her quick, minute course adjustments kept jerking Thaal and the captain in the rear compartment back and forth. Thaal decided not to criticize her now. The woman would kill for him if he ordered her to.

The captain, on the other hand, looked like he didn't have the guts to kill a game fowl to feed his troops. Offering bad news had made him wince again and again.

He offered more. "They began a search right away for the alien, what's-his-name."

"Embassy-Who-Climbs. He's from this planet and we're not, so technically *we're* the aliens. Have they found him?"

"Yes, sir . . . *dead*."

"Dead, how?" Thaal's mind flashed on tremendous volumes of gems that might never see the sunlight.

The captain's voice fell to a whisper, the tone of a child telling ghost stories. "They say he'd been ripped open from inside. His internal organs, his brains, his eyes—all *gone*. And whatever did it to him is still on the loose. Maybe still on the base, waiting to attack."

Thaal stared hard at the captain. "You weren't ever in a combat unit, were you, son?"

"No, sir. Comms. Then public relations."

"I can tell. Well, find the parasite and kill it. Now, back to the X-wing assault. You're sure they read *Phanan*."

"Yes, sir."

"What are our losses?"

"Colonel Gidders's shuttle. Six E-wings on the ground and two in space. One pilot dead, one suffering exposure from going extravehicular. And the base-side access shaft to the mine is destroyed. They targeted it specifically."

Thaal felt anger swelling up inside him. "Wraith Squadron."

"Sir?" The pilot glanced over her shoulder at the general. "We're getting word that the civilian authorities are at the Kura City mine access. In force. Facts are sketchy."

"Head for that access, Lieutenant. I'll put my foot on that situation personally, before it turns into a problem."

"Yes, sir."

Voort and Myri reached groundside before the flight of starfighters from Rimsaw Station, now visible on their sensors, came within visual range. The X-wing pilots switched off their transponders and returned to terrain-following mode, joining ordinary airspeeder traffic en route to the courthouse plaza.

Ahead, the distinctive three-story redstone courthouse building came into view. Lights blinked from in front of the nearby army-surplus business facing the plaza—city guard airspeeders, a dozen at least, plus medical speeders.

The open-air market in the plaza itself was almost deserted. A large crowd of pedestrians had accumulated near those vehicles.

Voort slapped the side of his helmet. "Stupid, stupid, *stupid*."

"What is it, One?"

"I missed a variable! Of course word might leak out that it was Ledina Chott being rescued from the army-surplus place. And of course people would congregate there. All our witnesses. *Stupid*. Fire me, Two, and take over."

"I can't. You fired me first."

They came in for a landing on the lawn of the courthouse, almost unnoticed. Voort reactivated his transponder, then issued Dustbin a command that would initiate a memory wipe in the R5 unit. In her starfighter, Myri was doing the same with her transponder and her R2. The memory wipes were an unfortunate but necessary precaution—now no investigator could obtain information about Voort or Myri from their astromechs.

Their black airspeeder glided across the lawn to set down just ahead of them. Voort swung down from his cockpit, saw Myri was down already, and sprinted for the speeder. He and Myri boarded from either side into the back compartment.

Trey accelerated away from the starfighters. He glanced back at Voort. "Where to, Leader?"

"Very funny." Voort was too tense to feel amused. "Give me the bad news first."

Trey shook his head. "I have no bad news."

"There's *always* bad news."

Drikall turned to answer that. "Despite an emergency scrubbing and some potent industrial deodorants, Stage Boy smells really bad."

"If that's the worst thing we're facing, we're doing great. For once."

They pulled up beside a tent at the very edge of the open market. The tent, decorated with broad green and white vertical stripes, had a sign out front reading: YOUR FUTURE REVEALED. A smaller sign, handwritten, tacked beneath it, read: CLOSED FOR MEAL. WE PREDICT YOU WILL RETURN IN ONE HOUR.

Voort made sure his veil was still in place, then exited the speeder. He took a look around. He could see stalls and ground-vehicle trailers with hucksters in them, but no customers. He ducked as if to avoid the attention of the hucksters and followed Myri into the tent. "At least we have *some* witnesses to our arrival."

She sealed the flap behind them. "Of course the sellers wouldn't leave their goods."

Inside the tent were tables with costume pieces atop them, chairs, two immobile droids—dressed in X-wing pilots' uniforms and veiled helmets—and Mulus. He rose and beamed at them. "Welcome to the changing booth. Are we go on my decoys?"

"We are go." Voort dropped his helmet in one chair, sat in another, and unsealed his boots.

Mulus held up a comlink and moved to the tent flap. He unsealed the flap and pressed a button on the comlink.

The two droids jerked into awareness and walked toward the flap. The more slender one immediately began speaking in the distinctive tones of a protocol droid. "As I was saying, we can only imagine what things taste like, but—oh, thank you, sir—but I think that properly cleaned oceanside sand looks scrumptious. Golden, gleaming sand." The two of them passed through the flap. "Don't you? Oh, dear, we seem to be clothed. I wonder how that happened?"

Mulus sealed the flap.

Voort tossed his boots aside and stood. He began to shed his pilot accoutrements. "Where's Lab Boy?"

"Getting final preparations done on the new scape-droid. He's obliged a mobile waste droid to be fitted with a comm-equipped projector, bought in this very market, atop it. I helped him subvert the droid. Poor boy's helpless with electronics." He picked up the generously cut porter's jumpsuit from the table beside him. "Your disguise."

"Forget it. We've got to lure back all the witnesses. The only way a porter can do that is by exploding. *Ledina Chott stole our witnesses.* Ungrateful girl." Voort unzipped his orange jumpsuit and stepped out of it, leaving him clad only in a black nightsuit.

"Well, we *did* kidnap her." Mulus dropped the porter's jumpsuit back on the table. "How are you going to get the witnesses back?"

"*I don't know.*"

"Speaking of Lab Boy, I think I deserve a Boy name for this operation."

Myri, now also down to her nightsuit, paused by a large box full of droid parts. "Gem Boy."

"I like it."

"Help her get suited up, Gem Boy." Instead of going out the front, Voort moved to the back tent wall, felt around until he found the rear exit Trey had prepared, and unsealed the slit. He stepped through into the market, and the slit sealed behind him.

He saw Scut immediately. The Yuuzhan Vong, wearing his human face with the flat-top hairstyle, was at the center of the market, working on his improvised scapedroid. The droid, chest-high, looked as though it could accommodate quite a lot of waste. New brackets on the top held a good-sized holoprojector and an auxiliary pack.

Voort trotted over. "Is it ready to go?" He looked around, fretful. In the skies to the east were numerous inbound dots—starfighters.

Scut shook his head. "I bought the holoprojector new. Its internal power pack has never been charged before. It's charging now. But it'll be a couple of minutes before it'll allow power through to the projector—"

"Never mind the explanation." Voort gestured to the distant crowd around the army-surplus business. "We have to lure them back here right now." Something caught his eye, a long black airspeeder, Galactic Alliance and army flags rippling from atop its front panels. It glided at ground level toward the crowd. "Thaal's here. We're almost out of time. He didn't even see the X-wings!"

Scut straightened, glanced at Voort. "Father lost your porter costume?"

"Father's doing fine. *Think*."

"*You* think. I build meticulously. I've never improvised."

Voort growled. He took a look around, assessing resources.

Stalls and trailers selling goods—meat rolls, jewelry, entertainment recordings, products with Ledina Chott's face on them among the other recordings. A big stall selling souvenirs—from the spot the Wraiths had rented. Voort considered setting it on fire. A raised octagon of natural wood five meters across with three buskers, street musicians, all of them human and professionally pretty, playing for credcoins, now just talking among themselves because there was no one to listen. A new-model speeder bike in red with a salesman standing, helpful and hopeful, beside it. A gleaming gold protocol droid, a black courier's bag hung on a strap over her shoulder, wandering aimlessly, apparently enjoying the weather.

In a place like this, Face Loran had evidently killed two dangerous men, improvising the kills. Voort's mind flailed around for the inspiration that clearly came so easily to Face. He withered inside.

Then numbers clicked into place in his head. Decibel levels. Ticket sales reported for Ledina Chott's upcoming concert. Voort turned to look at the musicians.

He held out a hand to Scut. "Give me a credcard. One with a thousand on it at least."

Without looking up from his droid work, Scut passed him a credcard.

Voort approached the musicians. They were human—two men, one woman, all dressed in a wild diversity of colorful garments like space vagabonds. All three were dark-haired and very pale-skinned; perhaps they were indeed travelers who seldom set foot planetside. Around the woman's neck was a strap, holding before her a bank of small percussion heads. One man carried a stringed instrument; the other had a keyboard hung from a neck strap.

Voort stopped before them. "Excuse me."

They left off their conversation to look at him, surprised. The keyboardist answered. "You're a talking Gamorrean."

"I know that. All Gamorreans talk, actually. I'm the only one who speaks comprehensible Basic. I speak more languages than you three have arms and legs. But that's not important right now. Can you get a lot of volume out of those instruments?"

The one with the stringed instrument grinned. "We can blow you right out of your body stocking."

"That was on my mind, actually. Run this." He held out the credcard.

The keyboardist took it, plugged it into a slot on his keyboard, and eyed the number that popped up on the keyboard's little screen. He opened his mouth to tell Voort the number.

Voort cut him off. "I know what's on it. Now you do, too. You can have it, the whole amount. If you'll do everything I say for the next fifteen minutes."

The strings player shrugged, agreeable. "Do we call you Master?"

"Sure. Clear the stage. Stand here."

They leapt to obey. Voort took the stage, standing at its center. "Crank your volume to max and keep it there. I doubt you'll get a disturbing-the-peace citation, but if you do, that card will cover the fine without looking any smaller. I want music. *Dance* music. I want it to sound like a jungle full of passion. Woodwinds and drums."

"Yes, Master." The keyboardist looked at the others

and adjusted a slider bar to maximum output. "'Torrid Yavin.' One, two, three—"

On "four" they launched into a ragged but spirited rendition of the backbeat-driven dance mix that had been popular a dozen years before on Coruscant, an anthem for the rebuilding of the world. Voort, surprised by the sheer volume their portable instruments put out, took an involuntary step back.

Then he started dancing.

He began with humanoid-figure hieroglyphics from Ziost. He well remembered the images from the scientific journals. Every four beats, he assumed a pose simulating one of those eerie ideograms. He knew his black nightsuit would accentuate his poses, make him stand out more.

All around the plaza, heads began turning toward him.

Then starfighters began to land on the courthouse lawn.

CHAPTER THIRTY-SIX

The nervous captain reached Thaal's viewport. Thaal opened it for the man. "Well?"

The captain had to speak up in order to be heard over the musical din now erupting from the stage at the center of the plaza. "It's not good. They found the access to the storage center. And—"

"One more hesitation and I bust you to enlisted man."

"Sir, they found Ledina Chott in the lift. She'd been drugged and brought *here*."

Thaal felt his heart sink. "The Wraiths again."

"It's time to run for it, sir."

Thaal thought it over. If he left now, he could be Thadley Biolan in his suite in minutes. Colonel Gidders could do damage control, blame everything on the missing General Thaal. But Gidders didn't have the full resources of the army behind him. Thaal needed those resources to find the Wraiths, to stamp them out.

"Captain, Lieutenant, it's time to choose sides." Thaal let a hard tone creep into his voice. The pilot turned in her seat to look back at him.

"Gidders is a good soldier. Blame for the operation under Black Crest is going to fall on him. I'm going to make his time in prison short and pleasant, and when he gets out he's going to be a rich man. To accomplish all this, we have to hang together. I need to know you're on my team. Everyone on my team has a golden future in front of him, but sometimes it's hard going. Are you with me?"

The driver nodded at once. "Yes, sir."

The captain gulped but nodded. "I'm your man, General."

"Good. Captain, use your public relations skills and this credcard." Thaal passed him the card. "Get back in there and start spreading funds around. And information. Information that my inspection here was to check into rumors about Colonel Gidders. He's been under suspicion for some time for trafficking in the black market."

"Yes, sir."

"Sir?" The lieutenant pointed out the back viewport. Thaal twisted to look.

A flight of starfighters was in the process of landing on the courthouse lawn. Thaal saw stubby A-wing interceptors, E-wing escorts, a bulbous Aleph with its trailing thruster extensions, all in Starfighter Command gray.

And they were coming to ground around two X-wings that waited, their canopies up, on the lawn.

Thaal jammed his head out through the viewport. "Sorrel doesn't have any X-wings up at her base. Does she?"

"No, sir." The driver leaned out her own viewport. "And those have add-on hardpoints on their S-foils. Not regulation. Those are the ones that strafed the base."

"The Wraiths are here! In the mine, or watching. And we're going to find them and kill them."

There were more starfighters circling overhead, and Thaal now saw a shuttle descending—one with a Starfighter Command colonel's insignia on the side. "Stang, Sorrel's here. I've got to send her packing. Captain, put a layer of permacrete on the situation inside. Lieutenant, with me." He exited his vehicle and hurried toward the courthouse lawn.

He got there just as the shuttle was landing. He positioned himself near the starboard boarding door. The boarding ramp, unfolding from the side, narrowly missed his foot.

Colonel Sorrel was the first to descend. Thaal offered her a neutral look. "Kadana. You don't need to be here."

She flashed him a smile without any warmth. "Two mystery X-wings and two of Gidders's roving flyboys, as usual overstepping their bounds, buzz the civilian station, and it's somehow not my business? General, the secret to telling jokes is to make them funny first." She reached ground level and looked around. "We followed the X-wings' transponder signals here. This is now a Starfighter Command jurisdiction incident. I've already cleared that with the planetary government."

"Blast it, Kadana, they didn't just buzz my base. They destroyed a training squadron. Killed one of my pilots."

Kadana nodded absently. Troopers—a naval boarding party from the look of them—were descending behind her and lining up on the grass. She gestured to get their officer's attention. "Spread out through the plaza. Look for X-wing pilots and anyone suspicious."

Thaal forced himself not to sputter. "You brought the navy in on this?"

"And my own military police. General, it's a new era of interservice cooperation here on Kuratooine." She set out, her stride long and fast, toward the plaza. "What *is* that racket?"

For a moment, Thaal reconsidered his aide's recommendation. A quick walk back to his speeder would result in his safety.

No, he needed to see bound Wraiths, whatever they were, in front of him experiencing interrogation. In fact, Colonel Sorrel should be there beside them, strapped down and anticipating the end of her life for defying him.

Thaal set out after her.

He activated his comlink. "Chakham Command Center, this is General Thaal. I want a full company of troopers here, at the Old Kura City Courthouse Plaza . . . place . . . whatever it's called . . . to take charge of a situation. Ten minutes. Light a fire under their butts."

Voort danced as an audience of zero onlookers became a line of people, then deepened into a crowd.

An *enthusiastic* crowd. As he ran through a full-length version of the Twi'lek Strutters' Night, some onlookers began clapping in time.

He decided to reward them. He grabbed the torso of his nightsuit and yanked. The whole nightsuit—like so many Wraith garments, a breakaway design—came off in his hands, leaving him in dark undershorts and socks. He spun the garment over his head as he strutted, then threw it into the crowd. He launched into a set of muscleman flexes punctuated by fanny-wiggles.

It was working. Onlookers were still arriving, some of them at a run. The musicians were in their groove now, jamming with the skill of long experience. Voort had caught his own rhythm, old moves coming back to him.

And now pilots and troopers were streaming his way.

Voort began to feel something strange within him, something he hadn't felt in years.

He was . . . enjoying himself.

He began a series of provocative belly-rolls. Some in the crowd, ladies especially, offered a ragged cheer.

* * *

Thaymes grinned at what he was seeing on the monitor. "Stage Boy."

"Time for me to go on again?" Turman was still behind the black curtain.

"No. The general's headed toward the confrontation point."

"All by himself?"

"He's following the colonel. I think you convinced her."

"Of course I convinced her. I can convince any woman of anything."

"Not when you smell like that."

Turman took a couple of seconds to answer. "I'd kill you if you weren't right."

Just as Thaal caught up to Colonel Sorrel, not far from the edge of the crowd watching the nearly naked Gamorrean, a Starfighter Command military policeman approached Sorrel from the side. He saluted. "We found the pilots, Colonel. Two droids, one protocol, one a heavyweight hauler."

Before the colonel could answer, Thaal offered a growled reply. "They're decoys, idiot. Protocol droids don't fly starfighters or shoot at people."

Colonel Sorrel shot him an amused glance, then returned her attention to the MP. "The general knows all about decoys, Corporal. Detain the droids but continue your search."

"Yes, Colonel." He fled the general's presence.

"I can't think with that racket going." Thaal left the colonel's side and shoved his way through the crowd, up to the musicians. "Stop playing!"

They looked at him blankly.

"*Stop. Playing.*" Stang! It would not do to pull out his hold-out blaster and shoot them, not even a little.

Someone in the crowd bellowed loud enough that Thaal could hear him: "Hey, Lieutenant Joykill, move along." Others laughed.

But the musicians ceased playing.

The Gamorrean onstage, now covered in sweat, stopped dancing. He glared down at Thaal and spoke, raising his voice so all in the crowd could hear him. "What's the problem? Don't you support the fine arts?"

Startled, Thaal almost took a step back. "You're a talking Gamorrean."

The dancer threw his hands up and looked skyward as if imploring Skifter Station for intervention. "Why doesn't anybody think I *know* that?" He stared down at the general. "I'm Professor Voort saBinring, late of Ayceezee Public College."

"You need—"

"But you can call me Piggy. Everybody calls me Piggy."

"You need to shut—"

"I'm a war veteran here on my first vacation in years. And I've just made my professional dancing debut!"

The crowd cheered.

Now the Gamorrean turned to the crowd and raised an arm in celebration. "Kura City audiences are the best audiences in the city!"

The crowd cheered again. Then the cheer tapered off as the onlookers tried to figure out what he'd said.

Thaal jabbed a finger at the dancer. "One more word out of you and I'll bury you up to your neck in my drill yard." He turned away from the stage and took a deep breath.

Now, with the music cut off, at last he could think again.

His pilot sidled up. "Sir, the troopers are inbound from the base."

He nodded and rubbed at his temples. "Good, good."

Colonel Sorrel and two of her MPs joined him. Sorrel gave him an admonishing look. "He was pretty good. For a Gamorrean."

"I don't care. Colonel, I need you to do me a favor. In that spirit of interservice cooperation you mentioned. I'll count you as a personal friend and ally for the rest of my military career if you do. Just take your people out of here. I'll take charge of this situation. Do it for the sake of my dead pilot."

"*General Stavin Thaal.*" The voice was very loud, amplified. Thaal turned to look. So did the military personnel and civilians all over the plaza. Even the droids turned to look.

A squat droid rolled toward the general—a large mobile waste bin with some machinery on top. Above the droid floated a holographic image, that of a man.

Part of a man. The only portions of him that were human were his white hair and the right side of his face, one blue eye staring unblinking at Thaal. The rest of his head was mechanical. Below his face Thaal could glimpse the top of a Starfighter Command uniform, its cut and design four decades old.

Colonel Sorrel looked at the general. "Friend of yours?"

He shook his head. "This man is named Phanan. He was mutilated in the war against the Empire. He faked his death a long time back. Recently he's been . . . stalking me."

His pilot interposed herself between the droid and the general and drew her blaster. She took aim at the droid's wheels. "It might be carrying explosives."

"We'll find out." Sorrel gestured to a couple of MPs. When the droid came to a stop in front of the pilot, they approached, scanners in hand. Both looked over at the colonel and shook their heads. But the pilot resolutely stayed in the way.

"Every word the general says is true!" The hologram offered a partial smile. Only his right upper lip was flesh, so it was only a quarter smile. *"Except for one thing. He calls himself Stavin Thaal . . . but he lies. Stavin Thaal is dead. Colonel, you must take this imposter into custody."*

Thaal felt a little trickle of worry. He kept it from his face. "Lieutenant, shut that thing down."

The pilot took aim at the holoprojector.

One of the MPs lashed out, his rifle butt connecting with the lieutenant's wrist. The blaster dropped from her hand. She clutched at her wrist, then looked back at the general for orders.

"Like I said." Colonel Sorrel's voice was artificially sweet. "This is a Starfighter Command jurisdiction."

"That just ended your career." The general became aware that onlookers, made nervous by the MP's attack, were beginning to edge away. "All right, Lieutenant. We're going back to the base. We'll let the colonel play like she's in charge during her last day as an officer." He turned and immediately bumped into a gold protocol droid.

Rocked by the impact, she clutched at him for support. "Oh, I say, my apologies."

He gave her a shove. She fell, landing on the pavestones, careful to keep from crushing her courier's pouch beneath her. "Oh, my. Clearly one apology is not enough."

In the distance, Thaal could see the first speeder carrying his Pop-Dogs inbound. A few seconds of stalling and they would be here, a more potent force than Sorrel's MPs. Nothing Phanan could say would endanger his exit.

So Thaal turned back to his accuser. "Show your-self, Phanan. If you think I'm an imposter, despite the fact that I have to go through security screenings *every day*, you just step right up to my face and prove it."

"I think I can clear this up." The voice was female, pleasant, and very familiar to Thaal.

He spun. Ahead of him, moving through the crowd, a wrap of synthfur in gold around her shoulders, was his wife. She smiled and waved.

"Zehrinne?" Confusion and relief replaced the sense of worry. "What are you doing on Kuratooine?" When she reached him, Thaal embraced her.

"I'm here for the gambling. Skifter Station's reputa-tion has reached all the way to Coruscant." She wrapped her arms around his neck, gave his cheek a kiss. "But maybe I *should* denounce you. Revenge for divorcing me."

"Not funny."

"No, I suppose it's not." Zehrinne's voice trailed off and she stared intently into his face. She cupped his jaw with her hand.

Then she broke away. "This is *not* my husband. He's wearing false eye lenses and makeup." She took another step back, shock on her face. "What have you done with my husband?"

Thaal spun in the direction of his speeder as if he intended to walk away. But in turning he noted the position of every naval trooper and Starfighter Com-mand MP near him. And of Colonel Sorrel. And Zeh-rinne.

Then he turned back toward his wife. "You shouldn't have done that."

Zehrinne shrugged, dropping for a bare second the pretense that she was afraid and shocked.

Colonel Sorrel took a step forward. "General, I need to take you into custody pending—"

Thaal reached into the coat pocket where his hold-out blaster rested. Wouldn't the colonel and his lovely traitor of a wife be startled when he drew, aimed, and discharged it right into their faces.

CHAPTER THIRTY-SEVEN

On a distant rooftop, stretched out under a canopy of flexiplast matching the roof's protective surface, Wran stared through his scope at the four oncoming Pop-Dog personnel transport speeders. They were inbound from the south and had rounded the eastern slope of Black Crest Mountain moments before.

Mostly Wran stared at their undersides. The speeders were well up in the air, exposing the repulsors and thrusters lining their bellies.

He zeroed in on the lead vehicle's main repulsorlift unit, kept his aim on it, and fired.

His laser shot hit the unit, pierced it. He saw surprise on the distant face of the pilot. The speeder continued forward, its flight speed undiminished, but it nosed over into a too-rapid descent.

"Comm, Gun. One down." He switched his aim to the second speeder.

Thaymes's voice whispered from his earpiece: "Gun, Comm. I read."

The other three trooper carriers went evasive, banking and losing altitude, their pilots hoping to take cover behind intervening buildings. The maneuvers were sharp, catching some of the Pop-Dogs off guard; Wran saw three spill over the side of his new target.

He fired. A black hole appeared in the side armor shielding the motivators of his new target. He fired twice more, creating two more holes, before his laser rifle whined at him to indicate it was recharging.

His second target continued its controlled descent as if undamaged. Troopers in the bed opened fire on Wran's position—on the entire top floor of the building beneath him, in fact. But then the starboard side of the speeder, the side he'd perforated, dipped as though the repulsor-lifts there had failed. The vehicle went from horizontal to vertical in an instant, pitching everyone but the strapped-in pilot free. Then it went upside down as it dipped beneath the buildings two streets over.

Wran heard a crash from the vicinity of his first target, followed by the sound of metal crumpling from the direction of his second.

He looked around. No other transport speeders were in sight. They'd gone below cover. "Comm, Gun. Two got by me."

"Understood. Team Shellfish, you're up. Gun, they may be gunning for *you*. Get clear."

"I hear that."

The third transport rose like a submersible vessel cresting the ocean's surface as it came over the lip of Wran's building. Even before it leveled off into horizontal flight the vengeful Pop-Dogs in the back began pouring blasterfire into the canopy erected at the far edge. The canopy jittered and rattled as it was burned into a crisp black ruin.

The transport came to a stop a few meters away. Two Pop-Dogs leapt off, landing in a crouch on the roof, and ran up to the canopy. One covered it while the other yanked it clear. The others took aim.

But there was nothing beneath.

Their own engines kept them from hearing, from reacting in time, as two speeder bikes crested the same roof edge they had just crossed. The two speeder bikes flashed by overhead, piloted by a blond human woman and a cream-brown Wookiee female.

Each of them dropped something as she passed overhead, a globe that fell into the speeder's passenger bed.

Veteran Pop-Dogs dived away. Others, quicker to act than to think, aimed after the speeder bikes. One got off a first shot that missed the blond woman by a dozen meters.

Then the globes detonated, filling the air with unhealthy-looking yellow gas. It spread across the roof, coating the Pop-Dogs all around.

Rugged men and women who'd been trained to kill began coughing, clutching their eyes.

Two hundred meters away, the distance increasing, the blond woman spoke into her headset mike. "Ranger to Comm. Third speeder down. Location of fourth unknown."

"I read."

"Tell Drug Boy good work."

There was no weapon in Thaal's pocket. He groped for it, startled, for a moment.

It couldn't be gone. In the minutes since the last time he'd felt it, he'd performed no physical activity that could have dislodged it. And no one had been close enough to him to—

That protocol droid.

He ran. He slammed Colonel Sorrel out of the way and headed toward the oncoming Pop-Dog transports—

They were gone.

No, one was still incoming. Almost at ground level, it rounded a street corner and headed toward him.

There was a familiar *poomp* sound from the interior of a black speeder parked nearby. Thaal could only watch as the grenade, fired from a military-issue blaster rifle, arced toward the transport speeder, hit the pavement in front of it, and exploded into an immense yellow cloud. Unable to maneuver in time, the transport flew through it. It emerged with its surfaces and passengers all tinged yellow. The passengers began curling into balls, clutching their eyes, heaving.

Thaal watched as, its pilot temporarily blind, the speeder sailed past him, heading in a curved, erratic course toward the starfighters in front of the courthouse.

Footsteps behind him, shouts to stop—Thaal turned toward the nearest vehicle, a red speeder bike with a human salesman standing protectively nearby.

Thaal hit the alarmed-looking man, knocking him out of the way, and started up the swoop. It roared into life, its too-powerful engines perfect for testosterone-addled boys and middle-aged men.

Then Thaal felt the sting in his neck.

He ignored it and revved the thrusters.

Tried to, anyway. His hands stayed clutched, unmoving, on the control bars. His feet would not budge from the pedals. The speeder bike rose a meter into the air and began a slow, slow drift forward, pushed along only by a light breeze.

Colonel Sorrel drew alongside, pacing him at a slow walking speed. "Pending a full investigation into these events."

The crude scapedroid pulled up to Thaal's right, opposite her. "You will find his tan skin is makeup. Beneath, he's a more yellow color. The lenses he wears on his eyes match Thaal's retinal prints, but his true eyes do not. Textured false skin on his hands and feet bears Thaal's prints, but Thadley Biolan's prints lie beneath." Ton Phanan shook his head. "I don't know how long

Stavin Thaal has been dead . . . but it's clear this man killed him long, long ago." Then the image of Ton Phanan winked out.

Trey, in the front seat of the black speeder, set his blaster rifle aside. "Nice shot."

Drikall put his dart rifle away. "I thought so."

"No, I meant me." Trey started up the speeder and headed away from the plaza. "But you get points for brewing up a good tear gas."

"Thank you for your unstinting praise."

"Tear gas that I fired, with consummate accuracy . . ."

"You're ruining it for me."

In minutes it was done. Civilians crowded around the drifting speeder bike an MP held in place. Others waited for the inert improvised scapedroid to start talking again. More MPs and Kura City Guards arrived and argued with one another about who should be arresting whom. General Thaal remained sitting, paralyzed, on the swoop he'd intended to ride to freedom. Colonel Sorrel took a dampened rag to his cheek, wiping away tan makeup to reveal yellower skin beneath. Zehrinne Thaal stayed nearby, answering investigator questions, wearing an expression of intermixed anxiety and disinterest.

Two blocks away, Voort, wrapped in a traveler's cloak, boarded the delivery speeder.

Thaymes looked up and smiled as he entered. "We're extracting?"

"We're extracting."

"Stage Boy, it's curtain call."

The black curtain was swept away. Ton Phanan stood

on the other side, in the black-lined rear of the compartment, and stared imperiously at the other two.

Then he pulled his face off, revealing Turman's features beneath. "I need a bath."

"You do, in fact." Thaymes hit a comm preset. "Comm Boy to all boys and girls. We are extracting. Don't talk to strangers on your way back. Don't accept candy."

A narrow viewport into the front compartment slid open. Sharr peered back through it. "Say, Leader. What happened to your clothes?"

"Shut up." Voort took a seat back in the black-lined mini studio Turman had been using.

"You lost them again?"

"Leader to Mind Boy, shut up. You know I took them off dancing."

"So you stole your own clothes this time."

Voort sighed. "Yes, and I'll get myself back someday."

Scut, Mulus, and the gold protocol droid boarded. Scut and Mulus took seats. The droid pulled her faceplate away, revealing the features of Myri. "It's impossible to sit down in this thing."

Turman gave her a look that included no sympathy. "Lean against the back panel. Don't fall down when we decelerate."

Myri reached into her black courier's pouch and pulled out a small blaster pistol. "Anyone for a souvenir? The last blaster General Thaal will ever own."

Thaymes looked interested. "What do you want for it?"

"An X-wing."

"Forget it."

"We'll get you out of that." Scut rose and began disassembling Myri's exterior plates.

Mulus gave Voort a pleading look. "*Now* can you help me understand what just happened?"

Voort nodded. "I was confused for a long time. I didn't understand why Thaal didn't break and run to begin his transformation process. It clearly would take weeks or months, a time frame in which he'd be vulnerable to capture and discovery. Then I realized—he already *had*. Months ago. He'd been wearing makeup and traditional appliances to fool security measures while, underneath, he already *was* Thadley Biolan."

Mulus's eyes lit up. "Ahhh. So at any point, he could take off his disguise and it would be impossible to prove he was the traitorous General Thaal."

"So we brought him here and gave him reasons to stay Thaal—greed for your gems, then a need for revenge against 'Ton Phanan.' On and on until we had everything set up and he couldn't get away."

The vehicle rocked a little, then Wran appeared in the front viewport beside Sharr. "Leader. What happened to your clothes?"

Voort reached forward and slid the viewport closed.

Sharr slid it open again. "The other speeder and the speeder bikes are here."

Voort leaned back, interlacing his fingers behind his head. "Wraiths, let's fly." Then he looked skyward, though he had no idea whether Vandor-3 was in the direction of his stare. "All right, Bhindi. *Now* we've won."

CHAPTER THIRTY-EIGHT

It was one of the most secure buildings on Coruscant. Shaped and colored like a hard-boiled egg cut lengthwise, it stretched the distance of two city blocks. Its every window was made of ship's armor-grade transparisteel. Its every entrance was under the constant scrutiny of a droid guard working from one of its three security command centers.

So when the squat redheaded man in the Alliance general's uniform finished with the three-stage process to give him admittance to his own quarters, it was not odd that he looked a touch surprised to see a dead man in his social chamber, drinking his wine.

The redheaded man paused as if collecting his thoughts while the door slid shut behind him. "General Loran."

Face Loran, dressed from neck to foot in his usual black, set his wineglass aside on an end table. "General Maddeus."

Borath Maddeus, head of Galactic Alliance Security, moved cautiously into his own home. "I thought you were dead. I'm very pleased to be wrong for once."

"You didn't *really*."

Maddeus grinned, the expression broad across his

face. "Well, I worried that this time it might be true. Your speeder explodes spectacularly, there's genetic evidence of you all over the wreckage, your whole family disappears . . ." He moved to sit on the sofa situated at a right angle to Face's. "What on nine ice worlds happened that day?"

"Three assassins. Two followed me into a marketplace, and I dealt with them. I got back to my speeder, got in, and asked my onboard droid brain if the vehicle had been tampered with. Turned out it had, so I did something that would have gotten me in deep trouble with my wife if it had turned out not to be a bomb. I cut myself and bled all over the controls and pilot's seat."

"Hence the genetic evidence."

"Correct. I instructed the droid brain to wait one minute and then take off, fly to the nearest landing location up the avenue, and land, a task simple enough for its piloting functions to handle. I knew where the killers' speeder had landed, so I assumed I was under observation from that position, and I slid out the viewport on the opposite side of my speeder. I figured if it was a bomb, it would detonate within seconds, while if it was a tracking or eavesdropping device, the killers' speeder would remain in place long enough for me to creep close enough to get good identification details off it."

"And it took off, and exploded, without you." Maddeus nodded, approving.

"The killers' speeder took off, and I spent the next few minutes comming my home and two or three people I'd seen recently in order to give them a heads-up." Face's voice turned grim. "The third killer went to my quarters. Broke in as slickly as I broke in here and confronted my wife in our bedroom, where she was packing to leave. She shot him, a twin burn to the gut. He took a while to die. She said he kept murmuring."

"Begging for mercy?"

"Complaining that he couldn't find a Wookiee. I assume he was in shock." Face shrugged. "We disposed of the body, Wraith-style, and went into hiding. So I could carry out the final phases of my investigation on Coruscant."

Maddeus patted his breast pocket. "I have the official reports from Colonel Sorrel and others. They have some crazy details. Such as the fact that a Ton Phanan led the Wraiths. But no Wraiths have reported to me."

"They reported to me, once I let them know I was still alive. And Ton Phanan didn't report to you since he's been dead for decades."

"He really *is* dead."

Face nodded.

"So who were your agents in the field?"

"I'll get to that. We have a new problem." Face took a deep breath. "Here's the bad news. Though General Stavin Thaal is currently shown as being in detention in an Alliance Security holding facility, he has, in fact, recently escaped. I intend to find him and recapture him today."

Maddeus's face hardened into a mask of disbelief and disapproval. "You're joking."

"Not at all."

Maddeus rose and fished his comlink out from a trouser pocket. "I'll get a direct, live holocam feed of his cell. We'll see about this."

"Don't bother." Face rose, too. "You know he escaped, because you helped him escape. General, I accuse you of being a member of the so-called Lecersen Conspiracy. Don't reach for any other devices, as I'll have to assume you're going for a weapon."

Maddeus stared at his uninvited guest. Cold anger crept into his voice. "You know, Face, I'd heard that it was hard to stay friends with you. Now I find it's true."

"You want to hear my presentation? I spent all morning working on it."

"Please." Maddeus sat again.

Face began walking, pacing back and forth a few steps in front of his host's sofa. "You've been in Intelligence for about thirty years. It's hard to find out many details of your career—your official record is full of redacted details. Not surprising. Mine's like that, too. Anyway, among the redacted details are what you were doing throughout the Yuuzhan Vong War."

"I was building resistance cells on conquered and endangered worlds. Everyone knows that."

"Yes! But which worlds, and when?" Face stopped his lateral pacing and turned toward Maddeus. "Not on Coruscant. My old friend Baljos, who was here, coordinating the resistance, would have told me. But you were nearby . . . You're not in their official histories because, like most Intelligence officers, you prefer not to be chronicled. And you were never in the army, so you aren't on their official roster. But when Coruscant was about to fall, and then-Colonel Thaal floated the idea of setting up a resistance unit on Vandor-Three, you got behind the idea. Volunteered to help him set it up. I'm not speculating here—some of the old Pop-Dogs on Kuratooine are beginning to answer pointed questions. You're an honorary Pop-Dog, and Thaal owes a lot of his hero status to you. And he returned the favor by pushing hard for you to be the head of GA Security when it was time to sweep Belindi Kalenda off to obscurity."

Maddeus fingered his comlink. His face was impassive.

Face resumed his pacing. "No answer? No denial? Of course you won't admit to anything. I might be recording. Anything you say might lead to your conviction. As you wish. Where was I? Oh, yes, appointment to head of GA Security. Thaal knew that you and he were two of a kind, greedy pragmatists, so it didn't offend you at all when he offered to bring you into the Lecersen Conspiracy. Betray the Alliance, get a fat fee—say, a small planet, or a small continent on a rich planet, or whatever—for the simple task of betraying the Galactic Alliance. To a new Empire or the highest bidder."

Maddeus finally spoke. "How much of this bizarre theory have you discussed with others?"

Face stopped, turned back toward Maddeus, and barked out a laugh. "Here's where you're hoping I'll say, *No, I've naïvely kept all these facts to myself so that if I can be eliminated, you can go on as before.* General, I have full reports waiting on distant computers that will transmit if I fail to report in. And my wife knows. You know what she'll do if you try something with me? She'll go up in an X-wing and burn you to a cinder. And she'll let our daughter handle the trigger. Good practice for a sixteen-year-old girl. It's *over*, General. We found the special shipping crates HyperTech used to transport hypercomm units—with the coffin-sized shielded compartment in them, where your agent rode with anesthetic gas grenades. We found Thaal's private moon where the captured crews of all those hijacked ships have been serving as slave labor. Colonel Gidders on Kuratooine didn't take well to having Thaal lay the blame at his feet, so he's telling everything he knows, including special smuggling favors that could only have come about with the help of the head of Galactic Alliance Security. You're finished."

"Are you done with your speculating?"

"Am I?" Face looked as though he were thinking it over. "No, not quite. We were just at the point where you turn traitor. Later, when the conspiracy is revealed, you realize that you and Thaal haven't been outed by your surviving fellow conspirators. But you have to make sure that you're safe. So you call *me* in. You say, *I have some misgivings about General Thaal. Look into it, will you?* The idea being that if there's anything to find, I'll find it. But if I don't find anything, you and Thaal are as free as hawk-bats. And about as pretty. Where was I? Oh, yes. You were nice enough to give me a yacht, the *Quarren Eye,* with one of those compromised HyperTech hypercomm systems installed in it. I didn't know for sure it was compromised, at first. But I'd never trust a comlink someone else handed to me, even if it's wrapped up in a yacht. So what I did was form two Wraith groups, gave them nonoverlapping assignments, didn't tell them about each other, while I sent you reports describing a third group made up of dead and fictitious Wraiths. And then . . ."

Face paused for dramatic effect. "I'm assuming that you hadn't told Thaal you were doing this. And at some point you did. He's not as subtle as you are, so he made arrangements to wipe out the Wraiths, me first. Assassins come after me and I go into hiding. Search orders, implicitly kill orders, go out for the Wraiths whose names have only ever been mentioned across the yacht's hypercomm. And so I knew I had you. But in the first couple of days I was making sure my family wouldn't be found out, one of my two real teams, following up on an investigation I'd told them to ignore, met the other one." He shook his head, his expression rueful. "With sad results. Sadder for Thaal, though, in the long run. A vengeful Wraith is a very effective Wraith."

Maddeus's voice emerged as a grumble. "I didn't see that coming. The diverse Wraith units. That was a good tactic, Face. And you found us out."

Face's eyebrows shot up. "That was a *confession.* Oh, sacred day. I really am recording, you know."

Maddeus shrugged. "It doesn't matter. Even if you're transmitting live, I can kill you and get out of this complex by routes you're unaware of. I have safe houses, alternative identities, just like you. You've cost me a lot of money, Face, but not my freedom."

Face put on a mocking expression. "You know, killing me is the first part of that equation, and the hardest to accomplish. I can have my blaster in hand a lot faster than you can grab yours."

"My blaster's already in hand."

Face started to reply, but was interrupted by a noise— the clearing of a throat behind him. Slowly, he turned to look.

At the near end of the darkened hallway stood the silhouette of a burly man holding a blaster pistol. The man silently stepped forward. His face, coming into the glow rod light, was that of Stavin Thaal—rather, of the post-transformation Thadley Biolan. He wore civilian clothes, casual striped prints in red and yellow suited to an offworld tourist. He did not look happy.

Face raised his hands and turned back to look at Maddeus. "Oh." He chewed on his inner cheek for a moment. "Oops. The safe house where you were hiding him was *here,* wasn't it?"

"One floor down. With my personal security station, which is crewed around the chrono." Maddeus held up his comlink. "I activated it—a casual button-press of a preset while I was fidgeting—and alerted my personal security crew." Now he spoke into it. "Seal all exits from my quarters except the access to your station. Exterior holocams and security alerts set for maximum paranoia. We may be visited in a few minutes."

The voice that responded was buzzy but distinct: "Yes, sir."

Maddeus stood. "Stavin and I are going to leave now, Face. They'll find your body when they break in. Your wife can go up in as many X-wings as she likes. She'll never know where to shoot. Stavin, shoot him. Then we can go out and kill your wife if you like."

The former head of the army took a step into the social room, coming fully into the light. "I don't really want to."

"What?"

"I don't . . . I don't feel well." Thaal reached up to his neckline, tugged . . . and his facial features and hair peeled away, revealing a different man. He was far younger than Thaal, pleasant-looking, smiling. "Now I feel better."

Face lowered his hands. "Surprise."

Hours later, the sun was just cresting the nearest wall of skytowers when Face Loran walked, jauntily, from the main entrance to the vast, circular Senate Building, seat of Galactic Alliance government.

Thirteen people waited for him, seated on stone benches a hundred meters out in the plaza. Face waved and headed their way, navigating through pedestrian cross-traffic. He sometimes skipped like a child when he had an open stretch of permacrete before him.

He wrapped himself around his wife and daughter, then turned toward the others. "I can't believe you waited all this time."

Myri looked forlorn. "We were bored. Nobody was shooting at us. So we came here."

Piggy nodded. "It's the boss's duty to entertain us. You've let us down."

"Well, I'll entertain you now. Where are the speeders?"

Sharr perked up. "Should I steal us some?" At Face's arched eyebrow, he relented. "They're this way." He led the Wraiths westward across the plaza.

"So." Face took a look around, making sure that no other pedestrians were close enough to hear, pausing when any stranger momentarily moved too close. "After a full night of briefing and debriefing and explaining, I spent a couple of hours telling Chief of State Dorvan what we've been up to. I left out lots of details. Like your names."

Dia, tucked under his arm, looked up at him. "And?"

"And he offered me a desk job."

She smiled. "Head apologist for the Chief of State?"

"Head of Galactic Alliance Security."

"Excellent." That was Trey, and Face felt thumps against his back, pats of congratulation.

Dia made her face stern. "If you take it, you have to treat it as a desk job. No shooting. No personal spying."

He leaned to kiss her. "You're the only one I want to spy on."

"Deal."

"And I plan to accept the job. Now that I know my wife won't burn me to a cinder."

"Bhindi would be pleased." Sharr's voice was suddenly just a touch hoarse. "The way it ended. A venomous reptile rooted out from a position of high influence."

Myri sounded matter-of-fact. "Piggy getting back in dancing shape. She'd like that, too."

Drikall sounded more cheerful. "Jesmin has the monkey-lizard of her black-market investigation off her back."

Thaymes cocked his head, thinking. "Zehrinne Thaal gets her 'dead husband's' possessions. And things of Thadley Biolan's she can prove were Thaal's. A blow for vengeful discarded wives everywhere."

Piggy summed it up. "Not a bad set of results for Wraith Squadron's last hurrah."

"About that . . ." Face fell silent as they passed through the plaza's western exit arch, between two uniformed security troopers. "Keep it up, guys. I'm your new boss. Just saying." When the Wraiths were far enough away, he continued. "This wasn't a Wraith Squadron mission. Wraith Squadron ceased to be when it was decommissioned three years ago."

"True." Jesmin looked unconcerned.

"This was an action by a group of concerned civilians who never revealed who they were." They moved onto the ramp up to the next level of pedestrian walkways, and Face continued. "As such, it doesn't have to be your *last* hurrah."

The Wraiths looked at one another. Suspicious, Scut, in his flat-top human face, frowned at Face. "What exactly are you saying?"

"I'm saying that every intelligence agency has some unofficial elements. Of course, they aren't part of the agency budget, so they have to raise their own revenues."

Adra gave her father a concerned look. "Dad, should I be hearing any of this?"

"Of course not. Where was I? So a certain amount of theft and illicit trade is part of the job description. Reporting directly to me, of course."

Wran thumped Piggy on the back. "Voort's the boss."

"Call me Piggy. And I'm just a mathematics professor. And part-time dancer."

Huge hairy paws fell on Piggy's shoulders and he was spun around to face Huhunna. She seized his hands, held his right hand elevated and placed his left on her hip, then spun him away ahead on the walkway in a smooth gliding motion.

Face blinked after them. "I didn't know she could ballroom dance. Odd for a Wookiee."

Jesmin nodded. "We still have some things to learn about each other. I suggest we buy some breakfast and get started."

Scut glared at her. "*Buy* breakfast?"

"All right, steal it."

The Yuuzhan Vong nodded, mollified. "That's better."

Myri stared after Piggy and Huhunna as they danced. "Well, that's new."

Face glanced her way. "What is?"

"He's smiling."

Read on for an excerpt from

Star Wars: Crucible

by Troy Denning

Published by Del Rey Books

CHAPTER ONE

With lowlifes of every species from three-eyed Gran to four-armed Hekto standing belly-to-bar, the Red Ronto reminded Han Solo of that cantina back on Mos Eisley—the one where he had first met Luke Skywalker and Obi-Wan Kenobi all those years ago. Smoke hung in the air so thick and green he could taste it, and the bartender was pulling drinks from a tangle of pipes and spigots more complicated than a hyperdrive unit. There was even an all-Bith band onstage—though instead of upbeat jatz, they were blasting the room with outdated smazzo.

Usually, the driving bass and stabbing wailhorn made Han think of banging coolant lines. But today he was feeling it, and why not? This trip promised to be more getaway than mission, and he was looking forward to seeing his old friend Lando Calrissian again.

"I don't like it, Han," Leia said, raising her voice over the music. "It's not like Lando to be so late."

Han turned to look across the table, where Leia sat with a half-empty drink in front of her. Wearing a gray gunner's jacket over a white flight suit, she was—as always—the classiest female in the joint . . . and, despite a few laugh lines, still the most beautiful. He thumbed a control pad on the edge of the table, and the faint yellow radiance of a tranquillity screen rose around their booth. The screen was a rare touch of quality for a place like the Red Ronto but one Han appreciated as the raucous music faded to a muffled booming.

"Relax," he said. "When has Lando ever missed a rendezvous?"

"My point exactly. Maybe that pirate problem is more dangerous than he thought." Leia nodded toward the entrance. "And take a look at that miner over there. His Force aura is filled with anxiety."

Han followed her gaze toward a young olive-skinned human dressed in the dust-caked safety boots and moly-tex jumpsuit of an asteroid miner. With a nose just crooked enough to be rakish and a T-6 blaster pistol hanging from his side, the kid was clearly no stranger to a fight. But he was not exactly streetwise, either. He was just standing there in the doorway, squinting into dark corners while he remained silhouetted against the light behind him.

"He doesn't look like much of a threat," Han said. Still, he dropped a hand to his thigh holster and undid the retention strap. As a Jedi Knight, Leia felt things through the Force that Han could not sense at all, and he had long ago learned to trust her instincts. "Probably just some crew chief looking for new hires."

The miner's gaze stopped at the Solos' booth. He flashed a brash smile, then said something to the bartender and raised three fingers.

"He's looking for us, Han," Leia said. "This must have something to do with Lando."

"Could be," Han allowed, but he hoped Leia was wrong. Missed rendezvous and strange messengers were never a good sign.

Any lingering doubt about the miner's intentions vanished when the bartender handed him a bottle of Corellian Reserve with three glasses and he started in their direction. There was something in his bold stride and cocky grin that set Han on edge.

"Whoever he is, I don't like him," Han said. "He's way too sure of himself."

Leia smiled. "He reminds me of *you* at that age," she said. "I like him already."

Han shot her a scowl meant to suggest she needed an eye exam, and then the newcomer was at their table, stepping through the tranquillity screen. He placed the glasses on the table and opened the bottle.

"I hope you don't mind," he said, pouring. "But they keep a case of Reserve on hand for Lando, and I thought you might prefer it to the usual swill around here."

"You were right," Leia said, visibly relaxing at the mention of Lando's name. "Whom shall I thank?"

The miner placed a hand on his chest. "Omad Kaeg, at your service," he said, bowing. "*Captain* Omad Kaeg, owner and operator of the *Joyous Roamer,* one of the oldest and most profitable asteroid tugs in the Rift."

Han rolled his eyes at the overblown introduction, but Leia smiled. "It's a pleasure to meet you, Captain Kaeg." She motioned at the table. "Won't you join us?"

Kaeg flashed his brash smile again. "It would be an honor."

Instead of taking a seat where Leia had indicated, Kaeg leaned across the table to set his glass in the shadows on the far side of the booth—an obvious attempt to position himself where he could watch the door. Han quickly rose and allowed Kaeg into the back of the booth. If a stranger wanted to place himself in a crossfire zone between two Solos, Han wasn't going to argue.

"So, how do you know Lando?" Han asked, resuming his seat. "And where is he?"

"I know Lando from the miners' cooperative—and, of course, I supply his asteroid refinery on Sarnus." Kaeg's gray eyes slid toward the still-empty entrance, then back again. "I think he's at the refinery now. At least, that's where he wants you to meet him."

Han scowled. "*On* Sarnus?" The planet lay hidden deep in the Chiloon Rift—one of the densest, most difficult-to-navigate nebulae in the galaxy—and its actual coordinates were a matter of debate. "How the blazes does he expect us to find it?"

"That's why Lando sent me," Kaeg said. "To help."

Kaeg's hand dropped toward his thigh pocket, causing Han to draw his blaster and aim it at the kid's belly under the table. He wasn't taking any chances.

But Kaeg was only reaching for a portable holopad projector, which he placed on the table. "Let me show you what you'll be facing."

"Why not?" Han waved at the holopad with his free hand.

Kaeg tapped a command into the controls, and a two-meter band of braided shadow appeared above the pad. Shaped like a narrow wedge, the braid appeared to be coming undone in places, with wild blue wisps dangling down toward the corrosion-pitted tabletop and even into Han's ale tankard.

"This, of course, is a chart of the Chiloon Rift," Kaeg said.

He tapped another command, and a red dash appeared in the holomap, marking the cantina's location on Brink Station just outside the Rift. The dash quickly stretched into a line and began to coil through the tangled wisps of hot plasma that gave the Chiloon Rift its distinctive array of blue hues. Before long, it had twisted itself into a confusing snarl that ran vaguely toward the center of the nebula.

"And this is the best route to Lando's refinery on Sarnus," Kaeg said. "I've been doing my best to keep the charts accurate, but I'm afraid the last update was two standard days ago."

"Two *days*?" Han asked. With three kinds of hot plasma rolling around at near light speed, hyperspace lanes inside the Rift tended to open and close quickly—sometimes in *hours*. "That's the best you can do?"

"I'm sorry, but, yes," Kaeg said. "It's important to take it slow and careful in there. If you were to leave a hyperspace lane and punch through a plasma cloud, you would fry every circuit on your ship—including your navigation sensors."

"You don't say," Han said. Hitting a plasma pocket was one of the most basic dangers of nebula running, so it seemed to him that Kaeg was working way too hard to make sure he knew how dangerous it was to travel the Rift. "Thanks for the warning."

"No problem." Kaeg grinned, then let his gaze drift back toward the cantina door. "Any friend of Lando Calrissian's is a friend of mine."

Instead of answering, Han caught Leia's eye, then tipped his head ever so slightly toward their tablemate. She nodded and turned toward Kaeg. After forty years together, he knew she would understand what he was thinking—that something felt wrong with Kaeg's story.

"We appreciate your concern, Captain Kaeg." Leia's tone was warm but commanding, a sure sign that she was using the Force to encourage Kaeg to answer honestly. "But I still don't understand why Lando isn't here himself. When he asked us to look into the pirate problem in the Rift, he was quite insistent that he would meet us here at the Red Ronto personally."

Kaeg shrugged. "I'm sorry, but he didn't explain the change of plans. His message only said to meet you here and make sure you reached Sarnus." Continuing to watch the door with one eye, he paused, then spoke in a confidential tone. "But I don't blame you for hesitating. This trip could be very risky, especially for someone your age."

"Our *age*?" Han bristled. "You think we're old or something?"

Kaeg finally looked away from the door. "Uh . . . *no*?" he replied. "It's just that, uh—well, you *do* need pretty quick reflexes in the Chiloon Rift."

"It's called *experience*, kid," Han said. "Someday, you might have some yourself . . . if you live that long."

"No offense," Kaeg said, raising his hands. "I'm just worried about you heading in there alone."

"Don't let a few wrinkles fool you, Captain Kaeg," Leia said. "We can take care of ourselves."

Kaeg shook his head almost desperately. "You wouldn't say that if you had ever been inside the Rift," he said. "It isn't the kind of place you should go without a guide on your first visit. The plasma in there kills S-thread transmissions, so HoloNet transceivers are worthless—and even emergency transmitters aren't much good."

"What about the RiftMesh?" Han asked. "All that communications hardware, and you're telling me it doesn't work?"

"The 'Mesh works, but it's slow. It can take an hour for a beacon to relay a signal." Kaeg tapped the holopad controls again, and a multitude of tiny white points appeared in the holochart. "And it's not unusual for a message to pass through a thousand beacons before being picked up. Trust me, there's no lonelier place in the galaxy to be stranded."

"It's a wonder any rock grabbers go in there at all," Han replied. "I can't imagine a worse place to be dragging around half a billion tons of ore."

"It's worth it, my friend." Ignoring Han's sarcasm—or possibly missing it altogether—Kaeg flashed a square-toothed grin. "The tumblers in the Rift are fantastic, Han. There are more than anyone can count, and most are heavy and pretty."

By *tumblers*, Kaeg meant asteroids, Han knew. *Heavy and pretty* was slang for a high content of precious metals. According to Lando, the Chiloon Rift contained the largest and most bountiful asteroid field anywhere, with more capture-worthy tumblers than any other place in the galaxy. Unfortunately, its roiling clouds of plasma and a sudden infestation of pirates meant it was probably also the most dangerous.

"Which is why the pirates are hitting asteroid tugs instead of ingot convoys," Leia surmised. "The convoys have combat escorts, but the tugs are hauling all that valuable ore around alone, with no one to call for help."

Kaeg nodded eagerly. "It's terribly dangerous. You can send a message and go gray waiting for an answer." He winced almost immediately, then said, "No offense, of course."

"None taken," Leia said, a bit stiffly. "But with all of those asteroid tugs running around, I can't imagine the pirates coming after a small vessel like the *Falcon*."

Not seeming to notice how he was being tested, Kaeg shrugged and leaned forward. "Who knows?" he asked. "Even if the pirates aren't interested in the *Falcon*, there are many other dangers."

"And let me guess," Han said. "You're willing to make sure we have a safe trip—for the right price?"

"I could be persuaded to serve as your guide, yes," Kaeg said. "As I said, any friend of Lando Calrissian is a friend of mine."

"How very kind of you." Leia flashed a tight smile, and again Han knew what she was thinking. No trick was too low for a pirate gang, and one of their favorites was to slip a saboteur aboard the target vessel. "But you *still* haven't explained why Lando didn't meet us here himself."

"Your guess is as good as mine," Kaeg said. "As I mentioned, he didn't give a reason."

Han leaned toward Kaeg and pointed a finger at him. "You see, now, that's where your story falls apart. Lando isn't the kind of guy who fails to show with no explanation. He would've said why he couldn't make it."

Kaeg showed his palms in mock surrender. "Look, I've told you all I know." He focused his attention on Leia. "Lando kept the message short. I'm assuming that's because he didn't want everyone in the Rift to know his business."

"And why would *that* happen?" Leia asked. "Do you have a habit of breaking confidences?"

Kaeg scowled and shook his head. "Of course not," he said. "But I told you—Lando sent that message over the RiftMesh."

"And?" Han asked.

Kaeg sighed in exasperation. "You *really* don't understand how things work here," he said. "The RiftMesh is an open network—*open*, as in one single channel. Everybody listens, with nothing encrypted. If a message *is* encrypted, the beacons won't even relay it. That makes it tough to keep a secret, but it also makes life hard on the pirates. They can't coordinate a swarm attack if everybody is listening to their chatter over the RiftMesh."

"And that works?" Han asked.

Kaeg waggled a hand. "It's not perfect. The pirates find other ways to coordinate," he said. "But the 'Mesh is better than nothing. And it helps the rest of us track one another, so our tugs don't pile up when a good hyperspace lane opens."

Han turned to Leia. "That actually makes sense."

"As far as it goes." Leia did not take her eyes off Kaeg. "But he's been working pretty hard to get us to take him on, and that just doesn't make sense."

"Yeah, I know." Han glanced back at their confused-looking table companion. "Since when do tug captains have time to take on extra work as tour guides?"

The confusion vanished from Kaeg's face. "Is *that* all that's troubling you?" he asked. "My tug has been in for repairs for a month. That's how Lando knew I would be here to give you his message. And, quite honestly, I could use something to do."

Han considered this, then nodded and holstered his blaster. "Maybe we're being too hard on the kid," he said. "After all, he *did* know about Lando's stock of Corellian Reserve."

Leia continued to study Kaeg for a moment, no doubt scrutinizing him through the Force, then said, "Fair enough. But he's worried about something."

"Yes," Kaeg said. "I'm worried that you aren't going to let me guide you to Sarnus." He glanced toward the door again. "But if you don't want my help, you know how to use a holochart."

He started to rise.

"Not so fast, kid." Han grabbed Kaeg's arm. "You've been watching the door since you got here. You expecting someone?"

"Not anymore," Kaeg said, still watching the front of the cantina. "If you don't mind, I have things to do."

Han pulled the asteroid miner back down, then followed his gaze and saw a huge, scaly green figure entering the cantina. The reptiloid was so tall he had to duck as he stepped through the entrance, and his thick arms hung from shoulders so broad that they rubbed both sides of the doorframe. His spiny skull crest almost scraped the ceiling, and a thick tail swept the floor behind him. The creature stopped just inside the room, vertical pupils dilating to diamonds as his pale eyes adjusted to the dim light.

"Who's *that*?" Han asked, keeping one eye on the newcomer.

"No one you'd ever want to meet." Kaeg slid into the

back of the booth and slumped down in the shadows. "One of the Nargons."

"Who are the Nargons?" Leia asked. "I'm not familiar with that species."

"Lucky you," Kaeg said, sinking even deeper into his seat. "You should try to keep it that way."

"Care to explain why?" Han asked. "And while you're at it, maybe why you're hiding from that one?"

As Han spoke, two more Nargons ducked through the door, their big hands hanging close to the blasters in their knee holsters. They stepped forward to flank the first one and began to scan the cantina interior.

Kaeg was careful to avoid looking in their direction. "Who says I'm hiding?"

"Kid, I was ducking bounty hunters before your grandfather met your grandmother." As Han spoke, the first Nargon's gaze reached their table and stopped. "I know the signs, so answer the question—or you're on your own."

Kaeg's brow shot up. "You would back me?"

"Assuming you're really a friend of Lando's," Leia said cautiously, "and *if* you start being honest with us. Then, yes, we have your back."

The first Nargon said something to his companions. They eased away in different directions, one going to the far end of the bar, the other drawing angry glares as he jostled his way into the opposite corner.

Kaeg swallowed hard. "Deal."

"Good," Han said. "Tell us what you know about Nargons." He reached over and tapped the holopad controls, and the chart dissolved in a rain of sparkles. "Like, where do they come from?"

"Kark if I know," Kaeg said. "I never saw them before the new outfit brought them in, when the pirates grew so bad."

"New outfit?" Han asked. He was no expert on the

Chiloon Rift, but he knew the miners here were mostly independent operators whose families had been in the business for generations. "*What* new outfit?"

Kaeg's lip curled in distaste. "Galactic Exploitation Technologies," he said. "GET. You know them?"

Han had never heard of GET, but he didn't bother to ask for details. His attention was fixed on the entrance, where two more figures were just stepping through the doorway. Unlike the Nargons, this pair was not an exotic species. Standing less than two meters tall, with shoulders no broader than Han's, they were almost certainly human. But they were also wearing full suits of colored armor and blocky helmets with opaque visors, and that could mean only one thing.

"Mandalorians!" Leia whispered.

"Yeah." Han hated Mandalorians. Like their leader, Boba Fett, they had a bad habit of selling their fighting skills to the highest bidder—and the highest bidder was almost always on the side opposite Han. He turned to Kaeg. "What are Mandos doing here?"

"They work security for GET. They're handlers for the Nargons." As Kaeg spoke, the first Nargon leaned down to say something to the taller Mandalorian. "Is this going to be a problem? Because if you can't deal with Mandalorians, then you really can't deal—"

"Relax, kid," Han said. "We can deal with Mandos. We can deal with *anything* in this room."

Kaeg looked doubtful. "Tell me that after you figure out what a Nargon is."

The first Nargon raised a long arm and pointed toward their booth, then fell in behind the two Mandalorians as they crossed the room. The muffled rhythms of the smazzo music continued to reverberate through the tranquillity screen, but the cantina fell otherwise uneasy and still. Judging by all the worried brows and averted eyes, Han half expected the other patrons to clear out.

Instead, most remained in their seats, and the miners in the crowd turned to glare openly as the trio passed.

"Not real popular, are they?" Han remarked.

"Nobody likes rock jumpers," Kaeg said. "Galactic Exploitation came in fast and hard with a whole fleet of those giant asteroid crushers. Trouble is, vessels that big aren't nimble enough to run the Rift—and even if they were, GET crews have no nose."

"No nose?" Leia asked.

Kaeg scowled. "You need a sixth sense to operate here," he said. "Outsiders can't smell good rock, and they can't see a lane getting ready to open. They have no feel for how the Rift moves."

"So they trail independent operators instead," Han said. "And then push in on your finds."

Kaeg nodded. "*Push in* is one way to say it. *Steal* is another."

"And when did that start?" Leia asked.

"About a standard year ago. GET showed up a little before the pirate problem erupted in such a big way." Kaeg's face clouded with anger. "And we're pretty sure GET is buying from pirates, too."

Leia shot Han a look that suggested she found the timing as suspicious as he did, and he asked, "What makes you say that?"

"Where else can you take a stolen asteroid?" Kaeg asked. "GET bought up all the small refineries. Now their only real competition in the Rift is Lando's operation on Sarnus, and *he* would never buy from pirates."

Before Han could agree, the Mandalorians arrived with the lead Nargon. Too huge to fit completely inside the tranquillity partition, the reptiloid stopped halfway through and loomed over Leia, who seemed untroubled by the gold static dancing over his scales. The short Mandalorian—a squat fellow in yellow armor—came to

Han's side and stood with one hand resting on his holstered blaster.

The taller Mandalorian placed a chair at the table across from Kaeg, then removed his helmet and sat. He had dark curly hair and a burn-scarred face that appeared half melted along the left side. Barely glancing at the Solos, he placed the helmet in front of him, then folded his hands on top and leaned toward Kaeg.

"Skipping out on your marker, Kaeg?" he asked. "I took you for smarter than that."

"I'm not skipping out on anything, Scarn." Kaeg's voice was a little too hard to be natural. "I'm just catching a ride so I can get what I owe you."

A muffled snort sounded inside the helmet of the shorter Mandalorian, and Scarn sneered. "Why do I doubt that?"

"Look, you know what those pirates did to my tug," Kaeg said. "There's no way she's leaving the repair docks for another two weeks, minimum."

Scarn shrugged. "So?"

"So I'll be back for her," Kaeg said. "But it's going to take more credits than I had *before* our game to pay for repairs. I'm heading to Sarnus to make arrangements. I'll get what I owe you at the same time."

"Arrangements with Calrissian?" Scarn rubbed his chin just long enough to pretend he was thinking about it, then shook his head. "I don't think so. We don't like Calrissian, and he doesn't like us. We'll do this another way."

"That's the only way we're going to do it," Kaeg said. "I'm not giving you the *Roamer*—that ship has been in my family for two hundred years."

Kaeg overtly dropped his hand below the table, and Han tried not to wince. Hinting at violence was usually a bad idea when you were outnumbered and outflanked. But at least he was feeling better about the kid's story.

Gambling debts he could understand. He'd had a few himself, and the debt explained why Kaeg was so eager to get off Brink Station.

Han rested a hand on his own holstered blaster and tried to look bored, as though firefights against armored Mandalorians backed by overgrown lizards were a common occurrence for him . . . and, really, that wasn't much of an exaggeration.

The Nargon hissed and started to pull the blaster from his knee holster, but Scarn called the reptiloid off with a two-fingered wave.

"There's no need for anyone to get hurt today." The undamaged half of his face smiled at Kaeg. "The last thing I want is that crate of corrosion you call an asteroid tug."

It was hard to say whether Kaeg's frown was one of confusion or outrage. "The *Roamer* may not look like much, but she's all pull," he said. "She's dragged moons out of orbit."

Scarn looked unimpressed. "If you say so. But I have another idea." He extended a hand toward his Mandalorian subordinate. "Jakal?"

Jakal withdrew a pair of folded flimsies from a pouch on his equipment belt and handed them to Scarn.

Scarn unfolded the sheets and pushed them toward Kaeg. "Considering the size of your marker, that's more than fair."

Kaeg eyed the flimsies skeptically, then reluctantly picked them up and began to read. Scarn waited with a bored expression, as though the kid's consent was irrelevant to what was about to happen. Han kept his hand on his blaster grip and watched the Nargon watch him. Jakal's helmet pivoted from side to side as he kept an eye on the rest of the miners in the cantina, who were all carefully observing the situation at Kaeg's table. The other two Nargons continued to stand guard in opposite corners of the room, their tails bumping the walls as they, too, scanned the crowd. But no one was watching Leia, who was probably the most dangerous person in the Red Ronto.

Maybe the situation wasn't as bad as it looked.

Kaeg was still on the first page when he stopped reading and looked across the table. "Galactic Exploitation wants my family's share of the miners' cooperative?"

Scarn nodded. "That's right," he said. "You sign your share over to GET, then GET pays me, and your debt is settled. Simple."

Kaeg looked more confused than alarmed. "Why?"

Scarn shrugged. "All I know is, the bosses want to join your little co-op," he said. "Maybe they're worried one of their yachts will need to be rescued or repaired or something."

"Then they can pay for an associate membership." Kaeg tossed the flimsies in the middle of the table. "I'm not giving you a founder's share. I'd be run out the Rift."

Scarn's expression grew cold. "Either you put your thumb in the verification box, or Qizak here rips your arm off and does it for you. Your choice."

A nervous sheen came to Kaeg's lip, but he looked into the Nargon's eyes and managed to fake being calm. "Just so you know, Qizak, you touch me and you die. Clear?"

Qizak bared a fang, then looked to Scarn. "*Now*, boss?"

Leia raised a hand. "Hold that thought, Qizak." Her voice was calm and soothing, the way it always was when she made a Force suggestion. "There's no rush here."

The Nargon studied her, as though considering whether to rip her limb from limb or to simply bite off her head.

Leia ignored the glare and focused on Scarn. "How much does Omad owe, *Ver'alor*?"

The eye on the good side of Scarn's face flashed at her use of the Mandalorian word for *lieutenant*. But the eye on the scarred side merely pivoted in her direction, its cybernetic cornea fogging as it adjusted focus.

Scarn studied Leia in silence. His sneer of contempt suggested that he had no idea she was Princess Leia Organa Solo, sister to Jedi Grand Master Luke Skywalker, and a famous Jedi Knight herself. And if Scarn hadn't recognized Leia, it was a pretty good bet he didn't realize that her companion was Han Solo, one of the finest gamblers in the galaxy—and someone who would know how a cybernetic eye might be used to cheat a kid in a high-stakes sabacc game.

Finally, Scarn asked, "What do you care? You his mother or something?"

Leia's eyes grew hard. "Or something," she said. "All you need to know is that I'm a friend who might be willing to cover his debt . . . once you tell me how much it is."

She pointed at the transfer document and used the Force to summon both pieces of flimsi into her hand.

Scarn's jaw dropped, then his gaze snapped back to Kaeg. "If you think hiring some old Jedi castoff will get you out of your marker—"

"She's not exactly a castoff," Kaeg interrupted. "But you'll get your money, Scarn. Omad Kaeg is no shirker."

"Yeah, but he *is* kind of a rube," Han said. He looked Scarn square in his artificial eye, but when he spoke, it was to Kaeg. "Omad, the next time you play sabacc, make sure it's not with someone who has a cybernetic eye. Those things can be programmed to cheat in about a hundred ways."

Kaeg's voice turned angry. "You have a cybernetic eye, Scarn?"

"He didn't mention that?" Han shook his head and continued to watch Scarn. "You see, now that's just bad form."

Scarn's face grew stormy. "You calling me a cheater?" His voice sounded exactly like the voices of all the other cheaters Han had spotted over the years—well-rehearsed outrage with no real astonishment or confusion. "Because you weren't even there."

"No, but Omad was." Being careful not to look away from Scarn, Han nodded toward Kaeg. "What do you think, kid? Fair game or not?"

It was Leia who answered. "*Not*, I think." Her eyes remained on the flimsi. "Omad, a million credits on a *marker*? Really?"

"I needed to pay for repairs," Kaeg explained. "And I'm usually very good at sabacc."

"Oh, I can see that," Han said. He was starting to wonder about the convenient timing of the pirate attack on Kaeg's ship—and he was starting to get angry. "And I'll bet after the pirates had you limping back into the station, someone at the bar was buying drinks and talking about the Mando sucker in the back room."

"As a matter of fact, yes." Kaeg sounded embarrassed. "How did you know?"

"It's an old trick, Omad." Leia's voice was kind. "Han has fallen for it himself a few times."

"You have?" Kaeg asked. "Han Solo?"

"No need to talk about that now," Han said. *A few times* was exaggerating, but he knew Leia was just trying to keep Kaeg from starting a fight she didn't think they would win. Deciding she was probably right, he shifted his gaze back to Scarn. "So now that we know your marker is no good, why don't you sign it paid—"

"I didn't cheat," Scarn said, sounding a little *too* insistent. He raised a thumb to the damaged side of his face, then popped out his cybernetic eye and slapped the device on the table. "Check it yourself."

Han barely glanced at the thing. "I'd rather check the eye you used during the game."

"That *is* the one I used."

Scarn's tone remained aggressive and hostile, but the mere fact that he had switched from intimidation to arguing his innocence told Han the balance of power had shifted. Scarn recognized the Solo name, and he was no more eager to start a fight with Han and Leia than *they* were to start one with him and his Nargons.

"Maybe that's the cybernetic eye you were using," Han said, "and maybe it's not. But you didn't tell the kid you had one, and you gotta admit that looks bad." When Scarn didn't argue, Han extended a hand. "So give me the kid's marker, and we'll put all this behind us."

Scarn remained silent and looked around the table, no doubt weighing his chances of actually leaving with Kaeg's thumbprint against the likelihood of surviving a fight. Han risked a quick peek in Leia's direction and was rewarded with a subtle nod. She could feel in the Force that Scarn was worried, and *worried* meant they were going to avoid a battle.

Then Kaeg asked, "What about the rest?"

"The rest of what?" Han asked, confused.

"I lost ten thousand credits *before* I signed that marker," Kaeg said. "It was all the money I had."

Han frowned. "You took your last ten thousand credits to a sabacc table?"

"I didn't see another choice," Kaeg said. "And don't tell me *you* haven't done the same thing."

"That was different," Han said.

He glanced over at Scarn and caught him glaring at Kaeg in fiery disbelief. There was no way the Mandalorian was going to return the ten thousand credits, probably because most of it had already been spent. Han shifted his gaze back to Kaeg.

"Look, kid, ten thousand credits may seem like a lot right now, but it's not worth starting a firefight over. Why don't you think of it as tuition?"

"No," Kaeg said, glaring at Scarn. "Nobody cheats Omad Kaeg."

"Omad," Leia said gently, "*we*'re going to pay you for serving as our guide. It will be more than you lost, I promise."

Kaeg shook his head. "It's not about the credits. These Out-Rifters come pushing in here, thinking they can just take what's ours." In a move so fast it was barely visible, he laid his blaster on the table, his finger on the trigger and the emitter nozzle pointed in Scarn's direction. "It's time they learned different."

Han groaned but slipped his own blaster out of its holster and placed it on the table with a finger on the trigger. Scarn did the same, while Jakal pulled his weapon and held it nozzle-down, ready to swing into action against Han or Kaeg. Leia simply laid the transfer document in front of her and dropped one hand onto her lap, where it would be close to her lightsaber. The Nargon watched them all and snarled.

When no one actually opened fire, Han let out his breath and shifted his gaze back and forth between Kaeg and Scarn. "Look, guys, things can go two ways from here," he said. "Either everyone in our little circle dies, or you two come to an understanding and we all walk away. Which will it be?"

Kaeg stared into Scarn's remaining eye. "I'm good with dying."

"Then why are you talking instead of blasting?" Scarn asked. Without awaiting a reply, he turned to Han. "Jakal is going to put his blaster away and hand over that marker. Then we're done here. Clear?"

"What about the kid's ten thousand?" Han didn't really expect to get it back, but he wanted Kaeg to understand that some mistakes couldn't be fixed, that sometimes the only smart move was to cut your losses and move on. "Jakal going to hand that over, too?"

Scarn shook his head. "The ten thousand is gone," he said. "You think I'd be out here on the edge of nothing, wrangling a bunch of overgrown lizards, if I didn't have problems of my own?"

The question made Qizak's skull crest stand erect, and the Nargon studied Scarn with an expression that seemed half appetite and half anger. Han contemplated the display for a moment, wondering just how much obedience the Mandalorian could truly expect from his *overgrown lizards*, then turned to Kaeg.

Kaeg sighed and took the finger off his blaster's trigger. "Fine." He held a hand out toward Jakal. "Give me the marker."

Jakal holstered his weapon, then pulled another flimsi from his belt pouch and tossed it in the middle of the table.

And that was when Qizak said, *"Coward."*

Scarn craned his neck to glare up at the Nargon. "Did you say something?" he demanded. "Did I *tell* you to say something?"

Qizak ignored the question and pointed to the unsigned transfer document, still lying in front of Leia. "The bosses need Kaeg's share," he said. "That is the plan they have."

Kaeg's eyes flashed in outrage. *"Plan?"*

Shaking his head in frustration, Han said, "Yeah, kid, *plan*. I'll explain later." Hoping to keep the situation from erupting into a firefight, he turned back to Scarn. "Like you said, we're done here. Go."

Qizak pointed a scaly talon at the transfer document. "When Kaeg gives his share to the bosses."

"No, *now*," Scarn said, rising. "I give the orders. You—"

A green blur flashed past Han's face, ending the rebuke with a wet crackle that sent Scarn sailing back with a caved-in face. The blur hung motionless long enough to identify it as a scaly green elbow, then shot forward again as Qizak grabbed Kaeg's wrist.

Jakal cursed in Mandalorian and reached for his blaster again—then went down in a crash of metal and snapping bone as the Nargon's huge tail smashed his knees. Han stared. *How do we stop this thing?*

By then Qizak was dragging Kaeg's hand toward the transfer document. Han checked the other Nargons and found them both in their corners, still watching the crowd rather than the trouble at the booth. Good. If they were worried about the other patrons getting involved, it would take them longer to react. That gave the Solos ten or twelve seconds to even the odds—maybe longer, if the miners really did jump into the fight.

Han pointed his blaster at Qizak's head. "Hey, Finhead. Let—"

A green streak came sweeping toward Han's arm. He pulled the trigger, and a single bolt ricocheted off Qizak's temple. Then a scaly wrist cracked into Han's elbow; his entire arm fell numb, and the blaster went flying.

From the other side of the booth came the *snap-hiss* of an igniting lightsaber. The acrid stench of burning scales filled the air. Qizak roared and whirled toward a spray of blue embers that made no sense, and then an amputated forearm dropped onto the table, trailing smoke and sparks.

Sparks?

Too desperate to wonder, Han launched himself at Qizak, burying his shoulder in the Nargon's flank and pumping his legs, driving through like a smashball player making a perfect tackle.

Qizak barely teetered.

But the huge alien *did* look toward Han, and that gave Leia the half second she needed to jump onto the booth seat. Her lightsaber whined and crackled, and Qizak's remaining arm dropped next to the first. Two arms, maybe three seconds. Not fast enough. Han drove harder, trying to push the Nargon off balance . . . or at least distract him.

Leia buried her lightsaber in Qizak's side. The Nargon roared and pivoted away, but not to retreat. Remembering how the lizard had smashed Jakal's knees, Han threw himself down on the huge tail, slowing it just enough to give Leia time to roll onto the table. The lightsaber fell silent for an instant, then sizzled back to life.

Qizak let out an anguished bellow, then his tail whipped in the opposite direction. Han went tumbling and came to a rest against a flailing heap of armor— Jakal, writhing with two broken legs. Han spun and reached for the Mandalorian's blaster—then discovered that his numb hand lacked the strength to wrench the weapon from Jakal's grasp.

Jakal pulled it free and started to swing the nozzle toward Han.

"Are you crazy?" Han jerked his thumb toward Qizak. "He's the one who smashed Scarn's face!"

Jakal paused, and Han used his good hand to snatch the blaster away. So far, the fight had lasted six, maybe seven seconds. The other Nargons would join in soon. A tremendous banging sounded from the booth, and suddenly Leia was trapped against the wall as the armless Qizak tried to kick the table aside to get at her. Kaeg stood next to her, pouring blaster fire into the lizard's chest, but the bolts bounced away with little effect.

"What *are* those things?" Han gasped.

Jakal might have groaned something like *scaled death*,

but Han was already attacking Qizak from behind, firing with his off-hand. The storm of ricochets was so thick, he did not realize he was caught in a crossfire until he stood and nearly lost his head to the bolts screeching in from two different directions.

Han dived and began to kick himself across the floor behind Qizak. The bolts had to be coming from the other Nargons, blasting on the run as they tried to push through the panicked crowd to help their companion. But who would do that—fire into a brawl when their buddy was right in the middle of it?

He continued to squeeze his own trigger, pushing himself toward Qizak's flank and firing toward the smoking hole Leia had opened in the Nargon's ribs. Finally, he saw a bolt disappear into the dark circle.

And *that* drew a reaction. Qizak spun as though hit by a blaster cannon, pupils diamond-shaped and wide open. Gray smoke began to billow from his chest, followed by blue spurting blood and something that looked like beads of molten metal. The Nargon lurched toward Han, his legs starting to shudder and spasm as he prepared to stomp his attacker into a greasy smear.

Leia came leaping over the tabletop, her lightsaber flashing and sizzling as she batted blaster bolts back toward the other Nargons. She pivoted in midair, bringing her bright blade around in a horizontal arc. Qizak's head came off and went bouncing across the durasteel floor.

Han saw the body falling and tried to roll away, but he was too slow. The huge corpse crashed down atop him, and the air left his lungs.

In the next instant, the weight vanished. He saw Leia crouching at his feet, one arm outstretched as she used the Force to send Qizak's body flying into a charging Nargon.

"You okay, flyboy?" she asked.

"I'm—" Han had to stop. His chest hurt something fierce, and the breath had definitely been knocked out of him. Still, he managed to get his feet under him. "Fine. I think."

Kaeg scrambled from beneath the table. A flurry of blaster bolts nearly took his head off. He cried out in surprise, then waved an arm toward a dark corner.

"Emergency exit!"

He scrambled away, staying low and not looking back.

Han did not follow immediately. Recalling the strange sparks that had sprayed from Qizak's arm as Leia amputated it, he grabbed one of the limbs off the table—and was so surprised by its weight that he nearly dropped it. He flipped the stump around and saw that, instead of bone, the Nargon's flesh was attached to a thick metallic pipe with just room enough for a bundle of fiber-optic filaments.

"Han!"

Leia used the Force to send the last Nargon stumbling back toward the bar, then grabbed Han by the arm and raced down a short passage, past the refreshers and out through an open iris hatch. It wasn't until Kaeg sealed the hatch behind them and blasted the controls that she finally released Han's arm and took a good look at what he was carrying.

"Really, Han?" She rolled her eyes in disbelief. *"Souvenirs?"*

STAR WARS
THE OLD REPUBLIC

IN A GALAXY DIVIDED
YOU MUST CHOOSE A SIDE

CREATE YOUR OWN EPIC STORY

IN THIS HIGHLY ANTICIPATED

MULTI-PLAYER ONLINE VIDEOGAME

YOUR SAGA BEGINS AT
WWW.STARWARSTHEOLDREPUBLIC.COM